The
BRIDGE
of
PEACE

Books by Cindy Woodsmall

ADA'S HOUSE SERIES
The Hope of Refuge
The Bridge of Peace
(Book 3 coming in fall 2011)

The Sound of Sleigh Bells

SISTERS OF THE QUILT SERIES
When the Heart Cries
When the Morning Comes
When the Soul Mends

NONFICTION
Plain Wisdom
(coming in spring 2011)

The BRIDGE of PEACE

AN ADA'S HOUSE NOVEL

CINDY WOODSMALL

WATERBROOK
PRESS

THE BRIDGE OF PEACE
PUBLISHED BY WATERBROOK PRESS
12265 Oracle Boulevard, Suite 200
Colorado Springs, Colorado 80921

The characters and events in this book are fictional, and any resemblance to actual persons or events is coincidental.

ISBN 978-1-61664-891-6

Published in the United States by WaterBrook Multnomah, an imprint of the Crown Publishing Group, a division of Random House Inc., New York.

WATERBROOK and its deer colophon are registered trademarks of Random House Inc.

Printed in the United States of America

*In loving memory of the best, most dedicated
teacher in my life—my mom.*

*You were strong, gentle, wise, and flawed. You taught me to
read, write, and never give up on God. You taught me to
cherish friendships, be stalwart in hardships, and take great
pleasure in the little things life offers. I am grateful for
everything you took time to teach me, and I'm grateful for
everything I learned while you were simply being you.
It was your passing that caused me to begin writing,
for when I lost you, I lost a part of me.
I'll miss you forever.*

One

Quiet hung in the air inside the one-room schoolhouse as the children waited on Lena's next action. The curiosity she loved to stir in her scholars now filled their minds in ways she wished she could erase. The hush wasn't out of respect or desk work or learning.

Staring into defiant eyes, she stood. "Return to your seat, Peter."

With his back to the other students, he leaned across her oak desk. "Make me." The threat in his voice was undeniable. She'd spoken to his parents about his behavior, but they'd believed that their son was only kidding and that she was taking his words and actions all wrong.

Nothing about the conduct of this six-foot man-child hinted at humor. He wasn't teasing, but he was toying with her—like her barn cats did with field mice before killing their prey.

Feeling as unsightly as a wounded rodent was part of daily life for her. It even slipped into her dreams on a regular basis. But Lena was no mouse. When dealing with Peter, her will battled with her emotions. The teacher in her wanted to find a way to reach inside him, to get beyond the prejudices and surliness and find something of value. The rest of her simply wished he'd never moved to Dry Lake.

Still, she believed that most people had hidden wealth, good things within that made them more worthy than they appeared on the outside. For reasons that had nothing to do with Peter, she had to hold on to that belief.

She offered a teacher-friendly smile. "The assignment stands, and it's due tomorrow. Take your seat, please."

He slid her well-organized papers onto the floor and crawled onto her desk and sat. At fifteen he was the oldest student she'd ever taught—or *tried* to teach. He should have graduated sixteen months ago from an Amish school in Ohio, where he'd lived before moving to Dry Lake. Although she had no idea what happened to put him so far behind in his studies, he seemed to think *she* was the problem.

It would be easier to tap into his better self, or at least better behavior, if there was someone to send him to when he got this bad. During her *rumschpringe,* her running-around years, she'd used her freedoms to attend public high school. When her public school teachers faced a difficult student like Peter, they sent him to another teacher, a counselor, or a principal. If there was another adult nearby, Peter probably wouldn't consider it a game to try to take control of her class. Maybe she needed to talk about this situation with her *Englischer* friend Samantha. Surely with her degree in psychology and her working this year as a school counselor, she would know some helpful tips.

"At your desk, Peter."

"I'm not doing the work, and I better not get a zero."

She swallowed and drew a breath, refusing the temptation to scream at him. "You have the right to decide your actions, or maybe a better word is *inactions,* but you do not have the right to insist on what grade I can give." Hoping to continue with class, Lena walked around the desk and settled her attention on the first-grade students.

"Who has their penmanship papers done?" Her three first-grade scholars raised their hands. "Good."

She could feel Peter behind her, seething with anger that had little to do with her. Wondering if she should face him or keep her focus on teaching, she took Marilyn's spiral-bound notebook in hand and began looking over the young girl's work. "To your desk, Peter," she repeated as she made a smiley face at the top of Marilyn's page.

His breath was hot on the back of her neck as he whispered, "You won't win, so don't even try."

The threat unleashed her anger, and suddenly she became its slave. Even while telling herself to ignore him as he was finally making his way toward his desk, she spun around. "You're a bully, Peter. Do you understand that about yourself?"

His face and eyes became like stone. "I'll convince the school board you're the problem. They're already whispering behind your back about how to get rid of you. I bet they only hired you because they felt sorry for you. I mean, what else would someone like you do, marry?"

His personal attack caused a storm of insecurities about her looks to rise within. But that aside, she was sure he was wrong about the school board wanting to get rid of her. She'd made one good-sized error they'd not been pleased with, but surely…

He slapped the side of his face really hard and laughed. "Look, I'm making my face blotchy like Teacher Lena's."

The younger students looked horrified as he mocked her. Some of the older boys laughed, but most were clearly embarrassed for her. Peter kept smacking the side of his face, egging on the class to laugh at his antics.

"Mandy and Rachel,"—Lena looked to the oldest girls in the class— "please take everyone outside for a brief recess."

Peter sat on her desk again, but at least he'd hushed. Smirking, but silent. The room filled with the sounds of desks shifting slightly and the rustle of clothing and soft, padded shoes as her scholars went outside. Willing her irritation to calm, she took several deep breaths and focused her thoughts on what could be accomplished with patience and effort. Good memories of teaching moved into her mind. At twenty-three years old, she'd been teaching for five years, and with only a few exceptions, she'd basked in the fulfillment of it.

Soon her scholars were outside, and the room was quiet.

"I don't want to embarrass you in front of the class, Peter. I only wish you'd show that same respect to me. If you want to color the side of your face to match mine, there are still a few blueberries on the vine out back, but nothing you do to your face will alter the real problem, will it?"

"Not unless you quit."

"How will getting a new teacher solve anything? Why don't you try fighting against the part of you that has no regard for your future."

"I hate this place." He picked up a book and hurled it across the room.

Lena flinched as the text hit the ground, but she forced her voice to remain calm. "I understand that learning doesn't come easy for you, but I can help you overcome—"

"Learning comes plenty easy," Peter interrupted. "I just ain't interested."

She knew he struggled to learn, and maybe Samantha would have some suggestions about this too, but Lena's best chance of reaching him wouldn't be found in trying to make him admit to his difficulties. "Why not?"

"What do you care?"

"If I knew why, maybe I could help change how you feel."

He rolled his eyes. "I don't want your help. *Mamm* says I can't stop coming to school just because of my age, so I just want to pass the eighth grade this time and get out of here."

"Then do your work. If you're struggling, I'll help you."

"You teachers are all alike. You say that, but…"

Piercing screams of young girls vibrated the room, and Lena moved to the window. Aaron Blank's meanspirited bull stood mere feet from the ragged fence that separated the pasture from the playground. Elmer, a third-grade student, seemed to be harassing the animal with two eighth-grade students egging him on. She hurried past desks and ran outside. The older students banged on the metal gate with their hands while cheering for Elmer. The third grader poked a stick against the angry creature's face and nose while the younger girls squealed with fear and excitement.

Enraged, the Holstein tossed his head back and forth, slinging spit and mucus as it stormed at the stick, coming closer to the fence with each move.

"Boys, stop that right now." While Lena hurried toward the boys, the older girls left the first and second graders at the swing set and ran toward them as well. Clearly the girls hadn't been watching this group. Aaron had promised her that he'd fix the fence and keep this bull out of the pasture that bordered the school. Moving to a spot between the angry bull and the students, Lena took the stick from Elmer. She gestured for the children to back up. "Everyone return to the classroom. We'll discuss this inside."

As Mandy and Rachel encouraged the others to go inside, Lena turned to look at the bull. The massive creature could easily plow through the pitiful wire fence.

"One would think they'd know better," she mumbled quietly, taking a few moments of serenity to gather herself. "Why would they do such a thing?" She glanced up to see Peter standing in the doorway, watching her. He was probably hoping the bull would come through the fence and destroy her. She sighed. *I think I'm looking at the source of influence over those other boys.* After a quick, silent prayer of thanks for everyone's safety, she tossed the stick onto the woodpile and headed inside. Her students often hit a baseball or sometimes even a volleyball into this field and went after it. What if someone had done so today while others had that bull riled?

It was time for a lesson in using good sense. Surely even Peter couldn't keep them from seeing the wisdom of not provoking the bull. But Peter had many of them viewing her with as much disrespect as he did. How she looked had nothing to do with the job in front of her—arming her scholars with skills that would serve them all their lives and keeping them safe while they were in her care.

After school she'd drop off a few of the children at their homes and then do something refreshing before going to see Aaron about keeping that bull away from the schoolhouse.

❦

As Grey left his barn and crossed the driveway, he smelled supper cooking—probably fried chicken by the aroma of it. Pieces of freshly mowed grass that were almost too small to see were scattered throughout the lawn. The porch and walkways were spotless, and the windows sparkled as the sun moved low on the horizon. A familiar, tainted feeling rose within him as he opened the screen door to his home.

His wife stood beside the oven, scouring a nearby countertop. She glanced at the clock and then to him. "Hey." Her eyes moved over his clothing, and he knew the quick study of his outfit was to assess just how dirty he was today. She returned to the task in front of her.

"Hi." He set his lunchpail in the sink. "Where's Ivan?"

"At your Mamm's."

He nodded. The light in their five-year-old son's eyes strengthened Grey. After he removed the plastic containers from his lunchpail, he rinsed them. "Been there all day?"

"Just since he got up from his nap. Supper will be ready by the time you're showered."

Inside her softly spoken sentence, he'd been dismissed and given respectful instructions to come to the table clean. He needed to bathe and change clothes before the school board meeting anyway, so he went to his bedroom. While working in the cabinetry shop, he'd seen Lena Kauffman drop children off at the Mast house. He'd considered stepping out and speaking to her for a minute to try to get a feel for her side of the complaints the Benders were lodging against her. But if she knew the board was meeting to discuss those criticisms, she'd want to attend. Michael Blank, his father-in-law and the chairman of the school board, had said earlier this week that he intended to discover if the Benders had any real justification for their grumbling before he was willing to share any of the negative talk with Lena. Grey appreciated Michael's reasoning, but he doubted that Lena would. As a kid she'd had a fierce temper when pushed. It'd been many a year since Grey had seen it, so he was confident that hadn't played into Michael's decision.

The memory of Lena's brother provoking her beyond her control probably still stood out in a lot of people's memories. Her temper made her an easy target and caused her brother to declare war, so the harassment of Lennie became a full-time game as she was growing up. One time her brother had brought Grey and a group of friends with him on a romp through the woods. Soon enough they'd taken over an abandoned tree house. They were teens, around sixteen years old, and wanted a private place to get away from their parents, a place to talk freely and smoke a cigarette. But the playhouse was Lennie's, complete with books, papers, and a diary.

She must have heard their voices because she called out to them. When her brother realized she was climbing up the rope ladder, he'd shaken her loose, causing her to fall. Rather than going home, she raged at them while trying to climb the ladder again. Once she'd been dumped again, some of the guys pulled the ladder inside the tree house and dangled her diary and books over the sides. She'd thrown rocks at them, calling out the worst things her ten-year-old mind knew to say—that they all stunk and they looked like old mares. One of the guys began reading from her journal. Lennie's eyes filled with tears as she screamed for him to stop. Feeling sorry for her, Grey had freed her diary from the tormentors. He tossed it to her, but she kept throwing rocks through the oversized window frames until she pinged her brother a good one.

"Rumschpringe teens." Grey sighed. It was amazing the Amish community hadn't imploded from the turmoil they caused.

The dimness of the fading day settled over the quiet space as he entered the bedroom. Beige sheers fluttered gently in the late September breeze. The bedspread was tucked crisp and perfect with the pillows adjusted just so, and not one item sat on the top of his dresser. He moved into the bathroom and turned on the shower. His razors. His toothbrush. His shaving cream. His combs. All lined up perfectly on a rectangular piece of white linen.

Plush, clean towels were stacked neatly on a shelf. He grabbed one, hung it on the peg near the shower stall and peeled out of his clothes. Feeling tempted for a moment to leave his stuff on the floor, he mumbled to himself to grow up. Elsie wouldn't say a word. Conversations didn't pass the threshold of the bedroom. Ever.

As the hot water and soap rinsed the day's grime from his body, he wondered if she ever missed him.

The discomfort of the thought drained his energy. For too long he'd searched his mind and heart for answers. At twenty-eight he no longer had much youthful nonsense in him. He tried to think and act like a considerate man, but whatever was wrong lay outside his grasp to understand. Was it his fault? Was it hers? He didn't know, and sometimes he was so weary he didn't care.

But giving up would only break them worse.

Sing for me, Grey.

The memory haunted him. How long had it been since she'd wanted him to sing for her? He turned off the shower and grabbed his towel. He knew of only one possible answer for their marriage—an avenue that might bring relief—but he'd have to be willing to publicly embarrass her and himself to pursue it. There had to be another way to find answers.

Two

Deborah closed her eyes, trying to block out a reality she could not yet welcome. Heat from the gas-powered stove continued to pour into the kitchen as it had since before daylight. The orders for baked goods were almost done for the day. With her eyelids shut tight, she tried to still the fresh ache.

Not one breath of air came through the open windows or screen door.

Still. Dry. Unmoving.

Exactly like her life.

He'd left.

Not only the faith. And his friends. And his mother, Ada.

But her.

Three months ago. Some days she could feel beyond the blackness and laugh again. But now was not one of them, not after receiving a note from him in today's mail. He hadn't actually written to her as much as sent money along with a scribbled apology. His admission of regret only stirred hurt and anger. He wasn't coming back. She wanted to burn the cash he'd sent. But how could she? She and his mother needed money. Badly.

The Amish community would help her and Ada if they knew of their plight. She and Ada had discussed telling their people, but now they couldn't accept anyone's hard-earned money since Mahlon had sent cash. She might not be able to make herself burn it, but she wouldn't use it. And when she told Ada about the *gift*, Ada would agree that they couldn't use it. They were on their own now. Truth was, in ways they'd not realized until after Mahlon left, they'd been on their own for a really long time.

She slid her hand inside her hidden pocket, feeling the envelope thick with twenties. Once again, Mahlon had made life harder for her and his mother.

Drawing a deep breath, she opened her eyes, grabbed the bowl of frosting, and scraped up the last dollop of it and dropped it onto the cake.

The kitchen door swung open, and Cara waltzed into the room, her Amish dress spattered with paint and much of her short hair coming loose from its stubby ponytail and sticking out around her prayer *Kapp*. The young woman carried the confidence of being happy and loved, making Deborah wonder if she'd ever feel that way again. Deborah's brother Ephraim was thirty-two when he found love for the first time in his life. And even though he broke up with Deborah's closest friend in order to pursue the Englischer girl, Deborah had grown to love Cara too.

Cara glanced through the screen door, and Deborah knew she was checking on her daughter. "You about done?" She grabbed an apple out of the refrigerator, walking and talking much like the Bronx-raised Englischer she was. Or rather *was* until recently.

Deborah motioned at the load of dishes in the sink. "No. You?"

"For the day, yes. Though I'll never be done painting as long as the little elves keep building onto this old house each night while we sleep. Do you know how long it takes to paint the inside of a two-foot-wide, nine-foot-deep space? What did they do with a room like that in the eighteen hundreds? Show it to relatives as a guest bedroom? It'd keep down on guests, right?"

Cara's nonsense made Deborah smile, and she longed to be free to enjoy her days again.

Cara took a bite of apple and sat on the countertop. "Is Ada out purchasing ingredients for tomorrow's baking orders?"

"*Ya.*"

"If I help you finish up, will you go to Dry Lake with me?"

Wondering whether to tell Cara she'd received a note from Mahlon, Deborah continued smoothing the frosting over the cake.

Cara finished her apple and then tossed it across the room and into the trash can. "Hellooooo?" She dipped her finger into the bowl and scraped some frosting off the side.

"Hmm?"

Cara licked her finger, hopped off the counter, and fixed herself a glass of water. "You made two of those cakes?"

"Ya. It's a new recipe, and I'm taking one by Select Bakery and one by Sweet Delights as a sample of a new item on our list."

Cara moved next to Deborah and nudged her shoulder against Deborah's. "It's one of those really bad days, huh?"

Deborah's eyes stung with tears, but she didn't respond.

"I expect grief will come and go for a while, but any idea why you're feeling smothered by it today?"

Deborah pulled the envelope from her pocket and held it up. "Mahlon," she whispered.

Cara's eyes grew large with concern. "Oh no." Her words came out slowly. "Deborah, I...I'm sorry." Cara pulled Deborah into a hug. The tone of Cara's voice and the warmth of her understanding surrounded her like no one else's could. Cara knew loss and imprisonment of circumstances a thousand times greater than Deborah did. Cara placed her hands on Deborah's shoulders. "Do you want to share what he said?"

It seemed a little odd how careful Cara was being with her words. Then again, maybe she thought Mahlon wrote to say he was coming back so she was withholding what she'd like to call him. Deborah passed her the envelope.

Cara pulled out the note and cash. She ignored the money and read the message. "Dearest Deborah, I hope you are well. I'm so very, very sorry for the pain I've caused you and Mamm. Please allow me to ease my guilt by helping you financially. Mahlon." Cara rolled her eyes, but she said nothing.

The note sounded just as detached as Mahlon had been in the weeks leading up to his disappearance. Hearing it aloud brought back so many memories, and Deborah felt stupid for not seeing the obvious until he humiliated her in front of everyone.

Cara replaced the money and note in the envelope. She again hugged Deborah and stayed there. The pain didn't ease, but hope trickled in. "Patience, Deb," Cara whispered. "Just keep muddling through. The pain always fades at some point."

Deborah swallowed and tried to pull strength from somewhere inside her. She took a step back. *"Denki."*

The back door swung open, and Lori ran inside with muddy hands and an even muddier dog. "Better Days!" Cara grabbed the dog by the collar. "Out."

"Mom, you'll hurt his feelings."

"He'll survive." She shoved the dog outside and closed the screen door. "Although you may not. What have you been doing?"

"Mississippi mud cakes. Want to try one?"

Cara glanced apologetically to Deborah and shrugged. "It's probably as good as the frosting Deborah just made."

"Really, Mom?" Lori's dark brown eyes reflected excitement.

"Afraid so."

"What?" Deborah scraped frosting off the knife with her finger and tasted the fluffy stuff. "Oh, yuck!" She snatched the cake off the counter and slammed it into the trash can. "What on earth happened?" She grabbed the second cake stand and headed for the can.

Cara took hold of the sides of the stand. "What are you doing?"

"Tossing it out."

"You're going to let a perfectly gorgeous cake go to waste when we could use it to trick someone?"

As if rust had broken from Deborah's face, she smiled freely and released the stand.

Cara set it on the counter. "I vote we give it to Ephraim."

"Maybe. Did you know that my good friend Lena has long been considered the queen of pranks?"

"The schoolteacher in Dry Lake?"

Deborah nodded. "Remember the van wreck Ephraim told you about? The one our mother died in?"

"Yeah."

"Lena's mother was killed too, and Ada's husband, and seven others from the community, including your *Daadi*—your grandfather. It was awful for months. Anyway, Lena—who was about eleven by then, I think—had been looking for some way to make people smile again, especially her *Daed*. While in Philadelphia with an aunt, she found a plastic thing that looked just like a little pat of butter at a gag store. Her Daed never ate his biscuit or peas until the butter he'd put on them had melted. According to Lena, she put two hot *buttered* biscuits on his plate. He opened a biscuit and saw the little pat of butter, closed it, and waited for it to melt. Between getting other foods, sipping on his drink, and chatting, he checked the biscuit several times over the next five or six minutes. Finally he poked the butter, asking why it hadn't melted. When he touched it and realized it was plastic, he broke into an uproar of laughter. She said he laughed until tears rolled down his cheeks. There's been no stopping her since...except she hasn't pulled anything on me since Mahlon left."

"Then Lena it is."

"She hasn't been stumped or tricked in years. I'm not sure she'll fall for it."

"She might this time. It won't be expected." Cara dusted flour from Deborah's black apron. "An unspoken truce was called the day Mahlon left. She wouldn't dream of you pulling this on purpose. If we handle it right and slice a piece for her while we visit, she'll probably eat nearly a whole slice, just to be nice."

"You know, I fear for my brother sometimes." Deborah giggled, feeling sadness loosen its death grip.

Cara's laughter came from a spring of contentment within her, and Deborah enjoyed a refreshing sip. Cara wasn't even close to being someone Deborah would have chosen for her brother. She'd been raised as an Englischer in foster care and often struggled to accept the Plain ways. She behaved like a sharp-tongued heathen sometimes without even realizing it, but as odd as it seemed, Ephraim respected her deeply. The longer Deborah knew her, the more she understood why her brother had finally fallen in love.

Deborah smoothed Cara's hair back and tried to pin the short strands where they'd stay under the prayer Kapp. It was no use.

Cara tucked a strand behind her ear. "Since no one's pulled a prank since Jerk Face left, I say it's time to end the truce."

"Mom, Ephraim won't like that you're calling names. Who's Jerk Face, anyway?"

"It doesn't matter." Cara turned to Deborah. "Does it?"

Deborah took a cleansing breath. "No, it…he doesn't."

They both knew it wasn't true. Not yet. Maybe not ever.

Cara mocked a frown. "What'd you do wrong to make that frosting taste so bad?"

"I don't know. Is the cake itself just as bad?"

They moved to the tossed-out cake. Cara jabbed a fork in the very center of it, where it hadn't touched any part of the trash can. She took a tiny nibble and shuddered. "It's both frosting and cake."

"So what'd I do?"

Cara made a face. "Salt."

"Too much salt?" Deborah glanced to her work station. "How did I manage that?"

Cara shrugged.

Trying to recall what she'd done, Deborah went to the canisters and opened the one that said sugar. If she'd been paying any attention, she'd have realized that it held salt. Lori had filled them for her earlier today, but when? How many items had she made using salt instead of sugar?

"Lori," Deborah spoke softly, "when did you refill these canisters?"

"Today."

"No, honey, I mean when today?"

Cara put her finger into the canister and then licked it. "Yep, that's salt."

Lori shrugged. "Did I do something wrong?"

Cara placed her hand on Lori's head. "Nothing that another lesson with Ada about being a good kitchen helper won't fix. Besides, seven-year-olds are supposed to make cute mistakes. It's part of your job description. Did you fill the canisters before or after school?"

"After. I did it when Deborah left to get the mail."

Deborah sighed. "And then Deborah read her note and sank onto the porch steps in a state of depression before eventually making her way back into the kitchen in a complete cloud of confusion."

"And she began talking about herself in third person too." Cara winked at her. "Lori, honey, why don't you go upstairs and get cleaned up while Deborah and I tackle this kitchen mess and start making a quick supper? Ada will be back soon, and then we'll eat."

Lori headed out of the kitchen, and soon the sound of her tromping up the steps echoed through the quiet home.

Deborah grabbed a few dirty utensils off the cabinet and tossed them into the sink. "Ingredients in the wrong canister or not, I should have recognized the difference between salt and sugar."

"It's not a big deal, Deb."

She rinsed her hands and dried them. "Ya, it is. Money's even tighter than you know. Ada doesn't want to talk about it, but she's making deliveries to all three bakeries because we can't afford to hire a driver. Hitching and unhitching the horse and wagon, along with her making the deliveries every day, cuts into our baking time, so our workday is getting longer and longer, but we've got fewer goods to sell."

"I thought the bakeries paid for the courier."

"They did…sort of. I mean they were taking money out of our profit to pay for them, so Ada's getting that money, and we're making the deliveries ourselves. Lately she has to wait until we make a few bucks off what we sold in order to buy supplies for the next round of baking."

"So"—Cara shrugged—"Jerk Face sent you money today. Use it."

"I'll starve first." Deborah couldn't believe her own tone as she spoke—or the determination she felt.

"Your brother wouldn't like that plan."

"You cannot tell Ephraim." She motioned to the six-foot stainless steel commercial oven. "He's already done too much for us. This place was unlivable until he gave so generously."

"I…I didn't realize he was the one…"

"Well he was. A few others pitched in a little, but in this economy there are too many in our community who are hurting. I can't ask them for help when Mahlon sent us money. Ada and I will have to succeed…or fail…on our own."

Three

Lena climbed the wooden steps of her home and walked inside. Quietness greeted her. As she set her grading book and student papers on the table, a nearby mirror caught her eye. She moved to the wall hatrack with the oval mirror and looked at herself. Tears stung as she studied the bluish-purple stain that began halfway down her right cheek and continued down the side of her neck. She placed her hand over her birthmark. The width of her fingers all pressed together covered it with a little room to spare.

Was the birthmark all people saw?

Vivid memories of overhearing her brother's friends saying they felt sorry for her added to the hurt. In her teen years and before she joined the faith, she'd tried covering up the stain with different shades of concealer and foundation makeup. She'd never found one that could cover the blotch, only ones that streaked or made it look orange rather than blue. She wondered if Peter had seen how deeply he'd cut her today or if her well-rehearsed poker face hid the truth like she hoped.

The back door opened. "Lena, you home?" her Daed called out.

Studying herself, she removed her hand and angled her head a little one way and then the other. "Ya."

She could tell by his footsteps that he'd headed straight for the mud sink near the back door.

The sound of water coming on and his scrubbing up barely registered as she traced the mark. Thoughts of her mother came to her. She'd died a long time ago, but the memory of standing in the flower garden, crying in her Mamm's arms, played out in front of her. Lena hadn't been more than nine years old, and some of the boys at school had taunted her about her looks. They'd said she'd die an *Alt Maedel*—an old maid. Even now Lena could feel the warmth of her mother's love as she'd placed a rose in Lena's hand. *When the time is right, you'll be drawn to the right man. And he'll be drawn to you. He'll see beyond the mark, and he'll love you deeper and higher than most men are capable of. I promise you that.*

It wasn't like Lena wanted just any man, but oh how she dreamed of finding a good man, of having sons and daughters fill their home. The love stored inside her longed for him to show up. But not one man had even looked her way. How would she find the right one if none gave her a chance? She wanted to be under the wisdom and strength and leadership of a good husband, just like her people believed was right. She believed it too, but had God marked her for a different life yet not removed her desire for a husband?

Upstairs, hidden inside her hope chest, she had a very old but still well-loved list of her favorite children's names. The idea of never having a family of her own scared her.

"You didn't come out to the shop to see me when you got home." Her Daed came into the room, drying his face on a guest towel. He scrubbed the towel over his mostly brown beard with a few gray hairs peeping through. It didn't matter that he'd been widowed for thirteen years; once married, a man grew a beard and kept it the rest of his life. "At least greet your poor dog. She is begging for a little attention." He pointed at Nicky, who had managed to come into the room without her noticing. Nicky watched Lena's every move while her whole body wriggled in hopes of being petted.

She patted Nicky's head. Her dog stood and slowly turned in circles as if chasing her tail, making it easy for Lena to stroke her from head to tail without moving her hand.

Daed dried his hands. "I was hoping for a fresh cup of coffee between now and dinner."

Lena tried to shake the sickening feeling in the pit of her stomach. "Sure thing, Daed. Do you need a little something else to hold you until dinner is ready?"

"Nope, just a cup of coffee with you." He tossed her the dishtowel. "Then I need to get back to the shop before and again after dinner. The owners of Bissett's would like the kitchen table and chairs done by tomorrow if possible." He paused. "You look a little pale. You feeling okay?"

"Ya." She wouldn't tell him, or anyone else, what weighed heavy on her. He and others would try to assure her she was beautiful and the mark wasn't all that noticeable. Why bother? She wouldn't feel any better by people saying things they felt obligated to say.

Suddenly ready for time in her flower garden, she tossed the towel back at him. "I have things I'd like to do tonight too, as well as things I must do, so I'll get dinner started now."

❧

With the harness in one hand and a cube of sugar in the other, Cara eased toward Rosie, talking to her as she drew closer. But Rosie kept moving just out of reach. This reminded her of trying to catch a cab in New York on a Saturday night. She could see them, but they wouldn't stop for her. She knew so little about horses. Maybe the old girl didn't want to work on such a beautiful fall day. Cara sang softly while holding out her palm. Finally Rosie grew more interested in getting the sugar than in avoiding Cara. A moment after the horse's soft lips grasped the sugar from Cara's palm, she slid the rope harness on her.

She led her across the field and into the barn. Once inside Cara guided the horse to stand between the shafts of the buggy. "Easy girl." She patted her, but the mare shifted nervously. Cara bent forward to place the bridle on her, but Rosie jerked her head, hitting the side of Cara's face. Struggling to keep her balance, she managed to get the bridle in place. She threw the leather strappy thing over the horse's neck and attached the rigmarole that hooked into the bellybands. Ada had told her the names of this stuff. So had Ephraim, but none of it stuck in her brain. Couldn't one thing about being Amish be easy?

Forcing herself to focus, she continued connecting this thing to that until she was finally ready to stick the shaves into their holders on each side of Rosie. Once she'd threaded the leads through the rings, she was done connecting the horse to the buggy...maybe. She studied her work for a moment, wondering if she'd remembered each step. The gear sat a little odd. Cara angled her head a bit. That seemed to make it look straighter. She shrugged, hoping that everything was connected right or at least that everything *important* was connected.

Once Rosie was hitched to the buggy, Cara went inside. Ada stood beside Lori as they refilled the canisters with the correct ingredients. Better Days sat on the floor, watching Lori and Ada like he was trying to understand their words. What could be seen of Ada's light brown hair from around the head covering shined like she was still a young woman. At forty-three her face had no lines and her skin was vibrant. Cara bet she'd had very oily skin when younger and now she was reaping the benefits. "You be good for Ada." Cara kissed the top of Lori's head.

"Ada's gonna teach me how to wash, dry, and iron a prayer Kapp."

Ada shrugged. "One of you two needs to know how to care for the coverings."

"Yep, you're right." She missed being able to ruffle Lori's hair, so she tugged on one of the strings to her Kapp. "Did you guys want to go to Dry Lake with me and Deb?"

"You girls will be out too late for me." Ada placed the lid on the sugar canister. "I need to be up long before dawn again tomorrow."

Lori took the remaining sugar to the pantry. "Not me, Mom. Takes longer to get there and back than we get to see 'From. I hate that."

"Okay. If that's what you want to do." Cara kissed the top of her head again, feeling the starched prayer covering against her lips.

Deborah came into the kitchen, pinning a clean apron in place.

"There you are." Cara gestured toward the back door. "The horse is ready. Are you?"

She grabbed the cake box. "Ya."

They said their good-byes to Ada and Lori and went to the barn. When Deborah walked into the barn, she stopped and turned to Cara. "Harnessed her by yourself, did you?"

Cara tilted her head to the left. "If you do your head like this, it's not so bad."

Deborah angled her head and then her body. "Ya, you're right." She stepped into the driver's side, but once they were on the road, she held out the reins to Cara.

Cara shook her head. "You're the one in the driver's seat. What are you doing?"

"We're not in a car. And it's time you learn to drive…Amish style."

Cara folded her arms. "You drive. I'll ride."

"Did you rig this thing to separate from the horse while I'm driving it?"

"No. Of course not."

"Then take the reins."

Cara took them. The straps of leather felt totally different in her hands now that the horse was trudging along. She and the horse jolted when a van zoomed around them, but she continued heading toward Dry Lake. The cool fall air begged Cara to open her heart and soak in the very joy of being alive.

The sensation was new and exhilarating, making her wonder how long it would last. She knew that life offered no one a break for very long.

The sounds of town were far behind them now, and as much as she was enjoying the ride, she couldn't stop thinking about seeing Ephraim.

When she came to a fairly steep slope, she tried to gain speed so they could make it up the next hill, but Rosie seemed uninterested in going faster. "I've never driven anything before. But I know that a car or truck can't hear or care when the owners yell at it. Will Rosie?"

"Probably not, given that she never listens, but there are some things you just don't do as an Amish person, and yelling like a maniac in public is one of them. Once you're married, I'm sure Ephraim will appreciate it if you can hold on to that tradition."

Cara chuckled. "Now that's good info to know."

Deborah scrunched her forehead. "Did I miss something?"

"You said the Amish have no problem with me yelling at my horse or my husband as long as it's not in public."

"That's not what I meant."

"I'm pretty sure it's what you said."

"Poor Ephraim."

Cara chuckled. "What about Rosie?"

Deborah looked a bit lost for a moment, and then she laughed. "Knowing Rosie, I'm more inclined to say, 'Poor Cara.' Of course, you'll figure that out as time goes on."

The ride seemed to be pulling Deborah out of that dark hole Mahlon had dug inside her, so Cara did what she could to keep the silly banter going. By the time they'd traveled for nearly an hour, she almost had the hang of driving a rig.

"You need to slow down so you can take the next right turn up ahead."

Cara slapped the reins against the horse's back, making it gain speed. "You've got to be kidding. I didn't drive all this way to see Lena first."

"Fine. But I'm not delivering this cake on my own."

"Why not?"

"There are several rules to pulling a prank, but only two you need to understand right now. One, whoever thought of the prank must be in on delivering it. Two, no one goes alone."

"I'll repeat myself, why not?"

"Because, afterward, telling what took place isn't nearly as fun as re-living it together. Don't you know anything about pranks?"

Cara pulled into the driveway of Ephraim's cabinetry shop. "Nope. Pranks are for rich girls." She set the brake. "And you can trust me, Deb. In every way that matters—faith, family, friends, food, and shelter—you grew up rich." She hopped down and strode to the entryway of the huge warehouse-type shop.

Ephraim. He stood near the center of the vast building, scrubbing sandpaper over a cabinet that was sitting on a pair of sawhorses. Dark blue pants. Light blue shirt. Brown suspenders. Although it was a couple of hours before dark, he had lit several gas pole lamps. Under the glow of them, his hair looked more reddish brown than the usual strawberry blond.

The glimpse of him filled her soul. She'd once been so empty, and now it was as if he'd stolen the awfulness of her past and buried it somewhere. But it'd taken more than his physical strength to help her. He'd given up everything for a season—had been shunned and disgraced, all the while hiding the truth from her of what he was going through. And sacrificing.

He stirred her in ways she didn't figure the Amish were familiar with—physical desire. But she bridled it and tried to behave like an up-standing Amish woman.

Deborah nudged her, whispering, "Is this what you meant by seeing him?"

Cara took a deep breath. "No, but I could stay right here all day and just watch him."

"We have a cake to deliver."

Ephraim looked up, a gorgeous smile instantly erasing the blankness that'd been there moments before. He tossed the sandpaper onto the cabi-net and headed for her. Cara moved to him and wrapped her arms around his waist. The warmth and power of his hands made her feel both strong and weak. How was that possible?

He released her. "I wasn't expecting a visit."

"Deborah brought something for Lena. And I said I'd go with her to deliver it."

He looked past Cara and seemed to notice his sister for the first time. "Hi, Deborah."

"Hey. I think I'll go say hello to everyone at Daed's. Meet you at the buggy in ten?"

"You're only here for ten minutes?" Ephraim looked disappointed.

"No, we're coming back after we see Lena for a bit."

"Good. That'll give me a chance to finish up here and catch a shower."

Movement inside the office area of the shop caught her attention. *Anna Mary.*

Ephraim's ex-girlfriend stood in his office with the phone to her ear. Anna Mary knew the language, customs, and all the ways of the Amish. Cara knew almost nothing. If she'd been raised here as her mom had wanted, she would've grown up knowing all the Amish ways too. Anna Mary put the receiver in its cradle, blew out the kerosene lamp, and came out of the office. The moment she saw Deborah, her eyes lit up, and she hurried over to her friend. She engulfed her in a hug the way best friends do. The two whispered something before Anna Mary turned toward Cara and Ephraim. "Hi, Cara. How are you?"

"Hello. I'm good. You?" The words caught in her throat and tumbled out sounding rather frozen. Ephraim traced his fingers along the side and back of her neck until settling his hand there.

"She came to use the community phone."

Embarrassed that he felt the need to reassure her, she forced a smile and turned to Anna Mary. "I...I hope everything is okay."

"Ya, just making plans to visit one of my sisters who doesn't live in Dry Lake."

Cara shifted, trying to think of how to make small talk with her. "That sounds like fun."

"Ya, should be."

"I'll see you at the buggy in ten." Deborah waved, and then she and Anna Mary left the building.

Ephraim squared himself in front of her and placed both his hands on her face. "I'm glad you're here." He kissed her forehead before gazing into her eyes. "I have something I want to show you." He led her to his office. After he lit the kerosene lamp, he passed her a paper with a drawing on it.

"It's a sketch of a floor plan, right?"

"Ya. Plans for our new house."

"Ours? But you already own one."

"We," Ephraim corrected and then waited.

Her throat felt dry, but she made herself say it. *"We* own one."

"Ya, but it has one bedroom, two if we make that storage space into a room for Lori. Plus, I thought we might want to build elsewhere on the property, maybe not so close to my Daed and stepmother."

Her hurt from moments earlier shrank, and feathery-light contentment filled the gap. She didn't have much in the way of good memories from her past, but she had a future. "But I like your…" She cleared her throat. *"Our* house. You built it yourself. Just those hardwood floors you put in from some old barn are too much a part of you to leave behind."

He gave that 'I understand' smile of his. "But it's awfully small."

"If we make the living room into bedrooms, it'll work."

"You're going to be a demanding wife, aren't you?"

She studied him for a moment, wanting to know if he was teasing her. His eyes reflected amusement and love, and she felt his pleasure with her thaw a little more of her heart.

"I could probably build a set of stairs and add a couple of rooms above the main floor if living there is what you really want."

What she ached for more than anything else was for them to marry…

soon. But Amish rules said that she couldn't go through instruction until spring and that they couldn't marry until next year's wedding season. Because she'd been raised an outsider and had only been living as an Amish woman for a short while, the bishop had the power to make them wait several years, if he wanted to.

Ephraim laid the sketch on his desk. "Your plan will cost us a lot less money and keep me close to the shop, so it's great for me. I was thinking it might not be so wonderful for you. You're not used to having a large, somewhat intrusive family living next-door."

She shrugged. "I can hold my own without you having to build us a new house."

"Okay. We'll wait on building a place. In a few years we'll both be ready for a bigger one."

Longing to feel his lips against hers, she settled for giving him a kiss on the cheek. "I'm not interested in where we live or how big and comfy the house is. I just want to be your wife."

Four

Lena knelt and dug her bare hands into the dirt, loosening the ground around her aster plants. Nicky lay near her, stretched out in the warm sun while dozing contentedly. The sight of blossoms and petals renewed and connected her to hope.

She scooped her own concoction of mulch, fertilizer, and potting soil out of a bucket and onto the needed areas. The feel and smell of the earth, along with the beauty of the flowers—the delicate blooms and the rich shades of the purples, blues, and pinks—soothed her frazzled nerves.

While trying to get over the hurt, she looked for some answers for Peter. But even if she did discover a way for him to learn, would he accept her help? He discounted her as a worthy being. Getting past that wouldn't be easy, especially as he constantly made it easier for her to want little to do with him.

If she didn't need to go see Aaron later tonight, she'd visit her friend Samantha. She and Samantha had met while Lena attended public school for a few years. Despite getting together only a couple of times a year and Samantha's Englischer lifestyle, the women had a lot in common. In her work as a school counselor, Samantha always had a trick or two for dealing with difficult schoolchildren. Surely Samantha could help Lena push past Peter's stinging remarks and find a way to reach him.

"Lennie?"

Her brother Allen called to her. His rather craggy voice sounded just like her other brothers, but without a glance she always knew when it was him. Only a handful of people called her Lennie—Allen and two of his best buddies. While still kneeling on the lush grass, she turned to see him walking toward her. "Ya?"

"I guess you didn't hear me calling you. Is it noisy out here today?"

She wiped her forehead with the back of her wrist. "Extremely so inside my head. Did you want something?"

"No. Just checkin' on you."

"I'm good, thanks."

"Wow, are these from your greenhouse?"

She cleared her throat, refusing to laugh at her brother. He always meant well, but the man noticed almost nothing about her flower beds. It'd be her best guess that this was the first time he'd seen her asters, and she'd planted them here as seedlings two springs ago. "At one time they were from my greenhouse, ya."

"I dropped by to visit you and Daed and was surprised you weren't eating supper with him. If I cooked a meal, I'd eat it."

"You sure about that? Because if *you* cooked a meal…"

He chuckled. "Okay, fine, Teacher Lena. If I were you and cooked a meal, I'd eat it."

As sisters went, Lena had cooked a lot of meals for Allen over the years. After their Mamm died when Lena was ten, she began learning from her older sisters how to cook and run the house. Their community was never the same after that day—her brother most of all.

The day after their mother was killed, Lena heard odd noises coming from the attic. When she climbed the stairs, she found her big brother sobbing. He looked up and saw her, and she expected him to usher out threats and throw things at her. But there Allen was, sixteen years old, sitting on the floor of the attic, crying uncontrollably. When he caught his breath, he stammered through an apology for all his years of being mean to her, and then they cried together. Slowly he'd grown into a man worth having around, but like all her siblings, he had a family of his own now.

A rig turned into their driveway and ambled toward the house. Just the sight of Deborah Mast refreshed Lena's spirits. Cara sat beside her. Lena hadn't had much chance to get to know her yet.

Allen grabbed his suspenders. "Mahlon bailed on Deborah, and Ephraim broke up with Anna Mary for an outsider. For a while I feared all your closest friends would marry off, leaving you feeling like an outcast, but with all that heartache going on, maybe never dating isn't such a bad thing."

With soil covering Lena's hands, she stood. "I know you were trying to say something nice, but…" She wiped her hands down the front of Allen's shirt, pressing hard as she did so. "That's all I have to say on the matter."

"Lennie, Emily's going to shake the rafters when she sees this," Allen complained as he brushed off his shirt, taking extra time on the ground-in dirt.

Lena chuckled and walked toward the buggy, Nicky quietly shadowing every step she took. "Now this is a pleasant surprise."

Deborah brought the horse to a halt, got out, and hugged Lena. Cara climbed out, holding on to a cake box.

"Hi, Cara." Lena wasn't sure whether to hug Cara or offer to shake her hand or just speak. No one but Ephraim really knew Cara. Since she now lived in Hope Crossing with Deborah and Ada, they were getting to know her. The rest of the Amish community was still grappling, trying to get past the awkwardness of Ephraim breaking up with one of their own to welcome an Englischer stranger into the fold. People left the Amish faith to join the world, but she'd never seen it work in reverse—although she'd heard of a few Englischers who'd spent months or a couple of years aiming to join, only to change their minds.

"Hey, Lena." Cara passed the box to Deborah.

"We brought you something." Deborah gave it to Lena. "I made two cakes with that recipe you gave me and brought you one."

"Well, that's very sweet and thoughtful. Denki."

"Yep, that's me." Deborah placed her arm around Lena's shoulder. "Let's go in and share a bite. I want your opinion."

"I wouldn't care for any right now, but I'll cut a slice for each of you."

"Not care for any?" Deborah glanced to Cara. "How can you turn down my dessert? Ada is one of the best cooks ever, and she's trained me for years."

"Personally," Allen said, having followed Lena from the garden, "I think she's had a rough day at school." With a glint in his eyes, he continued to brush dirt off his shirt, clearly letting Lena know he was telling Deborah as a payback for rubbing dirt on him. "Lennie, I'm going on home."

"By all means, go home." She kept a straight face as he chuckled.

Deborah guided her toward the house. "You need to try this cake. It'll make me happy if you do."

"I'm really not the least bit hungry. I'll have some later tonight. May I cut a slice for you two?"

Deborah and Cara glanced at each other and shook their heads.

"We've already had plenty of the other one. Some of the scholars giving you trouble at school?" Deborah asked.

"Scholars?" Cara's brows scrunched. "I know you are not talking about a class full of Rhodes scholars, so what is it?"

"That's what you call students," Deborah said. "We call them that too sometimes, but mostly we call them scholars. So are they being difficult, Lena?"

"A few." They walked up the porch steps and into the house. Nicky zipped past them, heading for her doggy bed next to the stove.

Once they were in the kitchen, Cara took a seat at the island. "It's a one-room schoolhouse with Amish kids. How bad can they be?"

Lena set the box on the counter. "Just because we dress plain and live simple doesn't mean some of our youth don't push every boundary there is." She scrubbed her hands, taking note that her Daed had washed the dishes. After grabbing a kitchen towel out of a drawer, she sat on a barstool across from Deborah and Cara. Lena settled in, enjoying the banter.

After they'd talked for a while, Deborah gestured toward the cake. "You sure you don't want to try a bite?"

"I'll use the cake as a treat when the hard parts of the day are over."

"What else needs to be done?" Cara asked.

"I have to see Aaron about his bull. It's getting into the field nearest the school."

Deborah made a face. "Again?"

"Ya."

Deborah splayed her hands against the countertop. "We'd better go. You have things to do, and Cara didn't travel for an hour with me just to spend her evening waiting to see when you're going to eat that cake."

"Again with the cake. What is it with you tonight?" Lena rose.

Cara brushed wisps of hair out of her face as she got up. "Lena, about that ca—"

"Cara." Deborah jumped up. "We need to go." She took Cara by the hand and pulled her toward the door. "We only had a minute to stop by. We went by Ephraim's first, and I gave him my word I'd have Cara back real quicklike."

Lena followed them onto the porch. Deborah shooed Cara to the rig and then gave Lena a quick hug. "Good to see you."

If Lena didn't know better, she'd be convinced Deborah was pulling some sort of prank on her. And it'd be a welcome relief if she felt up to pulling pranks again. "You didn't even let me and Cara say a proper good-bye. Have you been spending too much time in a hot kitchen lately?"

"Maybe. But come see us in Hope Crossing this weekend if you can. Then you can say anything you wish to either of us. Bye."

Perplexed, Lena remained on the porch. Maybe Deborah just realized it was getting late. "Bye."

After watching Deborah and Cara's buggy pull onto the road, Lena knew she couldn't delay going to Aaron's any longer. She went inside and washed her face before putting on a clean apron. After hurrying to the barn, she hitched her horse to the carriage. But before she left, she went back inside and grabbed the box containing the cake. She knew that talking to Aaron for the third time about his bull being in the wrong pasture would be easier if she had a gift in hand. Passing him one of Deborah's desserts was a perfect plan, and surely Deborah wouldn't mind the cake being used as a peace offering.

When she pulled into the Blanks' lane, she noticed three rigs with horses tied to a couple of hitching posts. Clearly the Blanks had company, but all she needed to do was speak to Aaron for a moment. She looped Happy Girl's reins around a small tree, grabbed the box containing the cake, and headed for the house. She knocked on the front door and waited.

Dora Blank opened the door. "Lena." The fifty-something woman glanced behind her as if unsure what to do. "Were we expecting you?"

Lena held up the cake. "I need to see Aaron."

"Oh." She took a step back.

The moment Lena walked inside she understood Dora's cool reception. The members of the school board—Michael Blank, Enos Beiler, Jake Fisher, and Grey Graber—were sitting at the large kitchen table. Three wives, including Dora, were with their husbands. Grey's wife, who was Dora and Michael's daughter, wasn't there. For reasons Lena could only guess at, Elsie always avoided the school board gatherings. Maybe the meetings were too high-spirited for her more gentle nature.

The group appeared to be engaged in a serious conversation with Peter's Mamm and Daed—Crist and Mollie Bender—and with Sylvan and Lillian Detweiler. She wouldn't blame the Detweilers for being set against her. Her brief lapse in judgment last May could have cost them their oldest son's life. Their son John and his three siblings had left their lunches at home. If she'd had enough food from her lunch as well as other scholars' to feed them, as she'd done in the past, she'd have given it to them. But that day she'd only brought an apple, and she'd given it to the youngest Detweiler. No one else had extra in their pails either, so rather than letting them go hungry, she'd hitched her horse to its rig and told John to go back for the lunches. The Detweiler place is only a short distance from the school. But he must have been daydreaming, because her horse took over and automatically headed for home, her home, which meant the rig came to a four-way stop. Once at the four-way stop, John realized he'd gone the wrong way and slapped the reins on the horse's back without realizing that he didn't have the right of way and that a vehicle was coming. The car almost slid sideways trying to stop, and it nipped the back of the buggy, toppling the rig. Her horse came loose from the buggy and ran on home. John had a few bumps and bruises, and the people in the car took him home. It'd been a foolish mistake on her part, and the board had put her on probation for this school year, but surely they weren't still reviewing that incident.

"She's not fit, and every one of you know it," Peter's Mamm said.

"Michael," Dora called, stopping the conversation cold.

In only a brief moment the looks on their faces turned from one of studious consideration to awkward remorse. "Lena." Michael stood. "Would you care to join us?"

Join them? If they'd wanted her here, they would have invited her. Besides, she needed fresh air. She was good at her job, and she loved teaching. That was all she'd ever wanted to do, and no one had ever taken a teaching position at a younger age than she had. Would they take it from her because of Peter's nonsense and her one mistake with John Detweiler? "No...no thank you. I didn't mean to interrupt. I was looking for Aaron."

Michael placed his hands on the table, looking stiff and in pain. "I think he's still at the barn. We almost never see him before bedtime anymore, not since I hurt my back and can't do much farm work."

"He...he's"—Dora stammered— "sleeping there some nights. But you're free to go down and look for him."

"Denki." Shaken, Lena hurried outside, still holding the box with the cake in it. She drew in air, trying to fill her lungs. It wasn't so much that they were having a meeting but that they were having it behind her back. Couldn't they have told her about it and said she didn't need to come? Still determined to do what she'd come here for, she strode toward the barn. It only took a few seconds to figure out Aaron wasn't there. She went back to her horse, removed the reins from the small tree, and climbed into the buggy.

"Lennie?" Grey's smooth voice caused her to stop. He hurried over to the buggy. "You okay?"

She tried to swallow her embarrassment. "I've certainly been better."

"Michael saw no reason to upset you with these complaints. We're just hearing them out. If we have any concerns when tonight's over, we'll talk to you."

"It seems I should get a say in front of my accusers."

"You will, if it comes to that."

"It has come to that, Grey. Don't you think I need someone in there to defend me?"

He studied her, as if waiting for her to answer her own question.

And then she knew. He'd do a better job defending her than she would. Where she might get riled and make matters worse, he wouldn't. He'd never failed to stand up for her since becoming a member of the school board a few years ago. It was possible he defended her out of pity. She'd certainly overheard him saying he felt sorry for her on more than one occasion when they were young. The thought stung. Maybe Peter was more right than she was willing to admit. She took a deep breath, refusing to allow her fears and insecurity to get the best of her. Whatever Grey's motivation, he wouldn't let rumors or nonsense cloud the school board's judgment. She hoped he took her side because he trusted and respected her as a teacher, but she couldn't ask. If that wasn't his reasoning, what answer could he possibly give except denial? She drew a deep breath and decided to tease. "You better do a good job in there, Grey, or I'm tellin' Daed."

He laughed and tipped his hat. "No doubts on that one, Lennie."

She slapped the horse's back, trying to assure herself she wouldn't lose her job.

Before she got to the end of the lane, she spotted an Amish man in a nearby field. She watched as he walked with purpose toward a large patch of woods. She directed the rig off the beaten path and toward where the man was headed. She soon saw what he saw—a cabin, one that used to be for farmhands. He went inside. It was on Blank property, so Aaron might be there. She'd forgotten about the old cabin sitting in the woods, just out of sight. An Englischer family had owned this farm about seven years ago, before the Blanks moved from Ohio. And then Grey met his future wife— Elsie Blank.

Lena's rig groaned as she went down the rough path and stopped in front of the place. Music blared, and electric lights shined through the windows. Four or five horses grazed nearby, but an old, half-rusted car sat in the dirt driveway.

A hangout.

Since there were no electric lines running to the place, she assumed a generator provided the power. Its existence as a hangout was news to her. Probably a secret from all the parents too.

She took the cake with her and knocked on the screen door. "Hello?" She raised her voice over the din of music.

From the door she could see the living room, where young men lounged in chairs and couches or sat on the floor. One guy, with a beer in hand, turned toward the screen door. "No one in Amish costume welcome. Thanks anyway."

"I'm looking for Aaron Blank. Is he here?"

A girl in a tank top and jeans came to the door. Lena didn't recognize her, so she could be a rumschpringe Amish from another community, but more than likely she was an Englischer girl.

"Hi." She unlatched the screen door. "Come on in."

"Is Aaron around?"

"Uh, well." She turned back toward the others. "Come on, guys. Stop goofing off and help the woman."

One of the guys stood and took a long drink of beer before belching. "I'll get him." He went to a door and pounded on it. "Aaron! Somebody's here to see ya."

The group returned to their lounging around as if Lena weren't standing there. Aaron came out, rubbing his eyes like he'd been asleep. She couldn't imagine sleeping with all this noise. He staggered a few times, but he made his way to her. "Lena, hi. What's up?"

"Lena?" a man's voice boomed. "As in Kauffman?" Disbelief and sarcasm marked his voice as he stood up so he could see her better. When he rose, something small and metallic fell from his lap and onto the floor, but he didn't notice. "It is you. Has to be." He wiped his cheek several times as if trying to remove her birthmark from his face. "You fit the description."

Unsure who he was but quite confident he was drunk, Lena ignored the man. "Aaron, we talked about this before, but we still have a problem."

"What?" The drunk scowled at her. "Making my brother miserable during school ain't enough? Now you're gonna come here and pick on my friend Aaron?"

The drunk had to be Peter's brother. She knew all her other scholars' families. She stayed focused on Aaron. "The bull was in the field next to the schoolhouse."

"So?" the drunk barked.

Lena didn't answer him. "Aaron, surely you know how dangerous that is. The Nicols owned this farm for generations and always kept bulls and steers out of the pasture closest to the school." She held the cake out to him. "Please."

Aaron stared at the box.

"It's a cake."

He smelled of stale beer as he took it from her. "Ya, ya, you're right. I'm sure a fence needs mending. I'll see to it that it doesn't happen again."

"What?" Peter's brother took a step, sending the object he'd dropped earlier skidding across the linoleum floor. Lena looked down when it bumped her shoe.

A pocket watch?

He came toward the doorway. "You are kidding me. There's a fence there, right?"

"Of course," Aaron said, "but sometimes the boys hit their baseballs or volleyballs into that field during recess."

"Yeah?" the drunk scoffed. "If she knew how to control a class, inside or outside the schoolhouse, it wouldn't be a problem."

"I'm Lena Kauffman." She held out her hand. "And you are?"

"Not interested." He walked off.

"Sorry, Lena," Aaron mumbled. "Dwayne's had a case too many."

Lena reached for the watch and noticed it looked like the one her Daed had lost. But it couldn't be. It'd been missing for months. She'd never really thought her Daed lost it. For a while she wondered if Cara entered their unlocked home and took it, along with a huge roll of tens. She'd been suspected of a few burglaries when she'd first arrived in Dry Lake, but she had proven the accusations were false.

Lena picked up the watch, opened it, and read the inscription: *To Israel with love.*

She held it out toward Dwayne. "This is my Daed's watch."

"What?" Dwayne gawked at her.

"My Daed lost his watch last spring. It was the last gift my mother gave him before she died."

"Well, that's a real sad story and all, but I found it along the shoulder of a road when walking, and it's mine now." He reached for it, but Lena clutched it tightly and put her hand behind her back.

"I'm glad you found it, and I'll give you a reasonable reward, but it's my Daed's watch."

Dwayne hovered over her, swaying back and forth. What was it with these Bender men, Peter and Dwayne, that they liked to stand so close while peering down at her? Aaron set the cake on an end table. "Clearly it's her Daed's. Just let her have it."

"Oh, I'll be more than glad to let her have it."

His words were as immature and threatening as Peter's, but she wasn't giving up the watch. It meant too much to her Daed, and he'd not stopped searching for it yet.

Aaron stepped between them. *"Kumm."* He motioned Lena to the door. "Keep the watch. But it'd be good if you didn't come back here again. I'll see to it the bull stays out of that field, okay?"

"Denki, Aaron." Clutching her Daed's watch, she went to her carriage.

Five

Grey walked out of his bedroom at the same time Elsie walked out of hers. Startled and a bit curious what had kept her in her room past daylight, he stopped in his tracks. They stood in their small hallway, staring at each other under the soft glow of early morn. His shirt was not yet buttoned, and his suspenders were attached to his pants and dangling near his knees. She stood as erect and graceful as a deer when watching for danger. Each part of her clothing was tended to as perfectly as women did on their wedding day.

Sing for me, Grey. The memory of their earlier years echoed inside the emptiness of who they now were.

She lowered her gaze. "May I fix you breakfast?"

The question came at him most mornings, as if she were giving him a choice. It didn't matter that he hated breakfast. A wife cooked each meal for her family. At one time he'd thought it was her way of showing respect, maybe even love, but he knew better now.

"Ya."

While she moved about the kitchen, he sat at the table, reading the newspaper.

Saturday. Regardless of what he did to use up the day, Saturdays were a reminder of the emptiness between them. The aroma of bacon frying filled the room. Sunlight and cool air streamed in through the open windows. He and Elsie were in the same room, about to sit at the same table.

Those things made it look and smell as if normal life went on inside this house.

The clock ticked louder by the minute, telling him time was moving, and yet he wasn't. He and Elsie were in the same place they'd been for at least three years. With each week and month that passed, he was getting farther and farther from all chance of contentment. He'd let go of wanting happiness quite a while ago. But life was too long to live it like this, wasn't it? He closed his newspaper and set it to the side. "Any plans for today?"

"Usual. You?"

The morning begged to be enjoyed, and he knew what they needed to do. "I'm taking Ivan fishing. Would you like to go?"

"There's work to be done."

"There always is, and it'll still be waitin' after we've caught a few fish."

Cracking another raw egg into a bowl, she shook her head. She beat the eggs mercilessly with the whisk, but one would have to know her well to notice the slight, sharp movements as she dumped them into the pan and set the glass bowl firmly, but not too loudly, into the sink. She didn't let her movements reflect too much emotion. If she did, he could point it out and try to get her to open up.

She'd held her silence for years, never saying what really ailed her. Her complaints ranged from not liking the way he breathed to not understanding how he could get so dirty during a workday. If he dared to hum, she'd walk out. But, contrary to how he'd felt over the last few years, he wasn't a fool. When one person picked apart everything about another, the things being mentioned weren't really the problem. They were the side effects.

He understood the grief that had captured her when she gave birth to a stillborn son. He'd mourned the loss deeply, but it'd been three years since then. Did that painful time still cling to her? Her response to burying their second son hadn't seemed much different than her reaction to Ivan's birth. Perhaps that's how she dealt with pregnancy hormones, or maybe it was just her ways. Without them talking, he had no way of knowing.

When he tried to unravel the binding that held them prisoner, she grew more distant, more quiet. So as she carefully and yet sharply plunked his plate in front of him, he wasn't going to ask what was wrong. It could be that she wanted the work done before he went fishing, or that she resented that both Ivan and Grey would return with dirty clothes smelling of fish, or that he'd leave some fish scales in the yard after cleaning them. Even if he asked or tried to prod her to talk, they'd land in the same place they always did—only with a little more deadness between them each time.

No matter what or where they were right now, he still held on to hope that one day they'd really talk and she'd decide to accept her disappointments in being married to him, own up to her part of where they were and why, and be willing to start from there.

It'd taken him a long time to be willing to forget blame and simply start from where they were, but he'd done it. Could she?

"Daed!" Ivan stood in the doorway to the kitchen, a huge smile on his little face. His feety-pajamas covered all but his neck and head. One sleeve hung empty from his elbow down.

His little boy ran to him, and Grey scooped him up. "Ivan." He ruffled his hair and pulled him close, whispering good morning and his love in the only language the little boy spoke, Pennsylvania Dutch.

Ivan hung on tight. *"Du bischt daheem!"*

"Ya, witt fische geh?" Grey agreed that he was at home today and asked Ivan if he wanted to go fishing.

Ivan turned and slapped the table with his one hand, yelling, "Ya!"

"Ivan," Elsie scolded him. *"Net im Haus. Is sell so hatt zu verschteh?"*

Grey flinched as his wife fussed, *Not in the house. Is it that hard to understand?* "He's just excited." Grey aimed to keep his voice even as he spoke to Elsie in English. Ivan hadn't been taught much English yet, but even a child years younger than Ivan could pick up on tone.

"There are rules, Husband. Even for a little boy without an arm. You're not helping by indulging him. When will you see that?"

Ignoring her, Grey sat Ivan on the table facing him. *"Bischt hungerich?"* He nodded, letting Grey know he was hungry.

"Gut. Mir esse un no gehne mir."

Ivan's eyes lit up when Grey told him they'd eat and then go. Without looking at Grey, Elsie set a plate of food for Ivan on the table and returned to the sink. He studied his wife. "Elsie." He waited until she turned to him. Except for the dullness in her eyes, she looked much like she had the day he'd married her nearly six years ago. "Go with us. You could sit on a blanket and watch. Or pick wildflowers. We could share a lunch and maybe even a laugh."

Instead of her usual shake of the head and mumbling a "no thank you," her eyes welled with tears. "And then what will we share? Lies? Dreams we know can't come true?"

His heart quickened. Had she just shared a hint of what separated them? He stared at her, trying to understand what she might mean. "Lies?"

A cold, hauntingly familiar look covered her face. Silence suffocated his hope, but he held her gaze. "Surely believing in dreams would be better than this reality we're in."

The hurt in her eyes was clear, but he thought he caught a hint of her wanting to say more. From the moment he'd seen her in the hallway, she seemed less distant than usual. Did something in her want to open up? Wouldn't that be as vast and high as the heavens—for them to talk and plant some type of seed that didn't grow discouragement and sorrow?

He put Ivan in his chair and placed his food in front of him. He walked over to her, standing so close he could smell the lilac soap he'd given her for her birthday. "Talk to me," he whispered.

She grabbed a cloth and started wiping the counters. "You two go."

"We will." He took her by the arm, and she gazed up at him. "Why do we live like this, Elsie? Even if you married me for all the wrong reasons, why can't we let that go and embrace life as it is?"

Fresh tears filled her eyes. How long had it been since he'd seen her care?

"Please, talk to me."

Ivan finished the food on his plate, but Elsie remained still, staring out the window. The fact that she wasn't pulling away gave him more hope than he'd had in ages.

"You're wrong." Her words were barely audible. He waited, longing for her to say more, but she didn't.

"Okay," he whispered. "But why and when and how? And how do we fix it?"

"*Loss uns fische geh!*" Ivan declared loudly.

"*Ya, in paar Minudde.*" Although Grey assured Ivan that they'd go fishing in a few minutes, he kept his eyes glued to Elsie.

She shook her head, tears falling gently.

"Can't you just tell me some piece? I can't understand without words."

"I...I know. I...think about saying things." She laid her hand on her heart. "Words move through me like fish in a pond, but my pole has no hook, and I own no nets." She turned the water on, washed her face, and dried it on a kitchen towel.

Those few words were the most insight she'd given him in years, and now it was over. He could see it in her face. "We need help, Elsie."

"No." She stiffened, eyes wide, staring at him in horror. He'd never hinted at bringing in the support group before. She was such a private person that it'd tear her up inside to share with others their awful, ugly truth. He knew that about her, but wasn't the way they were living ripping her apart too? She probably took the idea of the council as his threatening her, but he saw it as the only option left. "Grey, please. Everyone will know everything if you do that."

"You know it's handled as privately as possible. Only the church leaders, the three chosen couples, and a few others would have to know. But even if the whole community learned of it, we need help."

"You have the right to tell on me, and God is your witness that I deserve it, but…please."

He stared out the kitchen window, wondering if being married would always be like this—no way to win, no way to forfeit, only a way to carry on.

Six

Standing beside the sink, Deborah counted out the last of the cash and shoved it into an envelope. The propane tank had to be filled early next week, or the gas stove would stop working. Thoughts of using the money Mahlon had sent tempted her. But how could she allow herself to use his money? He'd left them. Probably considered them a burden. Then he sent money?

Feeling caught in a thorn patch, she placed a stamp on the envelope and headed for the mailbox. She'd taken only a few steps when the back door opened. Ada smiled as she entered, but there was no happiness inside her greeting.

Deborah squared her shoulders, wanting to look strong for Ada. "You're done with deliveries already?"

Ada moved to a kitchen chair and sat. "Afraid not." She wiped perspiration from her forehead. "It was so much easier when the bakery sent a courier to pick up and deliver our goods."

"What happened?"

"Rosie went lame. I knew she was favoring her right front leg when I hitched her this morning. Anyway, I got our first delivery made and was halfway to the second when she refused to go any farther. At first I thought she was just being her usual obstinate self, but when I checked her out, I realized she'd thrown a shoe at some point, and her hoof is split pretty bad. It felt hot to me, so it's probably infected."

Deborah's skin tingled as stress crawled over her. Mahlon always took care of Ada's horses. Deborah hadn't even thought to look at the creature's hoofs, and they'd been taking the poor girl on paved roads to make deliveries and to go to Dry Lake and back. No creature deserved that kind of treatment. "Where is she?"

"Tied to a tree about a mile before Select Bakery. After she refused to go any farther, I made several trips back and forth, carrying as many boxed desserts as I could to the bakery. I took the most expensive and perishable ones, but cakes and pies get really heavy when toting them for a mile. I couldn't keep it up and knew we had to come up with a better plan, so I came on home."

Home. The reality around her didn't match the hopes she'd once had for this place.

Ada wiped another round of sweat from her brow. "Before leaving the bakery, I called Stoltzfus Blacksmith Shop. I know it's an hour away by carriage, but it's the only blacksmith I know. I didn't reach anybody, so I left a message."

"Okay, that's a start." Deborah poured Ada a glass of ice water. "Couldn't someone at the bakery drive to where the carriage is parked to pick up the rest of our goods?"

"That would only solve getting our goods to them. I haven't made the drop at Sweet Delights either. I asked the folks at Select Bakery if they could help me out. But two of their people always walk to work, and the other one's car is on the… She called it something. I didn't recognize the word, but someone dropped her off at work, and clearly her car doesn't work any better than my horse."

"Fritz," Deborah offered. "Cara uses the word." She wouldn't say it aloud, but the truth was, everything about her and Ada's lives was on the fritz. Was that how Mahlon felt? Like he'd never get ahead but was too trapped to do anything about it?

"Where is she?" Ada asked.

"Hmm?" Deborah looked up, wondering how long she'd been lost in her own thoughts. "Who?"

"Cara."

"Oh, ya. She and Lori are doing some yard sales. She called it window-shopping. I'm pretty sure she packed them a picnic lunch too and plans to spend the afternoon at Willow Park." Deborah reached her hand across the table. "I'll find the pushcart and get our goods to both bakeries. At least you made most of the deliveries to the farthest one out."

"I guess it's good they open first and want the items earliest."

"Maybe if I unhitch the mare and walk her slowly, she can make it to the barn without the need of borrowing someone's horse trailer." She slid the envelope with the money to pay the propane bill to Ada. "I better not pay that bill. Looks like we might need that cash today."

Ada took a sip of the water. "We made a few dollars today from what the bakeries sold yesterday but only enough to cover food for the next couple of days and fresh supplies for our next round of baking. I've got that birthday cake order for tonight, and I can't wait any longer to get started on it. If you can get the goods to the bakeries and the horse back home, we'll figure out everything else when you return."

"Ya, you're right. First things first." Deborah went to the barn, found the pushcart, and started walking toward Select Bakery.

The sting of feeling overwhelmed and incapable pricked her like hundreds of bees. Before Mahlon left her, she'd had confidence. She missed soaring on the winds, feeling strong and beautiful and hopeful. Had those feelings been a lie? Lately she messed up everything she touched, from making cakes to tending to their horse.

If this business failed, she hated to think what that would do to Ada. She'd lost her only child to the world.

The now-familiar questions started pounding at her again. *Why? Why didn't I know Mahlon wasn't in love with me? Why did life have to become so hard, so humiliating and lonely?*

She didn't hear anything from God. Maybe He couldn't be heard over the river of her own whining. As much as her bellyaching disgusted her, it didn't begin to express how she really felt. She wanted her life back. The one...the one Mahlon ran from?

It didn't make sense to want that.

She spotted the horse under a tree, waiting patiently to be rescued. Rosie had her right front hoof barely touching the ground. Deborah set the legs to the pushcart on the ground and moved to the horse, caressing her head and nose. The poor thing nuzzled against Deborah's touch. What an awful price Rosie was paying for Deborah and Ada's negligence.

"I can't seem to get anything right, Rosie." Deborah placed her forehead against the horse's, waiting on a peaceful thought or answer to float down and rescue her. It didn't.

She took a step back, longing to hear a whisper within her own soul. Something faint brushed her awareness. She knew this feeling. In the past this sensation swept over her when Mahlon was nearby, usually when he was watching her from a distance. She'd had it many times, but she didn't think she'd felt it since he left.

She stepped out from under the tree and looked up and down Main Street. A couple of women milled about, going nowhere in a hurry, and one man stood at the automated-teller machine outside the bank.

Mahlon wasn't there. Part of her wished he was. As much as he'd done to her, the biggest part of her still loved him. *How is that possible?*

"Hey, Deborah."

She jolted and looked behind her. Jonathan Stoltzfus, Mahlon's cousin, was astride his chestnut stallion, riding it bareback.

She wondered how she hadn't heard his horse coming up the side street behind her. "What are you doing here?"

Jonathan slid off his horse. "Ada left a message at the shop about an hour ago, saying you guys had a lame horse." He grinned and straightened his straw hat. "It took me about two, maybe three, seconds to realize there was a wagonload of desserts that needed rescuing."

The feeling of being caught in a briar patch eased. "I'm glad to know that I can always depend on you—as long as free desserts are involved."

"Never ever forget that, Little Debbie." He passed her the reins and moved to where Rosie stood. Within moments he had the horse's knee bent and part of her leg resting on his thigh while he inspected her hoof. "Ya, it's split and infected. She'll be out of commission for a while. I should've thought to check her shoes when I was at Ada's three weeks ago." He stood straight. "So, we need to connect Rosie's wagon to my horse without making the desserts slide into one another. Up for it?"

She doubted it. She'd do something stupid and mess everything up again.

Jonathan ran his hands down Rosie's shoulder and slowly moved past her fetlock, looking for other signs of injury.

"Ya. I guess."

Jonathan turned to face her. "If Rosie could talk, even she'd sound more confident than that."

She shrugged, trying to keep tears at bay.

He moved closer. "You want to talk about it?"

"There's nothing to say that you don't already know."

He lifted her chin, making her look him in the eyes. "We go way back, Deborah. I'd guess I realized you weren't so bad when I was in eighth grade and put a frog in your dress at school. You must've been in third grade at the time, just a little kid, and you didn't even tell the teacher on me."

"Ya." She remembered feeling the creature wriggle against her back, and she'd run out of the classroom without permission and danced around outside until that frog fell to the ground.

"Of course"—Jonathan folded his arms—"the day before, you'd used the backside of my homework to draw a picture on."

"You're the one who put it on my desk."

"I was busy and just set it down."

"And I made it more beautiful with swirly things and hearts and rainbows."

"Just what I wanted while standing in front of the class reading the report—the part facing them filled with girly stuff." He laughed, but she only shrugged. "Come on, Little Debbie. That image is worth a chuckle."

"How can I laugh about anything? All of me *believed* that Mahlon loved me. I thought he wanted a life with me…and every bit of that was a lie."

He rubbed his fingers across his shaven face, making a light sandpaper noise as he did. "Like you, I've known Mahlon my whole life. He loved you. You've got to know that's true. He was just…too immature and confused to deal with life."

When she didn't answer, he began fastening the rigging to his horse. That odd sensation washed over her again. She went to the sidewalk and studied the old town.

Across the street, more than a block away, a man stood watching her. *Is it possible?*

The hair on her arms and neck stood up. *Mahlon?*

Emotions pounded at her like hoofs from a dozen horses. What should she do? What did she want to do? Was it even him?

If it was…

Silence fell inside her, and emotions waited on the edge for an answer. Her own soul wanted to know, if it was him, then what?

When he left her, she quickly moved from beloved fiancée to the "humiliated one," and now she understood something about herself—she'd slipped from shock and mourning into a really bad place. And she had to fight her way free before she gave Mahlon the power to destroy even more of her life than he already had.

Jonathan peered in the direction she was staring. "What are we looking at?"

I have no idea. Even if the man was Mahlon, she still wouldn't know who she was seeing. "A creation of my imagination."

The man took a few steps toward her, and Deborah's heart went crazy. If it was Mahlon, she didn't want to face him. Not today. Not while she was a walking heap of...of...failure. He strode toward her, but his walk didn't look like Mahlon's slow, easy gait. Still, it could be him.

Whether or not the man she was looking at was Mahlon, he would return one day—probably with a wife and children. And he'd eventually walk right onto the porch of Ada's house and wait until they invited him in. When he did, she intended for her and Ada to own a very successful business. Somehow.

Jonathan brought his horse alongside her. The man was still too far away to know if it was Mahlon. A car pulled up in front of him and tooted the horn. The man seemed to be staring at her, but then he got into the vehicle.

"You ready to get moving?" Jonathan asked.

The car drove out of sight before she managed to look up at Jonathan. "Actually...I think I am."

Seven

With Ivan perched on his shoulders and a basket of fish in one hand and poles in the other, Grey walked toward home. He heard a woman saying one-syllable words—"Got ya," "No way," "I win," "I don't think so"—but he couldn't see her. He was on the road beside the Kauffman house, and by the sounds of it, Lennie was somewhere nearby, probably in the side yard or under a shade tree, playing a board game with her Daed. He kept walking, but still he didn't see either of them.

Ivan laughed.

"Was iss es?" Grey waited, expecting his son to point or tell him what he was laughing at, but the boy broke into a long cackle. A little concerned he might fall, Grey dropped the basket of fish and his poles and steadied his son's shaking body. He glanced around the yard and saw what his son was watching.

Lennie and her dog. Nicky was facing her, squatting low. When Lennie made a playful step toward Nicky, the dog ran in huge circles before stopping. Nicky then squatted again, ready to lunge toward or run from. Lennie ran toward her. The dog took off, but not before Lennie touched her side. "Ha, I won."

The dog barked like mad, as if arguing with Lennie's announcement of victory. Nicky ran several circles and squatted low on her front legs, her tail lifted high in the air, wagging. Lennie danced around, her fists taut as she made circles with them in rhythm. "Oh no. I won. Game done."

Nicky ran at her, stopped abruptly, barked, and then took off. While teasing the dog and hopping around, Lennie caught a glimpse of Grey. The victory dance ended midstep. Her eyes grew large, and something between embarrassment and amusement played across her face.

"Teacher Lena." Grey nodded once. "What are you doing?"

She gained control over her surprise. *"Wie bischt du Heit?"* She straightened, asking Ivan how he was today.

"Hund!" Ivan chirped loudly.

"Ya, en verhuddelder Hund."

Ivan laughed at Lennie saying she had a confused dog.

Before he'd married, Grey raised dogs, and one year Lennie's Daed had asked Grey to keep an eye out for a particularly good dog for her, one that matched a whole list of things she would like in a pet. By the time Nicky was eight weeks old, Grey knew she'd make a perfect dog for Lennie. Grey thought Nicky was the best kind of dog—a mixed breed. She had a little Chow, Labrador retriever, and Australian Shepherd in her, and weighed about fifty pounds fully mature.

Lennie dusted off her hands. "Any news from the board I need to know about?"

"No. We got it all settled."

She nodded, crossed the yard, and held out her hand for Ivan's. He placed his inside hers. She talked to him in Pennsylvania Dutch, telling him that he was growing fast and that he'd be in her class, ready to learn how to read and write, by this time next year.

"Haldscht Schul fer die Handikap?" Ivan asked.

Startled, Grey found it hard to catch his breath. *Did she teach at a school for the handicapped?* He was sure his eyes mirrored the same confusion as Lennie's.

She looked at Ivan and told him no.

"Ich geh in die Handikap Schul," Ivan said.

Grey couldn't believe his son's words. What made him think he would go to the handicap school?

Lennie searched Grey's eyes for a moment. Feeling insulted by whoever had told his son that, Grey lifted him off his shoulders and held him. His son was small for his age and missing part of an arm, and if Grey dared to be painfully honest, Ivan was a good bit less mature than most five-year-olds, but none of that qualified him to attend a school for the handicapped. Speaking in Pennsylvania Dutch, Grey asked who'd told him he was going to the handicap school.

"Mamm."

Anger—years of it—swooped through Grey. Their son was missing part of one arm. What would possess his wife to tell him he needed to go to a school for the handicapped?

Silently fighting offense as he never had before, he felt displaced, as if he weren't really there. Yet he noticed every movement and heard every word. Lennie held out her arms for Ivan, asking if he wanted to pet the doggy. Ivan went to her. She gently commanded Nicky to lie down. The dog obeyed, and Lennie knelt beside Ivan while they petted the dog and talked about her fur being soft, like a rabbit's.

When Grey regained his ability to move, he picked up the basket. "He'll go to our local school."

Lennie stood. "I…I'm sure she's only thinking of his best interest."

"Oh, ya, sure." Grey doubted that his effort to conceal his frame of mind hid anything at all.

Lennie shrugged. "It's nearly a year away yet."

"Ya." Grey motioned for Ivan. *"Kumm mol, loss uns geh."* As soon as Grey said, *Come on, let's go,* his little boy hurried to him, telling Lennie bye.

He put Ivan on his shoulders again. Lena grabbed the poles off the ground and passed them to him. He mumbled his thanks and started walking. Hard. Fast. Unforgiving.

The closer he got to his house, the more resentment woke inside him. When he came to the sidewalk that led to his front door, he walked straight past it. He didn't trust what he might say…or how he'd say it.

He and Elsie were fragile. Although he was hard-pressed to imagine how they could be more distant than they already were, he didn't doubt it was possible. Ignoring his intense desire to set her straight about their son, he took Ivan with him and kept walking.

"Daed? *Heem geh?*" Ivan asked.

Needing to answer his son's question about where they were going, Grey quickly decided on his destination. He told him they were going to the cabinetry shop. They often went there on Saturday afternoons, and Ivan enjoyed it. With Grey's long strides and his taking shortcuts through several fields, he was soon on Mast property.

As he approached the shop, he heard the air compressor running, followed by bursts of noise as nails were shot into wood. When he crossed the threshold, he saw Ephraim inside a frame of what would eventually be a standing pantry. He'd like to talk to Ephraim, but he wouldn't. His burdens were between him and Elsie.

Ephraim glanced up and gave a nod before continuing with his work.

A few moments later Ephraim walked to the generator and turned off the compressor. "Been to the pond, huh?"

Grey set the fishing tackle on the concrete floor. "Ya." He took Ivan off his shoulders. His son went to the barrel of scraps and pulled out blocks of wood to build with.

"Grab that crown molding for me, will ya?" Ephraim asked.

Grey brought four sections to him.

Ephraim passed him a piece of sandpaper. "The Wertzes want this same molding to run along the wall from the top of the pantry to the floor. It works in spite of the wave that's in the Wertzes' walls, but I could use your help coping these inside corners to fit against the pantry. I was at their place earlier, so I've already measured and marked everything accordingly."

Grey gave a nod, and they began sanding the wood.

"I appreciate you coming in on Saturdays and helping here and there."

Grey didn't want to admit that he was using this time today to avoid going home, so he nodded again.

"If you ever have something you want to tell me…"

He shook his head. "Can't. But thanks."

The two worked in silence for a while.

Then Ephraim laid the wood to the side. "Cara didn't trust me at all at first. Did you know that?"

"No."

The sound of Ivan smacking wood against the concrete floor echoed through the room.

Ephraim rested against the workbench. "All I remember thinking about her at first was that I wanted her out of Dry Lake before anyone else could catch wind of who she was. When I had to step up and speak to the police to keep her and Lori from being separated, I realized she wasn't just an inconvenience who had showed up in my life at the worst time ever. She was a real person who hadn't been given a break in a really long time." Ephraim shrugged. "I think the only reason I recognized that in her is because I'd seen it in you time and again."

The weight around him grew stronger, pressing in like he was caught under deep water. "I…we need help," Grey whispered, releasing years of hidden truth. "I…can't imagine going on like this, and there is no way out. You know that." Grey's eyes burned, and he glanced across the room at his son. Ivan had surrounded himself with blocks of scrap wood and was stacking them as high as he could. "We've been in separate rooms for years. She refuses to talk about anything. How can I make that work?"

"Separate…" The look on Ephraim's face and the tone of his voice held alarm and distress, and Grey found comfort in it. With that one awful word, Ephraim understood Grey's isolation and the impassable cinder-block wall surrounding him and Elsie. "Why?"

"I don't know, at least not the real reason. There are times when I'm not sure I care anymore." Grey clasped his hands around his head. "Maybe I'm pushing her away."

"What makes you say that?"

"It…" He lowered his hands and walked to the doublewide open door. Gazing out over the fields, he tried to find the courage to confess. "The regret began without my permission… I'd wake at night, or maybe it woke me, but I wish we'd never married."

Ephraim moved next to him. "It can't be all that uncommon for people to feel that way sometimes."

He stared off in the distance, wishing he hadn't started this conversation and yet too desperate to keep it all inside any longer. "If she's picking up on how I feel, maybe I carry more blame than I think I do."

"Or maybe she's causing those feelings. Whatever's going on, there have to be answers."

He turned around to check on Ivan before he looked straight at Ephraim. "I'm so stinking mad at her right now that I'm afraid to go home. Just before I came here, Ivan said she plans on sending him to the handicap school." Grey smacked the metal frame of the door with the palm of his hand. "As the head of our home, I have final say about where he goes, but why would she tell him that? Is he not perfect enough for her? Does she want to hide him from our district?" Even though Ivan didn't understand much English and was at the far end of the building, Grey had whispered his words. "The closest school of that kind is nearly two hours away. We'd have to move, and I'd have to find a new job. If I thought he needed it, I'd do it. Is she seeing him wrong, or am I?"

The sound of wooden blocks tumbling made both Ephraim and Grey look at Ivan. He stood in the middle of strewn blocks, kicking them.

"I know he's a little immature, but—"

"Grey," Ephraim interrupted, "if we sent every immature first grader to the handicap school, a lot of us would've gone there. Including me."

"He's smart. I know he is."

"He seems bright to me."

"Then why would his own mother want to send him there?"

"Don't know. He's suppose to start school next year, right?"

"Ya."

"If I were you, I'd refuse to argue about it. You need an outside opinion, and I'd bet Lena would be the best help. I could be biased, since she's my cousin, but she's really good at what she does—understanding and helping her scholars. If she spent an afternoon testing him, like she does her first-grade students right before they start school, she could tell you how close he is to lining up with the other children his age. And she could probably let you know how much of a handicap he has because of his missing arm."

"I hadn't thought of that. She'd be honest too. She can always be trusted for that, but I don't know if Elsie will hear her."

Ephraim placed his hand on Grey's shoulder. "I find it hard to believe, but you still care what your wife thinks."

He gave a nod before he turned to study the fields, willing wisdom and direction to come to him. "The one thing I've learned about being married is that how I feel changes nothing. Ever."

"Whatever you do will be tough, but maybe what love you two do have is tougher."

Ephraim's words butted against the constant negative whispers inside Grey—the ones that spoke to him of defeat over and over again.

Love never fails.

He caught a glimpse of understanding, as if seeing inside an unfamiliar room for a brief moment. Love had a hope all its own.

"Daed?" Ivan tugged at Grey's pant leg. "Heem geh?"

Feeling tears sting his eyes, Grey lifted his son and held him close. *"Ya, loss uns Heemet geh."* He looked to Ephraim. "It's time I go on home now."

Eight

In her jeans and with her short crop of hair down, Cara continued reading the Sunday paper, enjoying the slower pace of between Sundays. Lori sat on a kitchen stool beside her, giggling over the comics. Cara hadn't seen Ada or Deborah yet this morning, although she knew they were up. A fresh pot of coffee and a small fire in the potbelly stove had greeted her and Lori when they'd entered the kitchen about thirty minutes ago.

Deborah walked into the kitchen looking every bit as Amish as she did on the other six days of the week, except she had on a white organdy apron that didn't cover the top half of her dress. Her hair was fixed just so. She made living Amish look easy. *"Guder Marye."* Deborah bid a good morning before grabbing the poker. She opened the lid to the potbelly stove and stirred the embers. "We don't want this burning for long, but we needed a little something to remove the nip in the air. I take it you're not going to Dry Lake with us for services this morning?"

Cara bit her tongue and shook her head. It was an off day, for Pete's sake. Besides, she had yard work to do. While shopping at yard sales yesterday, she'd found an item she wanted but didn't have the money for. An older woman at the sale offered to buy the item for Cara in exchange for some yard work. So the two of them struck a deal, and by tonight Cara would have earned a fantastic gift for Lori. Of course it was used, but Lori wouldn't mind that part—if she even noticed it.

Deborah fixed herself a cup of coffee. "Ada will be down in a minute.

We're leaving extra early so I can visit my family first. You're welcome to join us. We'll stay for the meal afterward and probably visit until midafternoon."

"Nope, we're good. Thanks." Cara liked between Sundays ever so much more than church Sundays. Ephraim had church today in Dry Lake, and he would come to Hope Crossing next Sunday to go to church with her, Lori, Ada, and Deborah. But so far he'd not pressed her to come to Dry Lake on her off Sundays. She appreciated that. It was enough for her that she sat through three hours of unintelligible preaching every other Sunday. Of course Ephraim understood the language spoken during the service, and he'd grown up attending three-hour services.

What possessed the Amish to have such long services anyway? But sometimes, when a few Pennsylvania words that she understood were strung together, she found it exciting. And those rare moments helped move the service from hair-pulling boring to slightly interesting.

Deborah sipped her drink. "Just as well, I suppose. The meeting will be held at the Lantzes' today."

"Lantz?" Cara tried to hide the snarl she felt. "As in Anna Mary Lantz?"

"Ya. It's at her parents' place."

Anna Mary's parents—just the thought of them set her on edge. Their deceit had ruined Cara's mother's life and had opened the floodgates of bad luck. It'd overflowed into Cara's life and even Lori's, yet the Lantzes were still members in good standing. She'd never understand the Amish ways. Not ever.

"But if you don't go… Well, I just want some backup when Lena returns the favor for our prank on her."

"She won't pull anything on a Sunday during church, will she?"

"No, not during the service but maybe afterward."

"Good luck with that, Deb." Cara patted her on the shoulder.

"You're awful. The plan was yours after all."

Cara shrugged. "Yeah, but Lori and I met an old woman yesterday. She lives a few doors down, and we're going to her house in a little bit."

"To visit?" Deborah asked.

"Sort of. I'll tell you the rest when we get back." She placed her index finger over her lips before pointing at Lori. "It's a surprise."

"But you're not wearing that, are you?"

Cara looked down at her clothes. "Yep. It's my off day. I'm comfortable. And I'm in my rumschpringe."

"Well, now, see, you're a little wrong. It's the Lord's Day. You've already admitted that dresses are just as comfortable as jeans. And the rumschpringe doesn't apply to you since its purpose is for freedom to find a spouse and you've found one."

Cara rolled her eyes. "Hair pinned back and prayer Kapp too?"

"You don't have to, but do you think wearing only part of our Amish apparel is a good idea?"

"I guess not." She sighed. "Great."

Ada walked into the kitchen, wearing what looked like a new burgundy dress under a new apron. Cara whistled.

Ada's cheeks grew pink. "Don't be ridiculous, Cara."

"Oh, so there isn't a man in Dry Lake you're hoping to look good for?" Cara continued to tease.

Deborah's face radiated behind her mostly hidden smile, and Cara knew she hoped the same thing for Ada.

"That's more than enough, girls," Ada said firmly before she took a chair. "I feel too old for such nonsense."

"You're not old. Don't you know forty is the new thirty?" When Ada looked torn between amusement and true embarrassment, Cara decided to change the subject. "How are you getting there if the horse is lame?"

A car horn tooted, and Cara had the answer to her question. A driver was picking them up.

"Ephraim's driver for the cabinetry shop stopped by yesterday and volunteered to come get us and bring us back home today without charge, so we took him up on it." Deborah gave Lori a quick hug. "You be good."

"*Gut is was ich bescht duh.*" Lori beamed at her, saying something along the lines of, "Good is what I do best."

Ada gave Cara a hug. "The way you see me and tease, you do make me feel younger." She took a step back. "I don't know how we'd have gotten through these past few months without you."

"Denki." Cara winked. "Be sure to bring Ephraim back with you, okay?"

"You think we or *anybody* could stop him?"

"I hope not."

After she closed the door behind them, she scurried upstairs and changed her clothes. By this afternoon she'd have helped an elderly woman and bartered for something Lori had only dreamed of. Excitement coursed through her. She couldn't remember when she'd had the ability to give Lori something truly special.

Grey stood at the sink with a cup of coffee in one hand while reading a newspaper he wished he hadn't picked up. The words made his heart thud with longing and…and jealousy? The Amish Mennonite newspaper had been neatly tucked in its rack since last Wednesday. While walking past it, he'd spied his own name—Benjamin Graber. Folks called him Grey, but Benjamin was his given name. So the newspaper had caught his attention, and he'd grabbed it to see what the man who shared his name had been up to. The impulse had seemed innocent enough. But now here he stood, flooded with emotions.

"Reading the paper on a Sunday before church?" Elsie asked.

He heard her complaint, but he continued reading the article. The man who shared his name lived in Ohio with his wife. It was common for the Amish to have the same given name and surnames. That was part of the reason for his nickname. According to the article, this Benjamin had been married for three decades, and he and his wife finished each other's sentences, laughed easily, and shared their heartaches freely. They'd enjoyed blessings and suffered losses by leaning on each other.

Grey set his coffee and paper on the counter and stared out the kitchen window. How did he and Elsie get to such a miserable place? Each of them living in their own world, yet they shared the greatest bond this planet had to offer—marriage vows. And a beautiful child as proof of that unity.

But it was as if they stood on opposite sides of a wide canyon. They could see each other, but even when shouting across the chasm, they couldn't understand much, if anything, of what the other one said, and there seemed to be no way to cross over.

When he'd come home last night, he'd tried to keep to himself what he'd learned of Elsie's intention to send Ivan to a special school. His thoughts were still lingering on the words *love never fails,* but when she'd grumbled about his clothes smelling like fish and about his wasting too much of the day on nonsense, he'd snapped at her, saying that Ivan would go to the local school. She'd stood in front of him speechless, looking frustrated by his anger. They'd muddled through the rest of the evening, offering stilted half sentences when conversation couldn't be avoided. The moment Ivan was in his bed for the night, he'd retired to his bedroom, closing the door behind him without another word being spoken. Never had such a gulf existed between them as the one last night.

When he stopped gazing out the window, he saw Elsie skimming the article he'd just read. Pursing her lips, she slid the paper onto the table. Then she went to the refrigerator and grabbed several large blocks of cheese. It was their contribution to the after-service meal. "It's almost time for us to leave for church. Is the horse hitched?"

Were her hands trembling?

"Is that all you have to say?"

She dumped his coffee in the sink. "It's a church day. And if we don't leave soon, we'll be late."

"Ya." Grey took his hat from the coatrack. "It wouldn't do for anyone to think we're less than perfect." Sunlight and cool air filled his senses when he stepped outside, but as he continued to fight and grumble with his wife, he seemed less able to enjoy the simple things. He went to the barn, got the horse out of the stall, and began harnessing her.

At the start of their marriage, only a few feet had separated them. Normal things—like not knowing or understanding each other's ways in certain areas—but he'd expected love to override those things. Wasn't embracing someone else's faults part of what friends did for each other? And marriage was supposed to be the best friendship of all.

His wife's shadow fell across the dirt floor of the barn. He led the horse and carriage toward her. Ivan stood beside her as she held a basket filled with cheese. "Whatever is going on inside that heart of yours, I can't go on living like this. Something has to change."

She started toward the buggy. "We need to go."

"Does anything I want even matter to you?"

Stopping abruptly, she lowered her gaze. "If you could just accept…"

He took the basket from her and set it inside the carriage. Was she waiting on him to finish her sentence like the other Benjamin Graber could for his wife? He had no clue what she might say. Back when they'd been married only a couple of months, he realized that he didn't understand her at all, because when she'd told him she was pregnant, he was excited. She wasn't.

After Ivan was born, she'd become distant and temperamental. He'd tried to help her by sharing her load of the work, making her breakfasts, and spending extra time with her. He didn't know if those things helped her, but within a year she was doing better. They began sharing a bed again. When their second son was stillborn, the grief had been unbearable.

By the time the intensity of their pain began to lift, he realized the distance between them was vast.

Elsie raised her eyes to his. "I made a vow to never tell you."

"Ivan." Grey pointed to the swing set in their backyard and told him to go play until he called him.

Ivan looked up at his mother. She didn't allow playing outside on Sundays until the afternoon. She said nothing, and he hurried toward the house.

"Whatever your secret, you've done a good job of keeping it. Too good. And if you knew how sick I am of how we live, you'd shout the secret from the rooftop."

She looked steely cold as she shrugged, and Grey wanted to shake her.

Slowly she went toward the buggy. "We'll be late."

"I don't care!"

She jolted, and embarrassment engraved itself on her face. He drew a breath and tried to keep his tone civil. "I may not be much of a husband in your eyes, but answer me this: don't I at least deserve to know what stands between us?"

She rubbed the center of her forehead. "Okay," she whispered. "I...I've always feared that the truth would finish destroying what little love you have for me."

He studied her, seeing raw ache under all her layers of organized perfection. Did the pain come from losing one son? Or from being married to Grey? As her husband, he should know. "What truth?"

"You know it, Grey. You just don't want to admit it."

"For the love of my sanity, Elsie, please stop talking in circles."

"Fine. You want to make me say it aloud? You want to make me take the blame? Then I will. We can't have more children. We *must* not. Not ever."

Alarm rang inside him, warning him not to let this conversation end until he understood. "Why?"

"Don't be absurd. You know why."

As he struggled to grasp what she meant, he took her by the arm. "Tell me why."

She pulled away. "Can't you see it? Ivan is missing part of one arm, and he…he's slow. When our second son was stillborn, the midwife told me something genetic was probably wrong with him. I can't…I won't have a family of children with physical and mental issues because I want to be with you. That's selfish."

Barely able to breathe, Grey leaned against a nearby wall for support. This was what separated them? He'd imagined hundreds of reasons over the years but never once thought of this.

Elsie moved to him. "I know I'm not an easy woman to love. And I'm not sure what I expected to happen to us when I started shutting you out, but I've only wanted to spare you."

He felt sure he should have compassion for her, but he didn't. "I had the right to know what caused you to behave as you do."

"Why? So you could change my mind, only for us to have another child that broke our hearts?"

"Ivan did not break my heart. He's a strong, healthy boy. And I don't think he's slow, not like that. And even if he is, no part of me enjoys him any less. Besides, what do you want from him? To be perfect? Like who? You? Me? May God spare him from our type of perfection, Elsie."

Needing to get away from her, he walked outside. He looked toward the house, making sure the best part of the last six years was still safe inside their yard. His little boy's blond hair shined like a white pillowcase in the sun. His hat lay on the ground, and his belly was on the seat of the swing as he dragged his lone hand lightly across the dirt.

Elsie walked to where he stood.

Grey couldn't even look at her. "You locked me out of your heart and our bedroom because you decided that was the best solution. You didn't ask your husband or the church leaders. Didn't seek out medical advice.

Didn't try to ease my loneliness by being honest. You did exactly as you chose." He turned to look her in the eyes.

"Grey, that's…that's not fair."

He pointed at her. "You do not have the right to talk to me about what's fair!" As he stood in his driveway yelling at his wife, Grey hated himself, hated who he'd become. For years he'd wanted them to talk, and now he couldn't gain control of his rage.

Studying him, their home, and their son, she seemed to waver in her position, as if some small bit of what he'd said might have merit. Part of him wanted to shake her. Part of him wished he could embrace her…and never let go.

He went toward the house. All these years he'd thought she didn't love him. He'd been convinced she regretted marrying him. He stopped and went back to her. "And it's not true. We do not have some defect that caused Ivan to have a deformed arm or caused our other son to be still-born. It's not us. Not you. Not me. Not who we are together. Those things just happen sometimes. That's all." He walked away again.

Elsie grabbed him by the arm. "It *is* true. Do you think I'd pull away from you if I didn't believe it? I'm trapped between a husband I love and a body that bears unsound children. Will you hold what I've done against me?"

"You've made our lives miserable, Elsie. And you had no right."

Tears fell, and she swiped them away. "Tell Ivan it's time for us to go."

Grey stared at her, remembering a hundred church Sundays of riding side by side while engulfed in loneliness and silence. Nothing carried weight like emptiness did. And it had stood between them most of their married years. Would they finally get to this point of her sharing her bur-den, regardless of how wrong she'd been, only to start over in the same dark, horrid place? "Why would you do this to us based on a guess?"

Her face was taut as she pursed her lips. "I…I…can't."

As he studied her, he saw more than just her failure. He saw his own.

His mind churned with memories, and he knew he'd made it too easy for her to shut him out. And his anger eased.

At twenty-seven, Elsie had lines of weariness creasing her face, and in that moment he felt the depth of her struggle to speak, and the heaviness of the guilt she felt, and the pain of the fears that rested on her day and night.

"We need help, Elsie."

"There's no help. There's only putting one foot in front of the other. You know that."

He used to think her no-nonsense personality would keep him straight. Now he'd give about anything to be able to get past that. "So you've stopped believing in hope altogether?" Ivan's voice carried on the wind as he sang loudly. Elsie's eyes moved to Grey's, and they shared a moment of parenting pleasure. They knew he was singing to God, not as a worship-type song, but as entertainment *for* God.

She watched their son, her eyes filling with tears. "You know that I…I have an aunt in Ohio…who…has five children with birth defects. After Ivan was born, she said that whatever is wrong with her, I must have the same thing." Tears trailed down her face.

Maybe she was right. Maybe they couldn't have completely healthy children. As his confidence waned, he reached out to put his arms around her.

She backed away. "I'm sorry for the way it is."

"We can't live on just a notion of yours. We never should have, and I won't let it continue. We've got to know for sure about Ivan, about our DNA. And then we'll make decisions from there."

She cleared her throat and gave a weak nod. "Don't, Grey. Please. The answers will not give us peace. It'll only bury the rest of what hope you have."

"I won't let fear stop us."

"Then truth will, and you will learn that I'm right."

Nothing they discovered would be any harder than coping with her years of silence.

Ivan hollered to them, asking why they weren't going to church.

They'd be more than thirty minutes late to a three-hour service, but Grey wanted to go. He had hope that it might offer some nugget to help him and Elsie.

Nine

After ringing the doorbell, Cara brushed strands of hair off her forehead. While waiting on the woman to answer the door, she surveyed her work. What had been an overgrown yard hours ago now looked manicured. She'd mowed and weeded. Lori had worked too. While they were hauling clippings and weeds to the mulch pit, Cara finally told her about the item they were working for—a beautiful bicycle.

She wasn't sure which Lori was the most excited about, the bike or the fact that they were working side by side to earn it.

The elderly woman came out of her home, eyes bright with appreciation. "Just look at this place." She turned to Lori. "You're a lucky little girl to have a mama who'd do all this for a bike."

Lori put her arms around Cara's waist and hugged her.

The woman motioned. "Come on. It's right inside the garage." They went down the steps. "I'm sure that's the last the yard will need for the season, but if you're around next spring and are interested in making money, stop on by. I have a yard boy, but by the time he can get here every few weeks, I need someone to bale hay rather than mow grass."

"It might be a good extra job for me, but I don't know right now. We can talk about it next spring, okay?"

"Sounds good." The woman went to a keypad and punched in several numbers, and the garage door opened. Motioning for Lori to follow her, she walked inside. "There it is."

Lori's eyes grew huge as she gaped at her mother. "It's...it's perfect!" She grabbed it by the handlebars and ran outside. The purple and pink metallic swirls glittered under the rays of sunlight. "Oh, Mom, this is just too cool." She straddled it and put her feet on the pedals. The bike fell to one side, and Lori jolted, putting her feet back on the concrete. "Teach me how to ride this thing."

Her daughter's excited voice rang out as she waved at the woman. "Thank you." Lori put her feet on the pedals again, and the wheels started turning.

Cara grabbed the bike's seat and smiled at the woman. "I...I better go."

The woman laughed. "I guess you better. Bye for now."

Cara ran on the sidewalk beside Lori, trying to give helpful instructions for how to find her balance. By the time they'd gone around the block once, Cara could let go of the seat for several seconds at a time. As they made their way around the block a second time, Cara only grabbed it when Lori was about to fall. Finally she released her and clapped as Lori rode about fifty feet before stopping herself.

Cara trotted to where she was. "That's great, honey. You are so good at this." They worked their way around the block for the third time, and as they approached Ada's House, she noticed two Amish men in front of the place, watching her.

Lori came to them first and stopped. Cara couldn't hear what her daughter was saying, but she could tell by her movements she was showing them her bike.

As Cara approached, she recognized them. One was a preacher from right here in Hope Crossing. The other was a bishop for several Amish communities: Dry Lake, Hope Crossing, and some other Amish district Cara wasn't familiar with. But he lived in Hope Crossing.

Cara straightened her prayer Kapp and tried to tuck loose strands of hair back into place before she stopped in front of them. "Hello."

"Hi, Cara."

She looked at the bishop. "I thought you'd be at the service in Dry Lake."

"I often am. Each district has visiting preachers from time to time, and they had plenty of preachers for today, so I stayed home. I went to the door, but it seems Deborah and Ada aren't here."

"They're attending the service in Dry Lake."

The bishop nodded as if that answered all sorts of questions he had. "Can we speak to you alone for a bit?"

Suddenly feeling unsure about what they might want, she turned to Lori. "You can ride up and down the sidewalk that leads to Ada's front porch."

"That's all? How about from here to the end of the block?"

"Not by yourself."

"But you can see me the whole way."

"Nope. You might keep right on going until you're in the middle of the street."

Lori started to argue, but Cara splayed her hand as if she was going to start counting. Lori nodded and began riding up the thirty-foot segment that led to Ada's front porch.

Cara took several breaths, glad not to be chasing that bike around the block. "So what's on your mind?"

"You're new to our ways, Cara. And you've been doing well. That's first and foremost to remember, but do you know what today is?"

"You mean aside from it being a between Sunday for those of us in Hope Crossing?"

The bishop shifted. "It is still a Sunday, and you were mowing someone's grass."

Her heart raced as she realized they'd come to correct her. "How do you know what I've been doing?"

"Someone saw you over an hour ago and came straight to us."

"Ah, so the Amish system of accountability depends greatly on tattletales."

The bishop scratched his beard, not looking even slightly perturbed at her retort. "Let's keep this friendly, Cara. You've made a couple of mistakes. That's all. If it helps, the person who told isn't Amish."

"Why would anyone do that?"

He shrugged, looking sympathetic. "People and motives are hard to figure, but we came as soon as we heard, in hopes of stopping you from doing anything else that might cause trouble for you."

"But I wasn't making any money, and mowing a yard isn't any more tiring than those boys playing baseball or volleyball on Sunday afternoons. That's allowed, right?"

"Ya, in the afternoon after they've had time to reflect on God," the preacher said.

Unable to accept their stance, Cara put one hand on her hip. Frustration circled round and round. "You're splitting hairs."

"It's our way not to work on Sunday. Surely Ephraim's shared that with you."

She did seem to remember him saying something about that. "Women fix food on Sundays, don't they?"

"We do as much preparation as possible on Saturdays, but fixing meals is allowed." The bishop's tone changed from one of explaining to one of slight frustration.

She squelched her irritation by counting. It was then that she realized what he meant by stopping her "from doing anything else that might cause trouble." If she hoped to be allowed to go through instruction starting late spring, she needed to stay in good standing with the church. They'd come over immediately to keep her from messing up her future plans. "Okay, fine. I won't do anything like this again."

"Good. And I...uh...well, when you talk to Ephraim, mention to him the type of lawn mower you used." He gave a nod as if they were ready to leave.

"Wait. Are you saying part of the reason you're here is because I used the wrong kind of mower?"

"I know how it probably sounds to you, but next time you mow grass, use a reel mower, not a gasoline-powered one."

Tinges of embarrassment began to mix with her anger. "But we use gas stoves."

"Natural gas is allowed to come into our homes through a propane tank. We don't use gasoline-powered anything—not cars, tractors, or lawn mowers."

"Well, Amish certainly ride in gas-powered vehicles."

"Sparingly so is the goal. Another, stricter goal is to avoid hiring a driver on a Sunday. The exceptions to that are situations like the one Ada is in, a widow wanting to return to her home community on church Sundays, or Ephraim, who catches a ride with a friend. Once we allow our people the right to hire a driver for absolute necessities, like medical needs or making a living, we do little to control what else a driver is hired for. We try to leave that up to their good judgment. But to hold on to our ways, we do not operate gas-powered machines ourselves."

As annoyance tried to get the best of her, she thought of Ephraim. Anything she said or did reflected on him. He'd withstood a shunning for her sake, and he deserved better than her arguing with the church leaders. "I'll use a reel mower next time."

A genuine smile began in the bishop's eyes and spread to his mouth. "Good. Very good. I'm pleased to have this kind of talk with you."

The preacher turned to the bishop and made a motion. The bishop shook his head.

She glanced from one bearded man to the other. "There's more, isn't there?"

The preacher turned to the bishop. "The longer you allow it, the more we look like hypocrites."

The bishop shook his head, and she could only guess he didn't want to say whatever the preacher wanted said.

"Well?" Her tone could cause frostbite, but she didn't care.

"Bicycles are forbidden," the preacher said.

The skin on her face burned. Finally, after years of poverty, she'd been able to give Lori something she wanted, something really, really nice. "What?" She crossed her arms. "No way. I'm not asking her to give that up."

"It's the way it is for members and their children. You have no choice."

She stared at the man. "Oh, there's always a choice."

"It's forbidden."

"Yeah? Well, that's just too stinking bad. This conversation is over."

❦

Deborah closed her eyes during the final prayer of the service, willing answers to come about how to make Ada's House a success. She'd sat through three sermons given by different men and the congregational songs she loved so dearly, all the while searching for solutions. The constant hunt had kept her up half the night, but she didn't have one new idea to show for it.

The service ended soon after the last song, and within minutes the home was a buzz of noisy activity as the hosts and many helpers began preparing for the after-service meal. Some of the adults held a quick discussion as to where they'd set up. The heat of summer was gone, and this early-October day seemed to be begging to be enjoyed, so Deborah hoped they'd decide to eat outdoors.

Jonathan held one end of a bench and Ephraim the other, waiting on directions.

"Let's set up outside," Rueben said.

The men quickly moved the wooden benches through the kitchen and out the front door. They would alter the underpinnings on half the benches, making those seats into tables. She helped the women hosts get the tables set and food laid out family style—homemade breads, sliced cheese, ham, cheese spread, peanut butter spread, pickles, red beets, and seasoned pretzels, along with some raw veggies and a few fruits.

Soon Rueben had the ministers seated as well as the oldest men in the district. While they began eating, Deborah helped the Lantz women set a table for the oldest women in the district. As soon as the group who'd been seated first was finished, women swooped in and cleaned off the tables. Deborah and Anna Mary washed rounds of dishes while fresh bread and cheese were sliced and the makings for sandwiches were placed for the next group to eat. Just as the married men and women sat separately during church and the meal, the single men sat separated from the single women, but later tonight the singles would attend a singing. After they'd sung the good-bye song, they would mingle at will while eating.

Deborah and Anna Mary stayed busy helping. Finally it was time for them to stop washing dishes and eat. Deborah dried her hands and passed the towel to her friend. A look passed between them, and she knew that neither of them enjoyed these Sunday mealtimes as they once had. She and Anna Mary used to feel that the after-service meal was a romantic lead-up to the Sunday night singings. They'd steal looks at their beaus, who sat at a nearby table, and share a smile or a nod. But that was over for both of them. Anna Mary had rarely caught Ephraim's attention during these times anyway, but Mahlon had always been attentive to Deborah, or at least he'd pretended to be.

Even after all Mahlon had dragged her through, she still couldn't make herself believe the depth of his deceit. He'd lived a double life, and the most awful thing about it was that Deborah had believed she knew him, understood him. They'd grown up together. Attended the same school. Spent their Sundays—

Jonathan's hazel eyes met hers, bringing her previous thoughts to a full stop. His pale blond hair hung below his straw hat, and his black suit fit snugly across his wide shoulders, making her wonder if he'd accidently worn one of his brother's jackets. What was the man doing watching her—setting her up for a prank? Lena had probably told him about the cake Deborah had given her, and now the two of them were plotting against her. He'd always treated her like a mix between a good friend and a kid sister, both of which made her easy prey for pranks and teasing.

When she and Anna Mary drew closer to the table, Lena waved for them to sit next to her. She sat next to Lena, but while she ate, her thoughts returned to Ada's House. What could she do to make it a success? Preoccupied with her search for answers, she quietly nibbled on her food.

Against the tradition of keeping to the men's table, Jonathan straddled the bench beside her. When she glanced around, she realized people were starting to leave for home. The official church time and its customary ways were over, so he was free to shift into a more relaxed mode. Jonathan and Lena chatted, but Deborah couldn't stop trying to figure out a solution for Ada's House. There had to be one. What was she overlooking?

Lena poked Deborah's side, making her look up. Deborah's Daed stood beside the table, and he must've said something, because he and several other men standing with him were seemingly waiting for an answer.

"He's glad you came," Jonathan mumbled while pouring ice water into her cup.

She nodded at her Daed. "Me too, Daed. You should come visit us in Hope Crossing and go to Sunday meetings with us when you're up to it." Her father smiled. Those few moments were very important. With other men around him, her Daed had stopped to acknowledge his pleasure with her, even though she was single and had moved out of his home and into another community. He'd given her a seal of approval during a church gathering in front of everyone. For her not to notice when he spoke would have been an insult. When he and the men walked off, she relaxed. Jonathan and Lena laughed softly.

"What are you two laughing at? It's not my fault my mind was elsewhere."

"Nope, it was your Daed's," Jonathan heckled.

On impulse she picked up her cup and tried to dump the contents on him. She leaned back just as he knocked it out of her hand, and they ended up dousing Lena.

Lena wiped her wet face and slung water at them. "Denki."

Deborah pointed at Jonathan, and he pointed at her, each blaming the other. Lena grabbed a napkin and soaked up some of the moisture from her dress.

Grey passed by, holding an empty glass with one hand and Ivan's hand with the other. "Taking showers after you've dressed for the day again, Lennie?"

"I keep forgetting which one comes first," Lena retorted. She raised an eyebrow at Deborah while trying to hide her smile. "Jonathan helps you save face, and you two do this to me? Some friends you guys are."

Deborah watched as Grey stopped near a small group of men and started talking. She'd seen him and Elsie come in really late. Elsie had shed a few tears during the service, and Deborah had said a silent prayer for them. They'd been married six years and had one child. That wasn't the norm for an Amish family, but no one asked them any questions. Since they'd buried a son, she was sure no one ever would ask—not even Grey's or Elsie's friends, siblings, or parents.

Ephraim moved closer. "I'd like to go to Hope Crossing as soon as we can. Robbie's coming by my place in just a little bit."

"Ada and me hoped to stay here longer than that."

Ephraim grabbed several clean napkins that were a few feet away and passed them to Lena. "If Ada wants to stay longer, Robbie can take her home later this afternoon. But I want as much time with Cara as I can get before the workweek starts again."

Deborah was sure he'd rather have skipped service and spent his morning with Cara. Next Sunday was a between one for Dry Lake but not for Hope Crossing. Deborah, Ada, and Cara would need to attend the service in Hope Crossing next week. Courting was always easier when both people lived in the same church district. Then they were free to spend every other Sunday visiting all day. "I'll let Ada know."

Ephraim left.

"Listen, Deborah," Jonathan said, "I have a horse I can loan you. He's young, about two and a half years, and a little too inexperienced to wait for long periods while harnessed and tethered somewhere, but he'll be perfect for what you need until Rosie is ready to return to work."

"You didn't mention anything about having an extra horse yesterday. How do you have one now?"

"Because I'm magical." He splayed his hands, moving them around in circles as if he were a magician. "Or because the man who owns him owes me money he can't pay, so I'm borrowing his horse for a spell."

"You're holding the man's horse hostage?"

"It's called bartering. You need to understand that concept, because if you use that horse, I want desserts. Lots of them."

Deborah looked at Lena and pointed at him. "How does he stay so thin when all he does is devise ways to get desserts?"

"Because his plans never work. How many goodies has he talked you out of so far?"

Deborah chuckled and held out her hand to Jonathan. "We have a deal."

He shook her hand. "I'll get paid this time. You can count on that, Little Debbie." Rather than releasing her hand, he tugged at it. "Come on. We can ride to my place, tie the colt to the back of the carriage, and head for Ada's."

Deborah rose. "You'll go with us too, won't you, Lena?"

Lena's eyes moved to Jonathan for a moment. "No, I...I have things I need to do."

Deborah studied her. Lena and Jonathan were usually inseparable on Sundays.

"Or I could go to my place and get the colt while you spend a little more time with your friends."

"Okay," Deborah agreed.

Deborah went inside and found Ada in the sunroom, talking with two women and two men. Waiting for a break in the conversation, she looked out one of the windows. Jonathan crossed the road to where most of the horses were tethered to the sides of hay wagons. A wagon loaded with fresh hay under a shade tree kept the horses happy until they were needed again.

The discussion paused, and Deborah quickly explained what was going on and asked Ada how she wanted to handle the afternoon. All but Israel excused themselves, saying they'd catch Ada in a minute but they needed to get their containers out of the kitchen first.

"Did you want to ride with me and Jonathan in the buggy or go with Ephraim in Robbie's truck?"

"When are you leaving, Deborah?" Israel asked.

"Pretty quickly. Maybe fifteen minutes?"

Was that a trace of disappointment on Israel's face? Deborah knew that he'd not courted anyone in the thirteen years since Lena's mother and the others had died. Ada hadn't either.

"Ada." Israel spoke softly. "If you want to stay and visit family and friends for a while, I don't mind taking you home later on."

"Oh no, I couldn't..."

Deborah placed her hand on Ada's back, pressing her fingers firmly and hoping Ada took the signal. "Since you're here and it's a visiting day... us girls will be fine for a couple of hours without you."

"But it'll take Israel two hours round trip."

Israel's eyes danced with laughter. "A minute or two more than that if I can beg a cup of coffee."

Ada's hands moved to her hips, and she huffed. "Coffee? Well, I guess there's probably some left in the percolator from this morning. Can I serve it to you cold, or must I warm it up first?"

Was Ada flirting? Deborah wanted to make a quick exit before she interrupted whatever it was these two were doing. She kissed Ada on the cheek. "See you later."

Ten

From Anna Mary's bedroom, Deborah kept watch out the window, waiting for Jonathan to return. Her girlfriends, all eight of them, talked nonstop, but there was no hint about the stunt Cara and Deborah had pulled on Lena. Deborah figured she'd better watch her back. Everyone seemed united in their innocence, as if Deborah and Cara hadn't brought a salty, yucky cake to Lena four days ago. Whatever their game plan, Deborah would try to be ready for it.

When Jonathan pulled into the driveway with the colt tethered to the back of the carriage, she gave everyone a hug and invited them to Hope Crossing when they had time. She hurried outside, and as soon as Jonathan saw her, he got out of the rig. He came around to her side and offered a supportive hand. Getting in and out of these boxes known as carriages, even with the little footstep, wasn't easy, but she'd never had someone help her before—except her Daed when she was a little girl.

"The chestnut colt looks really sturdy and energetic," Deborah commented as she sat.

"Ya, I think he's a good one." He made sure her dress was inside before he closed the door. He went to the driver's side and got in.

"I appreciate you loaning us a horse."

"My pleasure, Deborah."

"Especially when you're eating all those cakes and pies."

A wonderful smile filled his face as he slapped the reins against the horse's back. "Ya."

The horse picked up speed as they left the driveway, and so did Deborah's thoughts. There had to be a way to make Ada's House a success. As they passed the Graber house, she saw Grey just inside the barn, unfettering his horse. Elsie was walking up the sidewalk toward their home, looking every bit as unhappy as when she'd arrived at the service.

Jonathan took a deep breath. "This year the first of October is as beautiful as I've ever seen."

She didn't say anything, and he nudged her. "Do you live in Hope Crossing most of the time or inside your own thoughts?"

Deborah shrugged, trying to snap out of her reclusive mood.

Jonathan matched her shrug with a smile that said he was teasing. "Ever get tired of thinking about him?"

She bristled. "Actually, I wasn't thinking of him at all."

The surprise on Jonathan's face was sincere. "Oh...well...you are now."

She chuckled. "Not really. I want to make a success of Ada's House so badly I can't think of much else, except..."

"Except?"

"Elsie and Grey. I wonder about them."

Jonathan nodded. "There's a story between those two, a sad one seems like. And here I was hoping you were thinking about how to fill a huge order of baked goods for me."

It bothered her for a woman to be as unhappy as Elsie seemed. Grey was harder to read. He always had a little humor or a kind word to add to every conversation. "Do you ever watch married couples and wonder if they're happy?"

He looked from the road to her. "This is odd—I know it is—but I've been watching pairs since I was a kid. From the time they start seeing each other and on through years of being married. It's like a game of sorts. I pick who I think would make a good pair. Or when two people are seeing each other, I think, are they an okay, good, or great couple? Unfortunately, once I grew up, I had to add a group to my list called the fed-up couples."

"Wow, you're deeper and weirder than I thought."

"I agree, but it came natural. I must've been five when I started couple watching."

"So what'd you think of Grey and Elsie before they married?"

He slowed the rig as they came to a yield sign. "My observations are private. I've never told anyone what I think of a couple."

"Not even Lena?"

"Nope."

"Then it'll be our secret."

Jonathan studied her for a moment, as if deciding something. He nodded. "I hate to admit it, hated to feel it, but I thought Grey was making a poor choice. I couldn't quite put my finger on what bothered me about her then, but now I'd say that Elsie's chronically unhappy. Aren't there too many spells of sadness in life for a person to be unhappy before the bad days even arrive?"

"Ephraim and Anna Mary?"

"Both great people. Could have been moderately happy at least half of the time, in my opinion."

"Half of the time?"

"She's a little needy—nothing ridiculous, mind you—but Ephraim is a little leave-me-alone-ish. Not the best union but better than lots."

"Okay, what about Emma and Levi Riehl?"

"They're almost old enough to be my parents, so I wasn't around when they started seeing each other. But I think they fit like most solid couples do. They know how to help each other enjoy the good times and get through the tough ones."

"I can agree with that. What about Ephraim and Cara?"

Jonathan chuckled. "Now there is an odd, odd pair. And I think they'll always have some difficulty fitting in with the community as a couple, but within their home, within the relationship with just each other, I bet they'll be happier than any couple I've ever known."

"Actually, you're very good at this. I've thought similar things to everything you just said. So what did you think of me and Mahlon?"

"Not going there, Little Debbie."

"Why not?"

"Because I think you are really peculiar. You're just not the kind of girl I'd ever talk to or share a buggy with," Jonathan teased. "And if I tell you all that, you'll get out of my buggy, and then you won't be around for me to talk to."

Deborah chuckled and sat back, enjoying the company. She'd always taken pleasure in a few smiles, laughs, and pleasant snippets of conversations whenever Jonathan was around, but she'd never spent any time with just him. Once alone, Mahlon was rarely cheerful. He was deep…or maybe just secretive. But Mahlon aside, she'd never realized how fun Jonathan could be. "So, if I made you a gazillion desserts, what would you do with all of them?"

"Hmm, well, that's a good question. Let me think. Umm. Oh, I got it. I'd sell them. Yep. Well…I'd sell the ones I didn't eat. Or maybe I'd eat half of each one I sold. Whatever. But I'd set up a booth outside Ada's House, reel in Englischer tourists with my adorable Amish clothing, maybe offer a carriage ride or two, and then sell them every dessert you paid me with."

She laughed but stopped when his words caused an idea to pop into her head. "That's it! That's the answer I've been looking for!" Deborah grabbed Jonathan's arm and shook it so hard the whole buggy wobbled. "You are a smart man!"

"Now see, that's what I've been telling everybody for years. No one ever listens to me. You tell them, Little Debbie." He paused, looking amused and gentle and even a little unsure of himself. "So what was my brilliant idea, anyway?"

She took the reins from him and pulled onto the shoulder of the road. "I'm serious."

The everyday gentleness seen so easily on his face deepened. "Then I'm listening."

"I've been trying to figure out how to make Ada's House a success. We're in over our heads. We owe bills we didn't expect and can't pay. You know, new business-owning difficulties."

"I didn't know all that."

"Well, now you do. Just keep it between us. Okay?"

"Sure. But Ada is supposed to live there nearly rent free because of all the painting Cara's doing."

"Cara's done most of what she can, so this month's rent increases. Plus we need to pay for gas to heat the water and stove, food, phone, baking supplies, and water bills. The hay in the pasture will be dried up soon, and we'll need to supplement through buying hay and a lot more horse feed. Oh, and those boxes for putting the desserts in so we can take them to the bakeries get really expensive. Sometimes I see why Mahlon felt so under it all the time."

He shook his head. "Don't believe it. People are under a load, or two or three of them, at times. But running out like he did is—"

Deborah raised her hand. "Change of subject, please."

"Ya, you're right. So what was my brilliant idea?"

"I…I'm not sure."

Jonathan started laughing so hard his tanned face turned a captivating shade of pink. "Wow, I have such a great idea you have no idea what it is. I'm good."

Tears welled in her eyes as she laughed. Every time they looked at each other, they started laughing all over again. Finally they took a deep breath. What was so funny, anyway? Was it her excitement at his idea or his sense of humor or what?

"Jonathan," Deborah said firmly, "pay attention and help me sort this out."

He took the reins from her and pulled back onto the road. "You think better when riding in a buggy."

"I tend to believe you're right." The sounds of the horses' hoofs and the creaking of the carriage did seem to help her think. "Ada's House used to be an Amish home before Englischers bought it a long time ago. Now that we're in it, we're slowly fixing it up to look Amish again. It's near a busy town. Why can't we sell our own goods?"

"Like Ada's Coffee House or something?"

"No, I don't think so, but you're close. What else could we do?"

As they started throwing ideas at each other, Deborah wished she had paper and pen with her. Excitement and hope washed over her, scrubbing away some of the black stain Mahlon had left inside her.

Jonathan turned onto the road where Ada's House sat. Three Amish men, all dressed in their Sunday suits, stood on the sidewalk a few doors down from Ada's House. Ephraim was one of them. They rode past them, and Ephraim flailed his arms while talking, as if he was frustrated. "That doesn't look good, does it?"

"Not particularly."

"Cara was doing something today she wouldn't tell me about. Think she caused a problem?"

"Don't know, but your brother's awfully good at finding a balance between what Cara needs and what the church leaders want. It's pretty impressive."

"He's not that great at it. He was shunned for months and has been a member in good standing again for only a few weeks now."

"Ah, but he's no longer shunned, and he won the girl's heart. Don't sweat it, Little Debbie. No one thinks through issues more carefully before taking a step than your brother."

Realizing Jonathan was right, Deborah chose to stop worrying. Ada's House came into view. It still needed a lot of work, but Cara didn't have the ladders or supplies she needed to paint the eaves or most of the clapboard siding. Using the one ladder they did have, she'd painted the few shutters she could. And she had the porch looking perfect from ceiling to wooden floor.

As he slowed the rig, a faint idea tried to wriggle into Deborah's mind. Touching his hand, she studied the place. "Jon," she whispered, "keep going."

Without questioning her, he did.

Chills ran all over her. "Wait."

He came to a halt.

"Look at that dried-up cornfield."

He studied it and turned back to her, waiting.

"There's got to be something...you know...some..."

"Dried-up ears of corn?"

"No." She climbed down, crossed onto her neighbor's property, and entered the field.

Jonathan followed her. "Some women make dolls out of parts of cornstalks."

"Maybe." Deborah went deeper into the rows. The corn had been harvested, but the stalks remained. That stood out as very odd to her. The field didn't belong to an Amish person either. Suddenly, as clear as if God were passing her a picture book, she saw it. "A maze!" She spun around slowly. "And Amish-made cakes and pies and apple cider. Maybe other goodies too, along with pumpkins and hayrides. I know it's late in the season, being the first of October and all, but is it possible we could turn Ada's House into a pumpkin-patch-type place?"

"Now that is the best idea I've heard in a really, really long time." Jonathan's face radiated such pleasure and confidence in her. "Since it's too late to grow them yourself, you'd need to buy the pumpkins and have them hauled in. But the real problem is that a pumpkin patch is just needed for a month or so once a year."

Her mind spun like the wheels on a carriage. "Maybe we could find a special niche for each season."

His eyes grew large. "That's really good. Focus on the pumpkin patch idea. That's for the here and now."

Insecurity covered her like a blanket. "Ya, but can we lease the field, and even if we could, can me and Ada actually make money from our work? Will we know how to plan and organize for such a thing? Or will we just be taking on more bills?"

He stood inside that cornfield, studying her. "What does your heart say?"

"Part of it says try, and part of it says run." She moved in closer. "I want to try. But I've never felt so scared in all my life."

"Then do it while you're scared," he whispered, and the rustling of the wind carried his words round and round through the dry stalks. "I'll help you...if you want."

Eleven

Cara didn't know how far they'd gone when she finally began to have a reasonable thought or two enter her mind. She trotted along while Lori rode her bike. They kept going farther and farther from Ada's. Lori loved it, and she didn't know her mother was furious…and hurt. Stupid rule. She couldn't take the bike from Lori. Despite that, she'd been gone a long time, and Ephraim might be looking for her. "Lori, honey."

Lori stopped her bike.

"Let's head on back to Ada's now."

"Yeah, my legs are getting wobbly."

"That's my fault. We've gone too far. You want to walk for a bit?"

"No way."

They crossed a dozen streets on their way back, but soon enough they were on their block again.

Ephraim stood on the sidewalk, looking one direction and then the other. When he spotted her, he wasted no time getting to her.

"'From, look!" Lori chirped. "I got a new bike. Mama and me did it. And I'm good at riding, even in this dress. Watch me." Lori passed him and kept going.

Cara cupped her hands around her mouth. "Stop at Ada's, Lori. Don't go any farther."

"Okay." Lori's voice vibrated as she jolted along.

Ephraim studied her. "You okay?"

"I take it the men in black came to see you too."

"I spoke to them, ya."

Cara rolled her eyes and kept walking. Ephraim held out his hand for hers. She tucked her hands inside her folded arms. "What, you're not too embarrassed to hold my hand after I've spattered this horrible stain across the Amish?"

"Not today. Not ever." He tugged on her sleeve.

She unfolded her arms and slid her hand into his. Lori pulled onto the walkway that led to Ada's, dropped her bike, and ran into the house. Ephraim gently squeezed Cara's hand.

"You're not ashamed." Cara stopped. "Why?"

"Because I know you." They started up the walkway. "And I get it— the stumbles and mishaps." He shrugged. "Plain out, I expected a few to crop up."

"Look!" Lori ran back out the door with Deborah and Jonathan following close behind.

When Lori pointed to her bike, Deborah looked to Cara. "The surprise?"

"Yes!" Lori clapped her hands. "Isn't it great?"

"It's quite a...a surprise." Deborah searched her brother's eyes, clearly trying to figure out what to say. "Where did you get it?"

"Me and Mama mowed grass and picked weeds for it!"

Deborah's eyes grew large. "On a Sunday?"

"Yeah." Cara tugged at her dress. "And thanks for the great advice about changing out of my jeans and wearing my Amish clothes, Deb. It seemed to be a dead giveaway that I shouldn't be working on a Sunday, and someone told the church leaders."

"Oh dear." Deborah placed her hand over her mouth, trying to smother her laughter. "This isn't funny. I know it's not, but..." She glanced at Jonathan, who looked a little more sympathetic to Cara's troubles.

Clearly, Lori was too preoccupied with her bike to hear much of what the adults were saying.

Ephraim stepped forward. "You'll have to excuse my sister, Cara. She seems to be regaining her sense of humor…at the *totally* wrong time." He smiled at Deborah, letting her know he wasn't the least bit annoyed. "Lori, how about if we put the bike away for now and take Better Days for a walk?"

"Okay, but first I'm hungry. We've been gone all day. Mama just doesn't get hungry like me."

Deborah held out her hand for Lori's. "Kumm. I'll fix you something to eat."

"Can I take my bike inside with me?"

Ephraim nodded. "Ya."

Jonathan toted the bike inside as Lori jabbered about it the whole way.

Cara pulled her hand from Ephraim's. "I'm not asking her to give that up."

His gray-blue eyes stayed focused on her. "Let's talk about this later. You're tired and hungry and angry."

"Don't treat me like a kid. Even the church leaders didn't do that."

He took a seat on the porch steps. "I didn't mean to."

"The Amish don't ride bicycles?"

"Some do in other states. But you shouldn't see it happening here, not among the members."

"What's so wrong with a bike?"

"It's one of those old rules we've stuck by. They're a bit flashy, and they allow a person to travel a lot longer distances than a foot scooter." He shrugged. "I never said I agree with all the *Ordnung*. I just trust that for the most part the regulations are needed to protect our ways and help us stay close and accountable. Bikes are forbidden for us, and I can't change the rules or stop them from being enforced."

Her heart jumped. "I didn't get you in trouble again, did I?"

"Nope. This one's all yours. But the bishop and preacher's little talk with you is most of the discipline you'll get since you're not a member.

They'll want to talk again when you've had time to think. Did you really invite them to leave?"

Realizing just how snarky she'd been, she took a seat beside him. "I…I might have." She looped her arm inside of his. "Okay, fine. I definitely did. Will I ever get to the end of this list of rules?"

"You mean without breaking each one? Nah, I don't think so."

She sandwiched his hand between hers. "I can't ask her to give up her bike." He didn't respond, and her eyes filled with tears. "This just stinks. And it hurts too, not just a little either. All those years of having nothing— not even on Christmas—and then when I finally get to where I can give her something special…" Cara sighed. "I was so excited about today I couldn't sleep last night."

"I'm really sorry. I never once thought about the bike rule."

"It's a stupid one."

"Maybe. But it's there, and the rule is not open for debate."

"Now what?"

He leaned in and kissed her, his warm lips easing her anger and disappointment. With his forehead against hers, he drew a deep breath. "You mean everything to me, Cara." He whispered the words so softly, as if they came from a place deep within him. "That's all I know. You have to decide the rest for yourself."

"Some choice," she mumbled. If she didn't do it their way, she couldn't join the faith, and they couldn't marry. If he left the faith, he'd hurt his family, damage the business, and lose a huge part of himself. Over a bike?

❦

Grey tucked Ivan in for the night, sliding the covers gently over his son's arms as his little boy snuggled under their warmth. When Grey looked up, Elsie stood at the doorway. Surprise at seeing her there jarred him, but he kept his face expressionless.

He'd wrestled with his soul all day. A wave of forgiveness would come to him for a moment, but then realization of what she'd done would explode inside him like a volcano scattering ash so thick he couldn't see or feel anything but the aftereffects of the eruption. And now he fought to gain control of his will. He'd told her they'd find answers, but as the day wore on, all he'd found was hurt and resentment pounding inside him.

When he stood to leave the room, her eyes bore into him as they had all afternoon, willing him to understand. He understood. Her decisions had affected their lives like a cancer, and finally admitting what she'd done had not brought them closer. She seemed to think it should. After years of manipulating him through her silence and actions, she wanted him to understand and accept.

He went to the dresser, picked up the kerosene lantern, and motioned for her to leave the room. They walked into the hallway, and he passed the lantern to her. "Good night, Elsie." He turned to go into his room.

"You're furious with me."

Her words stopped him, and he stayed put as she went into her room and set the lantern on the nightstand. "I did what I thought was right. But even if I was wrong, this is how you forgive?"

She didn't get it, might not ever, and he couldn't make her. Remaining in the hallway with her standing beside her bed, he pulled the door closed. That door was the least of what blocked them from each other. She needed things from him he didn't possess—a way to build a bridge to cross the gulf that separated them. If he'd known how to build one, he'd have done it long, long ago. If one existed for him to cross over to her right now, he might burn it himself.

He walked to his back porch and took a seat on the stoop. The dark October air had a little nip to it. Voices carried from across the back field and beyond the creek bed. Allen's home sat on that piece of property. Like a lot of evenings, his friend's place was a bustle of activity.

"God, help me. I…I'm so angry with her." He put his head in his hands, torn between seeing his own faults and the bitterness he felt toward Elsie.

The back door squeaked as Elsie opened it. She stepped outside and pressed her back against the house, staring off in the distance. "I...I finally opened up, and now you're really angry. It's not fair, Grey."

Bitter thoughts washed over him. The moment Ivan was born missing part of one arm, fear began growing inside her. She should have told him... or at least someone.

She removed her Sunday apron. "What do you plan to do?"

"About us? I'm going to need some time. But I have a plan concerning Ivan and school."

She walked down the few steps and onto the grass before turning to face him. "He'll thrive in the Lancaster school for the handicapped. I know he will. And those children won't make fun of him. Rather than being at the bottom of the rung, he'll be at the top. Don't you want that for your son?"

"I want Lena to work with him."

"Lena?" Elsie scoffed. "She does not know Ivan like I do."

"She's the best teacher this district has ever had and my guess is probably the best Amish teacher in the state."

"Just because she attended a public school for a while doesn't make her a great teacher."

"Her reason for going is what makes the difference. She wanted to learn all she could so she'd be a good teacher. And she was a teacher's assistant of some type in a classroom for special-needs students. I trust that she'll know where Ivan should attend better than either of us does."

"You have that much confidence in her?"

"Ya."

"I worry she'll pick my mothering skills to pieces, given the chance. But if you're wanting an honest opinion, I've never seen her shy from speaking her mind when asked."

"You're afraid *Lena* will judge you? That's not her way. And you can't go on letting fear rule you and our family." Grey shifted. "Until today I didn't realize that's what holds us captive. But you did."

"You say that as though fear is some shadow that can be dispelled at will."

"And you treat it like it's a god to revere and bow down to."

"If Ivan is under her, she'll...know."

"Know?" That eerie feeling ran through him again, as if alerting him that what she was trying to say was important. "Know what?"

"About us...where you sleep."

How had he lived with her all these years and not known she was afraid of everything? "Ivan doesn't even know."

"But he will, given time."

While anger rumbled, he prayed. She had manipulated too much of their lives in order to hide her fears. No wonder she kept her distance emotionally as well as physically. She didn't want him to object to her reasoning.

One of the children at Allen's place let out a horrifying scream. *"Nee! Helf."*

Grey rose and moved closer to the creek bank.

Phoebe. Allen's youngest daughter. Grey stood too far away to see if she was hurt. Lennie flew out of her brother's house, running barefoot and like wildfire toward Phoebe. Lennie grabbed her up, clearly checking her out and talking to her. Phoebe wrapped her arms and legs around Lennie, sobbing. More adults came from around the corners of the house or from inside, hurrying toward the wailing. When Allen arrived, Lennie passed Phoebe to her Daed.

"Should you go?" Elsie asked.

The creek that separated their properties was fairly wide and deep. The only way to cross it was by horse. "I don't think so."

Allen looked up and waved. "Phoebe saw a raccoon coming toward her. We're fine."

"Okay, thanks," Grey hollered.

Phoebe raised her head and looked toward them. She hollered in Pennsylvania Dutch that she wasn't fine and that if Grey saw that thing again, he was to shoot it.

Allen laughed and patted her back. Soon the adults had rounded up all the children and taken them inside.

"You think it could be a rabid raccoon?"

"Doubtful. It obviously ran off when she screamed. It's a nocturnal creature hunting for food."

Elsie stood in the darkness, studying the sky. "Or God trying to tell me something I should have already known."

He didn't know what she meant, but he wouldn't bother to ask.

Tears welled in her eyes. "I didn't want you to know my genes were poor ones. I...I'm sorry."

Beyond her tears, he saw her self-righteousness begin to break, and a dusting of forgiveness settled over his heart.

❧

Under the starless night, Dwayne studied Lena's house. The chilly air seeped through his clothing. A dog perched its paws on a second-story windowsill and barked at him through a closed window. Dwayne set his toolbox next to the tree and stayed put, not caring what fit the dog threw. If they let the mutt outside, he'd slice its throat.

A woman came to the window, but the dark night shrouded his view. It was probably the stupid teacher herself. As far as he knew, only she and her Daed lived here. She opened the glass pane. The girl was an idiot and an ugly thorn in his flesh. He didn't put up with thorns. She seemed to spot him, and he propped against the tree and lit a cigarette.

He intended to get even, and she might as well know it now. Picking on his brother in class. Taking the watch back. That awful cake she brought to the cabin. It had to be poison, and Aaron refused to say a word about it to her. He said he knew Lena and it must be a joke of some type.

Dwayne spat on the ground. She knew exactly what she was doing, and so did he.

As he looked at her, new plans floated to him out of thin air. Deciding that a low profile would profit him more than giving himself away, he grabbed his toolbox and got off their property.

He walked the two miles to the schoolhouse and looked around. The playground was a perfect setting for causing trouble. He set his toolbox down, pulled out a pair of tin snips, and began working away at the chains that held up the swings. It might take a few times of someone swinging before the chain broke, but when it did, somebody would be hurt, and poor Teacher Lena would answer for it. It wasn't much, but it seemed like a perfect opening chapter to what he intended to be a very long book.

A cat meowed, drawing his attention. He tossed the tin snips into the toolbox. "Here kitty, kitty, kitty." The creature slowly came to him. Its soft, warm fur felt good against his cold hands. The cat purred as he rubbed her ears. "What are you doing hanging around an empty school? Maybe you've been out catching field mice. Now that you've seen me, you won't tell, will you?" He laughed and reached for the knife in his pocket. "I think not."

Twelve

Lena brought her horse to a stop near the schoolhouse barn. *"Zerick."* She repeated the word as the horse backed up until the small cart she'd ridden in today stood under the lean-to. The brisk ride in an open rig had done wonders for her. She'd finally shaken that eerie feeling she'd had since seeing a man staring at her house during the wee hours of the morning. Probably a drunk. Possibly a Peeping Tom. Usually both were harmless.

A fresh week lay ahead of her. The air smelled like fall, and leaves had begun to change color. She put her old mare in its small pasture, the one designed just for the teacher's horse. After she grabbed her goodies off the seat of the cart, she hurried into the school, wanting to get a fire started in the potbelly stove. Her scholars loved putting their lunches near a warm stove in cool weather. It wouldn't be cold enough to build a roaring fire and bank embers today—just a little one to knock the chill out of the air. But she'd brought homemade chocolate chip cookies, and when those got warm from sitting on the stove, she'd have a treat her scholars would work hard to earn.

She built the first fire of the year in her faithful old stove. After she set the cookie tin on top, she went to each student's desk and opened the spiral-bound notebook left there for her. She read the entries and left smiley faces, asked humorous questions, and shared a thought or two. These works didn't get a grade. Her students wrote to her whatever they wanted to, and she responded. Some wrote the beginning to made-up stories, and she'd finish the tale. Others shared events from their own life, but they didn't tell the whole story. That was her job. Their goal was to stump her so that the real ending was nothing like what she wrote. When they read them aloud, they shared the real ending and then read what she'd written. Their laughter never rang as loudly as when they read her responses. The older ones knew she cloaked her responses under the pretense of telling what probably took place. She spun yarns in hopes of making them love writing, reading, and using their imaginations.

She sat at Peter's desk, bracing herself for what he'd written to her.

I rided down the road on my way home aftr scool when I saw my
teacher in her yard plantin more flowers. I hate flowers. I'd ruther
be tended to than tend to somethin. But the teach must like them.
They don't like her. I know this cuz...

Wow. That wasn't a bad entry at all. Nothing biting or threatening. That improvement alone refreshed her. He'd written several sentences and spelled correctly most of the words she'd been working with him on. Definite improvement.

She tapped her pencil on the paper. *Hmm. I know this cuz...*

"Think, Lena." She put her pencil on the paper, hoping an answer would come that he'd enjoy.

I know this cuz...one day the petunias ran away from her
and chased after me.
Peter, Peter, petunia hater,
Didn't want flowers, but wanted something greater
Teacher Lena chased them down
When she caught them, they wilted to the ground.

"That's not good enough, Lena. *Kumm uff*, think." She tapped her pencil on the paper, looking about the room for inspiration. Surely she could think of a better little ditty than—

She noticed a pool of liquid under her desk. She stood and moved in closer. When she rounded the side of her table, she saw a white cat in her chair, covered in its own blood. The thick red syrup dripped onto the floor, making Lena's skin crawl. Her mouth went dry, and her body shook. Who would do such a thing?

Feeling dizzy and sick, she eased up to it and touched it. She jerked back, appalled at how death felt. Its stiff body sickened her, and she ran outside for fresh air. Teachers had some awfully mean tricks pulled on them at times, usually by the older boys in school or the ones who'd graduated not long ago. Drawing cool air into her lungs, she knew what had to be done—and before her students arrived. Ignoring her desire to sit down and cry, she hurried to the lean-to and grabbed a shovel and old towels that were usually reserved for craft days.

On the verge of being sick to her stomach, she moved the cat's body onto the blade of the shovel and carried it outside. Her body disobeyed her, trembling as she walked across the gravel driveway and to the far side of the lean-to. It seemed like the best burial spot. If anyone passed by while she dug the grave, they weren't likely to spot her between the huge tree and the far side of the lean-to. She eased the cat's body onto the ground and returned to her classroom. The next step was no easier—mopping up its blood. Trying to hurry so she could bury the cat and the bloody towels before anyone arrived, she couldn't keep her tears at bay.

Who would do this and why?

The older boys, and sometimes girls, could be pretty spiteful—seemingly angered by Amish restrictions and spurred into action by wild hormones, pettiness, and immaturity. But of all the nasty things she'd heard of over the years, mutilating someone's pet and leaving it bleeding in a teacher's chair was beyond normal. An occasional squirrel or deer's head might greet an unsuspecting teacher on the steps leading to the school. But someone's pet? She shuddered, trying to reason out who might've done this. The culprit could be from any district around here, not necessarily one of her students or former students. Even though she didn't have grandiose sentiments of how some students felt about her, she found it hard to believe any of her students, past or present, had the type of cruelty to do this. Still, thoughts of Peter's attitude toward her kept tumbling inside her. Surely he hadn't. She saw good inside him. Of course she saw meanness too.

The eerie feeling didn't leave her as she mopped up the blood and scrubbed the chair and floor until they looked clean again. After dumping the kindling out of its crate, she used it to carry the items outside. She grabbed the shovel and jammed it into the ground. Her body jolted, but the rocklike ground barely gave way. She slammed the blade into the edge of the earth again and again, making very little progress. Children's voices filled the air as they walked toward the schoolhouse. Buggies came and went as parents dropped their children off.

Should she run to get one of the Daeds to help her? A man could make quick work of this solid ground, but then her scholars would find out for sure, and it'd cause days of emotional unrest. Doubtful of her best course of action, she kept digging, hoping no one came looking for her. Once past the hardest-packed dirt, she made better progress and managed to carve a decent-sized hole.

"Lena." The door to the schoolhouse slammed as several scholars called to her. They'd begun hunting for her, but she needed only a few more minutes. Using the shovel, she tried to pick up the cat. She couldn't get the blade under it.

"Kumm uff." She tossed the shovel to the side and picked up the cat. As she laid it in the hole, Marilyn screamed. "Snowball! Why are you throwing my Snowball into the ground?"

The shrill sound of her youngest student's voice caused others to come running. Lena knelt in front of her. "She…she died, sweetie."

"No!" Tears streamed down the little girl's face as she reached for her cat. Lena stopped her.

Marilyn pulled away from Lena. "You can't throw my cat in the ground!"

Marilyn's older brother pushed through the crowd. Levi's emotions reflected across his nine-year-old face, and soon he was sobbing too. Lena directed them toward the schoolhouse. "Could one of you older boys please finish what I started?"

"What are we, your slaves?" Peter retorted.

Lena turned to Jacob, who gave a nod.

Lena knelt in front of Marilyn. "You need to go inside, but you can stay with Levi and sit on the reading couch. I'll be inside in just a few minutes, okay?"

Marilyn nodded and clung to her brother, crying as they walked toward the schoolhouse.

Lena lifted her head, ready to give loud instructions. "I want everyone to go inside and take a seat."

The children headed in that direction while Lena went to the hand pump. She lifted the handle and lowered it several times before water gushed out. After grabbing the soap dispenser out of its bucket, she scrubbed her hands and arms with a fury that could not remove the filth of what was taking place.

Mandy came back outside with a towel in hand. "Marilyn can't catch her breath. She seems to think you killed her cat, and she doesn't want to be thrown into a hole with some bloody towels when she dies."

Bracing herself for the long week ahead, Lena took the towel and dried her hands. "Let's go see what can be done to console—"

A piercing yell sliced straight through Lena. Had Jacob hurt himself while burying the cat?

Jacob came from the side of the lean-to. "What's wrong now?"

Too frazzled to even think, she headed for the playground area, followed by Mandy and Jacob. Elmer lay on the ground, crying. What was he doing out here? One glance at the swing set explained everything. The chain had broken, and based on where Elmer had landed, he'd been swinging really high.

"Stay put, and tell me what hurts."

"My arm!"

"Okay, lie still for just a moment, and let's make sure nothing else is hurt." She made a quick assessment just like her Red Cross classes had taught her. After running through her checklist and getting reasonable answers, she helped him to his feet.

"It hurts! Ow. Ow. Ow. Ow." Elmer's whining concerned her, but more than that, his hand had already begun to swell, and it had a slight blue tint to it.

"Can you move your fingers?"

As he wiggled them a little, her mind whirled with conflicting thoughts on what to do next. If she took him with her while going for help, someone else could get hurt, not to mention the emotional state Marilyn, Levi, and most of the class were in. Sending an older student might cause problems with the school board since she was on probation for a similar incident. Regardless of that, she couldn't leave. If she let one of the older children drive Elmer to the closest phone, and they didn't handle it like an adult, Elmer could have permanent damage done to his arm. Buggies hit potholes. Cars spooked horses. And if, in their nervousness, they drove too fast or too carelessly, more than just a child's limb could be in danger. She'd seen far too many incidents of that sort in her lifetime.

Deciding Mandy had the best head on her shoulders, she turned to her. "Can you drive my rig to Ephraim's place by yourself? He's got the closest phone. Tell him Elmer has fallen off a swing and may have broken his arm."

Upon hearing those words, Elmer started crying harder. Lena placed her hand on his head, comforting him. If he'd done as she'd said, he'd be at his desk safe and sound right now.

"Ya, I think so."

Lena moved in front of Mandy. "I need you to drive careful and deliberate. This isn't an emergency, but we need an Englischer driver and Elmer's parents so he can be taken to the doc in Shippensburg. Can you be very, very careful?"

She nodded.

"Jacob, hitch my horse to its rig, and then come directly inside. Is that clear?"

"Ya." Jacob's wide eyes told her he'd do exactly as she'd just demanded.

With her arm around Elmer, she guided him toward the schoolhouse.

No matter how she handled the next couple of hours, she'd hear from upset parents. If not tonight, then at the school board meeting next Tuesday. She'd have to explain these incidents and her actions.

And all she wanted to do was work with her students and teach, not be second-guessed by the parents.

※

Dwayne laughed so hard he almost choked on his dinner as Peter finished telling about the dead cat and Elmer getting hurt.

"That girl is sorely lacking in what it takes to be a good teacher." His Mamm pointed a finger at him. "But what happened to those children isn't funny, Dwayne." Mamm held a plate out to him, offering him more pot roast.

Dwayne slapped his brother on the back. "Does serve her right, though, don't it?"

Peter shrugged. "It's not like cats matter no way. They fill up the barns like mice and rats, and we shoot 'em, but I did feel a little bad for

Marilyn. She's terrified people are going to throw her in a dark hole if she dies."

No one said a word. Dwayne finished his meal and shoved his chair back from the table. "Don't be such a wuss, Peter. What do you care how anybody feels? Set a goal—like getting even with that teacher—and enjoy hitting the target. It's that easy."

"Dwayne," Mamm corrected, "watch your language, and we don't want to get even with her. I'd like to see her step down and get somebody in there who knows what she's doing. It's just like at our last Amish school. The teacher has no quality to her. That's all."

Daed pushed his empty plate away and propped his forearms on the table. "Now your mother was a great teacher in her day."

"Ya." Dwayne stood, wiping his mouth on his sleeve. "So we've heard." Unwilling to listen to any more stories about when his mother taught some twenty-five years ago, he walked out the back door and straight to the barn. At the back, under stacks of baled hay, he removed a Hot-Shot— his brand-new electric-current cattle prod. If that teacher thought a dead cat and a broken swing were problems, she hadn't driven a horse after it'd been on the receiving end of a Hot-Shot all night.

Thirteen

Deborah turned another page in the magazine, reading a true account of a family using a portion of their farm for a pumpkin patch. The aroma of shoofly pies and Amish bread pudding filled the kitchen as she waited on them to finish baking. Their commercial-sized oven had six shelves, all filled with pies, and their family-sized oven had the bread pudding.

Based on what she'd read, she and Ada could not do this venture alone, not even with Cara's help. "According to this article, we'll need a lookout tower of some sort."

From her position at the sink washing dishes, Ada glanced over her shoulder at Deborah. "A lookout tower?"

"Ya, it's a structure built in the middle of the cornfield maze. One of us can climb it to see the people inside the maze. If someone gets stuck, we can have a visual of them to send someone else in to lead them out, or we can give directions through a bullhorn. If you're selling baked goods and I have to go in to get them, who will come lead me out?"

Thoughts of all it'd take to set up a pumpkin patch kept running through her head. Unfortunately, she hadn't yet managed to secure use of the cornfield. She'd gone to the owner's house on Monday and Tuesday, but no one answered the door or appeared to be home. She'd had the same result this morning and intended to return again this evening, just like the other two days. Maybe they were on vacation.

Ada rinsed her hands and grabbed a dishtowel. "You're saying that like it's a joke, but you're really worried about getting lost in that maze, aren't you?"

It surprised her how well Ada read her sometimes. "A little." But the truth was, parts of her were terrified. Since Mahlon had left, she either felt grief or anxiety wadded up like a bale of hay smack in the middle of her chest most days. And she'd had enough.

When she heard voices and an odd noise, Deborah went to the back door and peered out. Not seeing anyone, she turned back to Ada.

Ada slung the dishtowel over her shoulder. "We'll get the hang of all this. I just know we will."

Jonathan's words ricocheted around inside her like one of those super bouncy balls her little brother bought from a vending machine in town. *Then do it while you're scared.* She'd never heard such perfect words in her life.

The buzzer went off. Deborah took the pies out of the oven and set them on a cooling rack. "There's so much to do, and we're six months behind before we even start. But I think our goal should be to do what we can this year—buy pumpkins to sell. Next year we'll grow them and let people pick them off the vine. We'll build a small maze if we can get use of the field and have a simple hayride—and really be ready for business next year. Do you agree?"

"Absolutely. I just hope the permits I have for operating my home business will cover what we need for a pumpkin patch."

"Ya. Robbie's taking me to the courthouse later this week." She tilted her head, listening to voices that seemed to be getting closer and the rhythmic echo of something being whacked.

Ada looked out a side window. "I think someone's in the cornfield, cutting stalks."

Deborah grabbed her sweater and ran out the front of the house, across the yard, and down the side alley until it opened up into the cornfield. There appeared to be about two Plain Mennonite men and one woman and then ten or so Englischer teens, all either cutting cornstalks or gathering them and hauling them to a nearby truck.

"Excuse me," Deborah called while hurrying toward them.

One of the men stopped cutting stalks. He looked about twenty-something and had dark brown hair. The woman passed an armload of stalks to a teen and then walked closer while dusting off her cape dress. Deborah hoped the right words would come to her by the time she stood directly in front of the man.

When she reached him, she drew a few deep breaths and straightened her apron. "I…I've been trying to reach the owner of this field."

The man jabbed the end of his machete into the ground. "An Englischer gentleman by the name of Carl Gilbert owns the field, but we work with a teen mission out of Harrisburg, and we rent the pasture from him."

"I'm Deborah Mast. My…business partner and I moved into the house that adjoins this property nearly four months ago, and I was hoping to rent this field with the stalks still standing."

"Business partner?" he asked.

"Ada. We bake goods for some local bakeries. But we hope to expand."

"Is she the older woman? And the man we see around here regularly, is he a partner too?"

"You've seen us?"

"I suppose a better question is, you haven't seen us? We harvested a lot of corn throughout the summer."

He would've had to set off dynamite for Deborah to notice anything but her own pain and confusion since moving in. "We…I…have been distracted. I apologize if in my state I was rude in any way. The older woman is Ada. The man is my brother. He lives in Dry Lake, and the younger woman is his fiancée."

He pulled a work glove off his right hand and held it out. "Ray Yoder." She shook his hand.

"And this is my mother, Joan." She had a pleasant smile as she nodded.

"Hi." Deborah returned the nod before focusing on Ray. "Any chance we could work something out?"

"We use this plot each year to teach inner-city teens about planting and growing and reaping. We do everything by hand, and right now we need these stalks for various fall festival events."

"There must be two acres here," Deborah defended. "Do you need all the stalks?"

His lips pursed, showing what might be amusement. "What we don't use, we sell to local churches and schools who need some fall festival decorations, and then that money goes for the mission. We do it each year, and it brings in decent money—for dried-up stalks, that is."

"I think I can match that money. I sure was hoping to build a maze—you know, with huge swatches missing all throughout it."

He scratched his head, looking thoughtful. "Yeah, I know what a maze is. You're thinking we could use the stalks from those cutout places to meet our real needs, and then you'd pay us for our losses in sales." He studied her. "How much you figure is reasonable to rent this cornfield?"

"I…I have no clue, and I don't actually have any money to pay you right now. But I will…at least I think I will, if you could…give me time."

"Now how can I turn down such a sure thing?" He suppressed a smile.

"I know how I sound, and I might not sleep tonight for feeling like I made a fool of myself asking to rent this field, but my concept for running a pumpkin patch is solid—a maze, hayrides, pumpkins, and baked goods to sell."

Joan pulled up the sleeves of her sweater past her elbows. "You don't sound foolish. A little inexperienced maybe."

Ray rubbed his chin and lower cheek, staring at the field. "Usually by this time I've arranged to have most of the stalks removed. It just hasn't worked out this year. Even today we only have a few who qualify to use machetes, and we only have a few hours to work." He made a clicking sound with his mouth. "I guess if you harvested the stalks from the swatches you clear and were willing to pay...*after* you've made your money from the pumpkin patch, I can rent this field to you for the difference in sales."

"The difference between what you sell this year and what you sell when you clear the whole field?"

"Yes. My guess is that will be somewhere between a hundred and a hundred and fifty dollars."

She liked his willingness to treat her like a businessperson and not a confused girl. "That sounds great to me, although I don't have anything to base it on. Can I talk to Ada first?"

"Sure."

Deborah's heart beat a little faster. "Would you care to come inside and have a slice of pie and some coffee while I talk with her? Everyone can come in."

"That's an invite we'd never turn down," Ray said.

As they followed her into Ada's, she commanded herself to breathe. She'd just made a step in the right direction, and it'd paid off. Mahlon had broken her, but she'd begun to heal.

✦

The Amish health clinic buzzed with people. Grey rolled up his sleeve and held out his arm to the lab technician. She placed an elastic band around his bicep, swabbed the skin in front of his elbow, and pushed a needle into his arm.

"You've got great veins," the young woman said. "Your wife does too."

Grey looked to Elsie. Her faint smile reflected cautious optimism, and he winked at her. Whether they received good news or bad when the time came, they'd agreed to make changes so their daily lives could move out of the *miserable* stage. Marriage could be a lot of things and people still be able to make it work, but few survived living in gloom.

The lab technician removed a tube full of his blood from the syringe part and placed another tube inside it. They'd taken three vials of blood from Elsie.

Doctor Stone had set up this clinic because some leaders in Grey's community had sought him out before he finished his internship. Most Amish shied away from doctors, tests, and hospitals, but because Dr. Stone had been willing to learn about the Plain community and respected them, the people were becoming more open to seeking medical help. Grey trusted the man's opinion, but the doc had said little about their concerns. He'd asked a lot of questions and then focused on Elsie's side of the family. He uncovered the main reason why her aunt probably had so many children with birth defects. Her aunt was the fourth generation in a row who'd married a relative. But he'd agreed that it'd be best to run tests and then talk. Every word he said seemed to remove some of Elsie's fears and inject hope into her.

After snapping the third vial in place, the lab tech loosened the elastic on Grey's arm. "We'll send this off to the lab. Did the nurse or doctor tell you that it'll take about two months to get the results back for this type of test?"

"Ya."

Two months. He and Elsie had to wait two months before they'd learn the truth—either she'd been wrong all this time, or they had some tough realities to face.

"Okay." The woman placed gauze on his arm and removed the needle before securing the gauze with tape. "You're all done."

Grabbing his jacket off the coatrack, Grey unrolled his sleeve. He and Elsie walked down the hallway and signed out. After he paid cash for the visit, they went out the back entrance to where he'd parked the buggy. So far the most important discovery they'd made over the last four days was the acknowledgement that they…actually, *he* needed a way to get from his plot of ground to hers. That whole concept felt very foggy right now, but it'd given him a clear goal…sort of. She'd admitted she couldn't find it within herself to come to him—in any sense of what that might mean. But as they'd talked this week, she'd lowered a few of her walls and spoken more honestly than in the six previous years. If the blood work proved that she'd been right about their having a genetic issue, they would go to the bishop and ask for the right to use birth control. Grey had no idea what their chances were of getting permission, but what they most needed to happen between them had nothing to do with sex. He untied the reins from the hitching post, tossed them through the front open window of the buggy, and climbed inside. He accepted where they were as a couple, even where they might be years down the road.

Acceptance of what couldn't be changed was what couples did, wasn't it?

He drove down the side alley and waited until he could turn left. They rode through Shippensburg and kept going until they entered Dry Lake. He'd been so absorbed in his own thoughts, he'd not even tried to get her to talk.

Ahead of them, at the Dry Lake Amish School, children were either getting into buggies or leaving on foot. Lennie stood on the steps, waving and speaking to parents as they picked up their children. He'd been told about the trouble happening at the school. A meeting had been called for next Tuesday, but he'd barely given it a thought. Disgruntled parents were the norm some years. Lennie knew that going in. The school board covered three Amish schools. He knew the goings-on in dozens of other Amish districts as well, and Lennie had more stamina for the difficult parts than any other teacher he'd heard of. But he hadn't told Elsie about the scrapes happening under Lennie's watch. He didn't want her to doubt Lennie more than she already did.

As they approached, the schoolyard cleared out, and Lennie went inside. He knew firsthand that the scholars under Lennie left the eighth grade better educated than most. She'd turn flips through a graveyard if she thought it would help those students learn a reading, writing, or math lesson.

He looked to Elsie. "School's out. And Ivan's with Mamm. Do you want to drop by to talk to Lena now?"

Elsie stiffened and then surprised him when she eased her hand over his and nodded.

He pulled onto the graveled circular area and brought the rig to a stop.

She pulled her hand away. "I...I really do want the tests to say I've been wrong."

"I know." Grey got out of the buggy and tied the horse to the hitching post. "And I know you're nervous about this, but I think it'll do us both some good to get Lena's opinion about Ivan."

As he looped the reins onto the post, Elsie climbed out of the carriage. Once on the steps of the schoolhouse, Grey opened the screen door for Elsie and walked in behind her.

From behind her desk, Lennie stood.

"Hey, Lennie. You got a few minutes?"

"Ya. *Kummet rei.*" She stacked the papers up in front of her and slid them to the side.

Grey grabbed a couple of foldout chairs that were resting against the back wall. "We came to talk to you about Ivan."

Lennie shook Elsie's hand, welcoming her. But she and Grey went too far back for them to use any formalities. He leaned back in his chair and raised their questions about Ivan's development. Lennie's blue-green eyes reflected a lot of thoughts, but he knew she'd guard her words carefully.

She folded her hands, looking more like a teacher than his closest friend's kid sister. "When Ivan has been at my brother's, I've spent time with the children, and we've played all sorts of games over the years, and I've never once thought he might be slow." She angled her head, her sincerity shining through. "He's quite introspective."

"What's that mean?" Elsie asked.

"He thinks a lot and talks only a little. He feels deeply, but he's not one to share his thoughts or feelings easily. Basically he's the opposite of me, which will keep him out of a lot of trouble in school, probably in life." Lennie fidgeted with a pencil on her desk. "But don't let his quietness give you the impression he's not bright."

Elsie shifted in her chair. "But what about his arm? The other kids will tease him."

Lennie set the pencil down and smoothed her fingertips across the table. "I was certainly harassed about my birthmark. I still am some days. And I won't lie. It'll hurt him. I'll do what I can to stop the mockery. If the adults make too big a deal out of trying to control the children on the topic, we'll make things worse for him. But the best thing for Ivan is already taking place—his Daed believes in him."

Elsie blinked, looking guilt-ridden. "I…I didn't mean to not believe in—"

"Oh no." Lennie glanced to Grey, looking baffled. "That's not what I meant. Ivan is Grey's shadow on the weekends; that's so good for him. When he sees his Daed able to do stuff, I imagine he sees himself as able to do it."

"Oh, I get what you mean. So can you test him?" Elsie asked.

"Of course. I mean, it's not anything official like the public schools do, but it'll let us know what we'd like to know. Why don't you bring him by the house Saturday around eight and let him stay with me for a couple of hours? Jonathan and I are heading for Hope Crossing around ten."

Grey laced his fingers and popped his knuckles. "I missed working today, and Ephraim's really behind, so after I drop Ivan off with you, I'll go to the cabinetry shop. Can you and Jonathan bring him by there before leaving Dry Lake?"

"Sure."

"We'll be glad to pay you for your time," Elsie offered.

Lennie bit her bottom lip, hiding a smile as she kept her eyes focused on her desk for a moment. "Because your husband is my brother's friend, he pays quite regularly as it is. But now that you mention it, I do have something I'd like at the top of the list this year."

Elsie turned to him, a slight smile in place as she silently looked to understand. She stayed so secluded from his life she had no idea what Lena meant.

"She means the spring rounds Allen and I do at our house, his house, and Lena's house."

"Oh, ya."

Lennie pushed back from her desk, drawing the meeting to a close. "Wooden planters under the windows... I do believe this will be the third year in a row I've requested them."

Grey tipped his hat as he stood. "I'll make sure they get done in time for your spring planting of flowers. And we'll have Ivan at your place around eight. Thanks, Lennie."

"Anytime."

Grey folded the chairs. "Oh, there's a school board meeting Tuesday night, and the board would like you to be there."

Lennie opened a drawer and pulled out a set of keys. "Ya, I figured as much. Dump one dead cat in the ground..."

Her sarcasm caught Grey off guard, and he laughed loudly.

Lennie walked from behind her desk. Grey set the chairs against the wall, and he and Lennie followed Elsie outside.

"I could use a minute to share a school incident privately before that school board meeting begins."

Since wives were encouraged to attend the board meetings, Lennie's request had him curious.

"Now's as good a time as any." Grey turned to his wife. "Would you wait for me for just a few minutes?"

"Denki, Lena."

"*Gern gschehne.*"

When Elsie walked off, Lennie turned to him. "I didn't want to undermine her confidence concerning this school. The cat wasn't just dead, Grey. Its neck had been slashed, and it probably died a slow death as its blood drained onto my floor. Someone had placed it in my chair."

"What?" It seemed wrong that while some parents lodged complaints, she had to deal with difficult scholars and then defend every action to the board—and made hardly any money in the process.

"Ya." She went up the three steps to the door of the school and put a key inside what appeared to be a new lock. The whole mount rattled, and she had to pull and push the door several times to get the bolt to line up with the strike plate.

"Any idea who?"

"I just can't imagine anyone who's that angry with me or with the community—past or current schoolboys included."

"Anyone giving you a hard time in class?"

She finally got the door locked. "Well, ya. Peter Bender has times of being disrespectful and mulish toward assignments, but I don't believe he'd do such a thing."

"Because he's not capable, or because you don't want to believe he's capable?"

"Now how could I possibly know the answer to that question?"

"Fair enough. I'll check with some of the youth and see if they know anything." They walked toward his buggy. "Where's your horse and rig?"

"I walked. My horse is acting up, and, besides, I love walking in fall and spring whenever I can."

He opened the door to his carriage. "Care for a lift? We could drop you off on our way home."

"No, but thanks anyway."

He got in and hung one arm out the open window. "Install that lock yourself, did you, Lennie?"

"Oh, be quiet before I strap that lock to the door of your carriage."

He took the reins in hand. "Yes, Teacher Lena. But I'll bring tools one day next week and see if I can adjust that lock to work a little better." He tapped the reins against the horse's back and tried to keep a straight face. "Of course it may need an entire new door as well as a frame."

"Grey, stop teasing her." Elsie peered around him, checking on Lennie. He knew Lennie didn't mind. If she ever did, she'd definitely let him know.

Lennie put her hands on her hips, mocking offense before breaking into laughter. Grey and Elsie pulled onto the main road.

Elsie shook her head. "I can't believe you tease her as you do, but clearly she has no problem speaking her mind."

He laughed. "We used to aggravate her to no end just to hear her logic on the matter."

"She's an awfully pretty girl. I...I hate to admit it, but before today I only saw that birthmark. Aside from that one thing, she's flawless. I doubt if she's a teacher many more years."

"Maybe not."

"I've never seen eyes that color. I couldn't stop staring." Elsie rubbed just below her neck. "I...I didn't realize she'd spent so much time with Ivan."

Grey always invited Elsie to go with them when they visited Allen. "She's at her brother's place sometimes when Ivan and I visit."

"So when she said she doesn't think he's slow, it's got a real basis to it and not just her being nice."

Elsie saw Ivan so negatively. He didn't understand it, and he certainly didn't appreciate it. "It has a real basis. And you're right; Lena would be nice about Ivan, but she'd also be very straightforward."

"I...I wish we knew already."

It wasn't like Elsie to be so chatty. Going through the steps today to begin to find the truth had her talking and even hopeful, and for the first time in years, Grey began to feel optimistic about their marriage.

Fourteen

Lena rode beside Ivan as Jonathan brought the rig to a halt in front of Ephraim's shop. She didn't think Grey would be worried about his son, but testing him had taken longer than she'd planned on. Jonathan had made it clear he wasn't pleased that they were running late. A few days ago they'd agreed to leave Dry Lake and head for Hope Crossing at ten. Even so, it wasn't much past ten thirty.

Lena opened the door, but before she stepped out, Grey came out the doorway of the shop and walked to them. Ivan jumped down and ran to his Daed. Grey picked him up.

"We had a very productive couple of hours. He's a great kid."

Grey spoke to his son in Pennsylvania Dutch, asking if he wanted to help him work in the shop. Ivan nodded.

"How'd he do?" Grey asked in English so Ivan wouldn't understand.

"Good. Like everyone, he has strengths and weaknesses. I'd like to discuss it privately, but right now Jonathan is in a hurry to get to Hope Crossing. Why don't you and Elsie come by the school next week, and we can talk about my findings in great detail?"

"I…I sort of expected you to just tell me."

"I got the feeling that Elsie is hoping for a somewhat professional opinion, not viewpoints shared over a back fence…or in this case through the open door of a carriage while she's not around."

Grey chuckled. "You're right about that. Denki, Lennie. We'll both come to see you one day next week."

"You're welcome. And since I began this on a Saturday and won't wrap up the report until Monday morning, I should get the best window boxes you can create." She grabbed Ivan's straw hat off the carriage seat and held it out to Grey.

He took it and peered in at Jonathan. "Is she always so picky about how things are handled?"

"Oh, ya. When it comes to her class, she's pickier and more business-like than most men could tolerate."

She scowled playfully at Jonathan. Grey chuckled as he stepped back. She waved as Jonathan tapped the reins, and the horse started down the driveway.

Jonathan clicked his tongue, making the horse gain speed quickly. "I'm so ready to be in Hope Crossing."

"Believe me, I know." Feeling a little too cool, Lena fastened her side of the front window. Jonathan used to be patient and didn't mind plans changing or whiling away the hours on a free Saturday. His new focus on Deborah meant Lena would have to adjust. Clearly in his mind and heart, Lena had been sent to the backseat of the carriage. She and Jonathan were friends. That's all. But over the years they'd helped each other ward off the loneliness for someone special. All these years, even though he'd dated at will, it'd been their secret how much he cared for Deborah.

"Hey." Jonathan nudged her with his elbow. "I didn't mean to be selfish. I'm sorry."

"It's just happening quicker than I expected."

"What?"

"I went from being someone you hung out with on free weekends to simply an excuse for you to spend time around Deborah without looking like you're interested in her. I can't imagine where we'll be a few months from now. And all that's good. I'm glad for you. I am. It's just..."

Deep concern reflected in his eyes, and he slowed the rig. "You...don't feel...anything special...toward me, do you?"

Lena laughed. "Oh, heavens, no."

He laughed quietly. "Whew. You scared me, because the last thing I'd ever want is to hurt you. And I happen to know firsthand that a person can care about someone without the other one knowing it."

"It's not like that at all. You're supposed to know that. But I'm being demoted, and I thought I was ready, but it's harder than I expected."

"Ya, I can see that. Now that I think about it, it'd be that way for me too if you'd found someone before I did. I'll do better. Just tell me or kick me under the table or something."

Lena chuckled. "That I can do. I might even buy steel-toed shoes."

"Ouch." He clicked his tongue, urging the horse to pick up speed again. "And you know Deborah. It'll probably be another year before she even notices that other men besides Mahlon exist on this planet. We have plenty of time for you to adjust."

"Gut." She reached into the covered basket at her feet. "Care for a piece of peanut brittle?"

"Store bought?" He shrugged and took the canister. "I'm surprised it's not homemade, but sure." He opened the lid. Two five-foot cloth snakes leaped out of the can. He hollered and all but jumped out of his skin. Lena kept her composure and stayed focused looking out the window. "I'll get you for that, Lena Kauffman."

"You can try, Jonathan Stoltzfus." She pulled a felt hat lined with straw out of the basket. "I have a plan to trick Deborah. You in?"

"What all did you bring?"

"After the awful way my week started at school, I needed to self-medicate, so I hired a driver to take me to Philly, and I went to a gag store. I felt so much better afterward. Poorer, but better."

"I've heard self-medication can be dangerous."

"It is…for the other people in my life." Lena gave her best evil laugh.

"What happens if after you find someone, he doesn't approve of the money you've spent on gags?"

"I'll tell him that I'm very careful with money—giving, spending, and saving. I've tended to my Daed's home, laundry, and meals for half of my life. I help family and friends when they need it, and added to that, I began working full-time before I became a teacher. If I can't spend a little money on fun items without it being questioned, he needs to keep moving because I'm not interested. Besides, everyone who's single and works spends a few dollars here and there to enjoy something important to them. If this imaginary fellow doesn't admit to that, he's a hypocrite."

"Wow. Say you have an opinion?"

She laughed. "Always. Did you forget?" Her skin tingled from her overreaction. She longed for a husband and was willing to make sacrifices for the right person, but if any man thought he knew better how she should've handled her life while waiting for him, she wasn't interested. Period.

Jonathan adjusted his hat. "You are something else. If a man ever questions how you've spent your money, I'm leaving the state before you respond, okay?"

She laughed. "You best take him with you."

He chuckled and nodded several times. "So, aside from the various gags you're going to pull, what's the plan for Deborah?"

"She needs a scarecrow as a decoration for the cornfield maze, right?"

"Ya, I guess."

Lena pulled a painted flour sack over her head and flopped the felt hat lined with straw on her head. "Once I'm in my full outfit, you'll get me set up outside and tell Deborah you made a scarecrow for her. I'll do the rest after that."

Jonathan laughed. "Please remain my friend…because it's scary to think of you as an enemy."

Fifteen

Sitting in the cabinetry office, Grey shifted in his chair while on the phone with a potential client. For the first time in years, he didn't feel that work and Ivan were the only hopeful things in his life. Hope. It hung in the fall air itself—light, airy, brisk, colorful, and an indication that something had shifted within the universe.

"Ya," he answered the woman's question for the third time. "I understand you live in Kentucky. If we work out all the details, we'll stay in your area for a week at a time, coming home on the weekends, until the job is complete."

The office door opened, and surprise ran through Grey as his wife stepped inside. "I'll drop a packet of info in the mail to you tomorrow. If you like what you see, just give us a call back, and we'll go from there." As the woman confirmed her address and said good-bye, he stared at his wife. She'd never come to the shop except when church was held here. "Hi."

She removed a cloth from a plate. "I…I made some cookies."

"Denki." He took a cookie. "Is Ivan with you?"

She shook her head.

He took a bite of the cookie. *Pumpkin spice.* "Oh, that's good."

She smiled and ran her fingers along the messy desk, looking at the various sets of plans. Piecing together his wife's actions, he had a suspicion of what was on her mind. She wanted to meet with Lena and get the results concerning Ivan. Grey stole a look at the clock. "School's not out for more than an hour yet."

Elsie didn't respond. She flipped through the calendar.

He took another bite of the cookie. "It's not likely she can step out of the school to talk with us."

Elsie kept her attention focused on the desk, but past her stoic nature, he saw disappointment.

The cookie seemed to lose some of its flavor as he tried to read her. "I guess we could go on and wait there until school is over. It's been quite a while since I saw her teaching methods in action anyway."

The muscles in Elsie's throat constricted as if she were swallowing or at least trying to.

Grey rose. "I…I think she'll have good news for us."

Elsie set the cookies on the desk and pressed her hands down the front of her neatly pressed apron. "I hope you're right."

He motioned for her to leave the office ahead of him. "Excited about being proved wrong?"

"Grey, that's just mean."

The way he breathed and moved no longer grated on her nerves, or at least not all her nerves, and for that he was very grateful. If that's all they had for a long while yet, he'd be satisfied, but in a place inside him where no one would ever know what he thought or how he felt, he longed for her to grow a sense of humor.

He spotted Ephraim. "I'm going out for a bit. I'll be back in a couple of hours and finish my work."

"Sure thing. I'll be here."

He got into the carriage Elsie had driven here, and they headed toward the school. The brilliance of the October sky and the gentle winds refreshed him as he thought about their future. The stiltedness between them still reigned, but his isolation had eased, and he dared to hope where they'd be in a few months or a year from now.

The schoolhouse looked like a photo—a one-room, white clapboard building surrounded by huge oaks with the leaves changing color, a playground with swings to one side, a turnaround driveway on the other, and a rolling pasture behind it. Had it been almost fifteen years since he'd graduated from that school?

He stopped on the far side of the lean-to, leaving room for the parents to pick up their children when school let out. He and Elsie got out and rounded the side of the outbuilding and walked toward the schoolhouse. A man's voice sounded angry, and Grey hurried closer, listening.

"I'm not doing it, and you can't make me. You're just too stupid to accept it."

Grey bounded up the steps and jerked the screen door open. Peter stood in the center of the classroom, inches from Lennie.

"What is going on here?" Grey strode into the room. "You!" He pointed at Peter. "Sit down." Grey stood there, daring Peter to do otherwise.

When Peter balked for a moment before taking his seat, Grey's blood pounded harder against his temples. "This behavior is not acceptable and will not be tolerated. Is that clear?"

"Ya," Peter mumbled.

"Excuse me? I had no problem hearing you earlier."

"Ya," Peter said clearly.

All eyes were on Grey, and he tried to gain control of himself, but this kid did not begin to understand the boundaries he'd crossed. "Elsie, would you take the other children outside for a few minutes? Lena and I need to talk with Peter. Then I want to talk to everyone."

Elsie motioned, and the children exited quietly and quickly.

Grey paced the room before feeling calm enough to grab two folding chairs. He set them next to Peter. "If you don't want to be at school, I can arrange for that."

Lennie took a seat. "I want you here, Peter. I really do think you're more capable of learning than a lot of boys your age. We just haven't fig-ured out *how* you learn best yet."

Grey blinked, trying to accept what Lennie had just said. Was she serious? "Before we do anything else, you give Lena an apology, a sincere one."

Peter looked at Lennie like she disgusted him.

Grey smacked the boy's desk. "You apologize now."

Peter folded his arms and stared at his desk.

Grey wanted to drag him out of the school and refuse him the right to return, but clearly Lennie felt differently. "We'll sit here until you can humble yourself enough to apologize."

Peter slumped in his desk, and Grey used the passing minutes to gain control of himself. Lennie sat there so poised, appearing ready to forgive and start with Peter again. As he considered her belief in others, he found it easier to calm down. Hadn't she had the same determined belief in her own brother?

Grey had been ready to give up on Allen during his wild days, but Lennie had never faltered. She never let him off the hook, always holding him responsible for his behavior, but at the same time she never quit believing he could become even more than she could imagine. And Allen became a good man. It wasn't who Peter was today that made her want to teach him. It was her belief in who he could become if he only wanted to.

Children's voices chanted and laughed from the playground. Lennie rose and went to the window.

She gasped. "Dear Father, no!" She spun around. "Grey! Go. Go." She pointed at the door, and they both ran.

He made it outside first and searched for what had her so upset but saw nothing.

Lennie passed him, pointing. "The pasture. The bull."

One glance and his body halted. His wife stood in the field some two hundred feet out, facing the bull while waving her arms. Two young boys were even farther out in the field.

"Get to the fence!" Elsie screamed at the boys while trying to distract the animal. The bull headed for his wife, and the boys ran for the closest fence, but they had hundreds of feet to cross before they'd get there.

Grey took off running and scaled the barbed-wire barrier with no effort.

Staying outside the fence, Lennie dashed to the area where the boys were heading. "Here!" she screamed while running, motioning for them. "Elsie, run a zigzag...a zigzag!"

"And head for the tree!" Grey clapped his hands. "Hey! Hey! Over here!" he screamed with all his might, trying to get the bull's attention.

The bull remained focused on Elsie, chasing her farther and farther from Grey.

"Elsie! Cut left! Go behind the tree!"

The bull picked up speed. All of Grey's motions seemed awkward and slow. As he continued running toward her, he watched the bull plow full force into his wife's back. Her body was lifted into the air, and then landed with a thud. The bull lowered his head and stomped her.

"No!" Grey rammed his shoulder into the bull's side, trying to get its attention. It didn't seem to even notice what he'd done. He kicked the bull's underbelly, and finally it turned. Grey cut right, hoping the bull would follow but not stomp on Elsie in the process. His idea worked. Sprinting toward the tree, he shifted right, then left, slowing the bull's ability to catch up to him. The bull snorted, slinging its head as it ran. Once behind the tree, he shifted one way and then the other, able to keep the bull from getting to him.

A quick glimpse of his wife made him want to scream out in pain. He'd made the bull follow him, but he couldn't help his wife. She lay sprawled on the ground, and Grey wanted to kill the stupid beast that separated the two of them. Lennie bolted for Elsie. While Lennie hurried across the field, Elsie slowly eased to her hands and knees, trying to get up.

The bull stomped and snorted, kicking up dust as it dodged one way and then the other, trying to get to him. He longed to get a good look at his wife, but every time he tried to see her, the bull came at him. Still he caught glimpses of her.

Elsie only looked addled and weak, but what had the two-thousand-pound, thick-skulled beast done to her insides? By the time Lennie arrived, Elsie had staggered to her feet. She wrapped her arm over Lennie's shoulder, and they made their way toward the fence.

His heart pounded like mad as he kept moving and screaming at the bull to keep its attention. It seemed to take Lennie and Elsie a week to get to the fence. Finally arriving, Elsie got on the ground and rolled under it.

The bull moved one way and then another, clearly wanting to get past the tree between them. Grey had to find a way to get to his wife. She needed medical help. He considered trying to outrun the bull, but the distance from here to the closest fence was too great. A clanging sound echoed again and again, and he realized he'd been hearing that noise since entering the pasture. From the backside of the field, near the broken fence, Grey saw the silhouette of a man coming toward him. The sun's rays hindered his view, but the man hollered and clanged metal objects together as he ran. When he drew close, the bull turned to the new distraction. Concern for whether the man could outrun the bull caused Grey to stay put.

"Go," the voice hollered while banging the objects together. "Get to safety, and take care of my sister."

Aaron.

The moment his brother-in-law had the creature's full attention, Grey ran for his wife.

❧

"Jacob." Lena crawled out of the field on her hands and knees. "Get Grey's horse. Unfasten it from the carriage, and remove everything but the bridle. Bring it here right away."

Elsie swayed, and Lena helped her ease to the ground, wishing Dry Lake didn't sit so far from a hospital. Dozens of thoughts competed for her attention as she tried to prioritize what needed to be done. No blood on Elsie's body. No bones protruding through the skin. Elsie quaked. Her lips had no color. Her eyes seemed unable to focus. Someone had to get to a phone and quick. "Mandy, you and Rachel take the children into the schoolhouse. Someone get me the blankets we use for sitting on during story time."

Mandy and Rachel began doing as they'd been told.

Jacob's voice broke through the commotion. "Get off the horse, Peter! She sent me."

Mounted on Grey's horse, Peter brought the animal to a stop about ten feet from her and Elsie. "I'll get to a phone and call for help. I'm faster on a horse," Peter said.

Torn between distrust and something unknown tugging at her, Lena shook her head. Mandy had taken a good bit of time to get to Ephraim's the other day, but she'd done the job as told. Jacob would too. Should she go herself? As horsemen went, she could outride all her siblings. She rose to her feet and took the horse by one rein.

Peter jerked at the reins, and the horse backed up. "I can do this." His voice cracked. "Please, let me do this."

For a brief moment Lena saw a repentant child who couldn't undo what his actions had set in motion. But did that make him trustworthy? She'd seen him ride bareback, and he could handle a horse better and go faster than she could. "Go. The closest phone is at Ephraim's shop, and tell him we need the parents to come get their children."

Grey leaped over the fence and knelt beside his wife. "Elsie." He drew deep breaths, too winded to speak.

Lena choked back her emotions. "I've sent...one of the boys to call for an ambulance. He's bareback on your horse."

Grey stroked his wife's face. "Can you tell me what hurts the most?"

Elsie tapped the center of her chest. "My heart." Tears rolled down the sides of her head. She licked her lips, giving color to her mouth. "All my married years of scrubbing and cleaning. All trying to make others see how perfect I was." She tugged at Grey's suspender. "In a week no one will ever be able to tell." She licked her lips again. "Except the one who's carried my imperfection with silence and honor."

"I'll scrub and clean every day," Grey murmured. "The cabinets and the walls and anything else while you recuperate."

Was that blood on her mouth? Rachel brought several blankets and held them out.

Lena took them. "Denki. Go on back now, and help the younger ones."

Rachel left. Lena knelt on the other side of Elsie and covered her with the blankets. She ran her finger over Elsie's wet lips. Blood. Hoping Elsie had only split the inside of her mouth when she hit the ground, Lena turned Elsie's head slightly, looking at her ear. Blood. She wiped the fluid from her earlobe and studied it, wishing...

Lena's eyes met Grey's. "No. Do you hear me? I said no."

His desperation broke her heart, and Lena's tears fell onto Elsie's grubby dress. Grey couldn't admit it, but they both knew Elsie was bleeding internally.

And there was nothing they could do but wait, hoping the ambulance would arrive in time.

Elsie shook as if she were in icy water. She closed her eyes, and Lena slapped the back of her hands. "She can't go to sleep. We've got to keep her awake." But Elsie didn't respond.

Grey sat on the ground, cradling her in his arms. "Elsie," he whispered, and she opened her eyes. "Don't you dare leave me now, not after..."

Elsie whispered something. Lena stood and slipped away unnoticed, praying help would arrive soon.

◖

Cold sweat covered Grey. His body shook, and his mind raged against what was happening. "You'll be okay, Elsie. Help's coming. Just...just stay with me. Please."

She closed her eyes.

"No. Stay awake. Listen to me...please." He tucked the blankets around her, feeling desperation like never before. His heart railed at him, despised him for not doing more for their marriage sooner.

Dear God, please. Don't let this happen to us. We've been such idiots. Forgive me.

Pleadings screamed inside him, but nothing changed his reality. He wiped a trickle of blood from the side of her mouth.

Please, God.

"Elsie," he called to her loudly, and she opened her eyes. "I need...us. Can't you feel that? Hang on. Just hang on."

She looped her hand through one suspender and tugged on it. "Tell... me...about the day...we...met."

Grey choked back tears, praying the ambulance would arrive soon. She wanted to talk about the past? He'd just begun having hope for their future. She had to survive this. She had to. "It was on a church Sunday, on a beautiful fall day like today. The windows at my house were open. Mamm and Daed had already gathered all my siblings and were in the buggy waiting for me, but I couldn't find my Sunday pants...or any others that would fit. I went to the window and hollered down at Mamm, 'I can't find my Sunday britches.'

"She shifted, looking a little nervous as she answered, 'Did you check in your dresser?' And I said, 'Ya.' And she said, 'Look in your closet, and maybe in the dirty clothes basket.'

"I searched through everything quickly, grabbed what I could find, and headed out the door. I walked outside, whistling like a man without a care."

She breathed a whispery laugh. "Then what happened?"

"Everyone in the buggy broke into laughter as I came outside wearing my pressed shirt, suspenders, dress shoes, Sunday jacket and hat…but no pants."

Elsie's breaths came in short, rapid spurts, but she smiled at the memory.

Grey wiped the back of his hand across his mouth, taking several deep breaths in hopes he could finish the story. "Then I looked up and saw that you and your family were passing the house, walking to church."

Her breathing came in shallow gasps. "Tell more."

"Then I tipped my hat at you as if nothing unusual was going on. You screamed and covered your eyes."

"Later…your Mamm s…s…said."

He pulled Elsie closer, trying to warm her. "Well my Mamm looked you up before the service to try to reassure you that wasn't a normal event in Dry Lake. She thought you and your family were visitors, but then we learned your Daed was trying to buy the old Englischer farmstead up the road a piece and was thinking about moving here from Ohio. She told you that I was keeping things light so no one would be mad at her about me not having pants and that I didn't usually run around in my boxers."

"M…m…more."

"Your eyes met mine, and you told me later that's when you knew you wanted to marry me. You wanted a man who…who…" Heaviness settled into his chest as he realized how badly he'd let her down all these years. "Had two good senses—ya, that's what you said—the sense to be himself and the sense to laugh instead of get mad. And I told you that when a person has chicken legs like I do, they have to have a sense of humor. And because you'd seen those scrappy legs and still weren't running away, I said you must be the right girl."

She swallowed. "You…find your good senses…again, Grey. You find them and don't let go."

"I will. You'll help me, right?" He placed his hand on her cheek, staring into her eyes. But as he held her, light faded from them, making her look… "Elsie!" He placed his hand on her neck, looking for a pulse. She had one, barely. "Elsie, listen to me."

Her body became heavier against him, but she didn't respond to his voice. Without looking at him again and without even a gasp or twitch, she exhaled. And never took another breath.

Sixteen

Inside the barn, Cara painted a strip of wainscot lying across sawhorses. She swayed to the music coming from her battery-operated radio.

"'From!" Lori squealed as she ran out of the barn, Better Days yapping at her heels.

In Hope Crossing on a Monday afternoon? Cara turned. Ephraim was on foot, which meant Robbie must have dropped him off out front. Lori ran to him and jumped into his arms. Rather than his usual quick swing of her body into the air as he shared a bit of banter, he pulled her close, one hand embracing her head as all movement halted. He kissed her head and set her feet on the ground.

When he stopped in the doorway of the barn, his focus didn't budge from Cara. Realizing the radio was not acceptable, she went to the bale of hay where it sat and turned it off. He said nothing.

Cara shrugged. "I…I just wanted to hear some familiar tunes."

"Mama's been dancin'."

"Just a little," Cara added quickly. "There's good news, though. I didn't set up my work station in the yard like I'd wanted to on this gorgeous day, so no one but Lori heard the music or saw me."

"I tried tellin' her not to, 'From. She never listens to me."

Cara found Lori's exasperation with her cute, but Ephraim's face held emotions she'd not seen before. Had she taxed his patience too much?

"I…I'm not a member, so music is okay until I begin my instruction, right?"

Without answering, he walked to her and pulled her into a hug. He held her in a way he never had before. His warm embrace renewed her spirits even more than the beautiful October day.

"I had to see you, had to feel you in my arms." His deep voice sounded different today.

Lori squeezed between them. "Yuck." She put a hand on each of them and pushed them away from each other.

Ephraim playfully nudged her back before kissing Cara gently on the cheek.

"I'll say it again. Yuck." Lori hurried out of the barn.

"Hey," Ephraim called to her. "Run inside and tell Ada we're going for a long walk."

"Yes!" Lori whispered loudly. "You want me to grab our picnic blanket?"

"Ya."

"And make some sandwiches?"

"Ya." Ephraim's eyes never moved from Cara, and she knew he'd come to tell her something.

"What kind?"

Cara snapped her fingers. "Lori, just go."

Lori put her hands on her hips. "I was just asking 'From, Mom."

"Mind your tone, Lori," Ephraim corrected her.

Lori lowered her hands, looking hurt. She walked into the barn and wrapped her arms around Cara's waist. "Sorry."

Cara bent and kissed the top of her head. "Forgiven. Now take off."

Without asking anything else, Lori and Better Days ran through the backyard and into the house.

Ephraim moved to the radio and picked it up. He turned it around as if inspecting it. "You're finding it harder to give up the Englischer ways rather than easier."

It wasn't a question, so she decided not to respond. Of course it was hard. She missed having electricity and her choice of clothing, but of late those preferences seemed a lot easier to give up than music and television. The new fall season of shows had been going for a couple of weeks now, and she didn't even know if *Survivor* was still in the lineup. She'd never owned a television, but the restaurant where she'd worked had them hanging from the ceilings. And today while listening to a rock station, she'd heard half a dozen new songs—good ones.

He set the radio back down on the bale of hay. "I don't care about bikes or music or you dancing. When I lived among Englischers those few years, I could see how tough it'd be to live Amish if one hadn't been raised that way." He moved to her. "But the longer it takes you to accept our ways, the more likely it is that church leaders won't think you're ready to join the faith, and then it'll be even longer before we can marry." Ephraim slowly brought his face to hers, as if letting all of her—her mind, will, heart, and body—awaken to what he was trying to tell her. He kissed her long and slow. "And I want to marry you…as soon as possible."

When he released her, she could barely think. "I…I didn't think Amish…had feelings like that. I thought they…you were too practical."

Ephraim backed away, drawing a deep breath. "What you don't understand about people of faith is sort of baffling." He took her hand into his. "I've got some bad news. Grey's wife died this afternoon. Attacked by a bull. She had massive internal injuries."

"Ephraim, I'm so sorry. Do I know her?"

He shook his head. "Elsie was a quiet woman who avoided gatherings as much as possible and kept to herself even when she attended church. But Grey is…bad right now." Ephraim reflected a sadness that made Cara hurt for him. "The whole community is. The schoolchildren saw the incident."

"What? That's horrible. I…I…" She wrapped her arms around him, aching for the children and their parents.

"The bull belonged to Elsie's brother Aaron. Aaron got his hunting rifle and shot the bull—again and again and again. Elsie died before the ambulance arrived, but Grey rode with her to the hospital. Friends and family hired a driver so they could meet him there. He and Elsie have one child, a five-year-old son, who doesn't know yet. Grey will tell him when he returns to Dry Lake, but I imagine Grey has forms and reports to fill out, so that will be hours from now. It's bad, Cara."

They tightened their hold on each other.

"I know you're not at ease in Dry Lake, running into your estranged relatives and all, but I'd like for you to come stay for a few days. You and Lori and Ada can stay at my place, and I'll stay at the shop."

"Ada and Deborah have a business to run."

"They'll close their doors for a few days, as will most Amish businesses in and around Dry Lake."

"Stop all business?" The idea sounded bizarre. People took time off from work, as little time as possible, but life never slowed. When her husband died, one of the most painful realities was that life never paused. New York didn't care. The restaurant he'd once managed had replaced him when he could no longer work, and on the day he died, she received a two-week notice to move out of the apartment that belonged to the owners of the restaurant. "Okay, I'll come...and try my best not to embarrass you."

"I'm going to keep saying it until you believe me. I will never feel that way. Not ever." He took her by the hand, and they began walking toward the house. He hollered for Lori.

She stuck her head out the back door. "Be there in a minute. Jonathan's helping me make sandwiches."

Cara shielded her eyes from the sunlight. "Jonathan's here?"

"Ya."

They walked back into the barn. Ephraim sat on a bale of hay and picked up the radio. "He came with me to tell Deborah and Ada. The driver will take them on to Dry Lake as soon as Deborah and Ada are packed. I imagine Lena needs Deborah about now."

"Why's Lena taking it so hard? Oh, you said the schoolchildren saw, and she's their teacher." Grief settled over Cara, and she began to understand how interwoven the Amish were.

"When one of the schoolboys arrived at the shop to use the phone and told me what had happened, I'd hoped it wasn't as bad as it sounded. I went to the school and learned that Elsie had died, and I felt sick for Grey and Ivan. But something else happened inside me. Something I'd never experienced before."

"What?"

He drew her hand to his lips and kissed it. "Over the years if someone died and I was seeing a girl, the news sobered my thinking. Every time. Beyond the sadness I'd think about the girl and know she wasn't who I wanted to spend the rest of my life with. Even if that day was my last day on earth, I was ready to walk away. Something about death made it clear. I…I always felt so shallow when that happened. Those types of events cause people to want to hold on to who they have. Today when the news hit, I felt vulnerable, and I needed you, longed to hold you and talk to you." He squeezed her hand. "I had to see you, to make sure you and Lori were safe, to reassure myself we will become a family." He stared at the radio.

"Then you arrived, and I'm…sneaking around and hanging on to some of my former ways."

"You're you, Cara. I don't want you to be anyone else, and we can be imperfect together, but it seems as if you own more of me than I do, and… yet other things possess your heart. I understand it, but it scares me. I need *you*, but what do you need?"

Wishing she could snap her fingers and change for him, she tugged on his hand, leading him out of the barn. "I'll adjust to living the Old Ways… I will."

Seventeen

Lena woke, startled from her nightmare. More exhausted than when she went to bed, she longed for her thoughts to settle. All she could do was doze and jerk awake after another dreadful dream. She kept reliving the trauma she'd witnessed less than sixteen hours ago.

What must the children be going through?

She pushed off the covers and sat upright. Grief weighed heavy, making her head spin.

And what about Grey?

He'd begun yesterday with a wife, his family intact, and a good road ahead of him. Today he was missing half of himself.

All night she'd dreamed of Elsie teetering on the edge of a rocky cliff and of Grey running to grab her. Instead they both plummeted. Elsie died instantly. Grey lay at the bottom of the gorge—broken, bloody, but unable to pass from this life to the next.

Nausea returned. She went to the window and opened it. Cold air rushed in. Nicky stretched and moaned, wagging her tail a few times before going back to sleep. Lena glanced through the open doorway, seeing Deborah in the adjoining bedroom, motionless under the quilts. A hired driver had brought two Amish families here from Ohio late last night, families Lena had never met before. They were friends of Elsie's family from Ohio, but Elsie's parents' home couldn't house any more people.

Lena breathed deeply, trying to rid herself of queasiness. It didn't matter how poorly she felt. There was much that needed doing. Foods of all sorts had to be prepared for Elsie's visiting relatives as well as for the day of the funeral. She closed the window, gathered clean clothes, and went into her bathroom. Maybe a warm shower would make her feel better. It usually helped, but after drying off and slipping into her dress, she still felt nauseated and weak. She pinned up her wet hair and secured her prayer Kapp in place.

It was just as well school was closed for the next few days. She knew nothing to say or do that would ease the shock and pain her pupils were going through. Urie and Tobias, the boys who'd snuck into the pasture, the ones who'd caused Elsie to become the bull's target so they could escape—how would they survive their guilt? And what about Peter? Would this cause him to completely give up?

When school was in session again, her scholars would need more help than she knew how to give. A tremor ran through her. The weeks ahead felt darker and colder than a winter's night.

And Grey… Would he ever feel warmth within his soul again?

Oh how she wished she could undo yesterday.

Before leaving the bedroom, she checked herself in the mirror, making sure she'd pinned everything correctly in place. She was descending the stairs when someone knocked on the back door. Nicky barked, running ahead of her. Lena told her to hush, and she obeyed. Since they'd had guests staying with them last night, Lena had lit a few kerosene nightlights, which illuminated the entryway. She told Nicky to stay. When she opened the door, Aaron Blank had his hand ready to knock again.

They both seemed too caught by surprise to speak.

Nicky barked.

"Hush," Lena scolded.

A faint aroma of alcohol surrounded him. He didn't have a jacket, and his short-sleeve shirt and pants flapped in the brisk winds. She hadn't even begun to consider his guilt.

"Kumm out of the cold."

But he didn't budge. Even in the dim glow of kerosene night-lights, his dark, bloodshot eyes held such remorse that Lena couldn't hold his gaze.

He removed his straw hat. "I...I...only did a half job fixing the fence...and now..."

Lena's heart twisted, and she tugged on his arm. "You made a mistake. Kumm. Get warm."

Aaron pulled her in a hug, and she felt him trembling. "My sister. I killed my own sister."

No words came to her. Only pain at what Aaron would carry for the rest of his life. She embraced him warmly. "Kumm." She took him by the arm, and he eased inside.

Nicky growled, and Lena snapped her fingers. "Go lay down."

With her tail tucked, Nicky went to her bed in the kitchen. Lena followed her, guiding Aaron as he staggered. She helped him to a chair. Dirt and stains covered his clothes, and she wondered where he'd left his coat.

"I...I need a bathroom."

"Sure." She pointed to the closest one. He'd been in it a few times in the past when church was held here, but she didn't imagine he could think clearly enough to remember.

He stood and stumbled his way into the half bath.

She added wood to the potbelly stove and set a pot of coffee on to brew. Kneeling in front of Nicky, she gave her a few doggy treats and then patted her head. "You do your job and get fussed at about it." Lena cuddled her nose in the palms of her hands. "Welcome to the real world, I suppose."

Nicky laid her head on the raised edge of her doggy bed, satisfied that Lena had doted on her. Aaron walked back into the room, looking a little better. He seemed to have washed his face and somehow scrubbed a bit of his drunkenness away.

"I...I shouldn't have come like this, Lena. You...you deserve better."

She ached for him. He wanted to be a good guy; she'd never doubted that. But so far he didn't have it in him to follow through. "So do you, Aaron. Kumm, sit. Coffee will be ready in a few minutes. Then we can talk."

He did as she'd requested. He took her hand in his and several times started to say something. But instead they sat in silence.

❦

Days had passed. Grey knew they had, but he hardly remembered any conversations he'd had with people. Tuning out the murmuring of the many voices within his home, he moved from one room to another. He couldn't hear when someone spoke to him, even when he tried, and he couldn't find the strength to try.

Everyone thought him to be a good husband who'd lost his wife. They didn't know the truth. No one but Ephraim knew the strain inside Grey's marriage, and Grey would never tell. He shouldn't have talked to Ephraim either. Elsie had a right to privacy. She had a right to a lot of things he hadn't given her.

He pulled a chair from the kitchen table, walked into the living room, and sat in front of his wife's open casket. Wearing the customary white apron and prayer Kapp that she'd worn on their wedding, she looked so much like she had six years ago.

What happened to us, Elsie?

That tormenting question never ceased pounding inside his heart. He blamed himself. Each tick of the clock had felt suffocating since the moment she'd died. He hadn't realized that even when he and Elsie were the most miserable, hope—constant, threadbare hope—kept him. Tomorrow a service would be held in his home and another one at the grave site. Then it'd be time to close the casket, lower her into the ground, and cover his future with dirt.

"I'm sorry, Elsie."

His Mamm placed her hand on his shoulder. "You need to come eat."

Even with the cooler temperatures of October, his house radiated with heat from all the baking the women had done. Someone with good sense had opened a few windows a couple of inches. But he didn't want food, or fresh air, or conversation. He wanted time alone. "Can you do me a favor, Mamm? After everyone's eaten, can you get them to go home? Take Ivan with you."

"You don't need to be alone, Son."

"Ya, I do. Can you do that for me?"

People had been here day and night. They'd filled his home even before he arrived from the hospital. He understood the Amish tradition, but he needed tonight by himself.

"Please, Mamm."

She nodded. "If you're sure."

"I am."

"Will you come say good-bye?"

"No," he whispered. "I'll see them all tomorrow before and after...the services, and I'll do as I need to then." He choked back his tears. His Mamm patted his shoulder.

After the meal and cleanup, his house grew quieter and quieter as people left. The sun slid behind the horizon. As darkness grew, Grey rose and lit the kerosene lamp. Elsie liked for him to go through their home each evening and light the gas pole lamps and kerosene lanterns.

Through all their silences had he noticed or appreciated the rhythm to their marriage? He returned to his chair. His guilt grew worse with each passing day, and he knew it'd just begun.

His only chance to make it right had ended, taking most of him with it.

Sing for me, Grey.

Her voice ran through him as clearly as the day they married. She'd asked that of him every day until Ivan was born. Tears filled his eyes. If he'd knelt before her and sung to her, without being asked, would she have told him sooner what separated them?

Sing for me, Grey.

He swallowed and straightened the collar of her dress. "Amazing Grace..." He began the song softly and sang louder with each verse, trying to drown out the condemnation in his own heart. Wind whipped through the room, billowing the curtains and threatening to damage the nearby houseplants. He shut the windows. Clouds moved quickly across the dark skies, bringing a sense that only darkness lurked beyond the gray.

Eighteen

Samantha drew a huge circle on the chalkboard. She pointed inside the circle. "This is where everything and everyone you love belongs. Can you begin telling me things to write inside this circle? Don't raise your hand. Just say it aloud."

Children began volunteering answers, slowly at first, but then the responses grew faster and louder, as did their laughter.

Nine days had passed since the incident, and Lena's heart pounded as she watched Samantha interact with her class. Her friend had read about Elsie's death in the local newspaper and stopped by Lena's place to check on her. After Samantha talked to her about posttraumatic stress disorder and other related issues, Lena asked if she'd come talk to her class.

Lena's own feelings were so jumbled she didn't know where to begin trying to sort them out. Hearing Grey sing to Elsie the night before he buried her made Lena teary-eyed every time she thought about it. She'd been in her brother's yard and as Grey's voice carried on the wind, she grew still and listened. She couldn't help Grey with his grief, but with Samantha's knowledge, Lena could make a difference for her scholars. Even Peter was responding well to Samantha.

The school days were long and filled with tears and confusion, but now Lena felt as if they'd do more than mark time off the calendar. She desperately wanted healing to take place.

Wrapped inside a winter coat and a woolen scarf, Deborah stayed warm. The stars shone brightly across the November sky as she slid another mini–pumpkin pie onto a customer's paper plate. The bite-sized pies were rather time-consuming to make but well worth the effort. Customers could purchase five different kinds and sample each flavor. Or they could buy a regular-sized pie to take home with them. After eating the mini-pies, guests often bought whole pies. The success of the last four weeks might not show up in an abundance of money. That remained to be seen. But she and Ada had learned so much about running this type of home business. If they could do this kind of production with so little time to prepare for it, she felt fairly confident they could run an even better pumpkin patch next year.

People armed with high-powered flashlights called to each other from inside the corn maze, and their laughter flowed. Cara stood in the tower, keeping watch and giving humor-filled verbal directions to those inside the maze as they moved from one stamp station to another. She honestly didn't know who had the most fun—Cara or the ones inside the cornfield.

A few feet away Ephraim ran the cash register. Lena came around the side of the house, bringing Deborah a stack of boxed pies. All the baked goodies were ones customers had ordered and paid for in Ada's kitchen. They'd pick them up at this cubicle since it was the last stop at the pumpkin patch before the guests headed home. People could also order and pay for baked goods from this station.

Lena grabbed an order off the counter and began to fill it.

Jonathan's voice carried softly through the air as he sang while driving the hay wagon toward its stop. His breath turned to vapor as it left his mouth. The riders were giggling and singing the little German ditty he taught each time. He brought the rig to a stop, hopped off, and chatted comfortably with kids and adults alike as he helped them down and pointed them in her direction. This was his last ride for the night. This group had been through the maze, gone on a hayride, and spent time with Ada in her kitchen, eating roasted pumpkin seeds and decorating cookies before eating them. In October the children decorated cookies to look like pumpkins and jack-o'-lanterns. Since November had begun, Ada had the customers decorate what she called turkey cookies, which sounded rather distasteful to Deborah, but the kids loved making a cookie look like a turkey.

When she and Ada had enough apples, they ran an apple press, where the children could squeeze out a tiny cup of their own cider. Ada used the pulp to make four-ounce jars of apple butter, which sold much better than they'd expected.

While counting out change to the person in front of him, Ephraim glanced up at Cara, who stood in the tower. He passed a written order for desserts to Deborah.

"I didn't expect her to love this type of work." Deborah read the slip of paper.

"Ich hab." Ephraim spoke the words *I did* quietly. He pulled out a large brown paper bag from under the counter and passed it to her. "It gives her a chance to connect with Englischers on stuff I know almost nothing about—music, television shows, sports."

Deborah opened the bag, ready to fill it with baked goods. "She's crazy about you."

Concern reflected in Ephraim's eyes as he studied Cara for a moment before returning to his register. "I know." He looked at the next customer. "What can I get for you today?"

Folks who'd gotten off the last hayride were now picking out sugar pumpkins for making pies. Then they'd buy some baked goods and head for home. The group currently in the maze had already been on a hayride. Ada's House and Pumpkin Patch would close in less than thirty minutes. She finished filling the order and passed it to the woman. "Denki," Deborah said.

The woman put her nose at the edge of the boxed pies and breathed deeply. "Oh, this will be perfect for our ladies group tomorrow."

As Deborah said good-bye, she noticed Jonathan beside his horse, patting and talking to her. His eyes met Deborah's. He cocked his head, mouthing the words *Surprise for Lena*. He pointed at the barn. Deborah nodded. She hadn't forgotten. Lena would turn twenty-four tomorrow. Since tomorrow was Saturday, Lena would come help at Ada's House for a while, but then she'd spend tomorrow night with her family. So Deborah and Jonathan were giving her a surprise party—with the emphasis on the word *surprise*.

If all went well, they'd celebrate Lena's big day as soon as the last customer left. It'd be a mixture of gag gifts disguised as real presents. But what made this plan more fun was that the trick goods were ones Lena had purchased. With help from Jonathan, Deborah had confiscated the items from Lena's hidden stash.

Jonathan tipped his hat before leading the horse toward the barn. Time to take care of his horse and let her rest until tomorrow afternoon.

Lena nudged Deborah. "Customers at the far side of the pumpkin patch." Lena pointed. "I could go, but I think they need a bit of Deborah advice with the kiddos before the parents have an all-out fight on their hands."

"Oh, ya, sure."

While Lena filled another order, Deborah hurried across the yard and toward the pumpkin patch. Lena had told her that she had a way of working with siblings that kept everyone happy.

She drew a deep breath, taking in the cold air, the array of delicious smells, and the joy of having great friends and family. She'd always cherished them but never more than now. Lena hired a driver and helped Ada in the kitchen on the nights and weekends when she could get here. Ephraim made sure to be here on Friday and Saturday nights. Jonathan had stayed five days straight after Elsie's funeral, helping them make up for lost time. They had designed and cleared paths in the maze and built the tower, and each week he went with her to all the Amish farms, where she bought pumpkins. Cara pitched in as if she'd always been a part of the Amish community. They also baked and sold dozens and dozens of small loaves of Amish Friendship Bread, and she'd be surprised if they had any left to enjoy over a cup of hot chocolate when they closed for the night. But friendship bread to munch on or not, after the crowds were gone, she and her friends would sit in the living room and share events that took place at their stations. And they'd had crowds like this every night for the last four weeks. Clearly the fliers they'd posted in town and the ads they'd taken out in the newspaper were doing their job. She'd expected business to slow to nearly nothing after the Englischer celebration of Halloween passed, but she'd been wrong. If anything, business had picked up.

Her girlfriends she'd been close to most of her life came to help out when they could—Rachel, Linda, Nancy, Lydia, Frieda, and Esther. They had all come on three separate weekends, and it'd been way too much fun to call what they'd done actual work. Unfortunately Anna Mary hadn't come at all. She had a new beau in Lancaster, some ninety minutes away by car. Deborah missed her, but she understood.

"Hello." Deborah waved as she came toward the family. She looked at the girl sitting on the ground, crying. Her brother stood with his arms folded, grumbling about wanting a different pumpkin. "So what is it about that pumpkin that you like so much?" she asked the boy. Either she'd find a pumpkin that suited both of them, or she'd sell them two pumpkins at half price each. Customer service that guaranteed satisfaction seemed to be a main reason they had such great repeat business.

Grey sat in front of a roaring fire. He could feel its heat but still felt gripped by icy remorse, and he wished he knew how to break free. Was this how grief always worked? Did it enclose a person on all sides and never let up, even during sleep? Or was this worse because he'd been such a fool with his time?

Sprawled on the floor between him and the hearth, Ivan quietly played with his wooden toy horses.

"Daed? *Der Gaule kann nimmi schteh.*" Ivan rose and turned to him, telling his father that his horse couldn't stand up anymore. Its hoof had broken off.

Grey held the horse in his hand, wondering if he remembered how to carve little animals. He'd made these for Ivan's second birthday and hadn't carved anything like it since.

Ivan's eyes grew large for a moment, indicating that he'd thought of something. He scurried across the wood floors in his socks toward the back door.

Grey called after him, telling him it was wet outside.

Ivan said nothing as he slung open the back door.

Children. Their resilience astounded him. Ivan missed his Mamm. He crawled into Grey's lap and cried sometimes, but then Grey would read to him, or talk to him of Elsie, or get on the floor with him and play. Soon enough the intensity of Ivan's sadness would ease. Grey's regret hadn't dulled for one moment.

It seemed the most Grey could offer Ephraim at the cabinetry shop was to muddle through his work load. Grey's Mamm kept Ivan, and Grey worked as few hours as he could and still be able to pay bills. Even though Grey had no energy and no clear thoughts to help him accomplish much, Ivan only seemed to need him to be present. So Grey was there. He remembered a man once telling him that regret after a loved one died was like living in hell itself. At the time Grey hadn't understood.

"Daed, kumm."

Grey checked the clock almost wishing it was time to put Ivan down for the night. He had another two hours before Ivan's bedtime. As much as he longed for the ease of free time once Ivan was asleep, he knew that's when another night began, one that seemed to last forever. He rose and went out back.

Pointing to a tree branch, Ivan told his Daed to look. *"Guck."* He wanted a new horse carved from that branch.

Grey told him they couldn't cut that branch. That it would hurt the tree.

Across the yards, his and Allen's, he could see that every room in his friend's home seemed to have at least one kerosene lantern lit. The idea of visiting his friend pulled on him. Allen had come over every day since… Elsie had passed. He'd bring Grey a newspaper, or food from his kitchen, or just a few minutes of talk about the weather. Each time Allen would ask Grey to come for a visit. Since Ivan wanted more from Grey tonight than he could muster, maybe he should go. Ivan needed a distraction, and Allen's home always had children.

"Witt du ans Allen's geh?" Grey asked.

Ivan grabbed his Daed's hand, pulling him toward the steps that led to the yard.

"Whoa." Grey pointed at Ivan's sock-covered feet. They went inside and put on their coats, hats, and boots.

Soon enough they were in the barn, and Grey hitched the horse to its carriage. Grey's home sat at the end of a long lane. No other homes could be seen from here, except Allen's. If Elsie had been so inclined, Grey would have built a bridge across the creek that separated his and Allen's places. But she liked seclusion—cherished it actually.

Maybe if he'd tried harder to understand her.

He couldn't stop the constant rehashing of old topics, so he didn't even try. But he felt as cold and damp on the inside as the weather around him. He hoped his heart would grow used to it so it'd feel normal rather than be this current unbearable pain.

He helped Ivan out of the buggy, and his son ran ahead of him. The boy knocked, and Allen opened the door, welcoming him. He heard the Kauffman clan cheer and clap when Ivan entered.

"Phoebe, Amos, look who's here," Allen called out.

Tears stung Grey's eyes as he led his horse to the lean-to, and he breathed a prayer of thankfulness. It seemed he had little to offer Ivan these days except the steadfastness of quiet love and being with him. But energetic love oozed from others and made up for what Grey could not give. When he stepped inside, everyone spoke a friendly hello just as they always did.

"Kumm." Allen hugged him. "We're just now finishing dinner. Can we fix you a plate?"

Grey shook his head. "We ate at Mamm's a few hours ago."

"You and everybody else had dinner at a reasonable time, I'm sure. We had to wait on Lennie, and she spent today in Hope Crossing at Ada's House and then got to running late."

Lennie stuck her tongue out at Allen. "Watch it, big brother. It's my party, and I'll make you cry if I want to."

Grey helped Ivan out of his coat and then took off his own and hung them on the coatrack. The humor and camaraderie in the Kauffman household caused him to take a deep breath for the first time in a month.

"Kumm," Phoebe said to Ivan before running upstairs. Ivan ran behind her.

While still sitting, Israel pulled the chair out for Grey. "Did what Lena said make sense to anyone?" Israel asked.

Grey took a seat, knowing conversations in Allen's household ran in every direction at once. He always enjoyed the lively banter.

"It's a twist on lyrics to a song," Lennie answered her Daed. "You've heard it when in stores and such. Haven't you? 'It's my party, and I'll cry if...'"

Israel held up his hand. "From your rumschpringe days?"

Allen's wife, Emily, brought a cake to the table.

"Ya." Lennie went to the counter and grabbed a dessert box. "My tenth-grade English teacher had us listen to songs in class and dissect the lyrics. We did that for a few minutes every day as a creative way to understand concise storytelling."

Emily cut a slice of cake and passed it to Grey. He rarely ate a cake he liked, so he passed it to Israel.

Israel took the plate and set it on the table in front of him. "I don't even want to know any of the lyrics. I still wake in a cold sweat when I think of what all you heard and saw while attending public school."

Emily passed Grey another piece of cake. He gave it to Allen.

"Me too." Allen mumbled around the cake. "I worry what the statute of limitations is for any trouble she caused while there."

Lennie set the dessert box in front of Grey, and when Emily tried to pass him another piece of cake, Lennie intercepted it. "No cake for Grey, Emily. Remember?"

"Oh," Emily said, "I always forget about that. Who doesn't like cake?"

"Grey," Allen offered.

Emily laid a hand on her stomach, and Grey realized she was expecting again. She didn't look too far along, but had someone told him, and he'd forgotten?

"With four little ones and one due this spring, I can't even keep straight what *I* like to eat and not eat." Emily giggled.

"I understand." Grey chose to ignore the pang of sadness that smacked him. He'd had such hopes of him and Elsie receiving good test results and finding healing from years of marital stress. Then they'd have had more children.

He put a hand on the box Lennie had set in front of him, but Allen stopped him. "I wouldn't open that if I were you."

Lennie took the container and opened it. "Allen, you're a big scaredy-cat." She passed the box back to Grey before going to the island and getting another dessert box. Grey took a cookie—chocolate chip oatmeal with pecans, his favorite.

He caught her eye, and the look on her face assured him it wasn't a coincidence. "Allen would have brought them by your place tomorrow, but since you're here, please take them with you." She set another dessert box next to Allen. "Just don't touch it, and you'll be safe, big brother."

"What kind is it?"

Lennie shrugged.

He picked it up and smelled it. "Lemon pound cake?"

"Deborah's?" Emily asked. But Lennie didn't respond.

Allen set the box on the table. "Lemon pound cake is my favorite."

Lennie took a bite of the chocolate cake. "I know."

He opened the box and screamed like a girl when four cloth-covered snakes pounced at him. Grey about choked on his cookie.

Lennie put her hand on Grey's shoulder. "*Now* it's a happy birthday."

"Man," Allen complained. "How come you do this to me and not Grey?"

Lennie raised an eyebrow and propped her chin in the palm of her hand. "Because he's not my brother, which means he didn't sow seeds that must be reaped."

Grey cleared his throat. "As a kid, she did warn you regularly that she'd spend the rest of her days getting you back."

"Ya, I did." Lennie waggled her eyebrows. "Besides, I need a favor from Grey."

Grey took another bite of his cookie. "Ah, that explains everything."

"No, not everything." Lennie reached into the box in front of him and stole a cookie. "You don't know the favor."

Conversations came and went as children ran in and out of the room. His grief remained thick and undeniable, but tonight gave him that moment of pardon he so desperately needed. Maybe he'd survive this season yet, at least with enough of him left so he could be a good Daed to

Ivan. That was all he wanted in life now—to be the kind of Daed he needed to be.

When most of the group scattered—the women to clearing the table and washing dishes and Allen to checking on the children upstairs—Grey remained at the table, trying to think clearly enough to hear Israel as he talked. It'd become so easy to stay lost in thought.

"*Grossdaadi.*" Phoebe called for her granddad, and Israel excused himself.

With the table empty of plates and flatware, Lennie walked over and began scrubbing it with a wet cloth. "You doing reasonably okay?"

Grateful at least one person refused to pretend his grief wasn't there, he considered her question. "What's reasonable?"

"Somewhere beyond complete agony and just shy of willing yourself to die, I'd think."

Did that mean how he felt landed in the normal range? He found that thought comforting. "Then I'm doing reasonably okay."

"*Gut.*"

"How are Urie and Tobias?"

She took a seat near him. "Pretty good, I think. At times I have to stop class and just let the scholars talk and cry and draw pictures. Whatever they need."

"And Peter?"

"Withdrawn and sullen. I…I'm still concerned about him. He carries a lot of guilt for being the reason you sent Elsie outside with the other students."

Grey didn't have the strength to talk about this. He carried enough guilt for both him and Peter. If he hadn't been so angry with Peter, he wouldn't have sent the others outside.

Grey shifted. "Elsie's parents said Aaron's taken to holing up in that cabin by himself most of the time."

"Ya, I heard."

"If losing a daughter wasn't enough for Michael and Dora, Aaron's making it worse. I've tried to talk to him, but…I don't know what to say or do."

"Ya, it's hard to figure, but it seems to me all we can focus on is what we can do." She reached down and picked up a wayward trick snake off the floor. "And it's important for you to pull as many stunts on Allen as possible. That may not help *you* much, but it'll do wonders for me." She softly mocked an evil laugh, patted his arm, and headed for the kitchen.

"Lennie."

She paused.

"You didn't tell me the favor."

"I need a donkey for this year's Christmas pageant."

"Real animals?"

"The class voted to do a live crèche."

Her energy for life contrasted with his, and he felt old and even more tired. "I don't own a donkey anymore. Haven't for years."

"Ya, I know. But you have a trailer for hauling creatures, and the Englischer family who bought your donkey will loan him out for a night, right?"

"Ya, probably so, but I'm beginning to think it'd been easier to have a gag pulled on me."

Her lips curved into a smile. "I'll be sure to keep that in mind."

Nineteen

Lena spread a little straw across a section of the schoolroom floor, mentally listing what else she needed to do for tonight's Christmas play. She checked the clock, hoping Grey hadn't forgotten. He'd been at Allen's two weeks ago when she dropped by, and she'd reminded him then about tonight. He'd forgotten all about the play but assured her he'd get the donkey here.

She'd let her scholars off school today so she'd have plenty of time to prepare. Since the Amish didn't take off extra days for Christmas break like the public schools did, she might get a few complaints from parents about her decision but surely not many.

Scholars were supposed to be off school only for Christmas Day and Second Christmas. She loved the Amish tradition of Second Christmas on December 26, which was treated like Christmas itself, only better in her opinion—more relaxed, more visiting time with friends and relatives. She moved to the potbelly stove and stoked the wood.

Someone clomped up the wooden steps. The door opened, and cold air swooshed inside as Grey entered.

"You're here in time."

"That I am." Without looking at her, he moved to the potbelly stove.

He hadn't been to this building since the day Elsie died, and seeing the stress etched across his face, Lena regretted asking this favor. Grey wasn't the same man who'd come to her school nearly eleven weeks ago. His voice was so deep and heavy with grief that it didn't even sound like his anymore. The circles under his eyes and the way he carried himself all spoke of a heartache she couldn't begin to understand.

Loneliness for a future mate swept over her like a nor'easter, but she couldn't imagine what it did to a man who'd lost his mate so very early in life.

He held his hands over the stove. "I put the donkey out back with the other animals." He looked around the place. "Where are all the desks?"

"We lugged them to the lean-to."

Her brothers and Daed had helped her move the desks into the lean-to and cover them with a tarp before they set up church benches and tables. She and her Daed had created the props—a mock stable complete with wooden stalls, a fence, and a cattle gate. The live animals waited outside, tethered to the nearby fence.

"This looks really…different." He took off his hat. "You've gone to a lot of trouble just for a play."

"It's not just a play. It's a reminder of the birth of Christ and all that we hold dear." Lena went to a box of goods sitting on a serving table. "So"—she got out a coffee cup and spoon and moved back to the wood stove—"will Ivan come tonight with his *Grossmammi* and Daadi?"

"Ya. I'm not staying."

Disappointment stung, but she tried to hide it. Lifting the percolator from the wood stove, she asked, "Coffee?"

"Ya."

She filled the cup and passed it to him before returning to the box. As she pulled out items and began to set the table, Grey put his mug on a bench and peeled out of his coat. "What can I help you do?"

His offer caught her off guard.

"The children will start arriving soon to get into their costumes." She passed him a box filled with goodies. "I'd like to have snacks set out for their parents to munch on."

He began unloading the items while she set various empty containers on the table. Without another word Grey opened a bag of chips and one of pretzels.

She tossed him a can of peanuts. "These too, please."

He opened them and dumped some in a couple of containers.

She set a cake box in front of him. "Would you get the cake out and put it down there?" She pointed to the far end of the table.

He looked at the box and pushed it her way. "You open it. I'll put it wherever you want it."

"You too?" She huffed at him and opened the box.

"I apologize, Lennie. I accused you unjustly."

She slid the cake his direction. "Just put it down there. There's a candle inside the box. Stick it in the top of the cake, will you?"

Keeping watch out of the corner of her eye, Lena took a few steps farther away from him. She'd intended to give the cake to Jonathan, and she hoped she didn't regret changing her mind.

As he tried to wedge the candle in place, the top of the cake popped open, and confetti sprang at him. But brightly colored paper wasn't all that landed on him. Icing did too, and she bit her bottom lip to keep from laughing.

He stared at her, frosting spattered across his shirt. The shock on his face struck her as hilarious, and she had to cover her mouth with both hands in order to stifle her laughter.

Watching her reaction, he chuckled. "What'd you do that for? If I don't eat cake, what makes you think I want to wear it?"

She moved in closer and swiped her finger through a dollop of frosting on his shirt before placing it in her mouth. "Who doesn't like cake?" As she feigned innocence, she was poking a little fun at her sister-in-law. The woman never remembered that Grey didn't like cake. Never.

"Lennie. I…I'm tellin'."

"You do that, Grey." She passed him several napkins. "And we'll see who's sorry then."

"Send me out in this cold weather to do you a favor, splatter my shirt with frosting, and then threaten me?"

"What are friends for?"

"Clearly they're to make *you* laugh. How much time did it take you to build that?"

Her Daed walked inside and glanced at Grey. "Man, Grey, I thought you didn't like cake. How'd you end up with it all over you?"

"Tricked by your daughter."

Israel looked at her.

Pretending complete innocence, Lena shrugged. "I have no idea what he's talking about, Daed."

Her Daed poured himself a cup of coffee. "She has no idea what you're talking about, Grey."

"And you believe her?"

"Of course I believe her. If she chooses not to cook, I have to."

Lena choked back laughter, liking the little bit of joy she saw in Grey's eyes. "So who are you going to tell now?"

"You win."

"Wow, you give up easily. I think I like that." Lena took a clean shirt from the huge stack of things she'd brought for tonight. She held it out to him.

He just stood there, looking leery of taking it.

"It'll fit."

"The school's oldest students are eighth-grade boys, so just why do you have an extra shirt with you that will fit me?"

"Because you and Jonathan are very close to the same size, and you happen to be wearing his cake."

A hint of his lopsided smile worked its way into his eyes, and his countenance seemed less heavy.

"Ah." He motioned at the split-rail fence, manger, and hay. "What is all that?"

"The temperature dropped, so the live crèche is taking place inside."

"All those animals are coming in?"

"Sure, why not?"

Grey looked to Lennie's father.

Her Daed shrugged. "You ever tried to change her mind about something?"

Grey shook his head. "Not and been successful. I'll just slip into a clean shirt and take a seat. This I gotta see."

Carrying a shoofly pie, Deborah stepped into Lena's packed classroom. Gas pole lamps were lit and placed in various areas of the room. She shivered, almost aching with cold after her long carriage ride from Hope Crossing. Ada, Cara, and Lori were already here, having arrived in Dry Lake a couple of hours ago via a warm car.

Jonathan had needed to come by carriage so he could return a rented horse to its owner in Dry Lake. Since Deborah's pie hadn't finished baking in time for her to come by car, she rode for an hour in Jonathan's carriage, enduring freezing temperatures. It hadn't snowed in a week, but a foot of the white stuff covered the grounds.

Lena stood at the far end of the room, helping her scholars get into their costumes and practice their lines. She didn't look a bit frazzled as dozens of children asked their teacher questions all at the same time. Actually...she appeared to be having a great time.

Jonathan's hand gently directed Deborah to step forward to allow the people behind them to get inside also.

Grey's parents spoke as they walked in with Ivan. The little boy quietly weaved around people, heading for the bench where his Daed sat. She'd seen Grey last week during the between Sunday when she came to Dry Lake to visit. Seeing Grey was like looking at a used, half-torn dessert box. You could tell he'd once held something good. Tonight he didn't seem as empty or as battered as he talked with people near him, but he kept glancing at the commotion around Lena.

"Little Debbie." Jonathan bent down, drawing closer to her ear as he spoke softly. "Are we waiting by this door for a reason?" His warm breath smelled of peppermint, and when she looked at him to see if he was harassing her or being sincere, she saw someone she didn't recognize. He removed his hat. "What?" His voice held a bit of confusion, but his hazel eyes reflected comfortableness with her.

Her heart turned a flip as the enormity of their friendship seemed to change shape.

"I...I need to set this pie on the table." While thoughts moved through her like loops of warm molasses, she worked her way through the crowd.

For months Jonathan had helped her at Ada's House, receiving small wages compared to the value of his skill and work hours. He'd been diligent and so much fun as they had built a business Deborah was proud of.

He still worked for his Daed, dividing his time between Dry Lake and Hope Crossing. But he'd also begun expanding the blacksmith business to the Amish in Hope Crossing and further east of them—all areas that were nearly impossible for his Daed to get to in a day of travel from Dry Lake. Since all his blacksmith equipment was in his work wagon, and he traveled to people's farms to shoe their horses, he spent the night at Ada's when he worked close by. But the last few months were not her only memories of his being generous with his time. Over the years he'd always offered help whenever she needed it, just as he had for Lena.

Jonathan came up beside her. "You feeling okay? Did you get too cold on the ride here?"

Making space for another dessert on the serving table, she didn't look up at him. Until this moment she'd thought no more of her relationship with him than of the ones she had with Lena, Cara, and Ada. He'd become as close to her as anyone ever had...except Mahlon.

He cupped his hand under her elbow. "Deborah?"

Mahlon's closeness had been a lie. All those years he'd only pretended. Thinking about that confused her more. Who was Jonathan—a good friend or a man who'd stepped up out of loyalty and duty in order to fill the gaping hole Mahlon had left?

She gazed into his eyes, suddenly desperate to understand the relationship between them. "What are we doing, Jon?"

His hazel eyes reminded her of Mahlon, and she could hear what he would've said—*We're attending a Christmas play. Now let's find a seat.* And like the fool she'd been, she'd let him avoid her questions and hide his true self behind her love.

A hint of uncertainty flitted through Jonathan's eyes before a smile crossed his lips. "I'm being a friend and hoping maybe one day you'll want more."

His words startled her, sending concern and shock through her. As a friend, Jonathan was safe. Dependable. And loads of fun. The truth stared at her, and why she hadn't seen it before, she didn't know. Whether as a friend, beau, or husband, he had plenty to offer any woman. Even in her self-absorbed ways, his qualities had been too obvious for her to be completely blind to them. But she realized a horrible thing about herself: outside the realm of friendship, she had nothing but confusion and distrust. Suspicion seeped from the wound Mahlon had left inside her. But how could she distrust Jonathan?

She pulled off her gloves. "Why?"

He blinked, glancing to the table for a moment as if bewildered by her question. "Why?"

The reason for her question seemed very clear to her. What motivated him to want more? Did he feel compelled to stay by her side out of a misplaced sense of honor? He might not even realize what drew him to offer such a thing to her.

Lena spoke loudly. "Please take your seats. If you haven't already enjoyed some refreshments, you can do so after our play. If you have enjoyed refreshments, you may do so again...after our play."

He fidgeted with his hat. "Let's talk about this when the play is over."

Neither of them could do anything else right now but plan to talk later. She spotted Ada sitting in the row in front of Grey. Cara and Ephraim were on one side of her, and a couple of empty seats on the other side were saved for Deborah and Jonathan. She and Jonathan walked toward them.

She moved onto the bench next to Ada. From Ephraim's lap, Lori waved at her. She couldn't help but find the image totally endearing.

When the play began, she casually turned and studied Jonathan, who remained focused on Lena and the makeshift stage. When did Jonathan begin hoping their friendship would become more? Is that what he really wanted? If so, how did she feel about him? She loved being his friend.

"You're staring," Jonathan whispered without taking his eyes off the front of the room.

Voices from the children in the play grew louder, and laughter rose and fell like wind on a blustery day, but she couldn't focus as her heart ran wild with fear. No matter who he was, she'd lose. As a friend, he'd find a girl one day and leave her. Just the thought made her miss him. Did he truly care? After her ordeal with Mahlon, she knew she didn't possess any way of discerning what disloyalties and lies existed in a man's heart.

Jonathan turned to her, his patience clearly evident. "I don't think we should try to figure out where we are or where we're going. It's too soon, and we don't need answers to our questions tonight. Or next month. Enjoy the play."

Boisterous laughter erupted, and they immediately shifted their focus. She didn't know what they'd missed, but mixed in with everyone else's chortles, she could hear Grey's. Dozens of children in costumes, sheep, and Lena's dog all stood inside the now half-fallen fence. She'd missed most of the play while lost in her own thoughts. Lena opened the back door, disappeared for a moment, and returned, pulling the lead to a donkey.

The room cackled as the wind from outside blew out a couple of the gas pole lamps and hay swirled in every direction. If Lena had brought other animals inside earlier, had the lamps gone out then too? Lena tugged, but the creature stopped in the doorway, only half of him inside the building. She moved behind the donkey and pushed. "Did somebody glue her hoofs?" Her voice radiated loudly from just outside.

Her dog barked, and the donkey jolted forward. Lena thudded to the floor. Nicky ran to her and licked her face before she jumped up, straightening her apron. Fresh laughter erupted. Lena picked up Marilyn and set her feet on a wooden crate next to the donkey's head. Lena kept one hand on Marilyn while patting the donkey as the girl recited her lines. When the donkey relieved itself, Marilyn seemed unbothered. "And then the angel said to them…" Marilyn paused. "I smell something."

Everyone broke into laughter.

Marilyn wrinkled her nose and tilted her head one way and then the other, trying to see where that aroma came from.

"Okay, honey, what did the angel say?"

Marilyn spoke loudly. "Then the angel…" She paused again. "You sure they had animals inside where Jesus was bornt?"

"Ya."

Marilyn seemed fully aware that she'd taken over the play, but Lena kept trying to refocus her attention. These plays were always endearing, usually even a little funny, but this time people were cackling without restraint.

The little girl held her nose with her finger and thumb. "Maybe that's why they prayed so much back then."

"I know it's why I'm praying so much right now," Lena added. "Can you say the rest of your lines?"

She nodded. "The angel said to them…" She paused once again. "Teacher Lena, I feel kinda sick."

"Me too." Lena glanced across the room and spotted Marilyn's parents. "Do you not have farm animals at your place, Joe?"

The hilarity rippling through the schoolroom warmed Deborah's heart. Lena had known the community needed this event tonight, even if the weather didn't allow for it to be held outside. And Grey hadn't stopped chuckling. As the play continued, so did the laughter. But by the time Lena drew the evening to a close, she had most people teary-eyed with the depth of what God had begun that night thousands of years ago.

Lena pointed to the back of the room. "We have a lot of refreshments. Please stay for as long as you like and enjoy."

Jonathan continued chuckling as he stood. "Lena is as free spirited as she is an out-and-out mess."

"The floor is a mess," Deborah said. "And now I have to stay and help her clean up."

"Ya, me too."

"I'll stay and pitch in," Grey said. "And I'll see to it Allen stays too."

"We'll be done in time to get some sleep before morning then. Denki." Deborah glanced around the room, noting all the work that needed to be done. "You sure?"

"Ya." Grey adjusted his shirt collar. "Jonathan, fair warning. Don't accept any cake Lennie tries to give you."

❦

Rage burned through Dwayne. How could Lena boldly stand in front of everyone unashamed of the mark God had cursed her with? He'd put a stop to her. In his time. In his own way. He folded his arms, still watching the stupid teacher as she helped the brats out of their costumes.

In spite of the applause she'd received, she disgusted most of the folks here. He fully believed that, but she didn't know it—going about her life like people actually cared for her. It sickened him.

After all his effort, the bull had mauled the wrong woman. It had altered his course, but it hadn't changed his plan.

Twenty

Lena moved closer, reaching for the item in Elsie's hand, but Elsie faded into a new world, taking Lena with her. Valleys. Oceans. Deserts. They moved from place to place, but no matter where they landed, Lena couldn't get close enough to take the item Elsie held out to her.

Lena didn't know what the package contained, but she knew Grey needed it. Determined to reach it, she fought her way through wind, sand, snow, and rainstorms. Weary of fighting while Elsie faded from one world to the next, Lena screamed at her, "If you want me to have it, then give it to me!"

Elsie held out the parcel. A round of knocks vibrated the air around her, and Lena found herself somewhere between awake and asleep. The longing inside her matched nothing she'd ever felt before.

"Lena." Her Daed tapped on the door.

She opened her eyes, realizing it'd all been a dream. Early morning sunlight streamed in through her bedroom windows as she tried to let go of all the emotions the dream had pumped into her.

"Kumm." She sat upright.

"You're not even up. This is a first." Behind his smile, she saw concern. "Should I have left you alone?"

"No." She stretched. "It's Second Christmas. I don't want to miss a minute of it because I socialized too much on Christmas Day. Besides, I'm glad you woke me. I was caught in a frustrating dream."

Maybe the dream meant nothing...or maybe it was her own subconscious reminding her she had yet to give Grey her report about Ivan.

"How long before you're ready to go?"

"Forty minutes, tops."

He started to close the door.

"Daed." Lena pushed back her quilt, feeling a little more like herself again. "Can we go a bit out of our way and stop by Grey's before heading to Ada's?"

"Grey's?"

"I need to take him something."

"It can't wait?"

She slid into her housecoat. "Careful, Daed. Your need to get maximum time out of this rare invite by Ada is showing."

He chuckled. "It is, isn't it?"

"Don't worry. I'll never tell her…as long as you take me by Grey's first."

"Get ready as quick as you can, and we'll go by there."

Lena hurried through a shower and dressing. Once fully ready, she knelt in front of her hope chest, opened the lid, and looked for the report she'd written. After Elsie had passed away, Lena tucked the papers in here, keeping them in the most private place of all. As her fingertips slid over quilts and kitchen utensils, she cringed at the fresh pangs of loneliness.

Twenty-four years old and not even a prospect.

She spotted the edge of the manila envelope and reached for it, but as she did, her tablet of children's names called to her. The contrast between her reality and what she longed for stung. Ignoring the mounting sentiments, she grabbed the report and closed the lid to the chest.

By the time she slid into her coat and went downstairs, her Daed had the carriage hitched. Nicky danced at the front door, clearly hoping to go with her again today. "Can you be good, even around Better Days?"

Nicky sat, as if to assure Lena of her excellent behavior. A shiver of excitement about going, or maybe dread of staying behind, ran through her dog.

"It wouldn't be Christmas without you tagging along, now would it? Kumm."

Nicky ran to the carriage and waited. Lena locked the front door and hurried down the steps. She opened the door to the buggy, and Nicky jumped in first. "Daed, you're in too big of a hurry. I didn't feed Nicky or get a cup of coffee."

"I fed the dog, and"—he reached under the front seat and passed her a thermos—"I'd never let you go without coffee. You get too grumpy."

She giggled. Her faults were plenty—opinionated, stubborn, and too direct at times, to name a few—but getting grumpy wasn't one of them, and he liked teasing her about that. She enjoyed his company, and he'd always been easy to live with. Her mother had adored him, and she wished he'd take a few steps toward finding someone again. "Ever thought of asking Ada out?"

He tapped the reins against the horse's back. "I…I talked to her about it once, a long time ago."

"She didn't want to?"

"It wasn't that…at least I don't think it was. See…Mahlon didn't like the idea of his Mamm remarrying. She thought he needed her to stay single, and she was willing to do that for him, so I didn't pursue her. Besides, I had plenty to keep me busy with a houseful of children."

"Ya, it kept all of us busy." Lena opened the thermos. The aroma stung her nostrils. She put the lid on quickly. "How many scoops of coffee did you use?"

"How many should I have used?"

"Daed." Lena clicked her tongue. "We've talked about this. Two scoops per pot."

"Then you have about three days' worth of scoops in that one jug."

"It's a good thing for you it's the thought that counts."

Her Daed drove down the long lane to Grey's home, and she was glad to see that his horse and rig were still there.

She got out, and Nicky rushed behind her as if afraid she might be left behind. When she stood on the doorstep, she pointed at Nicky. "Sit." Her dog obeyed, and Lena knocked on the door.

Grey opened it, looking surprised to see her. "Lennie, what are you doing here?"

She held up the manila envelope. "I came to give you the results from when I worked with Ivan."

"Oh, I…I…kumm rei." He stepped back. Nicky whined, still sitting where Lena had told her to. Grey motioned. "You too." The dog ran inside, and Grey closed the door, studying her. "Why today?"

"I…I'm actually not sure. I had a dream that reminded me about this, so here I am. I didn't know if I'd catch you."

"Ivan's sleeping in a bit, so I'm letting him rest. Today won't be easy."

"You're spending a good bit of it with Elsie's folks then."

"Ya."

Rumors said the Blanks were in a bad way emotionally. They were bitter and miserable and dragging down anyone around them. She couldn't imagine how hard that would be for Grey and Ivan. "Daed and I are spending most of today at Ada's."

"At Ada's?"

Lena held her index finger over her lips. "I think there might be a little attraction between them."

"Really? Your Daed's been without a wife for a long time now."

"Thirteen years last October. Same as for Ada."

"No one could forget that nightmare."

"Even all these years later I still miss Mamm so badly some days. I can't even imagine what you must be feeling."

"Ya, it's…it's tough." He held up a coffee mug. "Care for some brew?"

"Ya."

He poured her a cup and slid the sugar and cream toward her.

"Denki."

"Would you care to sit for a spell? And I'll ask your Daed to come in."

"I can't stay." She added sweetener and cream and stirred her drink. "And Daed won't come in this time. He wants me to keep it brief. But I can down a cup before leaving. Daed fixed the coffee this morning. I do believe he could live single the rest of his life and never get the hang of fixing anything but water." She took a sip. "Oh, now that's good coffee." She drank a little more before setting the cup down. "Ivan's bright, possibly one of the brightest children I've ever worked with." She passed him the envelope. He opened it and pulled out her report. While he read it, she sipped on her coffee.

"Horse neck, Lennie. I never would've figured this."

"I talked to my friend Samantha about it too. You remember her?"

"Ya, the Englischer girl who used to spend the night with you sometimes and make your Daed nervous that you might get pulled into the world."

"That's her. We're still friends and still get together occasionally. She finished her master's program last year, and this is her first year as a school counselor. I showed her the tests he took, and she agrees with me. It means he's as smart as he is cute, which is never a good combination for the girls' sakes. I imagine he's much like you were at that age, but since I was just a baby then, I can't recall what you looked or acted like."

"I remember the first time I saw you. My Mamm had gone to visit your Mamm. I'd have been nearly five by then. We walked into your Mamm's bedroom, where you'd been born the day before. Your Mamm was still in bed, and you were in her arms. Your Mamm patted the bed, and I climbed up beside her on my knees, getting a good look at you. I remember thinking you looked so little and helpless…and then you let out a scream that about made me wet my pants."

She giggled. "I still have that effect on Allen. Ask him."

He slid the report into its envelope. "I love Ivan the same, no matter whether he's brilliant or slow."

"I never doubted that."

"So you know where I'm coming from when I ask, if he's this bright, why does he seem slow and immature?"

"Maturity will happen. Seems to me his Daed was a short, scrawny kid until…when, eighteen years old?"

"Sixteen, thank you very much." He ran the last words together quickly, with mocked offense.

"Sixteen. And your maturity issues were physical, not emotional, but your son isn't yet six."

"Point taken."

"If you can stand my usual honesty, I think you might be doing too much for him. Your Daed had you doing chores at a young age. My first memory of you had to be when I was five or six. You were in the barn milking cows, tending horses, and cleaning stalls by yourself. I was smitten just watching you."

"Interesting."

"And I remained that way until the old age of seven."

"Clearly you fell in and out of being smitten easily, because I never knew."

He never knew. Not that time or when she was about to enter high school or when she turned eighteen. It'd been a long time since she'd remembered how badly she'd wanted him to have feelings for her like she had for him. But he hadn't, and when Elsie arrived in Dry Lake, he never looked back.

That's just not who they were. With only a minimum of pain and disappointment, she'd accepted that soon after Elsie had arrived.

Lena ran her finger around the rim of the mug. "Remember when Allen stole a pie from Mamm's windowsill? Later that day Mamm questioned him. He lied and said I'd taken it to feed to my dog. You knew the truth, and when you didn't take up for me, I…I hated you…for a while."

"Allen could beat me up. You couldn't. But that story explains a lot about your obsession to get back at people, using desserts."

She couldn't resist smiling as she saw hints of the man he'd been before Elsie died. That awful day removed all rays of light from his eyes like when the sun dropped past the horizon in winter. "My point is that I think you should give him more responsibilities in line with a five-year-old. Does he dress himself?"

"No. How can he?"

"He'll figure it out. He'll be missing that arm the rest of his life. He won't grow out of that. Let him struggle until he's learned ways to compensate. And when he goes to the shop with you, give him some small projects of his own, like organizing the hardware or sweeping up and such. Let him figure out how to do things with one arm."

Grey studied her, looking like he agreed with her bold statements.

She took another sip of coffee. "We all have a handicap. And every one of us had to figure out how to get work done."

"What's your handicap?"

Her face felt warm as thoughts of her birthmark embarrassed her. Had he become so used to the sight of her that he no longer noticed? She traced the spot with her fingers, wondering how men saw her. "Having to put up with you."

He tugged at her hand, pulling it away from her face. "Surely you don't think…"

She lowered her eyes and took a sip of her coffee.

"Lennie." He sounded so shocked. "You're striking. The day we came to see you, Elsie remarked about how beautiful you are."

Unsure how to change the subject, Lena only knew she'd never felt so uncomfortable around Grey. She was blemished. She accepted it. It seemed he'd accepted it too, a long time ago. Perhaps his reaction meant that he no longer felt sorry for her. She liked that thought, but to mention her looks in the same sentence as *striking* or *beautiful* was just wrong. She finished the last of her coffee. "I need to go. I just wanted to make sure you knew the truth about your son."

"I'm glad you did, especially today. I needed some good news." Grey took the envelope to a small, messy desk beside the back door. He shoved it into the plastic standing divider with a bunch of other mail. Rather than getting the envelope in, a stack of letters fell out and scattered on the floor. He grabbed them up, and then stopped suddenly as he studied a letter. Several moments later he tossed everything else onto the desk, but he continued to stare at the item in his hand.

She set her mug in the sink. "I shouldn't have stayed this long. If the carriage had a horn, I'm sure Daed would be using it by now."

Grey didn't look up. She motioned for Nicky and headed toward the door.

She paused. "Grey…are you okay?"

He slid his fingers over the address—Mr. and Mrs. Benjamin Graber. He slid the letter into his pants pocket. "Kumm, I'll walk you out and speak to your Daed."

❦

Grey stood on his driveway as the Kauffman rig drove out of sight. He reached into his pocket and pulled out the letter. It held the results of the DNA testing he and Elsie had done less than a week before she died. He'd thought about these findings several times, but he hadn't realized they'd come in. According to the postage date, it'd arrived here about eight weeks after Elsie died. His Mamm or Daed or a sibling had been bringing in the mail for him when they came for a visit.

The titles of Mr. and Mrs. stirred tornado-force winds inside him. Studying the envelope, he ambled back into the house. If he opened it, he'd know the truth. Had Elsie been in fear all those years for nothing? Or had she shut him out of her heart and out of their bedroom based on reasons he could live with?

He put his thumb under the seal of the envelope and tore a bit of it before stopping. If she were alive, they'd sit down together and open this. He could imagine the tension in the room, as the tests would have decided much of their future. But now that she was dead, did he really want to know what this envelope held?

She'd been wrong about Ivan. If she had shut out Grey without just cause, he'd wrestle with anger again. If the results said either of them had a genetic issue that caused their offspring to have defects, how would he feel then? When his grief eased, would some part of him feel relieved that her death had freed both of them?

Grey paced as anger rose within him. "God forbid!"

He couldn't change that their life together was over, but he could protect her memory and his heart. Still he ached to know the truth. She'd isolated him based on her fears. Had she been right?

Ivan walked into the kitchen, rubbing his eyes. *"Frehlich Zwedde Grischtdaag."* Ivan wished his Daed a Merry Second Christmas.

Grey tussled his son's hair. "Frehlich Zwedde Grischtdaag, Ivan."

His son kept going, heading for the bathroom.

Grey felt as trapped by this medical report as he'd been by Elsie behaving as if she disliked everything about him. He wouldn't chain himself to regret or resentment. He went to the stove and lit the gas flame. Whether Elsie had been right or wrong about them passing down bad DNA to their offspring, he'd never know. He held the letter over the flame. When it caught on fire, he moved to the kitchen sink and watched it burn. "I choose to be free of all that we didn't handle right."

He dropped it into the sink as the last of the paper turned to black ashes. He closed his eyes, feeling guilt begin to release its grip.

Twenty-One

Cara sat on the corner of her bed as Deborah tried to make her hair look like it should. Second Christmas, and Ada had Amish guests arriving soon. "It's no use trying to get it to stay in place, Deb."

"Well, there's no hiding that all you have is a stubby ponytail instead of a bun under your prayer Kapp. But with enough bobby pins and hair spray, we can make the sides stay in place...sort of. Even Englischers who come here from way outside Amish country take note of your hair. One woman had some sort of zoom lens on her camera and asked if she could take a photo of you while you were in the tower."

"Uh, lady, the sign out front clearly says no taking photos of the workers." Cara grabbed her prayer Kapp off the open Bible on her bed and passed it to Deborah. She read a few verses from the Bible regularly, but understanding most of it took knowing history and principles she wasn't familiar with yet. But she kept at it. "Was yesterday what Christmas was always like for you and Ephraim?"

"There were always presents, too much food, and lots of people we loved. Is that what you mean?"

"I...I guess. It just feels like I've entered a different country sometimes."

Deborah wove the last straight pin through strands of Cara's hair. "Well the fact that we kept forgetting to speak English probably has something to do with that feeling."

Cara stood and straightened her dress and apron while looking in the mirror. "It does fit nice."

"Ya, nicer than my dresses fit you. Ephraim knew what he was doing when he hired Lavina to make new dresses. Christmas present or not, a man paying for dresses to be made for his girl or wife, like Ephraim did, has to be a first."

Cara moved to the dresser, picked up another gift he'd given her, and opened it. She ran her fingers over the well-worn pages of *Sense and Sensibility*. The clothbound edition had been published in 1908, and Ephraim had given it to her yesterday for Christmas. From the moment she'd opened it, she'd sensed an odd stirring in her soul.

Ephraim loved books as much as she did. She'd noticed that the first night she slept in his home. Finding the gift had taken him time, effort, and money, but that was only part of what touched her so deeply. When she opened the book, the first sentences filled her like music used to, and she felt the beat of them thrum inside her. The feelings hadn't faded a bit since yesterday.

She used to love books above all else, but that was before she had to drop out of school in order to survive. After that, reading became a luxury she didn't have time for, and music had filled that void. Everywhere she worked, music came through the speakers or the music channels on television.

"He's said nothing about me not taking Lori's bike away." The texture of the off-white pages felt much like an infant's palm.

"What else did you think he'd do?"

"I...I expected at least a little bullying on the topic." She couldn't remember dealing with a man who hadn't bullied her in one way or another. Her husband had been a gentle man in a thousand ways, and she'd grown to love him deeply, but even he knew the fine art of cornering her—and because of it, she'd married him.

She read a line from Jane Austen's book: *Had he married a more amiable woman, he might have been made still more respectable than he was.* She wanted to be amiable for Ephraim's sake, to make him respected again in the community. To make him happier with her than he would have been with Anna Mary or any other woman.

As she skimmed some of the pages, she knew that everything that drew her to music, or to anything else not allowed by her future husband's people, could be found inside books. And she sensed that she might be able to let go of longing for non-Amish things. "I…I want to be able to commit to the Amish faith by springtime. I do."

Deborah smiled and embraced her. "My Daed always says that wanting to make the needed sacrifices and actually doing it is the main difference between those who have peace later in life and those who die in their regrets."

After she'd opened the book yesterday, she'd been unable to look at Ephraim without tears welling in her eyes. When she'd first thought about joining the faith, she had no idea that giving up music would be so hard. But in ways she hadn't realized, music had comforted her throughout her loneliest years in foster care. At fifteen, when she became a dancer at a bar, it'd been her first taste of having power over her circumstances. Her very pulse seemed to carry the beat of music, and it pulled on her so much more than the addiction she'd had for cigarettes. And yet her future husband had stumbled onto something that eased her craving.

Didn't books carry the many rhythms heard in music? Didn't the words inside a story stir the soul like a song? Books were not forbidden, and Ephraim had given her a way to be herself and yet live inside the boundaries placed around the faith.

He hadn't known what his gift would do for her, but now she wished to give him a gift that touched his heart just as much. She'd given him a few gifts yesterday—two new shirts she'd sewn for him, his favorite meal for Christmas lunch, and a card listing why she loved him. He'd seemed really touched by those gifts, but what else could she give that would do for him what he'd done for her?

Deborah pulled on her boots. "Ephraim will be here soon. If you want to get that special breakfast made, you'd better get moving."

Cara gently closed her book and set it back on the dresser. "Will Jonathan be here for breakfast?"

Lacing her boots, Deborah grimaced. "He's spending today with his family."

"The whole day?"

"Ya."

"Did you two ever talk things out?"

She tied a knot in the shoelaces. "No. I've decided he's right. Why force a talk about who we are and what I want from our relationship if I don't know how I feel or what I want? It's like backing myself into a corner to make a decision when I don't have to do that right now."

"Sounds wise to me."

"Ya, that's sort of what Ephraim did with you, isn't it?"

"Very much, only he had the added pressure of not knowing if I'd ever come to believe in God or be willing to join the Amish faith."

"He knew what he wanted, but he gave you room until you knew what you wanted. I really admired that. Mahlon never did that on any topic. He always encouraged me to believe about him what he wanted me to believe."

"I think that's the first time you've ever admitted a flaw in Mahlon."

"It feels wrong to compare him with anyone."

"But doesn't comparing mean we're thinking? Otherwise aren't we just accepting whatever others want us to believe?"

"So you think I need to assess the differences between Jonathan and Mahlon?"

"It's healthy, Deb. If we're not free to figure out the differences between men, aren't we judging them to all be alike?"

"One thing I've learned this year: men are not all alike."

Cara chuckled. "They are as different as fool's gold and twenty-four-karat gold. That's a valuable lesson to learn *before* you choose someone to marry."

"Mom!" The sounds of Lori stomping up the steps vibrated the antique doorknob.

Cara opened the door. "In here."

"Mom!" Lori hollered, sounding really miffed. Cara moved to the landing.

Lori's hands were on her hips. "Why didn't you tell me?"

"Tell you what?"

"You know what, Mom!" Lori's eyes filled with tears. Whatever Cara had done wrong this time had her daughter really angry.

The sounds of the front door opening caught her attention. Ephraim walked in. He smiled at Cara before glancing at Lori, who stood on the stairway with her back to him. "I shoulda been told!" Lori screamed. "I don't want that stupid old bike if it's not allowed."

"Oh." Cara's heart sank. "Okay."

Lori folded her arms, staring at Cara with huge tears in her eyes.

Ada stood at the bottom of the stairs. "I…I didn't mean to mention anything about bicycles. We were talking about the types of toys other Amish children got for Christmas, and when she asked why no one got a bike, I answered without thinking. I'm really sorry, Cara."

"It's okay, Ada."

"You ruined everything, Mom! Why didn't you tell me?"

"Lori." Ephraim's quiet tone caught Lori's attention. "You'll say your piece with respect or not at all."

Lori burst into tears, ran up the stairs, and slammed her bedroom door.

Trying to hide her embarrassment, Cara rolled her eyes. "I'm a horrible mother, I guess." She shrugged. "Merry Second Christmas, Ephraim."

"Ada. Deborah." He nodded at each one. Looking a little unsure of what he'd walked into, he climbed the steps. "Frehlich Zwedde Grischt-daag, Cara." He moved in closer, and Cara's heart pounded.

Deborah cleared her throat and hurried downstairs.

Ephraim studied Cara. "Hi."

"I guess I really messed up again."

Ephraim's eyes moved over her. "Blue is a good color on you."

"I should have told her about the bike."

He caressed her cheek. "Do you know how much I enjoyed yesterday?"

It'd been the best Christmas that Cara had ever had. It made it perfect to know it'd been memorable for him too. The warmth of his hand didn't compare to what he did to her heart. When he kissed her, she'd never felt so secure or loved.

He rested his forehead on hers. "That's a much better greeting."

She liked that he didn't let Lori's outburst rattle him. "She'll make a better Amish member than I will."

"If that's supposed to be a fair warning, I'll tell you again—I don't care that you're not Amish through and through. Our way of life comes easier for her. My guess is, when she's a teen and in her rumschpringe, she'll never waver in wanting to live Amish."

Propping one hand on her hip, Cara pulled back. "And you think I do?"

Ephraim's gorgeous gray-blue eyes revealed little emotion. "The thought has crossed my mind."

The door to Lori's bedroom creaked.

Cara looked around Ephraim to see her daughter peeking through the crack. "You want to talk?"

Keeping the door open just a little, Lori put her lips on the crack. "You shoulda told me."

"I didn't know, not until after we'd brought home the bike."

She opened the door a little more. "I don't want to fight."

Cara motioned for her. Lori ran to her and wrapped her arms around Cara's waist. "You mad at me?"

"No, Lorabean, I'm not."

"I like my bike, Mom."

Cara knelt. "I know. Me too."

"What are we gonna do?"

"I don't know, kiddo. What do you want to do?"

Lori looked at Ephraim and back to her mom and shrugged. "I guess I want to do the right thing."

Cara held her daughter, enjoying the feel of her little arms wrapped around her neck. "Okay. We will. But for now you go on down and give Ada a hug."

Lori nodded. She went to Ephraim. He picked her up and hugged her.

Lori pointed downstairs. "I made you something on the sewing machine you gave me for Christmas. Mom helped me learn how to work the foot pedal by myself."

He kissed her cheek. "You two can do anything you set your minds to. But you can't keep getting mad at your mom when she's doing her best. You don't want her getting mad at you when you're trying but you don't get it right, do you?"

While still in Ephraim's arms, Lori studied her mom. "Nee."

"*Gut. Bischt hungerich?*"

"Ya."

"*Geh, ess.*" He set Lori's feet on the floor, and she scurried down the steps.

Cara straightened her dress. She didn't know exactly what they'd said, but it was something about eating. She went into Lori's room and made her bed. Ephraim leaned against the doorframe.

"Four of my siblings got new scooters for Christmas. I bought one for Lori a few weeks ago. If you'd like to give that to her for Second Christmas, you can."

Cara placed Lori's favorite book on the nightstand. *Shoo-Fly Girl.*

She should be grateful Ephraim had bought a scooter to make up for her blunder, but she wasn't. She wanted to be the one to give Lori a really special riding toy. Instead she'd done something out of ignorance and needed her daughter's forgiveness. She'd hoped to make a lasting memory together—and she had, but not at all the one she'd planned.

Ephraim slid one hand into his pants pocket. "Your aunt Emma came by last night after I arrived home. She wanted me to let you know they were saving a place for the three of us at dinner. I got the impression she'd invited us earlier."

Startled, Cara tried to piece together the last conversation she'd had with Emma. "I remember her talking to me one night during Elsie's viewing. We were washing dishes at Grey's. But between her tossing in a few Pennsylvania Dutch words and all the commotion, I didn't catch enough words to know what she was talking about." She started out of the room.

Ephraim stood his ground, blocking the doorway. He studied her. "Does Lori know she has relatives in Dry Lake?"

She clicked her tongue and huffed.

"What?" Ephraim stood up straight.

"Nothing." She whisked past him and started down the stairs.

He put his hand on her arm. "There is too something. I know it. You know it. I just don't know what *it* is."

She didn't like standing two steps below him, so she pulled free of his hand and moved back to the landing. "You're patient and kind, and, God is my witness, I never knew good men like you existed, so I should probably keep my mouth shut and behave like a sweet Amish fiancée."

"Do us both a favor and don't."

"Okay, fine. No matter how much I change, it's never enough. Just this morning I began feeling like I could give up music. There is no way you could ever know how huge that is. And now you want me to care about people as if they're real family."

"They *are* real family, Cara."

"No, they are strangers that I've met—ones who left me stranded as a child in a bus station. It took years to give up believing in the people I kept hoping would show up for me, so don't be surprised if it takes years to learn how to let them into my life. I've told you before that I stopped accepting crumbs from tables long, long ago."

"They aren't offering crumbs."

She bit her tongue to keep curse words from slipping out. "Yes, they are. Their own children are grown, meaning time is easier to come by these days. Then I showed up in their driveway months ago and challenged them concerning their decisions. *Now* they want me to visit and hang out? And you're pushing me for them."

"I just asked if Lori knew she had relatives."

"Ephraim." She elongated his name with deep frustration. "Give me a break. Man alive, you don't bully, but you let your will be known."

"And so do you, Cara." His raised voice rattled through the old homestead. He closed his eyes for a moment. "Look, I understand you—where you're coming from, how and why you feel the way you do—but that doesn't keep me from having opinions of what I think you should do next. If I'm wanting too much to happen too soon, I have no doubt you'll say so." He angled his head, a touch of humor reflecting in his eyes. "And sometimes, like today, you can even tell me without cursing."

Cara shook her head, wondering how she could start an argument with someone she loved so completely. "I haven't told her."

"I figured."

"Yeah, but you just had to ask anyway, didn't you?"

"Okay, so you're right. It was more than just a question, but I'm trying, Cara."

She rested against the wall, wondering if she'd ever be all that he deserved. "Me too."

"I know." He moved in close, placing one hand on the wall beside her.

"Why is it so stinking important that I connect with my so-called family?"

He shrugged. "It's not important."

"Oh, I beg to differ, Ephraim Mast. It's very important to you. I just don't know what *it* is."

His gentle smile warmed her. "You won't like *it*."

"I'll survive. Say it, rich boy."

"Uprooting is in your blood. You began running at fifteen, and sometimes I...I'm concerned you haven't really stopped yet, only paused."

"And you think aunts and uncles that I barely know the names of and cousins I don't know at all have the power to change me?"

"Family has a way of causing roots to grow."

"That can be true, but we also know family can cause a person to put on her running shoes. Look at it that way, and you'll be fine."

He lifted her chin and kissed her. "If you stay, we stay. If you leave, we leave."

Her heart turned a flip. He wasn't talking about whether they'd stay at Ada's today or visit her relatives. He meant her joining the faith...or not.

The confidence in his eyes and mannerisms didn't fade. "Right?"

"I told you that I'll join the faith."

He didn't look convinced, but he nodded and stepped back before motioning for her to go downstairs ahead of him.

His insinuation of doubt had her heart pounding. Was she just having a reasonable amount of trouble adjusting to the Amish ways or was she wavering?

Twenty-Two

Lena wrote the date on the chalkboard, her steady hand drawing long loops out of Monday, January 8. A decade ago, on this same date, Allen had fallen from the barn loft and broken his ankle. The image of looking out the window and seeing Grey fight snowdrifts as he carried her brother to the Kauffman house still remained vivid. He seemed so strong that day.

She shouldn't be thinking of him, not like this. He stirred her, and she dared to wonder if one day, maybe a year or two from now, he might consider her. She'd witnessed a lot of single men in her days, and not one of them compared to Grey's quality. And so handsome. He didn't seem to mind her birthmark, and clearly she had the power to make him smile again. So maybe...

She faced her students in first through fourth grades. "Who can tell me what number could replace the word *January* and means the same thing?"

Elmer held up his hand. Lena pointed to him.

"The number one."

"Good." She began writing the different months of the year on the board in random order. With her peripheral view, she could see Peter studying the board. She'd given the older students a different assignment, but he learned best when simply observing the younger ones. She'd used this method a lot without him having a clue. "If we can use the number one in place of the word *January,* what number would we use for the month of June?"

No one answered, but Peter appeared to be thinking.

"If January is number one…," Lena said.

"June is the sixth month," Peter scoffed.

"Exactly." Lena smiled at him briefly. His mocking tone didn't bother her. He used it as a cover. But his lethargic ways did trouble her. He seemed tired all the time and rarely ate. "Scholars, when you've written the name of the month and its corresponding number beside it, please take it to my desk. Peter, would you sit at my desk and check the papers?"

Without even rolling his eyes, Peter moved to her desk. She went to him. Glad for a moment to talk to him quietly where no one else could hear them, she gave him a red pencil. "Lots of smiley faces. Focus on what they get right, and gently correct what they've gotten wrong."

Peter took the pencil from her. "If I have everyone getting this right by the end of today, can I have five points added to my last math test?"

The young man confused her. On one hand he cared about nothing. On the other a few points added to a test actually mattered. "That's too much unfair pressure for you and them. You're working with first graders also. Some of them have yet to fully grasp the concept of the twelve months of the year. But if you have the second, third, and fourth graders able to accomplish the goal by Friday, I'll absolutely give you those points."

His stone face reflected little, but he nodded.

Lena hesitated. "If you need anything, you can talk to me, or I can contact my friend Samantha for you."

Peter stared at the pencil in his hand. "Not everyone gives smiley faces or cares what a person got right, only what they got wrong."

"We can't live based on naysayers, Peter. We all have value and the right to find as much peace with ourselves and our flaws and weaknesses as possible. Why would forgiveness be so important to God if we didn't need it all the time? He knew we would need it from Him, but also from us for ourselves and for others. When we get peace with our weakest areas, we'll find new ways to build on our strongest areas."

Peter shrugged, but he seemed to like what she'd said.

The day flew by, and soon Lena stood outside the schoolhouse saying good-bye to her students. With freezing temperatures and high winds, she hadn't been a bit surprised when a parent, neighbor, or relative came to pick up every scholar. Once they were gone, she went back into the classroom and began grading papers. On nice days she took the work with her, but on days like today when she had a roaring fire in the potbelly stove, she liked to hang around until she could bank the embers. Not only did that make leaving less of a fire hazard, but it also made the room warmer in the morning and starting a fire much easier.

Through the frosted windows she saw the hazy shape of a buggy, and a man got out. Her heart thumped a few extra beats as hopes of seeing Grey became her first thought. The front door opened, and she stood. Aaron Blank removed his black felt hat, revealing hair the same color. Concern ran through her. He was a disheveled mess. His hands shook. Dark puffy circles ran under his eyes. And even at a distance he smelled of stale alcohol.

"I...I was talking to Dwayne a few weeks ago. He was griping about what Peter had told him, that you'd brought some psychologist woman in to talk to the scholars. Is that true?"

"Ya, I thought the children needed someone who knew a lot more about grief and trauma than I do. She's a counselor at the school I attended during my rumschpringe."

Aaron's dark brown eyes studied her before he tossed his hat on a desk and walked to the blackboard. "What kind of a person uses their running-around years to attend school?"

"Well, those Englischer kids would say a really dorky one."

Aaron turned to face her, a gentle smile on his lips. "It doesn't bother you what others think, does it?"

This unusual visit worried her. He seemed to be looking for answers, and she prayed for the right words. "Sure it bothers me. I just do my best to not let it rule me. It still hurts, every time. In my younger years, it'd sting so much I would cry myself to sleep. I find humor helps a lot and doing things I enjoy, like teaching."

He ran his hands across the dusty chalkboard and then rubbed his thumb over his fingertips. "You studied during your rumschpringe. Wanna guess what I did during mine?"

She didn't have to guess. His rumschpringe hadn't ended yet, because he hadn't joined the faith. Based on his age, he should have. His running-around years began either before or around the time he and his family moved here from Ohio, almost seven years ago. And based on glimpses she'd caught of his life, he'd gone from being an occasional-weekend teen-age drinker to a twenty-four-year-old man who stayed half drunk most of the time.

He moved within inches of her. "I need help, Lena, and I don't know who else to ask."

"You came to the right place. The counselor Dwayne told you about is a school psychologist. She can't help you, but she brought me a list of other counselors in case any of the adults in Dry Lake wanted to talk to someone." Lena sat in her chair and began looking through the drawers in her desk. "There's a place called the Better Path, I think." She found the paper. "Ya, that's the name. It's about forty miles from here. I'm not sure who runs it, but she said there's a Plain Mennonite counselor who's a young man like yourself, and he comes highly recommended in his field."

Aaron sat on her desk. "I've got to stop drinking, but I can't imagine how to do that. Daed and Mamm know I drink, but they don't have any clue how much or how often."

"I wish I knew what to say. All I know is you need to take care of you. It will hurt when they are forced to accept it, but at least you're also offering them hope by looking for help."

"They don't even know I'd been told about that fence or that Elsie's death is my fault. If I'd fixed it right when I had the chance…"

His heaviness wrapped around her, but she couldn't think of anything to say about the bull breaking through. "Aaron, if you can tune out what everyone thinks and feels toward you, can you see your way to finding answers?"

He moved to a window and stared at the back pasture where his sister had died three months ago. "Ya, I...I think I can...with the right help."

"Then for now, do what you need to for you. When you're well, you can make it up to them."

"Well." He let out a slow, heavy breath. "I haven't felt well in a really long time." When he turned to face her, his dark brown eyes were filled with tears. "I'm scared that I'll never get free."

"You can't erase how you've spent your rumschpringe or the day Elsie died. But if you win against this need to drink, you can change your future. I know you can." She wrote down the information about the Better Path and held it out to him.

He took it. "Dwayne said that my Daed came by here this morning before school started. What'd he want?"

She wondered how Dwayne knew about Michael coming here. "He came to let me know that there's a school board meeting next Monday."

"Can you imagine how my Daed will feel when he finds out I'd been warned about that bull?"

"Aaron, you thought you'd fixed the fence."

"Ya, while in some half-drunken state."

"He doesn't need to know that. It won't help anything. Just take care of yourself. I'll deal with the school board. But if I were you, I'd avoid Dwayne."

"Dwayne isn't so bad. He's a better man than I am. He's always in control, even when he drinks. He never overdoes it, never gets clobbered."

She feared his judgment concerning Dwayne would come back to haunt him, but she didn't think she could convince him. "You have a good heart, Aaron. And if you get sober, I'll bet you'll even find it."

He went to the desk where he'd dropped his hat. "Denki, Lena. You...

you've always been nice to me. I appreciate that a lot." Without another word he left.

As Aaron pulled away in his buggy, she hoped he'd do whatever it took to get free of past mistakes.

❧

Lena knocked on Crist and Mollie's door, wondering why the school board had chosen to meet here. They were Peter and Dwayne's parents, and she couldn't shake the feeling that she was entering the lions' den. She doubted Grey would come, but she hated the idea of facing opposition without his voice of reason.

Mollie let her in. "Lena." Mollie managed a short nod and motioned to the kitchen table.

Elsie's Mamm looked pale and almost as sad as the day her daughter was killed. All the school board members and their wives were here, except Grey. Dwayne was here too. She guessed it was futile to hope he might not be at a meeting being held in his own home. Sylvan and Lillian Detweiler were here too, which meant old criticisms were coming her way again.

Lena went to a chair and took a seat.

The Detweilers' complaints against her stemmed from the incident last year, the one that caused the board to put her on probation. It'd been such a foolish mistake on her part, but her alternative was to let four children go hungry.

Michael looked up from the papers in his hand. "Ah, Lena, you've arrived."

She'd arrived ten minutes before it was time for the meeting to begin and had managed to be the last one to get here, so she wondered if they'd had a meeting beforehand too.

He called the gathering to order, and Dwayne took a seat at the table. She was in his home, but she'd hoped he wouldn't stay for this part.

They bowed their heads in silent prayer.

Michael interlaced his fingers and placed his hands on the papers spread out in front of him. "Several parents have a lot of questions, but rather than having everyone come, Mollie and Crist will be their spokesmen. They've been gathering questions from parents, and we'd like you to respond to those questions. Since Grey isn't here to take notes, Jake will. It won't take long. Are you ready?"

"Ya."

Crist placed a piece of notebook paper on the table. Only half of it was filled. That gave Lena a little hope. "The first item the parents would like to know is about Elmer. He was on a swing when the chain broke, and he ended up in a cast. Why weren't you aware that the chains needed to be replaced?"

Michael shook his head. "She's not responsible for playground equipment. That's the board's job."

"I disagree," Crist said. "It's the board's job to replace the items. It's hers to inform you."

Michael shook his head and started to say something.

"I can answer his question," Lena offered.

"Okay, Lena, go ahead," Michael said.

"Those chains were only two years old. Not a one of them should have broken, but Daed and I changed them all out after Elmer's accident and before anyone else used a swing."

"Gut. Denki, Lena." Michael made a note.

Crist read the next item. "You buried one of your scholars' cats while the child begged you not to? Is that true?"

Michael lifted his hand. "Who wrote these questions? Lena deals with a large classroom of children, and we can't second-guess her every decision."

"I'd like to at least know where she found the cat," Crist said.

Lena glanced at Dwayne. "The cat's throat had been slit, and it was left in my chair. We all know that mean pranks are pulled on teachers from time to time. I tried to bury it before the children arrived. I guess I could have hidden it in the lean-to and buried it later, but I didn't."

"And you didn't bother to tell the school board that someone left a dead cat in the room? Shouldn't they have been informed?"

"I mentioned it to Grey within a few days of it happening."

Michael tapped his hand against the table. "That answers plenty. She did her job, and I'm sure Grey would have told us if...if...Elsie hadn't..." The sting of Michael losing his daughter had stolen the words from him.

Crist nodded. "Yes, you're right." He looked at Lena. "Were you aware that the bull had gotten into the pasture near the school before the day... of the incident?"

Lena cringed. "Ya."

Michael shifted. "I won't sit here and let anyone blame Lena. It's my field, and my son's bull. We're responsible. End of it. I've told the board for months there's nothing to talk to Lena about."

She ached for Michael. Like Aaron, he blamed himself.

Crist took a sip of water. "The parents would like to know if the school board approved Lena bringing a counselor, a psychologist of some sort, into the school to talk to the children after the incident."

Michael looked surprised. He angled his head toward her. "You brought in an outsider to talk to the scholars without permission?"

"I...I guess I did."

"You guess?" Dwayne scoffed. "You don't know?"

Lena straightened in her chair. "The children were traumatized, and I have a friend who is a school counselor. She only came in to help them sort through their feelings and to offer advice on dealing with trauma and shock. I never left the room while she talked. We did some exercises she suggested—drawing, talking, acting out how we feel. She said and did nothing against our beliefs. Nothing."

Michael breathed deeply. "That wasn't wise, Lena. An outsider we don't know, a psychologist no less, brought in to talk to our children? You had to know this was unacceptable."

Lena steadied her pounding heart. "The day of the incident I saw the trauma that took place in each child's heart and mind. I know Samantha Rogers from my days of attending public school, and I knew she'd have the expertise to help them."

"Peter is worse, not better," Mollie snapped.

Lena tried to find the right words. "That's not Samantha's fault. She did nothing that would make anyone worse. I...I think he's probably better than he would have been without the insights Samantha had to offer."

"I don't believe you," Mollie said.

Lena cleared her throat, trying to guard her tone. "Okay."

"Okay?" Mollie scoffed. "You think what you've done is okay?"

"I'm sorry it upset you, but I think it's been helpful for all the children."

"You're not even a little sorry." The oldest board member, Jake Fisher, scooted his chair forward, making an awful sound as he did. "We don't want some stranger who may not even be a believer offering the children of Dry Lake hope. Why would you step outside of our ways to do this your way?"

Lena steadied her tone, trying to remain respectful. "We allow firemen to come to the school and share their wisdom. They put on their full gear and teach the children how to respond to a fire. I thought Samantha could help in her own area, like they do."

Jake frowned. "So you didn't ask because we allow firemen to come into the school?"

"A problem came up, and then an opportunity for finding some relief surfaced, so I went for it."

"Went for it?" Dwayne's smug smile made her feel sick. "She talks more like a public school girl than an Amish one."

A wave of nods circled the room.

Michael took notes. "Lena, do not allow any outsider to come into the classroom without permission. Clear?"

"Ya."

He gathered his papers. "We can't decide a discipline tonight. I'm dealing with all I can right now. I might as well let you all know about Aaron. You'll hear about it elsewhere if I don't. He's…entered a rehabilitation center somewhere outside of Owl's Perch. I…I don't know what made him think he needed that kind of help, but he didn't ask my opinion. I can't see us trying to make a fair discipline call on this tonight." He grew still as he studied Lena. "I'm afraid you've crossed a line."

Dwayne scoffed, and all eyes moved to him. "I think you should ask Lena who suggested Aaron leave Dry Lake and see a shrink."

Aaron's mother straightened, looking more alert than she had since Lena arrived. Dora ran her fingers over her cheek. "What did you say to our son that made him leave his family when we needed him most?"

Lena's heart jumped, and she knew her face radiated guilt. "I…I know how this looks, but he came to me, and…I…I gave him some information."

"What *kind* of information?" Dora asked.

She wouldn't tell because Aaron might not want her to. "It was a private conversation. I…I was only trying to help."

Murmuring continued, and several board members asked her questions at the same time.

Michael's hand shook when he raised it to silence everyone. "Whatever conversation took place between Aaron and Lena isn't a school matter. Aaron may have chosen badly when deciding who to talk to, but no part of that can affect our decision concerning Lena as a teacher. And we're all too upset to have any sense of fairness in our decision of what discipline to hand down. I say we table this matter for at least a week. All in favor say aye."

A chorus of dull ayes echoed. "Any nays?"

No one said anything.

With his elbow on the table, Michael held his head in one hand. "You will remain under probation, and you are not to allow any Englischer inside the school without the board's permission. Is that clear?"

"Ya."

"We'll take all this under advisement and either let you know of another meeting or send you a letter with our decision. Your actions between now and then will be carefully scrutinized. I'm very concerned, Lena. Do you understand?" He spoke gently, but she saw hurt and anger in his countenance.

"Ya." Lena said her good-byes, grabbed her coat, and left. Cold wind slapped her in the face when she stepped outside. Her heart ached over the board's view of her, and she fought tears while making her way along the narrow path of cleared snow toward the barn. At least Michael refused to make a decision until he and the others calmed down, but the idea of losing her school stung. Her scholars needed that time with Samantha. But if she lost her school because of overreaching her authority, she'd never get another teaching position at any Amish school.

Twenty-Three

Wonderful smells of baked goods drifted throughout Ada's House, constantly reminding Deborah of all she had to be thankful for. She sat at the kitchen table, counting the money they'd made this week. Ada and Jonathan chatted quietly while Cara and Lori sat at the sewing machine making cloth dolls.

Deborah stacked the cash and checks together. "I just can't believe how well our business continues to do, and it's almost six weeks past Christmas."

Jonathan turned a chair around backward and straddled it. "Most of the snows have been perfect for sleigh rides this year. I think that's helped keep things really hopping around here."

"Ya, everything is just working so much better than I figured. But the truth is, we couldn't have done it without your constant help, Jon."

Cara laughed. "And some nights his big reward is getting to sleep in that awful room above the carriage house."

"Well, the upside is I've had a chance to expand the blacksmith business to places the horse and wagon can't reach from Dry Lake in one day."

Lori stayed focused as Ada and Cara helped her sew another faceless doll. Those sold great too, and Lori loved helping to make them.

Ada glanced up. "I never dreamed we'd stay this busy. We've sold every hope chest, coatrack, and side table that Israel made, and he's making more items for us."

Deborah slid the money into the deposit bag. "I hope I'm not all puffed up to think this, but I'm so pleased with us. We've come up with a theme for every season so far, and people have enjoyed each one."

Cara snipped loose threads off the doll in her hand. "We need to start working on a spring theme, but I'm not planting, hoeing, and harvesting according to the Old Ways. So if anyone mentions farming the Amish way at Ada's House, I'll scream."

"I've been mulling over the spring theme," Jonathan said. "And I think farming like the Amish is a great idea."

Cara screamed softly, making all of them giggle.

"It's just the first of February. We have a few more weeks of Amish Winter Wonderland to get through. We'll figure something out soon enough." Deborah removed her coat and Jonathan's from pegs near the back door. "I'm ready." She tossed Jonathan his jacket.

He caught it and opened the door for her. She grabbed her scarf, gloves, and winter bonnet off the shelf. Almost every Friday night, unless the temps were too cold, they walked to the bank to drop the money into the night depository.

Deborah put on her black bonnet, wrapped the knit scarf around her neck and lower face, and wriggled her hands into the leather gloves.

With his hands jammed inside his coat pockets, Jonathan nudged her with his shoulder. "Warm?"

"You know the answer to that," Deborah mumbled through the knit scarf.

"Did you put on the insulated underwear I brought you?"

"That's not for you to know." She pretended offense. "Where's your sense of respectability, young man?"

His quiet laugh warmed her more than all her layers of clothing. "Well, Little Debbie, I think working in a hot kitchen year round puts you at a disadvantage for dealing with cold weather. I could take the deposit to the bank for you."

"At least I wouldn't have to worry you might eat it before getting there."

"That's true enough."

She treasured his sense of humor, his willingness to exaggerate any fault, real or imagined, and laugh in a way that caused amusement itself to dance within her. He walked with confidence and lightheartedness. On a whim she slid her gloved hand into his coat pocket with his hand.

But he didn't laugh or make a joke as she'd expected. His features grew gentle, and he enveloped her hand in his.

"Ah, I'm much warmer now." Even as she teased him, unease ran through her. He'd been honest about how he felt, and it seemed inappropriate to flirt—to make him hope for things she remained unsure of wanting. But her hand in his felt so right that she couldn't make herself pull away.

They walked through the old town where tall brick buildings lined the sidewalks. Once in front of the bank, she pulled her hand free of Jonathan's and slid the thin bag through the deposit slot. When she turned around to leave, Jonathan stood directly in front of her.

He slowly lowered the knit scarf from around her lips. "I can think of something else that might warm you…us."

The aroma of aftershave clung to his hands, and his warm breath smelled of peppermint. Mesmerized by some invisible power, she couldn't respond. He slowly drew closer, and when his lips met hers, even her toes warmed. She moved her hands to his chest to push against him, but her hands disobeyed her and clutched the lapels of his wool coat. The gentleness of his hands against her face and his lips over hers caught her off guard. Never in her life had she experienced a kiss like this.

The kiss grew with each moment, leaving her breathless. When he eased his lips from hers and studied her, she leaned against the brick building for support.

"It's...awfully...hot out here." Deborah tried to make light of what had just happened, but her breathless, trembling words betrayed her.

She pulled the knit fabric over her lips and tried to catch her breath. He ran the back of his fingers across the scarf and her cheek. "Like summertime in February," he said softly.

Staring into his eyes, she understood that Jonathan had a way of making her feel totally secure and incredibly treasured. As she studied him, an odd and unwelcome sensation grabbed her senses. She closed her eyes, hoping it'd go away. It didn't. She sidestepped him, looking down the block. A man seemed to be looking right at them, and she knew he'd returned.

"Something wrong?"

The man eased into a side alley, disappearing completely.

Her legs shook. Was it really Mahlon or just her imagination, conjured up the moment she kissed another man? "Let's go back."

Jonathan glanced up the block and back to her. "You okay?"

Deborah wrapped her arms around herself and started walking. "Sure."

They walked home without talking. Once inside, the stiltedness between them made her want to tell what she'd seen...or thought she saw.

The wall clock showed that it wasn't yet nine, but Ada, Cara, and Lori apparently had retired to the upstairs. Deborah's eyes met Jonathan's. "I...I'm going on to my room now."

"Sure. Good night, Deb."

He turned to leave, to go to his room above the carriage house, then paused. "You want to talk about what spooked you?"

Her heart cinched into a knot. She'd reacted to his kiss with clear desire, and then she'd shut him out. Her behavior felt similar to the way Mahlon used to treat her. And embarrassment filled her as Jonathan wanted to face it openly. She took a shaky breath. "Just shadows of the past dogging me while I try to move forward."

He looked like he wanted to say more, but he tipped his hat and left. She outted the lanterns and stood in the darkness. Had Mahlon returned? The thought bounced around inside her head, confusing her more with each passing minute. She wouldn't know what she thought or felt until she knew whether it was him or not.

She eased into the foyer, looking up the steps for signs of light coming from under doorways. The only room with light was Cara's. She rarely settled down for sleep before midnight. Grabbing her coat and winter bonnet, Deborah went out the front door, moving quietly so no one heard her. While going down the walkway, she put her coat and hat on, but her insides felt colder than the night. The moon reflected brightly on patches of snow, but living in town didn't compare to the fields of undisturbed white at her Daed's place.

When a man moved out from behind a tree just a few feet away, Deborah gasped.

"Easy, Deb." Mahlon's familiar voice caught her. He'd cut his hair short, ridding himself of the curls he'd always hated. He wore a belt instead of suspenders, and his leather coat stood open as if the cold didn't bother him. He looked healthy and carefree.

"What are you doing here?"

"Checking on the two women I love." He shifted, looking surprisingly confident.

He loved her? "What do you want?"

"You."

She ached to say, *It's too late.* But as he stared at her, the words wouldn't leave her mouth. Something about him tugged at her, just as it always had. She should hate him. But all she could think of was that she had loved him before she'd even been old enough to know what love was. Her heart beat hard against her chest, pounding out the many, many feelings she'd had for him almost her whole life. "What does that mean?"

"I'm sorry I left, especially the way I did. I was so confused. I'm not anymore. And I love you. I always have. I want to come back and make it right."

"Make it right? I caught you sneaking off. When I confronted you, you rode off in a car with a friend, leaving me crying on the side of the road. You were a jerk to me and your Mamm, giving no thought to anyone but yourself."

He tilted his head, his quietness drawing her in as it always had. "A jerk doesn't care. I've never for one minute stopped caring."

"Then tell me why, Mahlon. You asked me to marry you, and then you ran off."

"No excuse." Mahlon lowered his head. "I…I messed up."

"No excuse? So either you still don't know, or you aren't telling."

He shoved his hands into his pants pocket. "You've changed since I left."

"Ya, I have. It's been almost eight months, and I've had to survive what you heaped on me. I doubt if you'll ever really know what you've done. You say you want to come back and make it right, but you're sneaking around in the dark, hiding your presence from everyone but me. Why?"

He stared at the ground before looking her in the eye. "I needed to see you alone. To have a chance to tell the full story. I've changed too, Deb. All for the better. I promise you that, but you'll have to give me an opportunity to prove it. I'm living not far from here. I'd like for us to talk, to cover some ground together, before my presence is known. Can you do that much for me?"

"You keeping secrets just never ends, does it?"

"I'm only asking for a few days. That's all."

She wanted to keep it a secret, but not for him. For her. It'd give her the freedom to figure out what she thought before everyone else started pulling at her to think and feel what they wanted her to. Even with her own reasons for doing this in place, she felt like a fool.

If she acted irrationally and Mahlon left again, Ada would pay. The man in front of her was Ada's only child. For any Amish woman, that alone carried a heartache that couldn't be erased. But if he returned, Ada's life would never feel lacking again. Deborah's presence and loyalty could only ease Ada's loss in a tiny way. Mahlon had the ability to erase Ada's sorrow and carry on her family line. "And if I never want to be in a relationship with you again, will you return anyway and rejoin the faith?"

He stared, his hazel eyes still holding power over her, and she hated herself for it. "Think about giving me a second chance, Deb. When you're ready to talk, leave a message for me with the cook at the Family Restaurant in town. I can tell you what you want to know. Just don't tell anyone else for now. Please."

Feeling a need to get inside before she gave him any more access to her heart again, she nodded. "Okay. For a little while." She started to walk off, but he caught her by the arm.

He gazed into her eyes, but she didn't know who stood in front of her—the man who'd always drawn her or a stranger. Or both. Had she ever known him?

His eyes misted. "Denki."

"I'm sorry, Mahlon, but I'm not doing this for you." She pulled free of his arm and headed for the porch, hoping she hadn't just created an opening for him that she didn't have the power to close. If Jonathan discovered that he'd returned and that she was keeping it a secret, Jonathan would walk away and never look back. As steady as sunrise in every season, Jonathan had no patience for girls who played games. He didn't need or ask for answers she didn't have, but he demanded honesty in a relationship.

She went inside and locked the door.

Why had she agreed to keep a secret for one man—a man who had proved unreliable—when it could ruin a promising relationship with someone worthy of her trust?

Twenty-Four

Lena moved the pot of heartland corn chowder from the stove onto the kitchen table, careful to square it on the hot pad.

Valentine's Day.

She set the flatware in its place and tucked a napkin beside it. In all her years since being old enough to be courted or to date, she'd never spent this holiday with just her Daed. At least one girlfriend and she had spent the evening eating chocolate candy and talking until the wee hours of the morning—that was the norm. One year when everyone else had a date, Jonathan had come over, and they'd played checkers, schemed new pranks to pull on people, and whiled away the hours just being pals. This year all her friends had someone special. She'd yet to find a man who interested her, except Grey. But when the time came, he could have any single woman, and he wouldn't consider her.

The sense of being different wrapped around her, and she seemed unable to shake it. The threat of losing her teaching position had made it easy for loneliness to carve its features all over her heart.

While moving the freshly baked bread onto the table, she heard the back door open, signaling her Daed's prompt arrival for dinner. His furniture shop stood less than twenty feet from their home, but she never had to call him—he came in early or on time. Except lately he'd missed a few dinners while he spent more and more time in Hope Crossing with Ada.

"These came for you." He passed her several envelopes. All but one were an odd size and color. He moved to the kitchen sink to wash up.

She set the other notes on the table and studied the business-sized envelope. Her hands felt clammy and her head swimmy. It didn't have a return address, but the handwriting was Michael's. The return address had been omitted on purpose. It wasn't from any one person. It came from the school board. Her heart pounding, she turned her back to her Daed, who remained at the sink, and quietly slid her finger under the loose seal and broke it. She pulled the neatly folded letter out and opened it.

Dear Lena,

We appreciate your years of service. You've been an excellent teacher, and we're aware that no position ever comes without issues, but it seems that you are having too much trouble submitting to the authority of the board. It is our decision that, starting with the next school year, you will be free to find a teaching position outside of Dry Lake. So that we do not hinder you from finding a new position, we will keep our decision confidential among the school board. You will have little trouble finding a teaching position elsewhere. Perhaps you will not find it so difficult to submit to the leadership of a different school board.

Sincerely,
Michael Blank
Enos Beiler
Jake Fisher

Grey hadn't signed it. Either he didn't agree with the decision, or he didn't know what was going on in his absence. She guessed he didn't know. Michael tried not to add more to a person's life than was absolutely necessary.

Her Daed finished drying his face on a kitchen towel. "From your friends, ya?"

Lena stuffed the letter and envelope into the hidden pocket of her apron, drew a shaky breath, and turned around. "Ya, they've remembered Valentine's Day." The envelopes on the table contained cards from each close friend—Deborah, Anna Mary, Rachel, Linda, Nancy, Lydia, Frieda, and Esther. And every one of them had beaus…again.

"Did you remember to send them cards?"

"Hmm?" Lena sat at the table and put the napkin in her lap. "Oh, ya. I did."

With the towel in hand, he took a seat. Lena choked back tears as they bowed their heads for the silent prayer. She tried to gain control of her emotions, but she wasn't ready for the bowed heads and closed eyes to be over when she heard her Daed's flatware shift. Trembling, she stood and dipped the corn chowder into a bowl for him.

He took it from her. "Smells great."

"Denki." She ladled soup into her bowl before sitting and passing him the bread.

"You're awfully quiet of late, Lena."

She nodded. How had she let this happen? What had she been thinking?

Her Daed's usually jovial features had a downward pull. "I spoke to Michael earlier today. He apologized to me for any unease their decision may be causing you. You can imagine his embarrassment when he realized I didn't know what he was talking about."

Unable to speak or eat, she shrugged.

"Are you in danger of losing your teaching position?"

"There are other places to teach."

"This school board covers three districts. If you aren't hired by them, no other district is close enough to get to by horse and buggy. You'd need to hire a driver or move."

She took a long drink of her water, hoping to get through dinner without falling apart.

Daed tore off a hunk of bread. "I didn't think the complaints against you that caused your probation last spring to be fair. It wasn't near the first time those children had come to school without their lunch. Every time you'd sent notes home, given them your lunch to share, and asked others to sacrifice part of their lunch. You had good reasons to send the oldest after the forgotten lunches—"

Lena raised both hands. "I know you side with me, and I appreciate it, but this has nothing to do with John going the wrong direction in my rig and getting hurt. I crossed a clear Amish line. I didn't view my actions as threatening, but the board does. I guess since going to public school, I don't see certain things as a hazard to our faith but as an opportunity to grow."

"What did you do?"

"Samantha came and talked to the class on a couple of occasions, trying to help the children cope with the trauma of seeing Elsie killed."

"Ach, Lena. You must've done it without going through proper channels. Why?"

"I told you why. I knew she'd be good for the class, and I…I invited her. I never let her be alone with any of the students. Everything she said was good and wise and helpful."

"Grey is the clearest, most balanced thinker on that board. What does he say?"

Lena pushed the full bowl of soup away from her. "He's not been to a meeting since Elsie died."

Her Daed stared at her, disbelief and frustration radiating from him. "That's not good for you, Lena. With him gone, those who are complaining will not be tempered."

"You're telling me things I know, Daed. Can we change the subject?"

"Sure. I've been taking different pieces of woodwork to Ada's place, and she's been selling them like hot cakes. I'm taking another load tomorrow. I'd thought about staying in Hope Crossing for a night or two. I've got friends there, and she needs help setting up some new adventures for springtime activities at Ada's House. But maybe it's not such a great time to be leaving you so much."

"Don't be ridiculous, please. I'm not a child."

"Ya, but—" Soft knocking sounds interrupted him. He went to the front door. Figuring someone had come to talk to him about furniture, Lena stayed put.

Her Daed walked back into the kitchen alone. "Peter Bender is on the porch, and he wants to talk to you. He didn't want to come in."

Lena grabbed her coat and hurried outside. Winds whipped through her clothes and up her dress, giving her chills. "Peter." She closed the front door. "What's going on?"

"I…I want to talk to that woman friend of yours, you know, the one who came to our classroom."

Suspicion filled her. Had Dwayne talked him into this? If she dared to bring Samantha into Peter's life after the board's letter, it would certainly be the end of her career. She'd never be allowed to teach at any school ever again. "Why?"

Peter shrugged, and under the silvery moonlight that reflected off the snow, she saw hostility etched on his face. He cleared his throat and sniffed. "I…I got to tell her some stuff I can't live with. I can't tell you or anyone else."

She had no doubt that Dwayne was setting her up. But Peter wasn't. To avoid the snare meant refusing to help Peter after she'd been the one to make the offer. Her throat closed and tears welled. "Ya. Okay." Her hands shook as she wiped tears off her face, hoping he didn't notice. "I'll try to reach her tomorrow and see if she will come out this way again. Can you talk to her here?"

He rubbed his nose and sniffed again. "Don't matter to me where as long as no one else can hear us."

"I can arrange for that. It might be best if you keep this just between us for now. Your parents need to know later on, but talking with Samantha a few times first is ideal."

"Sure. I won't say nothing to anybody." He looked like he wanted to hug her, and her heart melted.

"Go on home, Peter. It's too dark and too cold to be out like this."

He went down the steps and put his foot into the stirrup before pulling himself into the saddle. "Denki, Lena."

The trap set before her was clearly marked. "You're welcome, Peter."

❦

Deborah stood at the window in the dark living room, watching the street. Mahlon had asked for a few days. It'd been twelve. And he wanted more. She'd spoken to him twice. Each time hadn't been for more than thirty minutes—once when she took out the garbage late one night and once when she was feeding Rosie.

At least now she knew a few more things about him. He drove huge trucks across the States. He sincerely regretted giving in to his confusion and running off. And when not hauling, as he called it, he obviously spent his time watching the house. It unnerved her, and she avoided going out at night.

Since his first appearance, she'd felt every emotion over and over throughout each day—anger, resentment, confusion, compassion, and traces of desire. What she'd like to do is jerk him up by the collar and shout at him until he felt some of what he'd dumped on her.

The stairs creaked, and she jolted. Through the dark silence, Cara studied her. "Waiting for Mahlon to show?"

"I... You know?"

"He startled me one night when I'd gone to the barn for a drop cloth. He thought I was you."

"It's not what you think."

"Oh, I bet it's close enough."

"You can't be mad at me about this. You're the one who said I should compare."

Cara sat on the steps. "Do you have any idea what kind of a game he's pulled you into?"

Game?

She looked out the window. The moon dimly lit the yard, and memories of the hard work and successful nights of Ada's House seemed less of a victory now.

"It's not a game. Not for him or me."

"Can you at least admit what you're doing is dishonest?"

Deborah released the curtain and went to the foot of the steps. "He's a truck driver now. Aside from that, I don't even know what he's been doing since he left. Why did he leave? Why is he coming back? I don't want the answers he can give for Ada's sake or anyone else's. I need to know the truth of it for me."

"All reasonable things you could find out without sneaking around."

"I...I need this, Cara. Without pressure. Ephraim gave you time to figure things out. I just need a little time. Everybody has an opinion about Mahlon. They always did. I just want to think without anyone else's opinion crowding in. Surely you get that."

Cara sighed, and Deborah was confident she'd rolled her eyes too. Odd and infuriating as it was, Deborah still had feelings for him. But she couldn't decide if they were real or if they were a fantasy left over from her days of wanting to be his wife and bear his children. What kind of man joined the faith and then left, only to return? From the moment she saw him again, the questions looped together inside her, repeating endlessly, and occasionally a new one would join in, but she had no answers.

"And…and you know how hard it is to live this life. Maybe he…he just thought he wanted something else and then realized he didn't. You don't know. I don't know. But I *need* to find out."

Cara patted the step beside her, and Deborah sat down.

She put her arm around Deborah's shoulder and pulled her close. "Just do me one favor. Don't confuse rescuing love for the marrying kind of love."

Cara's words unleashed years of memories, all telling Deborah the real story. Sketches of her life with Mahlon since they were children connected inside her, clearing away the fog. She saw herself. She saw Mahlon. And she began to understand.

Tears filled her eyes, and peace eased the tightness in her chest. "I think maybe I do know him after all—at least some things about him."

Cara squeezed her shoulder, saying nothing.

Forgiveness slowly scrubbed the anger and confusion from her. "He needs me."

"Yeah, but what do you need?"

"To see Mahlon and talk, I think."

She just needed to leave a message for him at the Family Restaurant and arrange a meeting.

Twenty-Five

While Grey led his horse into Allen's barn, Ivan ran into the house. Grey took a deep breath. A hint of spring floated on the icy air as the sun began to set. The winter nights weren't as dark or as long or as cold as they had been. Patches of snow still lay on the ground, but spring would officially begin next week.

He'd survived winter. There were times when he could sense hope inside him, growing new roots and telling him he had a future. As he tossed some hay in a trough, he heard a noise as if a bucket had been knocked over.

"Hello?" He studied the dark barn. A shadowy figure darted out the side door. Grey hurried outside. A man, maybe Amish, clutched the mane of his horse, mounted it bareback, and took off. He returned to the barn, lit a kerosene lamp, and looked around. Nothing appeared to be missing, and there were no signs that the man had intended to set a fire. Feeling satisfied the person hadn't caused any harm, he put out the lamp and left.

As he approached Allen's house, Ivan appeared in the doorway, excitedly telling him Lena was here.

He didn't know why Ivan sounded so surprised. With Emily expecting a fifth child, Lennie had been here to help her most Saturday nights since Christmas. Lennie added her own flavor of pleasure to an evening.

He stepped inside. Allen smiled. "Glad you're here. I was going to come by your place in a bit."

Grey removed his coat and hat and hung them next to Ivan's. He'd tell Allen what he just saw when the two of them were alone. Lennie sat at the game table, surrounded by two nieces and two nephews. Allen's wife had a smile on her face, looking more energetic than she had in a while despite her due date being in two or three weeks. Ivan stood next to Lennie, studying small cards that were turned facedown on the table. They were playing the Memory Game.

Grey talked with Allen about the weather, planting spring crops, and business at the cabinetry shop. Ivan chose a card, glanced at it, and then picked up another one. He then passed them both to Lennie.

She giggled and tussled his hair. "You are too good at this."

Lennie glanced at Grey for the first time since he'd arrived. Her eyes held that familiar warmth, but she said nothing. He took a seat in the living room, choosing the chair that faced the children's game table. Allen grabbed the newspaper and sat on the couch.

"I'm planning a hunt. Care to go?" Allen asked.

"When?"

"Thought we'd leave this coming Wednesday and come home Saturday. I contacted Dugger earlier in the week to see if he has an empty cabin we can rent, and he does."

"I'll see if Ivan can stay with Mamm for those few days and let you know."

Rounds of applause came from the children's table. Lennie received several hugs before the children took off for the stairs. She remained there, turning the cards facedown. "You didn't even ask him what you'll be hunting."

Lennie didn't look up, but Grey knew she was speaking to him. "It's bird-hunting season. Does it matter the type?"

Her eyes moved to him, shining like emeralds in the glow of the kerosene lamp. "Don't bring back any quail."

"You don't like them?"

"I love quail."

Allen raised one eyebrow before opening his newspaper, looking determined to stay out of this conversation.

Realizing where this conversation was headed, Grey moved to a chair across from her. "So if you like them so much, we need to shoot 'em and bring 'em home to be cooked, canned, or frozen, right?" With the face of the small cards against the tabletop, he shifted them around until she had no idea what was where. She added the last cards to the table, and they began a fresh game.

She picked up a card and tried to find its match. Then she laid both of them down again. "If you shoot a quail, I'll…" She took another card, only this time she found its match, so she took another turn.

When it was his turn, he flipped over a card and then chose another one. "You'll what? Oh, wait. I've got it. You'll throw cake at me or make me ride for two hours in the freezing temps so I can do a favor for you."

"Have you ever listened to a quail?" She picked two cards, but they didn't match.

"It's hard to avoid hearing them in these parts." He lifted a card.

"They are a beautiful-sounding bird."

"Ya, but they're still just birds. They taste good too." He found its match and set it beside him.

"If you listen to a bobwhite, its melody might take you places without you ever leaving your yard."

"It's a bird, Lennie."

She gave a half shrug while winning several more cards.

"Are you actually serious?" He matched three sets before she took another turn.

"I can't imagine picking up a gun to kill anything, so my opinion isn't worth much to a hunter, but it's how I feel."

"How come I never knew this bothered you?"

She studied him, her eyes reflecting dozens of thoughts. "I began feeding quail a couple of years back, and then I saw one that had been shot but wasn't dead." She shuddered.

"Do you still capture critters that have worked their way into your house and release them outside?"

"Maybe."

He laughed and leaned the chair back on two legs. "Allen, we're going pheasant hunting." He lowered his chair. "Of course this means we need a bird dog. Can we borrow Nicky?"

"She's more of a butterfly dog."

"And you let her engage in that activity?"

She shrugged. "Not when I can stop it."

Allen folded the newspaper and tapped it against his leg. "Dugger has a bird dog we can use." Allen tossed the paper on the couch. "You can't listen to my sister, or we'd all be vegetarians."

Lennie clicked her tongue. "Or we could wait on you to fix a meal and starve to death."

Grey laughed. "So we won't go quail hunting. But, Lennie, you do know this means you have to clean and pluck the pheasants as a trade-off."

She won the last few rounds and tossed the cards onto the table in front of him. "If I was any good at plucking feathers off something, I'd have done it to Allen long ago."

He chuckled. "One minute she's sweet, and the next she's sassy as everything."

She stood. "One minute I was asking a favor, and the next I had what I wanted." She gave an evil laugh, then looked at the stairway. "I promised the young uns a game of indoor freeze tag."

When she was out of hearing range, Grey turned back to Allen. "Is she serious about the quail, or have I just been had—Lennie style?"

"I was only half listening and not watching her at all, so I don't know."

"Has she been feeding quail?"

Allen shrugged. "Not a clue. But if she has, we should find out where. Those will be some nice plump quail." Allen smiled. "Wouldn't she love that?"

"Listen." Grey lowered his voice. "There was a man in your barn when I put my horse up."

"A man? Any idea who?"

"None. He caught a glimpse of me and ran. Had a horse waiting near the barn."

Emily walked into the living room, drying her hands on a kitchen towel. She sat down and put her very swollen feet on the coffee table.

He and Allen dropped their discussion, and the conversation among the three of them ambled onto a dozen different topics as the children ran in and out of the room.

Emily held her hand out in front of her. Allen stood, took her by the hand, and gently helped her up. She whispered something to him before leaving the room, and he smiled.

Allen sat. "I'll keep an eye out, and if I see any signs of someone hanging around, I'll tell Emily. You haven't heard news about any trouble, have you?"

"No."

"The midwife gave Emily a cell phone last week in case she goes into labor."

"And you're planning a hunting trip?"

"She's yet to go into labor before her due date, but since you saw someone lurking around, I'm not going anywhere until I'm certain he's long, long gone."

🌿

Dwayne rode the horse hard for nearly a mile before he slowed. He struggled a bit to catch a decent breath. Grey had messed up everything.

Dwayne could've made the whole thing look like an out of control horse did the job. Lena finally had gone somewhere without that stupid dog of hers. He could have got her tonight, but then Grey showed up. Dwayne couldn't catch her in her own barn. When she drove a rig, her Daed hitched it for her in the mornings and brought it around to the front of the house. And he met her in the evenings when she arrived home. She arrived at school alone, but the lean-to stood open toward the road. That could mean witnesses.

Her brother's barn seemed perfect, and finally she didn't have the mutt with her. But Allen had come outside to meet her when she arrived. What was it with these men in her life? They treated her better than most dogs. It didn't make sense. Couldn't they see that God Himself hated her?

And she had no right to steal Peter's loyalty. None. He hated her so much he wanted to kill her now and be done with her.

All he had to do was find the right place and the right time.

Twenty-Six

Grey and Allen had talked for nearly an hour uninterrupted by children, who were upstairs with Lennie and Emily. That tended to be unusual, and Grey wondered if he should go up and see if he needed to rescue either or both of them.

Allen stretched and yawned. "I'm hoping Lennie and Emily come down and we play games soon. If I don't win a few rounds of spoons against Lennie tonight, I have to mow her grass all summer."

"I can't believe you bet against your sister, knowing she rarely loses at spoons. You're not as smart as I thought you were."

"You know, you've made that statement about me throughout most of my life. Seems like I'd hit bottom at some point and you couldn't think of me as any less smart."

"You're right." Grey chuckled. "I won't be caught thinking too highly of you again, no matter how low that is."

Bumps from upstairs rattled the ceiling as the children ran across the wooden floor. Bursts of laughter filtered down the stairway. As bedtime approached, Lennie had to be ready for one less child to be under her care, so he should get Ivan and head home. Normally, the adults took turns looking after the little ones, but for some reason she hadn't come back down.

Grey stood. "I need to go on home."

"No, stay," Allen said. "All you're going to do is tuck Ivan in and sit around by yourself. Let Ivan go to bed here. He can sleep over, and you can go home when we're finished winning against Lennie. I do not want to mow her yard all summer."

When he heard Lennie trying to settle the children down, he moved to the foot of the steps and hollered for Ivan. His son peeped over the railing, and Grey told him they needed to head for home in five minutes. Ivan nodded and then disappeared. Grey knew what would happen next. The boys would go in a bedroom and play very, very quietly in hopes of extending the visit. "Lennie?" Grey called.

"Ya."

"You need a hand?"

She came to the top of the stairs, carrying a suitcase.

"Maybe I should have offered to help sooner. You running away?"

She tossed the bag to him. It didn't have much in it, but it wasn't empty. Emily waddled onto the landing with her hands on the lower part of her back. Lennie helped her ease down the steps. Lurking strangers or not, Allen wouldn't be going hunting next week.

"Oh, Allen," Lennie sang softly once at the foot of the stairs. "Guess where you're going tonight."

Allen studied Emily. She shrugged. "My water broke. I called the midwife. She's got two others in labor, so she can't come here tonight. We're supposed to meet her at the clinic."

Allen stood. "You have yet to go into labor during the day."

"Are you complaining to the woman who's in labor?" Emily rubbed her lower back.

Grey chuckled. "The man's never as smart as he should be, Emily."

Lennie headed for the door. "I'll get the carriage."

"No." Allen hurried ahead of her. "I'll get it. Grey, you'll stay tonight and give Lennie a hand?"

"Ya, no problem."

Lennie looked at him and raised an eyebrow, but just as she opened her mouth to speak, a bump from upstairs vibrated the room. She took off even before the child let out a yelp. "I got it. We're fine. Go have a baby."

Emily chuckled. "Those children went wild with excitement when they saw my suitcase. I might just have an easier night of it than your sister will."

"Good. Serves her right." Allen winked at his wife.

Grey walked out with them and helped Emily get into the buggy. Once they were on their way, he went back inside. Lennie sat on the couch, reading to the children. All of Allen's children were dressed for bed. He assumed she'd done that earlier, unless she had a bit of a magician in her.

Ivan glanced up and then down again, clearly hoping his Daed wouldn't tell him it was time to leave. Grey took a seat and read the newspaper. The sense of belonging and friendship surrounded him, and he realized afresh all that he had to be thankful for.

Nearly an hour later he laid the newspaper in his lap. Lennie's reading had done its job. The children were relaxed and sleepy. Snuggled against Lennie, Phoebe had already fallen asleep. When Lennie closed the book, he moved to the couch and lifted Phoebe. Lennie put her index finger over her mouth, picked up little David, and motioned for the other children to follow her. Grey walked up the stairs behind them, enjoying the hushed serenity that now filled the home. Lennie went into the boys' room, and he walked into the girls' room. A kerosene lantern from inside the playroom gave off enough light so he could navigate around the strewn toys and books. Emily wasn't a fussbudget about tidiness. Her energy went into feeding and caring for her growing brood, not picking up toys. Six-year-old Katie crawled into the regular-sized bed. Grey pushed the covers back and slid Phoebe into the bed next to her sister.

"You'll leave a light on?" Katie mumbled as she rubbed her eyes.

"Ya." Grey went into the adjoining playroom and got the kerosene lantern. He turned the wick to its shortest length, causing the flame to barely give off light. Before leaving the room, he noticed a small circle of red tape on the floor. A doll sat in the center of it, holding a small piece of paper.

He moved to the night-light shelf in the girls' room and set the lamp on it. As he stepped out of their room, Lennie came out of the boys' room. "Ivan put on a pair of pajamas belonging to Amos, and all three boys are asleep."

"Time to relax." Grey motioned for her to go down the stairs ahead of him. The wooden steps creaked, reminding him of the age of this homestead. Grey had built his own place, but Allen had inherited his from a grandparent, who'd inherited it from a grandparent. A lot of family life had taken place here, and he wondered if any of them had dealt with as much marital unhappiness as he and Elsie had.

Another shard of isolation gouged at him. It never seemed to end. He'd once stood on a piece of earth by himself, able to see Elsie across a canyon, but he couldn't reach her. The sense of loneliness felt unbearable, but they could see each other, sometimes catch a few words as they yelled back and forth, and he always kept a smidgen of hope that he could build a bridge and cross over.

Lennie held a steamy cup of hot chocolate out to him. He took the cup, trying to clear his mind.

With a mug in hand, Lennie took a seat at the kitchen table. "You didn't stay tonight because I can't handle four children on my own."

Mulling over what to say, he sat down across from her. "No, but an extra pair of hands isn't such a bad thing, right?"

She raised an eyebrow while stirring her drink. "I'm the girl who helped replant the begonias, remember?"

Hiding a smile, he took a sip from his mug. "I was twelve, and it was a pop fly, bottom of the ninth, last out, and I caught it. Do you know what that means?"

"Ya, it means you ruined part of my mother's flower garden and

needed my help. We replanted that section with the same type and color
of begonias from Mamm's greenhouse." She tapped the spoon on the rim
of her mug before laying the utensil on the table. "You and I have a long
and odd relationship, ya? Sometimes I was the tagalong sister. Sometimes
the tattletale. Sometimes the confidante. Through it all you and I were
friends...with or without Allen. And I'd like to know why you've stayed
tonight."

As memories of good times eased his sadness, he realized anew how
much fun they'd had. Lennie had always mattered, and once she got past
the tattletale age, he'd never regretted letting her in on secrets.

She took a sip and licked the chocolate drink off her lips. "I don't need
a big brother. You miss Elsie, and I...miss Jonathan. And even though
those relationships don't begin to compare, because Elsie was your other
half, and Jonathan...well...he'll be someone else's other half eventually, we
both are feeling a little lost."

Jonathan not being around was probably another reason she'd spent
so many Saturday nights in the last few months helping her sister-in-law,
although she might have always spent Saturday nights with Allen and
Emily. He didn't know.

Grey turned the mug around and around, remembering parts of their
childhood and adolescent years. "Did you ever tell Allen about our conversation before you decided to go to public school?"

With the cup halfway to her lips, she paused. "You and he are still
friends, aren't you?"

Grey chuckled. He'd been nineteen and Lennie just fourteen when
they sat on her porch swing and talked for hours as she mulled over the
idea of attending public school. No one in her family, or in the district for
that matter, liked the idea. He'd sided with her on the topic. Right now,
she wanted that kind of honesty and friendship again. "I saw a man in the
barn when putting my horse in. He ran away, and it's probably nothing."

"Any idea who?"

"No."

"Why would anybody be hiding out in a barn and then run off?"

"I don't know. Why does anyone hide anywhere?"

"I didn't know people hid."

"Sure we do." He stared at the ripples of chocolate mixture in his cup. "People are good at hiding. Some run off. Some close themselves up in a room inside their own house. Some look right at folks while concealing who they really are." When he looked up, she seemed to be puzzled at the turn of the conversation, but he longed to tell her the truth. "I...I fall into that third category." He wanted to confess more than just his hypocrisy, but he couldn't make himself say anything else.

The serenity radiating from Lennie felt like a warm, inviting kitchen during a snowstorm. "Now that you've worded it that way, I can see where I hide things too. We certainly don't tell other people all that we're think-ing or feeling, do we?"

"No."

"I'm going to say something here because, like it or not, it needs to be said, okay?"

"I'm sure I've said worse things to myself already."

"Ya, me too." She paused. "If Elsie were here and you'd been the one to die, would she be free of guilt?"

Her words smashed against his guilty conscience.

Lennie brushed imaginary crumbs from the table as if unable to look at him while chipping away at who he'd become—a man encased in guilt. He'd been the head of his household, and what took place there could not be blamed on anyone else. Elsie had been at fault too, but it'd been his place to make everything right, and he hadn't.

Lennie raised her eyes to meet his. "Would you want her blaming herself like this?"

It hurt to think of Elsie having to survive her part in their unsuccess-ful marriage. He shook his head. But an unmarried person could never understand the confusing, complex relationship between a husband and wife. Until he lived it year after year, he never knew of the silent unity and the silent hostilities between couples. Vows were made in the presence of loved ones, and although no one warned them, they began a journey of expectations, disappointments, misunderstanding, and in his case…rejection while closeness slowly faded, leaving emptiness in its stead.

Unsure how honest to be, Grey searched for the right words. "You can't understand, and you shouldn't, not yet anyway…maybe not ever."

She angled her head, looking confident in her stand. "If I had done exactly as you have, would you want me pressured with the weight of this responsibility, or would you want me to let myself be free?"

He stared at her, unable to respond. Thinking about Lennie being under his same guilt, he gained some much needed balance.

She placed her hand over his. "If you'd want Elsie set free from her shortcomings and wrongs, then free yourself."

Getting complete freedom from his past wasn't as easy as making a decision. He nodded and cleared his throat, ready to change the subject. "Ephraim's hired a new man from Ohio. He starts next week."

She went to the stove and poured fresh hot chocolate into her mug. "Ya? Why's that?"

"Lots of reasons. Business is good. We never replaced Mahlon. As Ivan's only parent, I'm not willing to travel out of town much or work as many hours as I had been, not for the next couple of years."

"Makes sense. Have you met the man?"

"Ya. His name is Christian Miller. He arrived yesterday. Seems to be a nice guy. Single. He's about your age. Does good work. He'll live with the Benders until he can afford something on his own."

"The Benders? Does he know them?"

"I wondered the same thing, so I asked. Dwayne's Mamm and Christian's Mamm have a mutual friend, but until he arrived here, he'd never met the Benders personally."

He saw an unusual look in Lennie's eyes, and he wondered if she was interested in meeting Christian. Each spring Lennie organized an annual Picnic Basket Auction. Not only did it make extra funds for the school, but single couples throughout many districts had met during these functions. In the past Jonathan or a relative of hers bought Lennie's basket, which meant the two would go on a picnic together alone. With Jonathan seeing Deborah, maybe Grey should nudge Christian to bid on Lennie's basket. The idea didn't sit well—probably because he didn't know Christian and also because he didn't want to lose his and Lennie's free time together. Every time he was with her, she made life's burdens seem less heavy.

He took a drink of his hot chocolate. "You planning another auction this year?"

She shifted, looking uncomfortable. "I...I...ya. It's been in the works since fall, so I'll have it."

"You sound unsure."

She shrugged. "Odd year all the way around, I guess. But the classroom needs some items, like the ceiling-to-floor quality relief map and a battery-operated globe with an inner light that I've had my eye on for a few years now." She went to the game table and picked up the box of checkers. "I'm better at this than I used to be."

"Well I certainly hope so. You were what—fourteen the last time we played?"

"Sixteen, thank you very much." She mocked the words he'd said to her three months back.

"Hey, Lennie, what is that red circle of tape in the playroom?"

"Ah, it's part of the Circle of Peace game."

"What's that?"

She set the box on the table and opened it. "It's a game of truth telling. The person who steps inside it must only do so because they want to. No one can put someone there, but they can ask the person if they're willing.

By stepping inside, you're saying you trust the outcome is worth facing the dark parts of yourself."

"Who would want to play such a game?"

"Children who've lied but wish they were free to tell the truth. It's a safe place, because the one listening has agreed to forgive, keep the incident private, and help the person not need to lie next time."

"No wonder it's in the playroom. Only children would play that."

"You think?" Her brows tightened while she held his gaze. "Surely everyone needs to step inside a circle of peace at some point. I know I do. Even when telling the absolute truth, sometimes I later realize I'd been lying to myself."

She seemed to have no concept of the deceit that could take place between people. He hadn't known of such dishonesty either until he found himself caught in it. But if he'd voluntarily stood inside that circle, Elsie would not have listened. And he couldn't have made her tell the truth, circle or not. Once again he realized he'd taken on too much blame for what had taken place inside his home.

He opened the box of checkers. "Red or black?"

Twenty-Seven

Trying to remember all the right steps again, Cara hitched Rosie to the carriage, glad the old horse was back in good form. Birds flittered among the bare tree branches, singing loudly and exclaiming in their own way that spring had finally arrived.

"Just us, huh, Mom?" Lori stepped from one bale of hay to the next.

She and Lori had their coats buttoned tight and gloves on, but with April arriving in two days, the sunny skies and midforty temps had most folks moving about freely again.

"Yes, sweetie, this trip is just for us."

" 'Cause we're gonna talk. Right?"

"Yes." If Cara had known her daughter would get so excited to travel with just her, she'd have done it sooner.

"And we're gonna surprise 'From."

"I think so."

He might not be fully surprised since it was a Friday afternoon and he had to work late. She'd gone to see him a few times in the past when this happened. But she had packed her and Lori an overnight bag, so that would surprise him. Although she wasn't sure where they'd stay. Maybe his place and he could spend the night at his Daed's.

"I brought my story to show him, the one the teacher gave me an A plus on *and* a smiley face."

Cara chuckled. Teachers had so much power over children, and Cara didn't regret letting Lori leave public school to begin at the local Amish school. "Okay, grab your stuff and hop in."

Lori quickly did so, and they were on their way. Lori loved her Amish school and friends. But after being raised a New Yorker and now living among the Amish, her daughter didn't really fit in anywhere.

Neither did Cara, but she was a big girl and used to never fitting in. After her mother died and she entered foster care, she'd been treated like she had leprosy by a lot of the children at school. Even in foster care most of the kids had siblings they went to school with, and they stuck together. She'd slowly grown to despise those who had someone around with the same DNA. It seemed to be an invisible bond that everyone shared with someone—everyone but her.

Truth was, that's why she'd avoided connecting with her mama's family. They all had each other, and her insecurity kept stirring old resentments and fears. She hadn't known that, not until she read a passage in her mother's Bible this morning. Something about…it is not the natural children who are God's children, but it is the children of the promise who are…

It made her realize that, in a way, she was a promise to her mother's family. Her mother had promised to bring her back so her great-grandmother could raise her. Her mama died before that happened, but Ada had been praying for Cara all these years, and a hidden message inside Cara's mother's journal led her here. That was a promise of sorts, wasn't it? And God's promise to accept all those who came to Him also made her a part of this family—a quirky family to be sure with their strict codes of behavior and dress, but they were her family, and she was theirs.

"Lori, honey, remember when you were drawing in my mother's diary and discovered the name Dry Lake, Pennsylvania, had been written in it invisibly?"

She nodded. "We were at that bus station, and I sketched over a blank spot, and an address showed up."

"Yes, that's right. It led us here, and at first we lived in that barn."

"That's where I got Better Days. He was so small and furry and got milk from his mom. Remember?"

"Yes." The thought of it made her eyes burn with tears. God had been so faithful to lead them out of a stalker's grip and into Ephraim's arms—but it'd been a rough journey. "My mom used to live in Dry Lake."

"She did?"

"Yes, and she had brothers, several of them."

"Ephraim's got sisters, more than several."

"My mom's brothers are my uncles and your great-uncles." Cara began trying to piece things together for Lori. Until recently, as long as Lori had food and her mom, she took life as it came. Maybe that was Cara's fault, always running from a stalker and never able to tell her daughter why they had to uproot in the middle of the night or why she had to constantly change jobs and move to a worse apartment than the one before. Or maybe it was a blessing from God, one that had made Cara's life bearable.

She took the long route to Ephraim's so she could go up his lengthy back driveway. She looked down at her daughter, still too young to understand the complexities of family, but now Lori knew they had some roots. And Cara had been the one to tell her, not anyone else in the community. For all the frustrating rules of the Amish, she loved the heart of her people—most of them, anyway.

Her people.

Once on Ephraim's dirt drive, she brought the rig to a stop. "Do you want to drive the rig to Ephraim's?"

"Ya!"

Cara passed her the reins. The fields on each side of them were brown with a few patches of snow still clinging to the earth. An amber and purple glow covered them like a dome as the sun moved toward the horizon. Crows squawked while digging at dried vegetation. Gratefulness kept filling her until she felt like she might pop.

"Pull the reins back gently and say 'whoa.'"

Lori did as she said, tossed the reins at her the moment the horse stopped, and jumped down. "'From!" Her daughter took off running. "I drove the buggy!"

Ephraim came out of the shop and caught Lori before she plowed into him. He swung her through the air, and she was on his hip, deep in conversation, by the time Cara had hitched the horse to a post and walked to them.

Lori brushed wisps of loose hair from her face. "And I got aunts and uncles, my mom said."

"Ya, you do." Ephraim kissed Lori's cheek and put her down. He moved to Cara and engulfed her in a hug. He didn't soon let go either, and Cara knew he'd been waiting for this. He drew a deep breath. "I love you."

"Well, duh." She took a step back. "We got a few things to get straight, mister."

He laughed. "*You* are going to straighten *me* out on something? This I gotta hear."

She walked into the shop. "What's your favorite tool?"

"Why?"

"Don't ask questions. Just answer."

"It's hard to choose, but I guess the table saw."

"Show me."

He walked over to it.

"It's not a hand-held thing."

"Thus the name table saw. You're not going to try to teach me how to use it, are you?"

"Shut up, 'From, and tell me how it works."

"It runs off an air compressor, which is run by a battery-operated generator."

"If you had to give it up for me, would you?"

"Ya."

"Would you miss it?"

"Ya."

"Would you return to it and lose me in the process?"

"No."

"Would knowing that keep you from missing it?"

"You and leaving your ways is not even comparable."

"Yes it is." She grabbed him by the suspenders. "I'm always going to miss some things about my previous life, but I've made my decision, and you can't keep doubting me because I like talking to Englischers about television or music…or, in words you understand, talking to them about how much I used to enjoy my table saw and what all they're making with their table saws."

"I don't like this parallel at all. If Englischers have and use table saws like they have and use televisions, I'll be run out of business."

She laughed. "I believe this is where God intended me to be. I'm not messing that up for anything *draus in da Welt.*"

"Out in the world." His smile seemed never ending. "Very good, Cara."

"'From?'" She tugged on his suspenders.

"Ya?"

"Stop doubting where I'll land. I've landed. I have a lot more adjustments to make, but I'll make them."

"Yes ma'am."

"Now shut up and kiss me."

"Yes ma'am."

"Eeeew." Lori screeched and covered her eyes.

❦

Wearing the silky pajamas and housecoat Samantha had given her, Lena put the muffin tins in the sink to soak. As much as she loved teaching, she loved Saturdays and the freedom to start the day slowly and ease into it. She'd find a school district that would hire her, and she'd keep right on doing what she did best: teach. She'd made some mistakes. Who hadn't? But the complainers wanted something even they couldn't offer—exactness in all things all the time.

Her Daed stood. "Those were good muffins, Lena. Denki. I'm going out to get started."

She dried her hands and followed him out of the kitchen. He stopped at the coatrack and grabbed his straw hat. "You got plans for this morning?"

Lena slowly climbed the stairway. "Getting dressed, which I'm about to do, and then whiling away the hours like a single working woman should."

"You, dressed soon after dawn on a Saturday? I need to write this down in my journal." He smiled broadly and left the house.

Lena went to her room and slid out of her housecoat. The fleece throw blanket on her hope chest tempted her to wrap up in it and get a second cup of coffee. The wonderful thing about Saturday mornings was they were most often hers to do as she wanted. She grabbed the blanket, her Bible, the auction notebook, and a pen before heading back down the stairs.

She spread the stuff on the table, got another muffin and a cup of coffee, and relaxed against the kitchen chair. Wrapped in the fleece blanket, Lena opened her Bible.

She'd never enjoyed her weekends as much as she had recently. Not only did she have a new, two-week-old niece to adore; she had a good reason for spending a lot of time at Allen's. Helping Emily as much as possible after each birth was part of her life. And she stayed with her sisters and other sisters-in-law after they'd given birth too. But this time it'd become an unexpected pleasure. A fair amount of the evenings, Grey arrived in time for dinner, let Ivan go to sleep with Allen's children, and stayed until after midnight, playing games. Allen and Emily's enjoyment in his company ran deep. She'd been tempted numerous times to talk to him about the board's decision to let her go, but she hadn't. He didn't know about it, or he'd have apologized for their decision. But if Michael didn't want to burden Grey with the matter, she would respect that.

She tried to clear her mind of thoughts of Grey and focus on prayer and the Word. After a little while she nudged the open Bible to the side and grabbed the notebook for the auction. Trying to concentrate on her organizational lists spread out on the table was quite difficult. Grey filled her mind—his voice, eyes, sincerity, and even his rare grin. He was the only man she'd given ample opportunities to consider her, but he never did. When she'd gone to him to talk about attending public school, she'd hoped he would say, *Go, and when you're done, you'll be of a good age, and I'll be here waiting.* But he never showed an ounce of interest, not the romantic kind.

She traced her birthmark, wondering how he really saw her. He was past feeling sorry for her as he did when they were children, wasn't he? And what did he mean when he said he hid things while boldly looking at people? What would he have to hide, except his true thoughts concerning how he perceived people?

The question stung, especially since everything about him drew her. Would he ever see her as more than a friend? To marry a man like Grey would make up for all her years alone and be worth every unkind whisper she'd overheard about her being an old maid. Marriage happened young for Amish women. And courting even younger. If Grey slowly grew to love her, she might be twenty-eight or thirty before they were married. That'd be quite a wait, and she had no doubt that he would be well worth it, but could he ever care for her in that way?

That thought skewered her heart. She grabbed the bottle of her favorite lotion off the middle of the table and put a dollop in her hand. The creamy texture carried a mix of fragrant flowers as she spread it over her bare arms and hands. She drew a deep breath and tried to focus on the upcoming Picnic Basket Auction. She had to get her feelings for Grey in perspective. But it seemed that after all her years of pooling the love in her heart, waiting for a man to give it to, she now had no say over how she felt. He'd unknowingly opened the floodgates.

Elsie's rare quietness, beauty, and poise held Grey captive. When he could get past that loss, he might see that Lena had other things to offer, good and valuable things—like a powerful friendship, lots of laughter, and children. Years ago, before he married, Grey had said he wanted a lot of children. For whatever reason, Elsie only gave birth twice.

Since Lena wasn't graceful or gorgeous like Elsie, and Grey would always love Elsie more than her, maybe God would bless them in different ways, like them having a large and strong family. In her mind's eye, she could see his blue eyes and the joy she could bring to him—if he'd give her a chance.

Twenty-Eight

The new worker at the cabinetry shop, Christian, helped Grey load the buckboard with wood to take to Lennie's. April began tomorrow, and the warmth of spring had melted most of the snow. When Grey's Mamm asked to take Ivan to Lancaster for the day, Grey said yes, and he intended to use this free Saturday to make the window boxes he'd promised Lennie.

"Denki, Christian. I didn't realize you'd be here on a Saturday."

"Ya, me either." Christian's toothy grin came just short of laughter. "But Dwayne wanted to see inside the place, so I brought him over. What project are you working on today?"

"Just keeping a promise to the schoolteacher." Grey glanced toward the cabinetry shop, making sure Dwayne was still milling about inside. "Have you met Lena Kauffman yet?"

"I might have. I've met a lot of people in the two weeks I've been here."

"She's the schoolteacher."

Christian's brows knit. "Don't recall—"

Dwayne barreled out of the shop. "Sure you do," he said as if he'd been eavesdropping. "You saw her at church Sunday before last. The one with the stain on her face."

Christian looked at Grey and shook his head at Dwayne's crassness. "Ya. I talked to her for a spell. She's witty and nice looking."

Dwayne looked as if he'd just swallowed bad milk. "Are you crazy? She's not..." He stopped and then huffed. "Whatever."

"Her name is Lena." Grey slid another board into the wagon. "And as the local schoolteacher, she has a picnic basket auction every year. Single men bid on baskets filled with goods single women have made. Of course married women make baskets too, but only relatives—mostly husbands and children—bid on those."

"You're telling me she's not seeing anyone special?" Christian looked very interested in what he'd just learned.

"No," Grey answered, feeling unease grab his gut. Christian had been working with him and Ephraim for two weeks. Grey liked the man, and he'd thought about mentioning this to him before, but he kept getting a catch in his gut. He just figured he needed to know him better first. Today, as Grey looked forward to seeing Lennie, he'd wanted to ease some of her loneliness for Jonathan, but right now he wished he hadn't opened his mouth.

"So"—Christian closed the tailgate to the buckboard and fastened one side—"I could go to this auction, and if I won the bid on her basket, she and I could go on a date?"

"Ya." Grey fastened his side of the tailgate.

Dwayne crossed his arms. "You picking Christian out for her, or do you go around encouraging all the single guys to give her a chance?"

Grey had started this conversation at a really bad time. *If* he should've started it at all, he shouldn't have done so with Dwayne around. "I'm not picking anyone out. I just thought I'd mention the auction to the local newcomer."

Christian stayed focused on Grey. "She hasn't been to any singings since I've been here, 'cause I looked. So I figured she was taken."

Dwayne spat on the ground. "If you'd asked me, I'd told ya to..." He caught Grey's eye and then shrugged. "Never mind."

Grey didn't know what unkind remark Dwayne was going to say, but he had no more respect for Lennie than Peter did. Grey found it encouraging that Christian wasn't bothered one bit by what Dwayne thought.

Christian shifted, turning his back on Dwayne. "When is this picnic auction?"

With the rig loaded, Grey climbed up and took the reins in hand. Regardless of how he felt about starting this conversation, he couldn't undo what he'd begun. "The third Saturday in April."

Christian nodded. "In three weeks. Denki."

Grey slapped the reins without responding. The sick feeling in his gut didn't ease as he drove toward Lennie's, but he couldn't come up with what bothered him so much. It felt like jealousy, but that made no sense whatsoever. He pulled into her driveway and saw Israel in the side yard, applying stain to a freshly made coatrack. He hopped down and went to him. Lennie's dog came up to him, wagging her tail. He petted her. "Morning, Israel."

"Grey, what brings you out this way?"

"Mamm's got Ivan busy for today, so I'm using this time to keep a promise I made last fall. Lennie did some work for me in exchange for me making and mounting window boxes."

"You know, I remember her asking me to make her some of those a few years back." He chuckled. "I guess she gave up on me and came up with a new plan. She's inside somewhere. Go right on in. If you don't see her, just holler for her."

Grey went to the front door, tapped on it, and walked inside. He heard what sounded like a coffee cup chink against a plate in the kitchen, so he walked that way. When he caught a glimpse of Lennie, he stopped cold. The image engraved itself on his heart. Her long chestnut hair flowed. A fleece blanket had fallen off one shoulder, revealing a thin, bright pink strap and a lot of milky white skin. Clearly she hadn't dressed for the day, which meant she must still be in her sleeping clothes. He'd thought all Amish women wore white nightgowns from neck to ankle, but whatever she'd slept in, it wasn't a gown. Papers were spread out in front of her, and she had a pen in hand, looking every bit as gifted in intelligence as she was in beauty. Breakfast dishes and coffee cups still sat on the table.

Desire grabbed him. Lennie danced through him like she'd turned to vapor and entered his very being. How had he not realized what had been taking place within him since…since Christmas?

She took a deep breath and stretched, looking relaxed and absorbed in her own thoughts.

"Lennie."

She raised her eyes to his, and she seemed to awaken dreams he'd given up—dreams of unity, laughter, and hope with a woman. "Grey." Covering her bare shoulder with the blanket, she sat upright. "I…I didn't know you were coming."

He wrestled with guilt. What had he come here for, anyway—to build window boxes or to talk and laugh with Lennie? Right now, he knew the answer to that, but his wife had died in his arms not yet six months ago.

From her chair at the table, Lennie waved her hand. "Grey?"

He demanded his eyes move from her so that his lips could speak. "Uh, I…your Daed said for me to come in." He motioned toward the front door. "I brought the wood and saws to make window boxes."

"Ach, that's *wunderbaar*."

"Ya, I…I need to take measurements…of the window sashes."

"Sure. I'll get dressed. Have you eaten?"

He nodded.

"You can help yourself to a cup of coffee if you like. I'll just run upstairs."

When she stood, he noticed the long pink satiny pants peeking out from the wide gape in the blanket that ran down the front of her. She tugged at the fleece, trying to cover her immodesty. He lowered his head and stared at the floor as she hurried past him and up the stairs.

Her scent of lavender and roses and violets hung in the air. Trying to clear his head, he went outside and began unloading the wood. He wasn't ready to feel any sort of attraction for a woman. He had nothing left in him to give. Besides that, the feelings pouring into him were not who he and Lennie were. She'd been a constant in his life, but when did she seep past being a friend and sink into the deeper parts of his heart?

Thoughts of Elsie tore, and fear ate away. The idea of marriage terrified him. He never again wanted to give someone the power that came through the bonds of matrimony. But he hadn't known that until today. As hidden thoughts continued to reveal themselves, he understood one thing: he had nothing left to give to a marriage—the ideals of it, the struggles, the walls. He...couldn't.

Before he unloaded the last board, Lennie bounded out the front door—cape dress, black apron, and prayer Kapp in place. But none of that stopped his heart from pounding like crazy.

Nicky ran to her, and she knelt, patting her dog. "You might not know this because I kept it really quiet, but a couple of years back, right before school began, I injured my back and had to wear a plaster cast around my torso." She stood, looking rather serious. "It fit under my dress and wasn't noticeable at all. I had some tough eighth-grade students and wasn't sure how I'd corral them into being good for the year, especially since I couldn't move around too well. On that first day I had the windows and doors open, and a strong breeze kept flapping the ties to my prayer Kapp, so I took the stapler out and stapled the ties to my chest. Oddly enough, I had no trouble with discipline that year."

Grey held her gaze, feeling laughter stir as he watched humor dance in her eyes. "You're lying to me, Lennie Kauffman."

"Ya, but I made you smile." She interlaced her fingers and popped them.

He stared at her, awed at how she made him feel stronger than he was, rather than weaker. Surely she wanted no more from him than he could give—friendship. "You are something else."

"Ya, I am. So where do you want to start measuring first, upper-level windows or ground level?"

"I'm not very practiced at this, so let's start at the top. The extra distance will help hide the goof-ups from those looking at your home."

"Good thinking. Is that why my bedroom is on the top floor?"

He chuckled. The hours melted away too quickly as they worked together. She fixed them a quick lunch of leftovers from the night before, a beef stew and jalapeno cornbread, both of which were so good he asked for the recipe. Israel ate with them, and afterward he pitched in to help make window boxes. Grey wouldn't finish today, but a couple of hours next Saturday should do the trick. By evening they'd built, stained, and mounted six window planters. He still had to build two large ones for the front porch, but those would need extra care, so he'd get to them next week.

Lennie lined each wooden box with a mesh often used for screening porches. Then she passed him the stapler to secure them while she went to the greenhouse to get a bag of soil.

From inside the home at a ground-level window, he stapled the mesh in place.

Lennie came around the corner of the house. "Can you take this and fill them about three-fourths full of dirt?"

The top of her head was two feet below the bottom of the windowsill. He reached through the window, easily able to grab the top of the bag of soil as she held it up as high as she could. While he filled the box with dirt, she remained outside, using the squirt nozzle to pressure clean the screen that needed to go back in the window where he currently stood.

"Okay, these two are done." Grey shot one last staple into the mess. "Do you want us to put the screens back on now or wait until you've put flowers in them after the last frost?"

She gazed up at him, smudges of dirt on her face and stains on her dress and apron. Even with the heart of a woman, her countenance seemed like the carefree girl he'd always known her to be. "What's the prediction for the last frost this year?"

He set the bag of dirt in the windowsill and wiped his hands on his pants. "May fourth." Unable to see her, he leaned out the window. "Hey, where'd you…" His elbow knocked the bag of dirt over. He caught the bottom of it, but all that did was cause its contents to flow right on top of her.

She screamed. "Benjamin Graber, I'm telling!" She shook her head, dumping mounds of soil around her feet. He started laughing while she flapped her apron, ridding it of some dirt. She then used the underside of her apron to wipe off her face.

"Oh, ya, this is just really funny now." She glared at him. "You just wait until I tell." She cupped her hands around her mouth. "Daed!"

Her father came around the side of the house, took one glance at her, and applauded. She picked up the hose, wrapped her hands around the spray nozzle, and rotated it back and forth, pointing at her Daed and Grey.

Surely out of respect she wouldn't squirt her Daed, and Grey stood inside her home, with its polished floors, well-kept furniture, and white sheers, so he felt safe. "Ya? So just what are you going to—" Cold water smacked him in the face. While she continued soaking him, he slammed the window. She shifted and bombarded him from the next window right beside the first one. "Lennie!" Laughing too hard to catch his breath, he closed the next window.

The spray of water had caught potting soil off the top of the window planter and whisked it inside. Now soil and water covered a good bit of the floor, curtains, and cloth furniture. She stood outside with her hands on her hips and a thin layer of dark soil covering most of her. The waning rays of sunlight shone from behind her, making her appear to radiate white light. Those brief moments seemed to capture so many aspects of her nature—mischievous, playful, funny, innocent, and daring. "Never think you can predict a prankster, Grey," she yelled through the closed window.

Her Daed eased the hose from her and turned off the spigot. Grey opened the window.

"She has a motto." Israel studied his daughter, clearly amused. "I don't agree with it, but you see what it's like to try to control her."

"So what's this motto?"

Israel grabbed the screens to the window. "Things can be cleaned and replaced. Great moments cannot afford to be lost."

Lennie pointed at Grey's soaked clothing. "And that was a truly great moment."

Israel headed for his workshop. "I'll just put all the screens away until after she's planted flowers in those boxes."

Torn between who he should be as a recent widower, his raw doubts about marriage, and what he felt for Lennie, Grey knew why he was sorry he'd told Christian anything about her. He didn't want him seeing Lennie. He didn't want anyone having time alone with her.

Not anyone but him. Now how did that make any sense when he'd never have anything more to offer her than the friendship of their childhood?

Twenty-Nine

Deborah drove her rig toward town, passing stores and her bank before arriving at the restaurant. After tethering her horse to a hitching post, she walked across the parking lot. She pushed open the door and was greeted by the rattle of plates and waitresses carrying large trays of food. The smell of bacon and hamburgers added to Deborah's queasiness. She moved to an empty booth and slid to the middle of the seat.

The streetlights shone brightly against the blackness of night. A few people were walking along the sidewalk, cars stopped at the red light, and a couple of folks crossed the street. Town life had its own pace. Much more bustling than the farm she'd grown up on, and yet, compared to what Cara said New York City was like, it moved very slowly.

Slowly. That's how she'd let this mess with Mahlon drag out. He'd asked for a few days. It'd now been nine weeks. Nine weeks!

But she knew why she'd let it go on and on. Selfishness. That, and he'd written to his Mamm. The letter had made Ada so happy, so hopeful he might return, that Deborah couldn't find the strength to say anything to Mahlon that might cause him to leave. And for every week he'd stayed, she'd seen and understood more of who she was, what she wanted from life, and why she'd felt so drawn to him.

The bell on the restaurant jingled, and Mahlon walked in. His hazel eyes lit up as he walked to the booth. "Hi." He slid into his seat and stretched his hands over hers. "Thanks for coming again, Deb."

She stared at their entwined hands, hoping the right words came to her.

A waitress set a glass of ice water in front of her. Deborah freed her hands of his and took a sip, trying to settle her nerves. She hated how distant she'd been to Jonathan since the night he kissed her, but what else could she do? At least he'd been gone a fair amount lately with his blacksmith job. Right now he was staying several nights at a farm some twenty miles from here, shoeing a herd of horses.

Mahlon studied her—probably sizing her up and choosing his words.

As a long-distance truck driver, he hadn't been around all that much either. The absence of both men had given her time to think. When she did meet with Mahlon, he'd poured his heart out to her—promising her everything, including making Ada happy with a houseful of grandchildren.

She dipped her finger in the water and traced patterns with it on the table. Contrary to what she'd thought since Mahlon ran off, she did know him. And he knew her.

He wanted to give up his job as a truck driver and go through the steps to become a member of the Amish community in good standing again. He would return only to be shunned. Knowing that, she understood why he'd wanted time to talk to her before he made everyone else aware of his homecoming.

"I've done as you asked, Mahlon."

She'd listened to every word and taken time to think about them. It all made sense now. He'd felt trapped and overwhelmed. He was having panic attacks, but he couldn't say what he was feeling, in part because he didn't know what he was feeling or why. His Englischer friend had offered a way out, and in a state of depression, he'd jumped at it. Now that he was better, he regretted what he'd done. She'd listened. She'd heard. She'd made her decision.

"I sincerely understand why you left, but—"

"No. Don't say *but*. You…we need more time. It's just—"

"Mahlon!" she whispered loudly, elongating his name. Leaving as he did said so much more about him than he could bear to hear. She wouldn't share too much truth for fear of what it might do to him, but she was finished walking on eggshells for him. "It's time, Mahlon. I've kept your secret. I've listened. I've met with you. I've thought about all you've said until I can't stand to think about it anymore. You're not interested in letting me decide what I think. You want to make me see you exactly the way you've decided I should see you."

He stared at the table, unwilling to look at her. She hated that habit. He studied her intently when trying to read her, but otherwise he didn't look up. Truth was, the more time she spent with him, the more things she disliked about him. But Ada loved him, and because of that and because Deborah hurt for the issues he struggled with, she would remain kind and encouraging.

She took a deep breath, wishing he'd make this easier and knowing he wouldn't. "Now I need you to listen to me. Will you do that?"

"Sure. I'll do anything for you…for us." The positive words left his mouth, but dullness reflected in his eyes.

"You've spent so much of your life longing for what could have been. If only your Daed hadn't died. If only you hadn't seen the Twin Towers fall. If only you hadn't been born Amish. If only you could get free. You got free, Mahlon. And now you're thinking *if only* again. If only you could go back and undo. If only I was yours again. Your return isn't about you being in love with me. It's about who you are. I'm part of your new *if only* dream. I hope you return to the faith, Mahlon. Ada needs her only son in a way I can't fill. But…the truth is, I'm not in love with you, and what has died between us can never be revived, no matter how much time I give you."

Tears filled his eyes, and Deborah enveloped his hand in both of hers. He drew her hands to his lips. "How can you be so sure of yourself? I meant everything to you just a few months ago. We can get that back. I know you don't really trust that right now, but it's true."

According to the calendar, he'd been gone almost eight months before he began showing up here again. But it felt like years, based on what she'd learned. Deborah pulled her hands free of his and took a long drink of water. She'd said everything he needed to hear, but he wasn't listening. "Bye, Mahlon."

"You can't mean that."

"I'm sorry." She stood, and when he rose, she hugged him tightly. "You take care of you. And don't spend years wishing for what could have been if you hadn't left. Find what is and embrace it."

He looked confused and furious, but thankfully he didn't say anything. She started to leave and then remembered one more thing. "I won't keep any secrets for you from now on. If you want to tell your mother you're back before I do, I suggest you go see her tonight." She pulled the money out of her pocket that he'd given her since leaving Dry Lake. Laying it on the table, she felt like a piece of her soul had been given back to her. "Take care of yourself."

She hurried out the door and toward her rig, keeping her eyes on the rugged pothole-filled parking lot. Grief for hurting and disappointing him hovered over her. But she'd been fair. She'd listened and thought and prayed and considered. She hated being unable to help him, but she had no doubts she'd done the right thing for herself.

She glanced up at her buggy.

Jonathan.

He stood under the street lamp directly in front of her rig. He had no smile or warmth. "I got done earlier than expected, and Ada said you'd gone to town." He scoffed. "I wondered what would make you come to town alone after dark, so I came looking. Just wanted to make sure you got home safely."

She cringed at the idea of him seeing them through the plate glass window. "Jonathan, it's—"

He jerked open the buggy door. "Don't talk to me right now. Just get in."

She climbed in the passenger's side. A shudder ran through her when he got in and slammed the door. "I can—"

"How long has he been back?"

"Jonathan, would you please lis—"

"How long?" he interrupted.

She'd never seen him angry. His face held no expression, but the tautness of it seemed as unyielding as iron.

"Two months."

"Our own people think that if you have any interest in me, it's only because you can't have him. They think I'm a fool to be willing to accept whatever part of your heart Mahlon didn't take with him. The guys call it 'Mahlon's leftovers.'"

His insult slapped her, and she gasped. "That's mean, Jonathan."

"I'm telling you how it is for me. And I was willing to ignore everyone because I thought they didn't understand. How many times have you two met?"

"There's more to it than that. Will you listen?"

"Can't. Answer my questions first. How many times, Deborah?"

"Six. But he asked me not to say anything for—"

"Mahlon asked and you gave. That absolutely should not surprise me, and yet—"

"Let me explain!" she interrupted.

"More than angry, I'm disappointed. To see Mahlon secretly for any reason— I don't need to hear your explanations for that. You aren't who I thought you were." He stopped in front of Ada's House. "I'll put your horse and rig away before I leave."

She couldn't believe he'd dismissed her without even listening.

He got out, went around the buggy, and opened her door. He motioned for her to get out.

She didn't. "I know I was wrong."

"Good. Then we agree." He stared at her. "Don't make this any harder

than it has to be. Not telling me was the same as lying. I don't need to
know any more than that. Will he return? Will you give him another
chance? Is he asking you to leave with him? Is he just meeting to be
friends?" Jonathan shook his head. "It doesn't matter. The only thing that
matters is that you lied. I've played second fiddle to him all my life where
you're concerned, only then I knew it. This time you cheated me of the
right to decide."

Cheated him?

Getting out of the buggy, she found herself almost toe-to-toe with
him. She'd been so sure that what she'd done by seeing Mahlon secretly
was keep her word to him while discovering her own thoughts and heart.
And she'd done her best to get him to rejoin the faith, regardless of whether
she took him back.

"I…I didn't see it as cheating… He asked and…"

"Well, next time he asks, I won't be around to mind whether you do
his bidding." He sidestepped her and got into the buggy.

"Jon, I…I told him tonight I wouldn't see him anymore, and I
wouldn't keep his secret any longer either."

"Do you actually think that's supposed to make this any better? You
deceived me while giving him every chance. And you think that's a con-
solation? You have to be kidding yourself, Deborah."

She'd thought Mahlon abandoning her without warning was the
most heart-wrenching experience she would ever go through. That didn't
compare to the ache of losing Jonathan by her own actions.

❦

Lena poured Jonathan a cup of coffee. "Can I tell you what I think?"

He took the mug from her. "No."

She set the pot on the stove and pulled a pan of muffins out of the
oven. He'd jolted her out of bed over an hour ago. Even at seven o'clock,

she'd been sound asleep. Had he forgotten how much she loved slow-moving Saturday mornings? It seemed a reasonable perk to being unwed and childless.

They'd been talking for over an hour, and yet he held firm to his unwillingness to listen to reason. She'd seen him angry a few other times, and when he got this way, he stayed there. He'd peppered her with questions, wanting to know if Deborah had told her about Mahlon's return. Thankfully Deborah hadn't said a word to her, or Jonathan would be angry at her too. Most of his questions were aimed at trying to figure out if he knew Deborah at all.

Lena spread a kitchen towel over the bottom of a large bowl. "Deborah's five years younger than you and three years younger than me. She's cared about and tried to take care of Mahlon most of her life. Maybe she just got caught in a situation she didn't know how to handle."

"Do you think she still loves him?"

She dumped the muffins into the bowl and set them on the table. "I'm sure you could learn the answer to that if you'd talk to her." She held the container of food in front of him and placed her hand on his shoulder. "Eat."

He looked up at her. "In other words, fill my mouth and shut up."

She heard the front door open and her Daed's voice as he talked to Nicky.

"Exactly." She patted his shoulder.

Instead of her Daed entering the kitchen, Grey did. He looked from her to Jonathan.

Her Daed walked in after Grey. "I told you I thought she had company in here." He smiled. "How ya doing, Jonathan?"

"Good, Israel. You?"

Daed stole a muffin. "Better now."

Grey removed his hat. "I came to finish the job I started last Saturday."

Her Daed motioned. "Not before a cup of coffee. Come. Sit."

His silvery blue eyes held an unfamiliar look as he studied her. Was it possible he cared to some small degree and Jonathan being here bothered him, or did her hopes have her imagining nonsense? She'd told him months ago about missing Jonathan, but she had been clear he had never been a boyfriend or anything. Hadn't she? In the morning light, with Grey's presence filling the room, she couldn't recall.

"No, but denki." Grey brushed the inside rim of his hat against his pant leg. "I just wanted to warn Lena I was here. I'll be working outside that window mostly." He pointed to the kitchen window. "It won't take long. I made the boxes already. I didn't have any mesh, but all I need to do is add that and hang them." He said his good-byes and went outside.

He'd come inside with her Daed, not chancing another episode like they'd had last week. And he'd come to warn her he'd be on the porch and easily able to see inside. A gentleman, to be sure.

But as soon as she connected all those thoughts, a sensation inside her heart tugged, as if cautioning her that she didn't really know all there was to know about this man. It was a ridiculous feeling. Lena sat and stirred her coffee while trying to control her impulse to run after him and say things she shouldn't. Jonathan and her Daed talked about the weather and hunting for pheasants. If she went to Grey and said Jonathan was just a friend, would she totally embarrass herself?

Very likely so.

She could at least speak to him for a bit, maybe hint that Jonathan was just a friend. She stood. "I'll be back in a minute."

Her Daed grabbed a pair of work gloves off a shelf near the side door and passed them to her. "He left these last time. And he might think that mesh is in the shed instead of in the greenhouse."

"I'll tell him." With the gloves in hand, Lena hurried out the kitchen door. When she saw the door to the greenhouse open, she went inside. The glow of sunlight through the dome, the metal braces running an arc from one side to the other, the aroma of dirt, and the disarray of bags of soil, pots, and seedlings were a familiar mixture she cherished. She'd been thirteen and he eighteen the last time he'd entered her sanctuary. With scissors in hand, Grey had the bolt of screen spread over a rather messy bench. "I see you found it."

His movements stopped for a moment, but then he nodded without looking up.

"I...I figured you'd return to finish the job before planting time."

He made the last snip, freeing one good-sized piece of mesh from its bolt. "Ya, you'll be ready to plant flowers as soon as the first frost is past."

She held the gloves up. "Daed went with me to Allen's Saturday night. He brought these to give to you, but you never came by."

He put the bolt in the corner where he'd found it. "It's time I stay closer to home than I have been."

"He said there needs to be a bridge, and he'd have walked them over."

Grey flounced the mesh. "I better get done and be on my way."

Lena held the gloves out to him. When he grabbed them, she didn't let go. "I...think I may have left you with the wrong impression. See, Jonathan and I...well...he's just here to talk about his love life. That's what friends do."

"I think it's good you've remained friends."

"He's never been anything else. I know I've mentioned that I missed him before, but only because we've always hung out, and he's been seeing someone. Did I tell you that?"

Relief, if it was relief, flickered through his eyes. Whatever she'd seen, it lasted only a few moments. "It's too soon, Lennie."

"Oh...of...of course...I didn't mean that you felt...anything for me." Her cheeks burned with embarrassment, and she released the gloves.

He moved toward the door. Afraid it might be months before she got another quiet moment alone with him, she couldn't just let him walk out without telling him how she felt. She bolted in front of him, and he stopped abruptly.

"I...I'll...wait." Her heart pounded like crazy as she dared to cross all lines of common sense. "I won't say anything to anyone. Not a hint. And I know it's too soon for you to...really care, but if you think you might... one day...I...I'll wait...if you...want..."

He said nothing, and she couldn't read him. Her pulse raced as she stood before him so very vulnerable, and she felt lightheaded. When he didn't smile or nod, she knew she'd misread him earlier. His feelings did not match hers. Again.

She forced a smile. "Okay." Tears blurred her sight. "I...saw things I wanted to see. I'm sorry. I...guess I had to make a fool of myself over someone sooner or later. I trust you'll keep this between us."

He stared at the dirt floor. "Of course."

Desperate to be alone, Lena turned to go. He caught her by the hand, so gently that at first she thought she'd brushed a plant. Upon glancing down, she realized he held her hand.

He studied her. "I...I'm sorry, Lennie."

She tried to gain composure, but tears fell freely. "It's not your fault. I...I should've known."

She pulled free and hurried outside. Covering her birthmark, she went inside and straight to her room. She'd ruined everything—thrown her dignity down a well, embarrassed Grey, and ended all easygoing friendship between them. What a fool. She caught a glimpse of herself in the mirror. Her birthmark had flushed a shade darker and seemed to creep farther up her cheek, like a stamped reminder of who she really was.

Thirty

Deborah stood inside the walk-in pantry with a goal—to reorganize it. It's not what she should be doing. She needed to tell Ada the truth. Her conscience nudged, but it would hurt Ada so badly to know that her son was close by, or at least had been close by, and he hadn't bothered to come see her. It'd already been a week since Deborah had met Mahlon at the restaurant for the last time.

The spring rains pattered against the roof, windows, and siding. Not one customer had knocked on the door all day. It seemed as if God Himself were arranging time for Deborah to break the news to Ada.

Ada came to the pantry door and motioned to the shelves. "They look much like they did thirty minutes ago." She cupped her hand under Deborah's chin. "And you look much like a woman with a broken heart. Want to talk?"

"I don't want to. If…if I could keep it from you forever, I would."

Ada put her arm around Deborah. "Kumm, we've grown too close to hide truths from each other, no matter how painful they are."

Deborah held out a chair for Ada. "You sit. I'll fix us some tea."

Ada tilted her head, concern filling her eyes. Deborah added fresh water to the kettle, hoping she could hide from Ada many of her thoughts and feelings about Mahlon.

He'd taken up Deborah's time and energy, ruined what she had with Jonathan, and then disappeared, leaving her to pick up the pieces. Served her right, she supposed. Mahlon was who he was, and she'd dared to give him the benefit of the doubt, thinking she could make a difference in his choices. But it had never worked in the past, so why had she thought this time would be any different?

Mahlon's leftovers.

Maybe that had been true at first but no longer. And Jonathan shouldn't have said that to her, but it did help her see how her actions made Jonathan look if she had been seen with Mahlon.

She set two mugs on the table before dipping the tea-ball infusers into the canister of fresh tea leaves. Deborah didn't want Ada to know that Mahlon's selfishness in simply abandoning them had ended up setting Deborah free. Inside his quiet ways there stirred constant doubt and drama. He'd have a few days or weeks of accepting his circumstances with gratefulness, and then his turmoil would begin again. She saw that clearly now, and she thanked God she'd been spared from marrying him.

"The water's on to heat. And the tea balls are prepared. Come sit." Ada pulled out a chair and waited.

Deborah had stalled for as long as she could. "I don't know how to cushion what needs to be said."

"Just say it, child. Jonathan hasn't been here much lately. Are you at odds with my nephew and fear what that will do to our business?"

She missed Jonathan, but she had no concerns about the business. They had the money to hire someone to fill in for him as needed. "Mahlon returned."

Ada grabbed her hands. "Is he well?"

"Ya. I've met with him. He asked me not to say anything, so I didn't. But…I don't know where he is now, if he's living in Hope Crossing or moved on. He…he…said he wanted to rejoin the faith…if I'd have him."

Tears trailed Ada's cheeks. "My son wants to return?"

"I…I'm so sorry, Ada."

Confusion filled her eyes. "Sorry?"

Deborah fought tears. Ada had only heard that her son hoped to

rejoin the faith. "I tried to encourage him to return to the fold or at least…"
How could she tell Ada she'd all but begged him to visit her? "The last I
saw him was a week ago. I…fear he's moved on again."

"You met with him, had planned visits?"

The kettle began to whistle. Deborah went to the stove and turned off
the flame. "I did."

"What did he say?"

Deborah stood near her, pouring hot water in a mug. "He…wanted
things I can't give him, Ada. I…I'm sorry."

Ada covered her face and cried. As a storm of tears rolled over her
friend, Deborah moved back to the kitchen chair, feeling helpless.

"Was I such an awful Mamm he couldn't make himself come see me?"

"It's not you, Ada, just like he didn't leave me because of me."

"But he came back for you, right?"

Deborah nodded. "And he said he'd return to both of us and to the
faith if I'd still marry him."

Ada sobbed. After catching her breath, she smacked the tabletop.
"That boy! He should not have asked such a thing of you."

Deborah choked back tears. "I wish I could have done this for you,
Ada."

"I'd not have let you!" Ada stood and engulfed Deborah in a hug. "I
pray he returns. I do." She sobbed. "But I will not give you up to marry a
man who is so unsure of what he wants. Even you don't have the power to
make him happy. But you have it in you to be content and enjoy life, ya?"

"I don't seem to be very good at it, but I…I think so."

"That's not true, Deborah. You left your home in Dry Lake and
moved in with me because you have a good heart. We've had sadness this
year, but even then you kept working your way toward contentedness.
You're grateful too."

"And wimpy."

"Not wimpy. Gentle. Unkindness breaks your heart, leaving you addled for a while. But it is no surprise Mahlon found the world to be a cold place without you. And he knows the Old Ways are not enough unless you are by his side. I used to fear he'd come to his senses after he'd ruined his chance with you. My fears have come true, but he made his choice. Of course he changed his mind, but now you've made up yours."

"Jonathan saw me with Mahlon, and he's furious with me."

"You care for my nephew then?"

"I…I'm sorry. I know it's—"

"You owe me no apology. I take no offense, Deborah. Do you care for him?"

A glimmer of hurt showed in Ada's eyes, but Deborah trusted that their love would see them through the fresh damage Mahlon had heaped on them. She would turn twenty-two next month, and she finally knew what she wanted out of life: to trust God no matter what, to know herself, and to enjoy every piece of life possible—come floods or drought or anything in between.

And she wanted to earn Jonathan's respect back.

And then his love.

"Ya."

"He's more like Mahlon's Daed than Mahlon. My husband, Gerald, God rest his soul, was a good and faithful man. Patient and kind. And so much fun. He was steady and a blessing." She smiled. "Most of the time, anyway. But when he got mad, ach, there was no reasoning with him."

"Jonathan wouldn't even listen."

Ada sat. "Fix yourself a cup of tea and come sit. I'll tell you how to get him to listen."

❦

Grey stopped his horse at the hitching post beside the cemetery. A white split-rail fence surrounded it. He opened the gate and went inside. Rays of light poured through the thick white clouds. He went to his wife's grave site, removed his hat, and stared at the lush green grass.

The minutes ticked by. Birds sang. The aroma of spring surrounded him. The gift of life stared at him.

He cleared his throat. "I...I can't keep carrying the guilt for both of us. *We* made a mess of our marriage. We had our chance, Elsie. I tried. You know I did. After what we went through, the idea of marriage seemed too much to even think about again, but marriage isn't scary. Walls and lies and deceit are. It doesn't have to be that way, especially if friendship is the biggest part."

He shifted, glad this cemetery was out of view of the road as he spoke to the earth covering his wife's remains. "Maybe I shouldn't be ready to care for any woman, but I do. And I can't find hope for the future while wallowing in the guilt of the past. It wasn't all me. I lost sight of that after you...passed from this life."

What was it about a place that drew loved ones when it held only the remains of a physical body? He'd never come here and talked before today. But he had to get free of the guilt and fear that ate at him night and day.

Worse than those things, because of his sense of loyalty to Elsie and his fear of falling in love, he'd hurt Lennie. She'd shared her heart with him a week ago, and he'd let her believe he didn't care for her.

He closed his eyes. The air itself seemed to carry peace, and he drew a deep breath. Feeling as if he'd finally laid down the weight of both his and Elsie's guilt, he crouched and touched the grass over her burial spot. "I'm glad you're at peace, Elsie."

After a moment he went to his carriage. Rather than going home, he went by Lennie's. But Israel said she was at Allen's for the evening.

He tapped on the door. Allen opened it. "Hey, it's been a while since you were here on a Friday night. I didn't expect you to come by." He motioned. "Kumm."

Lennie stood at the sink, washing dishes. Some of the same notes he'd seen spread out on her kitchen table were now on Allen's table. All the children but the baby were in the living room, playing with a child-sized kitchen and eating ice cream.

Lennie looked up as if making sure he was okay. "Hi."

Taken aback, he barely managed a nod. He didn't know what he'd expected, but her reaction assured him that her heart of friendship overrode any other feelings taking place between them.

Emily waved the spoon in her hand before dipping it into the bowl in front of her. "Evening, Grey."

"Emily." He removed his hat. "I…I came to talk to Lennie."

"Ah, the Picnic Basket Auction is tomorrow." Allen took a seat at the table. "Has she roped you into helping with something on that project too? You might as well get used to being asked and learn how to say no. She's always busy with one project or another because she has no love life."

"Allen, please." Lennie dried her hands before glancing to Grey. "I think we've got everything settled. No need to discuss anything else."

She sounded kind and matter-of-fact.

Allen yawned. "Never even been on a date, that treasure hasn't, and at this rate she never will."

"Oh, she will all right." Emily smacked her husband's shoulder.

Never? Grey couldn't believe that, but he wouldn't ask.

"Allen." Lennie waited until he looked at her. "Shut up."

"I'm not trying to pick on you. I just think you need to try a little harder. After all your prep for running the Picnic Basket Auction tomorrow, did you fix a basket for someone to bid on?"

"It's the rules. If a woman over the age of seventeen walks into the schoolhouse, she must have a basket to auction off."

"Gut." Allen tossed a peanut into his mouth.

Grey fidgeted with his hat. "Lennie, can we talk?"

She picked up several papers and a pencil. "I really have a lot I need to get done for tomorrow."

Emily studied him for a moment. Then she looked at Lennie before standing and tugging on her husband's sleeve.

"What?" Allen mumbled.

"I need some help bathing the little ones. They have ice cream all over themselves."

"I thought Lennie was going to help with that."

"She has enough to do, and I just volunteered you."

He shrugged. "I'll be a while. Make yourself at home, Grey."

Waiting on Emily and Allen to get the children upstairs, Grey studied Lennie. She folded her arms, looking resigned to the discomfort he was causing.

The Amish traditions of courting or dating made it easy for young people to keep who they were seeing a complete secret. Grey had always assumed Lennie handled her private life discreetly. And maybe she did. Maybe Allen just didn't know.

As voices faded, she took a seat at the head of the table. "Look, Grey, I know you're sorry for what happened and that you feel bad about it. I appreciate your kindness, but I really don't need you coming here to explain it all more carefully."

Hoping the right words came to him, he placed his hat on the table in front of him and sat near her. "Lennie…I didn't come here for that reason."

The muffled sounds of water running in a tub and children prattling filled the room. He couldn't manage to say anything more.

She gathered some of the papers. "What then?"

"I…I…" He fidgeted with the rim of his hat. "I think I need a minute inside that circle of peace."

She laid the papers down and really looked at him for the first time. "You…have someone."

"No. What would make you say that?"

"If you're asking for pardon while you tell me a difficult truth, I just assumed…"

He put his hands over hers. "Lennie, could you stop jumping to the wrong conclusion for just a minute? See...I..." He shook his head. "Sorry. I'm really not very good at this."

"I can see that." She slid her hands free of his. "They're words, Grey. You choose them in your mind, and then you share them."

Her straightforwardness made him smile. "You were so open about how you feel toward me and what you were thinking. I wasn't ready to admit how I felt. You...you didn't read me wrong."

Disappointment reflected in her eyes. "Sorry, Grey, but I don't believe you. You're just saying that because you're a really nice guy."

"I know how I feel...how I felt before you came to me in the greenhouse."

Her eyes grew large, but it wasn't with excitement. It was wariness.

"You're not going to believe me?"

"I...I want to...of course."

"Good. Then it's settled." He angled his head, studying her. "Or is it?"

A slow, beautiful smile radiated from her. "I suppose it is, but it'll take months before it sinks in."

"Time we have. Actually we've got a lot of it ahead of us, and I know you said you'd wait, but maybe you should consider seeing other men— just to be sure your feelings...you know... aren't out of pity."

"You think *I* feel sorry for *you*?" She laughed. "Surely you can't believe that at twenty-four years old I don't know the difference between love and sympathy. I've waited a lifetime. And you should trust that I know what I want."

His eyes moved over every inch of her face. "I like the way you argue." He squeezed her hand.

"Are you sure you're sure?"

"You were better at accepting that I didn't care than you are at believing that I do."

Her hand eased to her birthmark, an unconscious move he'd bet. "I…I suppose I am."

He eased her hand away and caressed the mark. He ran his fingers down her neck, following the birthmark. When her eyes met his, he steadied his breathing. Gently guiding her closer, he breathed in the scent of lavender and roses. He kissed her cheek and brushed his lips across her skin until he reached her lips. Everything about her tender movements, including caressing his beard, spoke of being at ease with him. After receiving a kiss he'd never forget, he put some space between them.

Her eyes were closed. *"Duh net schtobbe."*

As she whispered *do not stop,* he wished the journey ahead of them wasn't such a long one. He had to be much more careful than they were being right now. Her reputation could easily be ruined if they didn't walk pure for at least another year. He placed his fingers under her chin, willing her to look at him.

"Lennie, we can't be careless. It doesn't matter how we feel. I'm still required to continue my period of mourning before I can court you or before anyone can know about us."

She shifted, sitting up straighter. "Ya. You're right." She ran her fingers over her lips. "That was amazing."

She was absolutely right about that. "We won't be able to see each other much. I can't come to your place just to visit you, and we can't go anywhere together. We can meet here some, but even that will have to slow down, or after our relationship is public, we'll be accused of using Allen's place in an inappropriate way."

"Your kiss was better than perfect. Did…I do it right?"

She had a way about her that fit him so perfectly. How had he never known that? "Was that your first kiss?"

She nodded. "And well, well worth waiting for."

A bump near the top of the stairs startled both of them. Moving his chair slightly, he straightened and put more distance between them.

She reached under the table and held his hand. "I know the period of mourning and propriety puts restraints on you. I don't mind...too much."

"It'll take being very careful and all of that time to win Allen's approval."

She frowned at him. "Why would he not approve?"

"Lennie?" The thumping sound of Allen coming down the stairs made Lennie jolt.

"Build us a bridge between your place and Allen's. Then you can walk over for a few minutes here and there, or come over while we're outside in the spring. Emily and I could bring over a dish of food. That way your visits don't have to be so formal or visible for others in the community to even notice."

Grey held on to her fingers for a moment longer. "I'll build us a bridge...in every way possible."

She grabbed her notebook and pencil. "What does *every way possible* mean?"

Allen walked into the kitchen and motioned Grey toward the sofa. "She's got work to do, and the living room is much more comfortable."

Grey rose, wishing they had time to really talk but at peace with the commitment between them. How had love for Lennie grown such deep roots in such a short time?

Thirty-One

Deborah stopped the carriage in front of Jonathan's home. She, Ada, and Cara had been at the school helping Lena set up for today, but as the morning wore on, she grew concerned that Jonathan might not come to the auction. Armed with Ada's sage advice, Deborah walked across the gravel drive and into his shop.

Jonathan glanced up, and a soft, hesitant smile drew her before he turned away, concealing his heart from hers. He continued working as if she weren't there. She'd not seen him in his leather apron and rawhide gloves in a long time. The apron was marred and stained, and his face had smudges of black, but those things only added to his rugged, handsome appearance. With a sturdy pair of tongs, he moved the horseshoe from the forge to the anvil. Still clutching the tongs with one hand, he began hammering, molding the metal to his will.

"Jon?"

He studied her for a moment before returning his focus to pounding the metal.

His Daed stepped out from a stall. "Well, hello, Deborah. We don't see you in these parts much anymore. You here for the auction?"

"Ya. I came to see Jonathan for a minute first." She waited, but Jonathan didn't stop pounding on the horseshoe. "I need to say a few things, and I think it's reasonable to ask you to hear me." She spoke above the noise.

He finally nodded. His Daed walked over to him and took the tongs and hammer. Jonathan removed his apron and walked outside with Deborah. She'd hoped they would go for a real walk, but he escorted her to the carriage and opened the door.

Although tempted to tell him he was being ridiculous and stubborn, she held on to Ada's advice. "From your perspective, you have every right to end our relationship. And I was wrong but not as wrong as you think."

"Wrong enough."

"I wanted time to think for myself. I did a selfish thing. I know that. I wanted to form my own opinion. Even more than that, I needed time to try to convince him to treat Ada right whether he returns to our faith or not. I didn't succeed, but I know I tried my best. And now we both know that I wouldn't have Mahlon back under any circumstances."

"So he did return to win you again."

Deborah climbed into the buggy. "He did. He said all the sweet, flowery things he's so capable of saying, including how he would rejoin the faith and how he wanted my help in giving grandchildren to Ada."

"That's some heavy temptation he tossed your way."

"No. It carried no temptation, although I expected it to." She drew a breath. "I would greatly appreciate your keeping what I've told you just between us. If he does decide to return and rejoin the faith, I don't want anyone else knowing what I just shared."

"Then you're still protecting him."

"I'm protecting us from being gossips and displeasing God. No part of me answers to Mahlon, but I do pray he finds his way. Hear me on this, Jon—I whisper thanks to God, even in my sleep, that I'm free of my promise to marry him."

He remained unmoving until a slow, easy smile radiated from him.

She took the reins in hand. "I have a picnic basket chock-full of your favorite foods. It'd be a shame if my Daed were the one to win the bid. It starts in twenty minutes. For years you've bought Lena's basket because she's your friend. If you refuse to forgive me as your girlfriend, I hope you will at least remain my friend."

He looked down at his clothing. "Twenty minutes?"

"Wear what you have on. I'm only picky about what's inside a man's heart. Nothing else matters." She studied the strength in his shoulders and arms and smiled. "Well, nothing else matters more than that." She slapped the reins against the horse's back, hoping that she'd begun regaining his respect and that he'd at least be her friend again.

❦

Grey stood in the back of the schoolroom, watching as Lennie spiced up the bidding with quips and humor and handed baskets to the auctioneer. There were times when she snatched the gavel and the battery-powered microphone from the auctioneer and managed to get twice the bid. Ivan sat next to Allen's oldest son. People came in and out freely, buying home-made lemonade and slices of cake from tables set up outside. All of today's proceeds would go into the teacher's fund.

As he watched Lennie, he could feel her lips against his. Since it'd been a first for her, he would have expected her to be self-conscious and unsure. She had no shyness. He liked that. But she did have insecurity about her looks. If he had the power to do it, he intended to scrub that lie out of her life even if it took years. He wished he were free to court her, free to treat her as she deserved. They'd already ventured past correctness for him as a widower. The only thing they hadn't done was make a public admission of it.

He couldn't cross that line. Lennie's reputation would be stained for a long, long time, because becoming involved with someone during their period of mourning was equal to adultery in the sight of many.

Grey jolted when Michael spoke to him. "I didn't expect to see you here today."

Too distracted to have a response, Grey simply shook his father-in-law's hand.

Michael blinked, as if keeping tears away. "I wouldn't have asked it of you, but it's right for all the members of the school board to be here. As chairman of it, I knew Dora and I needed to be here. Although Lena's…" Michael's voice softened as he said Lena's name, and Grey recognized the serious tone.

"She's what?"

Michael shook his head. "You haven't been coming to the meetings. When you're ready, we need to discuss what's going on."

"Michael Blank," Lennie called, "are you paying attention to the teacher?"

The room tittered with laughter.

Michael turned. "Ya, Teacher Lena, I heard every word you said." Michael winked at Grey.

"Well, now that's good. Did you wish to make the next bid on your wife's basket?"

Michael rubbed the back of his neck, clearly comfortable going along with Lennie's harassment. "Uh, the last bid was…"

"Fifty dollars," Lennie assured him.

"Fifty…" His eyes grew large. "I bid sixty."

"Sold!" Lennie exclaimed.

The room broke into laughter.

The auctioneer hit the gavel against his podium. "The first and last bid on Dora Blank's basket is sixty dollars."

Lennie motioned for him to take his seat.

Michael played along, lowering his head like a young man in trouble as he moved to the front of the room to sit beside his wife.

"Anyone else care to talk while the bidding is going on?" Lennie asked.

"Not me," Michael said. "I'm now penniless and can't afford to say a word."

Grey chuckled. Lennie could charm a snake right out of its skin when in this schoolroom. But the school board meetings never flowed as easily. Her nontraditional ways managed to get someone's hackles up all too often. And she'd stand her ground as if the Old Ways needed amending. He'd like to alter them himself about now and be free to see her at will. He looked around and saw Christian watching Lennie, probably ready to bid on her basket when it became available. Dwayne sat beside him.

Grey didn't like the idea of standing by while Christian won the bid and a date with Lennie. Her Daed or brothers might be willing to bid, but they'd drop out when a single man showed interest. He'd wanted to ask Allen to win the bid, but what excuse could Grey give for asking such a thing?

He looked around the room and saw Peter staring at him. He gave him a reassuring smile. He held no grudges against him. Peter nodded, not looking anything like the surly teen who six months ago stood in this very room and back-talked Lennie.

Several more baskets were bid on and sold. A few young men kept upping the bid when Cara's basket hit the block, making sure Ephraim had to pay dearly to share a picnic lunch with the woman he'd marry.

Lennie held up another basket. "Okay, this basket belongs to the beautiful and single Deborah Mast. Who will start the bidding?"

Deborah jumped to her feet.

Lennie frowned. "You're bidding on your own basket this year?"

Deborah hurried to the front. "I'm taking matters into my own hands, so to speak." She snatched her basket from Lennie.

Lennie picked out another basket.

Deborah motioned to her. "You haven't auctioned my basket."

"You took it and confused me, so I've moved on." Lennie raised an eyebrow and put one hand on her hip. "Anyone else here confused?"

Deborah shook her head. "I'm not a bit confused, haven't been for many months. Begin the bidding."

Lennie pointed the microphone near her mouth. "Okay, who will—"

"Everything in this basket is made from scratch," Deborah interrupted, pulling the microphone toward her as she spoke. "All the ingredients are fresh made, including the butter."

"Can I assume you made this with one person in mind?"

"Definitely."

"Couldn't you have written him a note about all this ahead of time and spared the rest of us?"

"That's not how the auction works."

"And this is?" Lennie asked. "Can we cut to the chase here? Jonathan, our good friend Deborah, who used only the best ingredients and no processed foods or leftovers whatsoever, would dearly love for you to win the bid. I suggest you aim high and end my misery."

Jonathan stood. "Three hundred dollars."

Cheers went up, and Deborah smiled broadly, laughing and blushing at the same time as she walked to Jonathan and delivered her basket.

The crowd in the room thinned out as some of the men paid for their baskets and left with a girlfriend, wife, daughter, or mother. Israel won the bid for Ada's basket, and they left. Soon Allen bought Emily's basket, and they left too. Grey moved to a bench, and his son sat beside him. With the sun shining brightly and today's temperature around seventy degrees, Lennie had the day she'd hoped for, a perfect time for picnics. The auctioneer and Lennie continued to take turns grabbing the baskets and asking for bids. As the event organizer, Lennie was called away to tend to some other business a couple of times. While she was elsewhere, the auctioneer took her basket from its place on the table behind him. There were only a few more baskets to bid on.

"The next basket belongs to our own Lena Kauffman."

Christian made the first offer. The moment Christian bid, Dwayne said something to him. Sammy, one of Lennie's older cousins, placed a bid while Christian and Dwayne seemed caught in an argument. Sammy had already bought and paid for his wife's basket, but with Israel and Allen gone, he seemed to be stepping in for them. Christian got up, bid again, and moved seats. Dwayne followed him.

Lennie hurried back into the room with a handful of twenties. He'd bet she'd had to take ones and fives out to her students who were running the lemonade and baked goods table.

Peter raised his ticket, showing the runner his number. "Fifty dollars."

Christian turned, clearly interested in who his competition was.

Dwayne stood. "No. You can't bid on her basket." He looked to Christian. "Or you either."

"Let's keep it calm, boys," the auctioneer said. "Anyone can bid."

"No!" Dwayne whirled around, looking at various people as if panicked. "She put poison in that food. I know she did. She tried to poison me and Aaron. If he were here, he'd tell you straight out."

Michael went down front. "What do you mean?"

"It's true," Dwayne cried out. "She brought us a cake that was poison. Aaron didn't want to make no fuss about it, so he threw it away quietlike."

"That's ridiculous." Lennie motioned. "Take a seat, Dwayne, or take yourself outside."

"Don't let her do this. Please," he pleaded.

"It's okay, young man." Michael put his hand on Dwayne's shoulder. "Just take a deep breath."

"I didn't want to say nothing out loud like this. I tried telling Christian private-like. You saw me. You got to believe me. So many people feel sorry for her because of that mark that they don't want to believe the truth about her."

Lennie placed her hand over her birthmark for a moment.

Grey's heart pounded like mad. "You're out of line, and I think it's time you leave."

"She's a liar and a deceiver." Dwayne sounded crazy, and Grey wondered if he realized that. But whether he was stable or not, Grey believed he knew Dwayne's purpose for bringing this up at this specific time—to cause Lennie as much trouble and embarrassment as possible.

Michael motioned toward the door. "Let's go outside, and we'll talk."

"No, I have to say this. I have to tell the truth. She's destroying men's lives one by one. Ask Peter. He don't want to admit it, but he knows she's a deceiver. At the last school board meeting, they told her never to bring a psychologist into the school again. So you know what she's doing instead? Bringing that woman from the Englischers' school into her house right after school is out, and Peter's been meeting with her behind Mamm and Daed's backs. I bet other students are too."

Grey couldn't believe that. Lennie was stubborn enough to do something her own way, but she wouldn't have hid it from him, would she?

Michael looked to Lennie. "Is this true?"

She didn't respond.

"Lena, we made our position very clear at the last meeting. Is what Dwayne says true?"

Confusion stirred. Lennie was in trouble with the board and had said nothing to him about it? He dismissed the nonsense. She didn't keep secrets from him.

Grey stood. "This isn't the right place or time."

"He's right," Michael said. "There are only three baskets left. If any of you intended to win the bid on one of the remaining baskets, please pay a reasonable fee, and let's end the auction now. I'd like to wrap up today's event and everyone go on home. We'll have a board meeting Monday night."

Lennie maintained control, smiling politely and thanking the first man who made his way down front to pay for one of the remaining baskets.

"Don't let her keep lying to you," Dwayne screamed before anyone left the room. "She knows exactly where Aaron is. She's the reason he went there. She's even chasing after Grey, almost as if she plotted for Elsie to be in that pasture with that bull while Grey stayed in this very classroom with her and Peter. Now Peter needs psychiatric help. Aaron is under the care of a doctor. What she's done eats them up inside, and if you don't stop her, she'll either run Grey crazy or seduce him." He motioned at Grey. "Grey's not falling for her tricks, though, because he's been asking other men to date her. He asked me and Christian. I think he was just hoping to find someone else for her to prey on so she'd leave him alone."

"Enough!" Grey strode to the front of the classroom.

Lennie stared at him in disbelief. "You...you did that?"

Michael and Dora waited for him to respond. If he assured Lennie of his love now, he'd break Elsie's parents all over again. He'd run Elsie's good name through the mud. And he'd ruin Lennie's reputation as well as his own. People inside the schoolhouse waited on him to respond. People who'd been outside had heard the shouting and come in.

She turned to Christian. "Did Grey ask you...to...date me?"

Christian looked at Grey, clearly unsure what to say.

"Well? Did he or not?"

Christian nodded.

Dwayne turned to his brother. "Peter, tell them it's true. Tell them you've been going to her place to see someone."

She folded her arms, trembling as if she were cold. "It's true." Her eyes met Grey's. She brushed her fingertips across her birthmark. The hurt reflected in her eyes pierced him.

She lifted her shoulders and walked out.

Everything inside him wanted to chase her, to make her hear him and trust his love for her. Surrounded by disapproving stares, he knew anything he did right now would harm her more. Dwayne's accusations against her character would die out—all but the one about her setting up meetings between Peter and the outsider.

Thirty-Two

He felt sorry for me? There was no other explanation for him asking other men to date her. His asking her to wait for him was a lie. He was hoping she'd find someone else. That's why he told her to date others. It had to be.

Tears burned Lena's eyes. She couldn't stay and help clean up. Others would need to remove the benches and load them into the wagon, get the desks out of the lean-to and set them up in the classroom, and restore order. She had to get out of here.

At the edge of the pasture, teen boys held attendant tickets that went with each horse and buggy. People were whispering as she passed them on her way to her rig.

He felt sorry for me.

She should have known that. She *had* known that.

A lonely widower and a marred old maid.

Why hadn't she admitted it for what it was?

Pain came in waves, reminding her of the newsreels she'd seen in public school showing the power of a surf during a category five hurricane. It battered against her, and her knees gave way. She staggered.

One of the teens started for her and stopped. "You okay, Lena?"

Willing her body to obey her, she got her footing. "Fine. Denki." She passed the gaggle of teens who stared and mumbled. They'd been students in past years, and they probably pitied her too. Probably laughed, wondering how she could ever expect a man to love her.

Her mother had been wrong. No man saw beyond her mark. None.

"Can we get your rig, Lena?" one of the teens asked. "Do you have your stub?"

She bit back the tears. "I'll get it myself. Denki."

And her job. She'd gone through a few years of public school just so she could be the best teacher possible, and now she'd lose this job in three weeks and probably couldn't get hired for another position anywhere.

After passing more than two dozen rigs that lined the fence, she untethered her Daed's horse. Her own horse had been too antsy to harness again today. Lena climbed into her carriage. She'd told herself not to look up, but she did anyway.

People filled the playground and schoolyard, staring at her, whispering. Grey stood with his hand on Ivan's shoulder, watching her. Fresh tears blurred her vision. Distress filled his features, and she knew he'd never intended to hurt her. Never meant for his loneliness to leave him so vulnerable that he'd make promises he didn't mean. The memory of following him out to the greenhouse burned through her. Clearly he hadn't been interested, but his guilt for hurting her must have convinced him to reach out to her.

And then he suggested she see other men.

She pulled onto the road, encouraging her horse to hurry home.

Grey would feel differently if she didn't have the birthmark. How many men would have asked to take her home from singings over the years if she'd had flawless skin like Elsie?

She lifted her face toward the sky, wishing relief would magically float from white clouds and ease her pain.

Oh, God, it hurts.

A mixed-up, half-remembered phrase from a song mocked her, and she thought of its name—"At Seventeen" by...by...Janis Ian.

Just listening to the ballad and deciphering the lyrics in English class had pained Lena. She had tried to avoid the boys' stares and pretend she didn't care. She hadn't wanted their attention, but something short of pity would have been welcome. When they did hang around, she ignored them, not trusting their intentions.

The melody of the song came to mind. The words were fragments she was surely recalling wrong, but they carried heartache anyway. *Those… with damaged faces…imagining lovers…*

She sobbed, begging the words to go away.

After pulling into the barn, she quickly brought the rig to a stop. She unfettered the horse, put her in a stall, and ran toward her house. Her Daed came around the side of the wraparound porch. "I didn't expect you this early. Forget something? Ada and I are on the porch swing, finishing our picnic lunch." He stopped. "You okay?"

"Fine, Daed. I just need to be alone, okay?" She didn't wait for a response before going inside and closing the heavy wooden door. Her dog jumped with excitement. Nicky's piercing yelps and quick jogs around her broke Lena's resolve. She ran upstairs to her room, closed the door, and melted to the floor. Nicky nudged her, accepting her fully. She imagined herself at eighty with her Daed long gone and some dog that would be Nicky the fourth or fifth keeping her company throughout the days and nights.

She pressed her hand down her flat stomach, closed her eyes, and let the tears flow.

❦

Cara held Ephraim's hand as they walked through the field and toward the road. Carrying the half-empty basket, he opened the cattle gate for her and then jiggled it to make sure the latch caught before they started walking again.

He slid his hand into hers again. "I'm glad you enjoy walking on pretty days."

"Next year I want to picnic inside the hedged area you like so much."

"The hiddy?"

"Yep."

"We could have spread our blanket there today if I'd known you preferred my private side yard to a spot by the creek."

"We're keeping the relationship above suspicion. The fact that other couples were sharing that same creek bank is a good thing. Besides, who did you share a meal with inside that hedged area last year?"

"Hey, you weren't even in Dry Lake last April. And the fact that I moved to New York to look for you thirteen years ago negates your right to harass me on this topic."

"Wow. Now that's a good argument, 'From. I'm impressed...and without a counterargument...for now. But I'll find one."

He mockingly sighed before he nudged her with his shoulder.

"Lori said that *hiddy* isn't a real word—English or Pennsylvania Dutch."

"I probably made it up years ago. It's slang for 'hidden place.'"

She wrapped her free hand around his arm. "I like the idea of us having a hidden place. We'll picnic there for sure next year."

"Even if it rains?"

"That sounds even more romantic."

He rolled his eyes playfully. "Women."

While they walked, a buggy came into sight. As the carriage grew close, Cara recognized the driver as someone from Ephraim's district, but she didn't remember his name. He slowed the rig. "Ephraim. Cara. Nice day for a picnic, huh?"

"Sure is, Sammy. You and the Mrs. not picnicking today?"

"I hung around and bid on Cousin Lena's basket for Israel—you know, just to make sure she had bidders. She had other bidders...for a while. Then it all went haywire. Anyway, I bought my wife's basket, but she's at home. Some of the little ones have a stomach bug."

"Sorry to hear that. Did you say something went wrong at the auction after we left?"

"Ya. When Lena's basket hit the auction block, a student bid on it. I thought that was real nice and all, but then Dwayne Bender stood up and shot all sorts of wild accusations at Lena. Accused her of poisoning a cake she gave to Aaron Blank—"

Cara's heart jolted. "A ruined cake?"

"Ya, and he said she's been chasing after Grey. Even hinted she might've plotted Elsie's death just to have him. Who's the new guy at your shop?"

"Christian," Ephraim offered.

"Ya, he was bidding on her basket too. Then after Dwayne said those things, Lena, Christian, and Grey ended up exchanging words, but the conversation made no sense to me. I think Grey must've encouraged Christian to date her. She was fit to be tied. About yelled at Grey over it. I don't know what all's going on, but I know Dwayne's got some serious problems to behave like that at a public function. Maybe Lena quit dating him and he's trying to get back at her. Seems like—"

"I…hate to interrupt," Cara said, "but I'd like to check on Lena."

"Sure, hop in. I'm going right by her place. It'll give me a chance to make sure her Daed or one of her brothers knows what's going on. They won't like this one bit."

Sammy and Ephraim talked about the upcoming spring planting and who was growing what this year. Her heart thumped like mad. If her prank had hurt Lena, she had to apologize immediately. Sammy stopped on the driveway in front of Lena's home. They wasted no time getting out. Through the screen door, Cara could see Israel pacing, and Ada was with him.

She tugged at Ephraim's arm. "I think the cake Lena gave Aaron is the one Deborah and I gave her as a prank."

"What?"

"Remember the night several months ago when your sister and I stopped by to see you at the shop and Anna Mary was there, making a phone call? We'd come to bring something to Lena."

"Ya."

"We brought her a ruined cake as a gag. She was going to see Aaron right after we left. She must've given it to him not knowing we'd pranked her."

Ephraim chuckled. "So your ability to get into trouble isn't confined to just breaking the Ordnung. That's good news, really."

She huffed. "Ephraim."

He turned away from Lena's house and coughed into his hand, trying to hide his laughter.

"You're awful."

"Hey, I'm not the one poisoning people. That'd be my fiancée…and little sister."

She stood on her tiptoes, kissed his cheek, and hurried up the steps to Lena's. Sammy was already inside, explaining things to Israel.

Israel looked beyond Sammy to Ephraim and Cara. "She came in upset and refused to talk."

"May I try?" Cara asked.

Israel gestured toward the steps.

"Which room?"

"Take a left at the top of the steps. First door on your right."

Cara hurried up the steps and tapped on the door. "Lena, it's Cara. I… I know this seems like a bad time, but I really need to tell you something."

Muffled sounds came through the door, and then Lena unlocked and opened it. Lena's eyes glistened with a hint of extra moisture and her cheeks looked as if she'd dried them moments earlier. Cara went inside and closed the door. "It's my fault about the cake. Deborah messed it up, and I talked her into using it as a prank."

Lena burst into tears. "I don't care about the cake."

"Oh." Cara tried to sift through the other information Sammy had shared.

"Aaron knows I didn't try to poison him. Dwayne's being a jerk."

Lena sat on her bed, wiping her tears. "He tried to pawn me off on other guys. Why?"

"Dwayne?"

"Heavens, no. Do you know why a man would do such a cruel thing?"

Cara didn't know who the man was, let alone why. "No."

"It's because of this." She clasped her hand over her birthmark. "It's always been because of this."

Cara sat next to her. Lena had no idea of her beauty, but Cara knew she couldn't change her opinion, not today anyway. "It won't always be. The younger you are, the more outward appearance matters. Then maturity hits...at least it does for most folks, and how a person looks is one of the last things people care about."

"But I lost him to someone perfect once before, and I accepted it within two weeks of them dating. This time...it's not the same." Lena brushed a stray tear off her face. "I'd like to be left alone, okay?"

Cara nodded. As she descended the stairs, she saw Grey through the screen door, and he was coming up the stairs to the house. Then she understood who Lena had been talking about. Grey knocked. Israel came out of the kitchen and went to the door.

"I'd like to talk to Lena."

Israel didn't budge for several moments. Then he looked to his daughter's room and back to Grey again. "You?"

"I need to talk to her, Israel."

"It's too early for you to be standing on the porch at any woman's house, Grey."

Early? Cara didn't understand.

"Go home," Israel demanded, "before the rumors of today damage Lena's reputation as a teacher and a woman."

Grey's eyes met Cara's. "She's too upset for anything to be accomplished right now."

He nodded and left.

Israel turned to Cara. "Anything I can do?"

Cara shook her head, wondering what it would have been like to have a dad.

❧

While Ivan played in the backyard, Grey paced along the creek bank. With too many pent-up emotions to just sit idle, he'd dug the footers for the bridge. Next week he'd put twenty-six feet of support beams in place from his property to Allen's and add concrete to keep them secure, hoping it'd offer him chances to speak with Lennie. By next Saturday he'd have the structure ready to bear the weight of all who used it. Nothing fancy. Plain. Simple. And it'd felt completely right to build it.

Lennie.

He'd so looked forward to knowing she might walk over, with Emily of course, and bring him a meal. The food wouldn't matter. Having a few minutes with her would. And he would cross it in hopes of seeing her, maybe catching a moment alone with her to sustain both of them during this forced separation.

But the secrets she'd hidden from him about what had taken place at the school board meetings and her connecting Peter with Samantha at her home bothered him. He couldn't bear getting involved with someone else who hid more of herself than she shared.

He knew that hidden things were issues to be worked out between couples, except they weren't a couple. He loved her, but that wasn't enough. It scared him to think of how often love alone wasn't enough to overcome the obstacles between a man and a woman.

It shouldn't be that way. That wasn't how God intended it to be. He said that love never failed, which meant that only Grey failed. Again. And again.

But he had to talk to her. He had to assure her...to let her know that his feelings for her were real. Why did she think the birthmark mattered? But she did. And he had to tell her otherwise.

How? He couldn't go see her after all the accusations Dwayne had fired at them. In those few minutes, in full view of more than half the community, Dwayne had spilled kerosene all around Grey and Lennie. One tiny spark between them, and the community would witness their private lives burst into flames. Lennie had handled her life so carefully while she waited for the right man. If Grey remained cautious, Dwayne's accusations would become less than nothing.

His actions over the next few days and weeks held the power to ruin two women's reputations—his deceased wife's and Lennie's. Did he owe it to Elsie to mourn her properly, letting everyone believe they had a strong marriage? Elsie always needed that from him. Even if he didn't owe it to Elsie, admitting that he now loved Lena would hurt Michael and Dora more than they could bear. Every person had a breaking point. He knew Michael and Dora were very close to theirs.

Lena had ignored the school board's mandate and arranged for Peter to disobey his parents' wishes. According to Michael, she'd given advice to Aaron she knew would cause trouble. If she wanted to look at why more men weren't beating down her door, she needed to skip the mirror and take a hard look at her stubbornness to do things her own way. The Amish community stayed strong through each person yielding their own desires for the sake of the community as a whole. There were other ways to get help for her class, Peter, and Aaron.

But he loved her spirit, her willingness to completely destroy her own standing to help someone. Her motivation was love, and she didn't stop because her standing might take hard hits in the process.

To him, that was worthy of his respect. But if he couldn't convince her of his love, his respect for her wouldn't matter.

Thirty-Three

Lena knew today, the Monday following the auction, would be tough to get through. At least yesterday had been a between Sunday, so she hadn't had to face anyone.

Too broken to sleep last night or to think well today, she did her best to keep the tears at bay and teach her scholars. She'd had to walk to school again today. Her once-spirited horse had crossed the line into flat-out unruly. While walking from her home to here, she'd seen people in buggies or working in their gardens and such. The whispers were endless, and her embarrassment complete. Although some waved, asking how she was doing, most kept their distance.

But she'd get beyond this. She'd read in the Bible one time that her life was hidden with Christ, so what people saw wasn't really her.

Or at least that's what she kept telling herself.

Besides, good teachers always had to set aside personal issues and keep reaching out. But after tonight's board meeting, she probably wouldn't be able to teach anywhere. With only three and a half weeks of school left, they'd let her finish out this year. But with Dwayne making the issues so public, she wouldn't be able to find a district that would hire her for next year. If the school board could only see how the counselor had helped Peter, they might not hold what she'd done against her. Samantha had helped release him from his anger and his thoughts of suicide.

She watched Peter. Between Saturday and today, he'd located that deep-seated anger she'd spent most of the year trying to remove. Whatever happened tonight at the board meeting, she knew she'd gambled and lost. Peter had talked to the counselor at her home twice a week for two months. To keep her Daed out of trouble, she'd timed the meetings to take place while he was away delivering furniture, most often to Ada's house. She'd seen progress in Peter, but it'd been destroyed somehow. Probably from the browbeating he'd taken from his brother and parents once he got home on Saturday.

With dread of tonight's meeting and such grief over playing a fool for Grey, she thought today might never end. Deborah had moved on after Mahlon left, and Lena kept promising her heart that she would too. But Deborah had men lined up wanting to court her. Lena? Well, she might have a chance at finding one good man if she could have the birthmark removed.

The clock struck three, and she dismissed the class for the day. Wishing she could remain at her desk, she went outside and greeted parents, trying to respond to them as if nothing were wrong. She helped the young ones get in buggies, but most of her scholars walked home in this type of weather. Before their excited voices faded in the distance, she saw a buggy carrying three men pull into the school's turnaround. The open carriage held the members of the school board—Michael, Enos, and Jake. All except Grey.

Michael brought the rig to a halt. "Lena, we'd like a word with you."

This couldn't be good news, not if the meeting was supposed to be tonight and they'd all come here now. While they got out of the carriage, she closed the school door. They could say whatever they came here for without her sitting in front of them like a frightened field mouse trapped by a cat.

She walked down the three steps and halfway to the rig and waited.

Michael stared behind the school at the pasture where his daughter had died six months ago. "Because of things we learned Saturday and after talking with folks today, we've canceled the meeting tonight. We think it best to say what needs to be said now. I see no need in having a meeting where Grey will try to defend your actions. He's done that for too many years, and the two of you should be ashamed."

Offense burned through her, and tears clouded her vision. "Do you dare hint that Grey and I had some sort of inappropriate relationship—that he was not faithful to Elsie nor I to God? That isn't true. Not even a flirtatious smile or a wink passed between us. He had no interest in anyone but your daughter. And I have never had an interest in someone God has given to another."

Michael stared at her for several moments. "Your reaction gives me hope."

"And I respectfully have grave concerns over yours."

Michael's face turned red. "You are far too opinionated, Lena Kauffman."

Lena's palms sweated, and her heart palpitated as she dared speak so boldly. "You've let a liar deceive you."

"Dwayne hasn't deceived us concerning your disobedience to the board's instructions. You overstepped your boundary and disobeyed our ruling." He held out an envelope. "You are dismissed from your position starting today."

His words struck her with the force of a roof collapsing, and her legs threatened to give way. "What?" She looked from one man to the next. "But I…I haven't sat before my accusers or been given a chance to speak."

"Mollie Bender will fill in for the rest of this year, and we'll find a new teacher for next year."

They'd chosen Dwayne and Peter's Mamm to fill in for her? The unfairness of it shook her, and she fought against tears. Unwilling to let them see even mist in her eyes, she gritted her teeth and gained control over her tear ducts. "Fine." Her heart pounding until she felt sick, she turned her back to them and began to walk off.

"You did this, Lena," Jake called after her. "In months to come, perhaps years, you will see that this is not our doing but yours."

The gravel under her feet crunched as she spun around and took several steps toward them. "And I'd do it again. Peter asked for help. He's old enough to graduate school in three weeks, old enough to go to work full-time, and old enough to begin the freedoms of his rumschpringe, where he'll dabble in the world's ways, but he's not old enough to know if he needs to talk to someone outside of our faith?"

Michael's face showed confusion as he listened to her reasoning. "That issue aside, you disobeyed us. We are your authority. We decide what's best."

"Or you refuse to hear reason and Dwayne decided for you."

"You dare stand here and mock us?"

"I dare to question you. There should have been a meeting where I could have answered the charges against me and lodged my own against Dwayne."

Michael studied the field, and she thought he might give in to her. The hurt and confusion on his face reminded her of the constant pain that tore at him. "We've made our decision, and it is final."

As she tried to absorb the loss, her mind swam with warm memories of the battles fought and won inside that classroom—just as battles were fought and won on every farm and in every home. Good seed was sown out of love and an abundant harvest prayed for, but even among the Amish the lines of right and wrong were not always clear. Should she have done nothing after Elsie's death and let the seeds of shock, grief, and guilt grow a crop unhindered and unchecked?

She didn't know, and she might not ever know. "I'll empty my desk."

After taking the few remaining gloves and sweaters out of the lost-and-found box, she set the container beside her desk. Word of her dismissal would spread quickly. By nightfall everyone would know she'd been released as the teacher. They'd think her a fool, if they didn't already. A silly, ugly, rebellious fool.

What most people thought was one thing, but knowing how Grey felt about her made it unbearable.

ﬡ

The smell of wood stain and the sounds of sawing and hammering inside the cabinetry shop were the most constant things in Grey's life. Since he'd been a teen, he'd worked here, first for Ephraim's Daed and then for Ephraim. He didn't seem to be much good at creating anything of substance outside of work, but inside these walls he built fine, sturdy items that would serve a purpose long after he'd left this earth.

When most of the young men had been out drinking and carousing, he'd stayed faithful to the Amish ways and honed his skills as a craftsman. He'd never been a girl chaser. It never interested him. So how was he now caught in forbidden circumstances and silently living outside the Old Ways?

He couldn't stop thinking about Lennie. The hurt she was experiencing tormented him. He'd spent most of yesterday writing her a letter. It seemed the only way to reach her without causing trouble. There was a chance it wouldn't get to her, but only a small one. Since her teen years, she was the one who took the mail inside most days. As far as he knew, she still did. Even if her Daed found the letter, Grey believed he'd give it to her. He might not approve, but Israel treated Lennie as a respected adult. He'd always let her make up her own mind, just like allowing her to go to public school.

"Grey," Ephraim called to him.

Michael, Jake, and Enos stood in the doorway of the shop. He went to them. If Cara wasn't in the office visiting Ephraim, he would have taken the men in there for privacy.

"We came to tell you there's not a school board meeting tonight," Jake said. "We decided it's best for everyone if you are not put in a situation where you feel the need to defend Lena."

"Am I being replaced?"

Jake shook his head. "No, but we met with Lena already…and we let her go."

"You what?"

"We voted, and we handled it, Grey," Michael said. "It didn't matter what was said at the meeting. She was on probation before she brought a psychologist into the school after Elsie died. We'd already told her she wouldn't be hired again for next year, and we'd hoped she could finish out the year. We'd—"

"Wait." Grey held up his hand. "You had reasons before this Saturday to let her know you wouldn't hire her again for next year? Why? And why wasn't I told?"

"You know that she was already on probation."

"I know she was the Detweilers' scapegoat, and all of you allowed it. That boy drove a rig back and forth to school half of that year. She let him go midday, and he was surely daydreaming while Lena's horse instinctively headed for her place. That accident caused no more than bumps and bruises. It certainly was not her fault. And what about his Mamm's fault for sending those four children to school time and time again without a lunch?"

"You defend her too heartily and too loudly," Enos said.

Michael straightened his straw hat. "Aside from the issue with the Detweilers, she was allowing more and more things to take place that should not have. The board had not approved the counselor who spoke to the class. And Elmer broke his arm while she was nowhere around. The parents had lost confidence in her, but we were going to let her finish the year. However, sneaking Peter in to see a counselor behind our backs and his parents' was too much. His parents thought he was staying after school to study. We didn't need your vote to have enough to dismiss her. We'd warned her not to allow that counselor into the school again, so she had the woman meet with Peter at her home right after school."

"She had a right to—"

"No," Michael interrupted. "She had a right to obey us, and she didn't. And she showed us no sign of remorse for her actions. I do not regret our decision. Mollie Bender will fill in until school is over."

"Mollie? Lena is let go without a hearing, based on trouble Dwayne stirred, and then you hire his Mamm?"

"Jake, Enos, will you wait for me in the carriage?" Michael asked and then waited until they were out of earshot. "I don't like what I see in you lately," he said softly. "You stand up for her as heartily as she does for you. You need to mind your step."

"I have minded my step. And I grow weary of it, Michael."

Without another word Michael left. Grey began pacing, trying to think what to do and how to do it. He didn't know exactly, but he had to see Lennie. Through the plate glass of the office, he saw Ephraim and Cara chatting.

He crossed the large room, tapped on the door, and went in. "They came to tell me that they've fired Lena. I've got to see her, but that could make everything worse."

Cara frowned. "Why would that make it worse for her?"

"It's like Israel said. It's too soon for me to be standing on the porch at any woman's house."

"You and Lena?" Lines creased Ephraim's face as Grey's words sank in.

"I thought you knew that already," Cara said. "You were there on Saturday when Israel wouldn't let Grey see Lena."

Ephraim studied her for a moment. "Ya, but I just thought Lena was too upset to see anyone because Grey had tried to get other men to date… Oh, now I see what's going on." He studied Grey for a minute. "I hope it works out for you two."

Grey nodded, glad Ephraim had no judgment against him—not that he had expected it.

Cara tapped her fingers on the arms of her chair. "I still don't get why Grey going to see her is a problem."

Ephraim quickly explained the ways of the Amish concerning remarriage.

Cara tucked a wisp of rogue hair under her prayer Kapp. "So it's unacceptable to become involved with someone any sooner than a year. Two years are appreciated?"

"Ya."

"Isn't there a verse somewhere in the New Testament that says once a spouse dies, the one left behind is free to remarry?" Cara asked.

"Free to, yes," Ephraim added. "But it's wisdom to wait, and it's the Amish way to push for that. Waiting honors the life of the person who died. It shows inner character and strength to remain alone, and it gives everyone who is grieving time to adjust to that loss before new people are brought into their lives as a family member."

"Everything is so messed up." Grey began to pace again. "And I don't know that I'm in a position to fix anything. I can't undo what the board has done, but she thinks I don't care. She thinks that birthmark keeps her from being beautiful and that I was pretending to care out of pity. How can she not know she's gorgeous?"

"Very, very easily." Cara cut a piece of electrical tape off its roll and put it across Grey's cheek, above his beard. "Wear that for a few weeks, or better yet let's fill in that space with a Sharpie. If you were a kid, everyone would look at that first and then at you. Half of them would make some sort of remark, make up a nickname, and never once let you forget it's there. And men can get away with such a mark much easier than a woman."

"There's no way that's kept men from courting her."

Cara played with the strings to her prayer Kapp. "Sometimes our heaviest baggage isn't who we are. It's who we think we are. And once we believe it, we unknowingly shape our lives after that belief."

Her words reached inside and yanked at his heart. Grey continued to help Lennie believe that lie by hiding behind the traditions of man. He wanted to protect her, but maybe all he was doing was making it easy for her to hold on to the lies she believed—just like he'd made it easy for Elsie to hold on to her lies. If he'd been willing to let everyone in the community think whatever he or she wanted to about their marriage, he'd have gotten help for them. He hadn't protected Elsie, not really.

His days of hiding and helping others hide were over.

"I've got to go."

His mind ran in a dozen directions as he drove his rig to Lennie's. He hurried up the steps and knocked. Nicky barked, but no one answered the door. She didn't appear to be home. He went to her Daed's shop. No one was there either. It was possible she had gone to Allen's, especially with her being upset. He climbed into his buggy, wondering what fireworks his presence at Allen's would cause.

After pulling into Allen's driveway, Grey hurried to the door and knocked.

Emily opened the door, took him by the hand, and squeezed it. "Grey, kumm."

"Is Lennie here?"

Allen walked into the room and stared at him in disbelief. "I cannot believe you're here."

Even as Grey stood inside Allen's home, memories of Lennie filled him—her voice, her sense of humor, her sincerity, determination, and stubbornness. One look into her eyes redefined love to him.

"I know how this must sound to you. And I understand why you feel like you do, but I'm in love with your sister."

"In love with her?" Allen pointed to the door, inviting Grey to leave. "This conversation is not taking place."

"I don't blame you for believing part of the lies Dwayne told. Too many people are, including Lennie. I didn't try to pawn her off. I knew she felt a little lonely and wasn't seeing anyone, so I mentioned to Christian that he could bid on her picnic basket at the auction."

"Christian moved here less than five weeks ago, so somewhere between then and now, you've fallen madly in love with my sister, and I'm supposed to trust your feelings on that matter. You're not in love with my sister. You're using her to feel less lonely. And I won't stand for it."

"Sometimes," Emily interjected, "when a spouse dies, the loved one left behind feels the connection of marriage for the rest of their life. Some marriages do not have that connection even when both are alive."

"What?" Allen's face twisted with disapproval.

Emily held up her index finger and left the room.

The air itself seemed to condemn Grey as Allen's eyes held complete disappointment. But as unreasonable as Allen could be at times, he respected his wife's opinion. Well, he usually did. Grey hoped this was one of those times.

Emily walked back into the room carrying a cracked and chipped teacup and saucer. "Elsie was my secret sister for sharing gifts one year. It wasn't like her to participate, but she did one time about three years ago. When I opened the gift and it was broken, she apologized and left the room. You can imagine how shaken someone like Elsie was to give a broken gift. I followed her, and through her tears she shared a few fragmented sentences, saying it hadn't been broken when she'd wrapped it, but it matched everything else she touched, including her marriage. She didn't say much else, but I was able to see into her world and Grey's." Emily closed her eyes. "Grey has been grieving the death of his marriage for many years."

Allen became completely still.

Emily placed the cup in her husband's hand. "He's been alone for a long time, husband. I believe he loves your sister—a good, solid love you can trust. Can you not look at those two and know in your heart they are right for each other?"

Allen studied the cup as if trying to see what Emily had seen. "I...I want you to stay away from my sister."

"I intend to do everything I can to let her know I love her. I don't care if everyone else stands against us, but you and I have been close friends our whole lives, and I know you love her like few brothers love a sibling."

"What you're doing is inexcusable. You used my home to get close to her. If what Emily says is true, then what I see is a man who knows how to hide who he really is from everyone, including his closest friend." Allen shook his head. "You were married to someone else yesterday. And today my sister is broken! You did this, and you want to call that love? If you don't leave her alone, our friendship is over!"

Allen's words were no idle threat.

"I'm sorry to hear that." Grey left.

Thirty-Four

Dwayne stood in his parents' home trying not to laugh as he listened to the good news. His heart thudded like a drum in his ears, pounding out the rhythm of hatred. But his genius had again proved itself. Lena was fired.

"They let her go because of me?" Peter asked.

"No, because she's an idiot," Dwayne added.

"Why do you have to hate everybody? What's she ever done to you?" Peter's whine grated on Dwayne's nerves.

"That's enough, boys," Mamm said. "I'll be the teacher for the rest of the year."

"From one idiot teacher to another," Dwayne mumbled.

"What did you say?" Mamm asked.

"If I'd wanted you to hear me, you would have. So where is she now?"

His Mamm shrugged. "Jake said she was at the school, cleaning out her desk."

And Dwayne knew she had walked to school. "I got better things to do than stand around talking about Lena."

He went to his room and eased the Hot-Shot from the top shelf in his closet. He'd need this.

His bedroom door swung open, and Peter's confused, almost blank face stared at him. "You think this is funny, don't you?"

"I think it's sad that you're too stupid to know when you hear good news."

"Why Lena? You've been gunning for her since we got here. Why?"

Dwayne slid the cattle prod back into its place. "Oh, I haven't gunned for her. Doubt if I will. Not a good idea." Dwayne moved to his bed and sat down. "You're taking it too hard. She's cursed. The whole community needs to be rid of her."

Peter grew stock-still. "What do you mean by that?"

Ire flew through Dwayne as he realized Peter no longer sided with him easily. Peter's betrayal wouldn't last long. He'd see to that. "You might like her, little brother, but she's done nothing to make you any brighter."

"Of course not. Nobody but you knows anything, do they?"

Dwayne rushed off his bed and shoved Peter to the floor. "Don't you ever think you can talk to me like that. You're too stupid to see she deserves what she gets. Make that mistake again, and I'll give you a flogging like never before."

Peter fought back, swinging and kicking, but Dwayne had fifty pounds on him. He pinned him facedown and pulled his arm up behind his back. A little more pressure, and it'd snap. "Stupid." Dwayne got off of him. "Get out!"

❦

Lena toted the cardboard box as the road continued to stretch before her. It surprised and disappointed her how few items she had to show for all her years of teaching. The weight of her pain seemed insufferable. She'd never envisioned leaving her beloved job like this.

Although her reality never supported her dreams, she'd always believed she'd end her time at the school due to getting married. Teachers never began a school year if they knew they were getting married during that wedding season. Most knew when school ended in May that they would marry during the next wedding season that fall. That made the end of the school year so joyous for the teachers, a special time Lena had celebrated with a lot of teacher friends at other Amish schools. Being the fool she was, she'd dared to believe it would happen to her one day.

Studying the fields for a distraction, she tried to keep her emotions in check. She'd not fall apart until she got home. She just wouldn't. Dwayne Bender thought he'd accomplished something special, but she knew her people. They had reason to be upset with her, and they were. But if he thought this would cause them to turn on her, he didn't know her community. They'd let the board members deal with the issues, and they'd accept their decision, but they'd also begin to see Dwayne for who he was. Life took patience. This wasn't over yet. It couldn't be.

Still…she couldn't stay here and watch them pity her. Sounds of leaves and twigs crunching made her study the patch of woods beside her. It didn't sound like squirrels or even deer. It seemed too loud and very rhythmic, like a person walking. She saw nothing, so she continued on. The noise seemed to be trailing each step she made. Pretending she heard nothing, she picked up her pace and then spun. A shadow of a man ducked behind a tree. Chills ran over her. She moved to the far side of the road, walking fast and looking for a stick or rock or something.

A little relief eased over her when she heard a horse and buggy approaching from behind. It slowed and eased up beside her. "Lennie."

She jolted, dropping her box. Glass shattered, making her cringe.

Grey stopped the rig and started to get out.

She waved him away. "Don't you dare get down to help me."

He stayed in the buggy. "I need to explain things. Let me give you a lift."

She stooped and gathered as many items as she could. Mostly the box contained gifts her scholars had given her—lots of red pencils with her name, various handmade containers for holding rubber bands and the like, and a now-broken vase.

"No." She refused to look at him.

"We need to talk, Lennie."

Gathering the larger shards of the vase, she remembered the day the class had given it to her. It'd been expensive, and they'd gone in together. She placed the pieces into the box. The sound of another buggy approaching caught her attention. "Go, before you're seen."

"I don't care. Anyone and everyone can think what they want to. I'm done hiding. And I'm finished with following the traditions. This is about us."

She didn't doubt his sincerity. But his motives betrayed him. He felt really bad for her and wanted to make it right. She continued to place most of her treasures into the box, but some had been too scattered to find. "Look, your decision to stop hiding stems from the same reason that motivated you to look for me Saturday night—you feel sorry for me. Just go away."

"Ach, kumm on," he complained. "Everything I said Friday night is true. Can't—"

"Stop," she hissed at him. "I don't believe you. Can you understand that?"

"No, I don't get it. I hear you, but it makes no sense for you to feel that way. None."

"Look, it was easy for me to get the wrong idea. I should've known you were just…being nice."

"We were drawn to each other—"

"Ya," she interrupted him again. "You to me because you were lonely and me to you because I was fool enough to believe you loved me."

"Len—"

The buggy coming toward them slowed.

Tears defied her and sprang to her eyes. "Just go. You hurt for me right now and want to make it all better, but that's not enough for me. Would it be for you? When the time is right, you'll find some flawless-skinned beauty and really fall in love."

"I…want you."

His words had the power to carry her into another world, and if she believed he meant it, she couldn't make herself stay away. Before she could open her mouth to speak, the approaching carriage rattled to a stop.

"Hi, Lena." Christian removed his hat. "Need a hand? I took off early today, hoping to catch you."

"I'd rather walk, but denki."

He glanced to Grey and then studied Lena. "Are you sure there isn't something I could help you with?"

She wrapped her arms around the oversized box. "I need to go."

"I guess it's 'cause I'm new to the district, but I don't understand much of what took place on Saturday, except that Dwayne's a jerk. I've been living at his house since arriving here, and I didn't need to see what happened Saturday to know that. Seems like you could at least go for a ride with me."

Noises came from the woods. She didn't want to go anywhere with either Grey or Christian, but she wasn't about to stay on this long stretch of isolated roadway.

"I could use a ride home."

"That's a good start." Christian opened the door and took the box from her.

She nodded to Grey. "Thanks for checking on me. You don't need to again." For a thousand reasons she could list without even pausing to think, she loved Grey. If he had loved her, they could have been unbelievably happy. She forced a smile. "I really am okay."

"I began a bridge."

She wished he would leave well enough alone. "And maybe one day, just from one neighbor to another, I'll cross it while at Allen's." She got in and closed the door.

Christian seemed quite amiable as he drove her home. But the trip lasted too long. Finally he pulled onto her driveway, got out, opened the buggy door for her, and helped her down.

He grabbed the box off the seat. "It's been a rough few days for you, so I'll leave for now, but maybe another time?"

She didn't want to be rude, but why was he doing this? Did he and Dwayne have some sort of bet going on? "I appreciate it, but no. I'm sorry."

He passed the container to her. "It was worth a try."

She went inside and set the box on an end table. Picking out parts of the broken vase, she was haunted by dozens of memories of being a teacher.

Moments later someone banged on the door. Grey, she suspected. Ignoring it, she continued digging for pieces. The door opened, and Grey eased inside.

"What do you think you're doing?"

"I...I'm not letting you hide or run."

Her face flushed. "Me? You're the one hiding your true self, and I know why you're doing it."

"I say you don't, but explain it to me."

"No. All you want is to pick apart my reasoning. You're a nice guy. Nice guys do too much to keep from hurting someone's feelings, including backing themselves into a relationship."

"Ridiculous! I don't know anyone who's that nice of a guy. Certainly not me."

The back door opened, and Nicky flew into the house, barking angrily at Grey as he raised his voice at Lena. A quick glance said her Daed had come in from the shop. "Something I can help with?"

Grey turned to him. "Your daughter is deaf. And if it's all the same with you, I'm not leaving until she hears me."

"I've heard you! You're the one not listening! Tell him to go home, Daed."

"What are you—five?" Grey asked. "Stand your own ground and talk to me like an adult. They're words, Lennie. Choose them in your mind and share them. Or is that only for students and people you want to mold into being who you think they need to be while you keep yourself in knots for not being perfect?"

Nicky growled at him and barked. Her Daed scolded the dog and pointed outside, but Nicky didn't obey.

Lena snapped her fingers. "Hush." Her dog quieted and sat. "My day has been bad enough without you coming here to argue!"

"Then stop arguing. Besides, do you think you'd be better off if I let you believe lies about how I feel?"

As Grey raised his voice again, Nicky growled at him. Daed looked from Lena to Grey. "I…I'll just be in my shop until one of you can hear the other. It's too loud in here for me."

Lena couldn't believe it. Her Daed had taken up for her all her life. He left, pulling the door securely behind him.

She tossed the broken pieces of vase back into the box. "I know things you don't think I know. Do you have any idea how many times I overheard you tell Allen that you felt sorry for me when I was growing up?"

"I never said that!"

"I know you did! You think I'm lying?"

Confusion lined his face as he studied her. "I don't remember…" He paced the room. "Wait. I do remember. Kumm on, Lennie. I meant I felt sorry for you because you had Allen for a brother. I was giving him a hard time for being such a pain."

"Why are you doing this? You never once felt anything for me until I threw myself at you, and even then you were busy trying to pawn me off on other men. You were hoping I'd find someone and leave you alone. You won't change my mind because I know the truth of it, Grey. Now just drop it and go home."

"You really think I would act interested because I'm nice?"

"Oh, I know better than that. Acting interested only came after you were lonely, and even then I had to chase after you and start crying."

He became still. "You…cared…before?"

"What? If you'd known, would you have altered your life to keep from hurting me?" She went to the front door and opened it.

He stood frozen, staring at her.

"Please, Grey."

Without another word he left.

Thirty-Five

After Grey tucked Ivan in for the night, he walked outside. The cool air vibrated with the sounds of spring. Stars shone brightly in an almost cloudless sky. He walked to the creek, looking at the unfinished bridge. Moonlight filtered through the trees and danced on the moving water.

All he could think about was Lennie. He could hear her voice as if she were picnicking outside with her family or playing in the yard with the children.

He'd never thought of her romantically when they were younger. She'd been fifteen when he was twenty. He thought a lot of her and even remembered thinking whoever married her would be a very blessed man, but he wasn't attracted to her. He'd never once considered that maybe it should be him.

He felt as if he'd been standing in a dark room filled with stuff. He couldn't make out what was in it, but it felt familiar. The journey he and Lennie had taken was like someone had lit a kerosene lamp on the other end of the house and walked toward him. The closer the person came to him, the more he could clearly see. Every shadowy object in the room became a memory or feeling he'd carelessly stored and each one revealed one thing—his complete and undeniable attraction to Lennie. But what he wanted from their relationship was more important to him than anything the physical draw could give. He wanted...no, he needed friendship, the kind he could never possess without her.

"God," he picked up a rock and tossed it into the creek. "I'm glad we argued. But she's hurting. It's been an unfair journey for her, unfair to lose her school, unfair for Dwayne to get away with his antics. Help her. Please intervene for her." Following the creek, he walked on. "I've done what I could to make her hear me. I need You to open her eyes and ears to the truth. Search my heart and let her know what's in it, Father. If she sees my love, nothing will ever separate us again."

Deborah surveyed Ada's House from her spot in the large booth on the lawn. It was a Thursday evening in late April, and Springtime at Ada's House was well under way. People were taking tours through the Amish homestead, buying crafts and furniture at will. Others were sitting in rocking chairs that lined the front porch. Many bought desserts and homemade ice cream. It'd been warm last weekend, but another springtime dip in temps made it feel a little nippy to eat ice cream, in Deborah's opinion. At least heavy coats were no longer needed.

Some of the older adults were playing rounds of checkers while visiting with each other. At the top of each hour, Ada and Lori led children in playing old-fashioned yard games. Ada's House was busy, but with the few extra helpers she'd hired, thankfully it wasn't panicky busy like last fall. Just right. She poured hot chocolate into a mug and went to the sidewalk near the road.

Jonathan pulled the hay wagon to a stop and jumped down.

"Hey, Little Debbie."

She passed him the cup and winked at him before moving to the tailgate to help folks get out.

As the last person stepped down, she thought she heard a phone ringing. Not someone's cell but the one in the shanty near Ada's barn. She turned to Jonathan. "Ada's phone?"

"I think so, but it won't be Lena. I'm sure it's someone wanting to know directions or hours. The answering machine we set up will handle it."

"I wish she'd call."

"Lena going to Philly whenever life becomes too painful started more than ten years ago. She's not one to call while she's gone."

"It just makes me sick to know how bad she's hurting."

"Me too. If I know her, she's doing what she needs to do to find some peace. Then she'll be back safe and sound." He pointed. "But it was a good idea to pull Israel into helping while she's gone. It's bound to help distract him."

Israel brought his rig to a halt. Jonathan passed her his mug and moved to the back of the hay wagon and helped people down. Deborah went to get Israel a cup of hot chocolate.

A lot of the visitors were new to Ada's House. But she found it encouraging to see so many regulars who began coming in the fall, like the man who stood at the booth chatting with Lori. She sat on the counter, talking nonstop.

He always wore threadbare clothes but spent a few dollars each time, buying something at the booth. He'd never gone inside, but he seemed to like catching a few words with Cara more than anyone else.

Deborah went behind the counter with Ephraim. While he rang up another sale, she spoke to him in Pennsylvania Dutch, asking if Cara had remembered to get the next batch of miniature pies out of the oven. He said that was what she was doing now. A few moments later Cara arrived.

"Oh, perfect timing. Let's set them on the far side of the register and then move them to the container."

The man tilted his head. "Did you make those?"

Cara wrinkled her nose. "Nope, but I kept them from burning."

He laughed. "How come all the Pennsylvania Dutch chattering stops when they speak to you?"

"Mom don't know it very well," Lori said before Cara could answer. "I'm doing pretty good learning it, though."

"Learning it?"

"We only been here a year. Moved from New York."

Cara placed her hand on Lori's head. "That's enough, Lorabean."

Lori nodded.

Cara pulled several whole lemons out of the hidden pocket of her apron. "We needed more lemon slices for hot tea, but I couldn't find the knife."

Deborah held it up. "Sorry. I snatched it."

"You want to see my dog, mister?" Lori pointed to the front porch where Better Days was tethered, watching folks peacefully and enjoying an occasional pat on the head. "Before I started learning the language, we was living in a barn 'cause we found the address of Dry Lake in a diary, but Mom didn't have no money for food or a house. But I didn't mind 'cause I found a whole litter of puppies."

The man blinked. "In…a barn, Cara?"

Cara studied the man, as if a little offended by him. She lifted her daughter and passed her to Ephraim. He nodded and took Lori inside. Deborah assumed he was going to give her a lecture on not telling strangers everything she knew. She moved each pie into the clear plastic display rack.

"I…I didn't mean to get your little girl in trouble. But…"

Deborah paused. Cara cut him a look, reminding Deborah of a side to her she rarely showed anymore.

"Too many questions," Cara assured the man.

He nodded. "Sorry. It's just odd to see…I mean, a woman your age not knowing the language."

"Whatever." Cara shifted. "You can't believe anything children say."

Jonathan walked up. "Uh, forget something, Little Debbie?"

"Oh, Israel's drink!" She passed it to Jon, who walked it back to Israel. Ada stood near the rig, talking with Israel.

"I don't mean to cause no problems. But…you weren't raised Amish?"

Cara paused, staring at him.

He lowered his eyes, his hands trembling as Deborah had seen them do before. "You're…clearly not happy with me, and it's my fault for being nosy." The man walked off and then turned back. "It's clear you don't want anybody knowing about your life. I…I won't say a word of what I know. Your mother wasn't the only one good at keeping secrets."

"My mother…" Cara didn't budge, and she didn't appear to Deborah to be breathing either.

The man weaved between folks until he arrived at the sidewalk and began hurrying away.

"My mother?" Cara's face twisted, and then shock registered. She went around the counter, skirted people, and stopped on the sidewalk. "Hey!"

Deborah followed her, but the man kept going.

"Mister, wait."

But he didn't. Deborah had no idea what Cara wanted, but Ephraim arrived.

Cara cupped her hands around her mouth. "Trevor Atwater!"

Already halfway down the block, the man stopped cold. He turned, and Cara just stared at him.

He waited, but Cara didn't budge.

Deborah placed her hand on Cara's shoulder. "Who?"

Cara closed her eyes, shaking her head. "We've seen him here half a dozen times since we opened, haven't we?"

"Ya, but who is he?"

Cara's breathing was labored. Ephraim stood beside her, saying nothing. The man started back toward them and then turned and walked away.

"I can't believe this. Is it possible?" Cara muttered.

Ephraim shrugged. "I…I don't know."

Israel moved ahead of Cara, staring after the man until he was out of sight. "The last time I saw him, he worked for your grandfather. It's been nearly thirty years since then, but it's him, Cara. All night I kept thinking I recognized him from somewhere."

"Who?" Deborah asked. No one answered her.

"Great." Cara clicked her tongue. "Another set of hurdles to trip over and land on my face." She rolled her eyes. "If he returns, I bet it won't be for a while. I think I spooked him."

"Ya, I think you did," Ephraim agreed.

Cara looked at Deborah, unwavering steeliness reflecting in her eyes. "That's my dad."

Her dad? The man who had abandoned her in a New York bus station? Tears welled in Deborah's eyes and she felt shaky, but Cara stood straight and calm and dry-eyed.

"It's almost time to close up," Ada said. "Let's wrap up a little early and try to enjoy some fellowship with just us. I think we all need it."

Ephraim angled his head, studying Cara. "You okay?"

"You know what?" Cara finally stopped staring at the place where the man had disappeared. "I'm not bad."

Thirty-Six

Late afternoon sunlight streamed through the open window, showing every flaw in Lena's face as she stared in the mirror. Folded inside her hands were glossy pamphlets she'd picked up in Philly earlier this week. She'd needed to get away by herself for a couple of nights, so she'd hired a driver to take her to a hotel. The sights, sounds, and aromas of the Amish specialties at Reading Terminal Market had helped her get this mess in perspective. She'd talked to a lot of Amish people she didn't know, and walked the endless aisles that were lined with booths, each one housing baked goods, fresh fruits or meats, fascinating Amish-made crafts, or deli-type restaurants—all under one roof.

While in Philly she'd also checked into having her birthmark removed. What she'd learned planted a serious temptation within her. There were treatments that could alter her looks. She opened one pamphlet and reread the info. Laser surgery. It stood a chance of removing or almost removing the birthmark. Most likely, however, since she was in her midtwenties, the procedure would only lighten it. But was this what she really wanted?

It didn't have the power to change anything between Grey and her because she'd always know the truth he couldn't admit. But it might change how she felt about herself and maybe make it easier to accept the rejection.

"Lena?" her Daed's voice came through her door.

She tucked the pamphlets inside her dresser along with the still-unopened letter Grey had sent to her. "Ya?"

He opened the door. "You sure you don't want to go to Ada's with me tomorrow?"

"Denki, Daed. I'm just not ready to mingle yet."

Her Daed moved to her bed and took a seat. "I wish your Mamm were here. She'd know what to say."

"There's nothing to say. I have to adjust."

"If you apologize for ignoring the board's instructions and give your word you won't do anything like that again, I think they might hire you for next year."

"You think I'm wrong."

"Ya. I love you just as much, but I don't think any teacher at any school could get away with doing what you did without being suspended or losing her job."

"But he needed help, and I made sure he got it."

"I know. You have a good heart. Even in this uproar, no one in the community doubts that. But you can't ignore our ways, or what a parent wants, or what the school board wants. You can't decide what's best all on your own. You wouldn't want me to do that. When we disagreed during your teen years, you threw a fit, insisting I get a woman's opinion. And since I was a single parent, I did. And you're right—Michael shouldn't have agreed to dismiss you without a hearing. Can you see how all this works?"

She shrugged. "Ya, I guess so."

He patted the bed, and she sat beside him. "Tell me about this matter with Grey."

Her eyes clouded with tears. It'd been six days since Dwayne had exploded at the auction and stirred rumors and caused her to lose her job. She hadn't stopped reliving the humiliation of it yet. "What have you heard?"

"Rumors are saying Dwayne is full of sour grapes because you caught him with my watch and made him give it back. His folks are offended at the accusation, but best I can tell no one is siding with Dwayne. As far as you and Grey, I don't suspect most know what's going on to have anything to say on the matter."

"Most?"

"I'd think someone knows what's going on. Someone always does." He pulled a letter out of his pocket and gave it to her. "Clearly it's not me."

She ran her fingers over the handwriting on the envelope. Grey had written to her again. "I love him, Daed. And I wish I didn't."

"Why?"

"I…I thought he loved me, but…" She traced the birthmark. "I'm thinking about trying to have it removed."

"Lena, every human has flaws. And all of us have to deal with those flaws in each other. Pride makes us want to be perfect outwardly, but nothing can make us perfect inside. Do you really want people awed by an outward appearance that will fade fast with age?"

"If I'd had any experience with men, I wouldn't have been so foolish or gullible with Grey. And if I were beautiful like Elsie, I would've had experience."

"Being flawless won't make him love you." He placed the letter in her hand. "Surely you know that. And I know that *if* Grey isn't in love with you, it has nothing to do with the birthmark."

"You aren't angry at the mess of tangled emotions going on between us when he's only been a widower for seven months?"

"You've had enough people angry with you this week, my dear girl." He stood. "Whatever you do from here, just remember how you would want to be honored if you were Elsie, okay?"

"But how do I know if he loves me or if he's just being nice because he feels sorry for me?"

"Through the same gift that strengthens every good relationship—time and communication." He strode to the doorway.

"Daed?"

He turned.

"Denki. Mamm couldn't have done any better."

He chuckled. "But she didn't burn everything she cooked."

"Again?"

He nodded. "We have no eggs left in the house, and tomorrow is muffin day."

Somewhere deep within, her sense of humor began to stir again. "Those poor chickens—all that work for nothing."

"Feel free to borrow my horse and go by Allen's to get some eggs. And if your horse doesn't settle down soon, we've got to sell her."

"I'm not ready to sell her. I'll try working with her now that I have more time."

"I need to get back to work. I'm taking a small load of furniture to Ada's tomorrow. Can you get the eggs?"

"I don't want to go anywhere yet. We'll just have oatmeal or something else in the morning."

"Sure thing."

Lena moved to her dresser and pulled out the first letter Grey had written to her. When she passed the mirror, she stopped. When had she started letting this birthmark completely define her worth?

She knew others who had obvious outward flaws. Did they want to change their looks too? Her thoughts drifted to Ivan. She would hurt all over if Ivan let what was missing on his body have final say about how he felt about the rest of his body. He'd have to live with having only half an arm his whole life. He could wear a prosthetic, but he'd still have a visible flaw…just like her. If she had her birthmark removed, what message would that send to him or to other people she loved?

She opened the first letter Grey had sent her.

My beautiful, sweet Lennie,

We've known each other forever, and yet it seems, in some ways, we
don't know each other very well at all. That doesn't surprise or
disappoint me. I look forward to understanding you better, to knowing more of your secrets and flaws and you knowing more of mine.

  You're as deep as those gorgeous eyes, as clever and witty and
unpredictable (in a good way) as anyone I've ever known. But I am
disappointed in one thing…that I have failed to help you see
yourself through my eyes.

  Please allow me to remedy that right now by sharing memories, thoughts, and truths of who you are to me.

  But first, I don't know why I wasn't drawn to you as a young
man, but I know it had nothing to do with outward appearances.
We were friends, and you were my closest friend's kid sister. You
were fifteen when I was twenty. Thankfully, men don't usually fall
for teen girls, but I think the reverse happens more easily. I've
always thought you were one of a kind—rare and worthy. When
you were seventeen, I remember thinking you'd become a beautiful
woman and would be a blessing to any man.

  Here's a story from our past—
  The big boys needed to find that baby frog before little Lennie
ate it… Can you remember that? I dare say no, but if you could,
you'd remember I was brave and strong and not the one who laid it
in your two-year-old lap as a gift in the first place. Okay, we've got
that straight, right?

She laughed, and tears flowed freely. What a pair they made. His
words continued until he'd filled three pages. He spoke of warm summer

nights and private conversations they'd shared and years of them just being friends. Then he shared his journey of falling in love with her—the closest female friend he'd ever had or ever hoped to have.

Was it possible he really did feel as he kept assuring her he did? With that thought pounding at her, she opened the second letter. He'd filled it with white petals from umpteen daisies.

My beautiful, sweet Lennie,

I found a field of daisies... I know they aren't blooming yet, but it's my story, and you aren't here to set me straight. So I found this field of daisies inside the florist shop and picked you a bouquet. After I paid for them at the cash register, I headed home. Along the way, and it's quite a ways to a store...I mean, a *field* like that, I decided to take one flower and do the "she loves me, she loves me not." Unfortunately, it landed on "she loves me not," so I tried another flower, and another, and another. Do you happen to have any daisies in your greenhouse? I'm in need of more.

Your friend, your confidant, your first kiss and, with all that is good in my life, I hope your last...

Somehow that sentence didn't work out as I'd hoped. I didn't mean your last kiss ever. I trust you know what I mean. And I trust as time gives you perspective, you know what you mean to me.

Grey

Feeling his hope and humor in each word, she closed the letter. Oh how she wanted to believe he meant every word. Feeling a little renewed strength, she decided to get out for a bit. They did need eggs for tomorrow, and she really would like to catch a glimpse of Grey.

After harnessing her Daed's horse to the buggy, she drove to Allen's.

Before going into his house, she walked to the far edge of the backyard. *The bridge.*

But it wasn't finished. Grey had set the timbers on the cement foundation and nailed half of the decking in place. The wood for the other half was neatly stacked on the half-built bridge. A toolbox lay on top of the stack. She studied it, wondering why he hadn't finished what he'd started. Across the creek and across Grey's backyard sat the home he'd built for him and Elsie. A few moments later his screen door popped open, and Grey stepped outside. He strode across the yard, his shoulders broad and squared. He had a spring in his step, one she hadn't seen in him in years, and she wondered when it had faded.

He studied her, as if soaking her in. "Lennie." His voice sent warmth running through her.

"Hi." She pointed to the bridge. "You didn't finish it."

"I realized that I can't be the one to finish it, so I did my part." He went to the center of it and opened the toolbox. "The hammer and nails are in here."

"I can see that."

He shrugged. "Whenever you're ready...if you're ever ready."

"I...I'm not."

"Okay." He closed the toolbox. "I didn't think you would be yet. I know how this must look to you, and I know what people are going to think, but we know what is between us. Truth of what exists between couples is all that matters."

His words pulled her, making her almost powerless to resist. But the man before her—with his perfect body, blue eyes, and gorgeous voice— couldn't really love her, could he?

Grey shifted. "So...how are you?"

"I don't really know. Confused, I guess." She shrugged. "And surprised. I mean we were really yelling at each other. I...I can't even believe it."

"Ya. I don't regret it, though. I left knowing you better."

"That's scary."

"You know me better too."

"That isn't as scary."

"Not for you. It is for me."

"Is this how relationships work?"

"Sometimes…maybe. I don't really care how they're supposed to work, only that ours does. You know?"

She sort of did, and she liked how he viewed relationships. But he knew everything about her, and there was something he wasn't telling her. Was it hidden feelings he didn't want her to know about or something else?

"Lennie!" Allen's craggy voice hollered. He hurried over to her. "I didn't know you were here. Kumm uff rei."

He told her to come in, but he had no greeting for Grey? She glanced from one man to the other.

"Kumm," he said again.

She looked at Grey. He and Allen had never been at odds. Grey must've told him, and Allen obviously didn't approve. He'd jeopardize his friendship with Allen for her?

Unwilling to make anything between Grey and Allen worse but wanting to share a sentiment, she thought of something. "I have daisies blooming in the greenhouse. In a few months I might relinquish them to you."

"I'm ready for them whenever you say they're ready."

"Oh, and you can make those flowers say anything you want them to if you know the trick."

"I know how to get the wrong answer. Will you show me how to get the right one?"

She liked the wordplay between them, and an image formed in her mind—moonlight filtering into a dark bedroom. Grey was on a bed, sitting with his back against several pillows, talking and laughing. She lay across the foot of the bed, chatting openly while snacking on something. The bond between them could not be seen by human eye, but even now she felt its magnitude. "I think maybe…someday."

He nodded. As she and Allen walked back toward the house, Allen turned, watched Grey for a moment, and waved.

Thirty-Seven

Dwayne sat in Michael's living room listening to Grey reason with the school board. Dwayne's hands shook with anger as he glared at Peter, and he fought to keep his mouth shut. He'd sown enough seeds of scandal against Lena that everyone ought to hold her suspect. When he prodded people a bit, they said they wanted to leave the matter in the school board's hands, insisting that everyone needed forgiveness over something they'd done in recent months. Bunch of idiots! Not a one took the bait about Lena planning Elsie's demise or chasing after Grey. Not a one! What really had him furious was that Michael had called a board meeting because Grey had insisted. And Grey had talked Peter into answering a few questions.

Grey sat in front of Peter, talking all serenelike. It made Dwayne sick. But Lena had better luck than he'd figured on. Some brother or friend or even her Daed always stepped between him and her, just like when he was tracking her in the woods the other day.

Peter finished explaining what Samantha did and said that week Lena had brought her into the school.

"Denki, Peter," Grey said. "Does anyone want to ask a question or make a comment about this aspect before I move on to another?"

One of the board member's wives spoke up. "Sounds to me like that woman offered a lot of clever ideas and wisdom for helping the children, but I heard nothing any of us would disagree with."

Grey chuckled. "Well said. Anyone else?"

The board members murmured among themselves and their wives, all nodding like hollow little bobbleheads.

Dwayne's Mamm put her hands on her hips. "That don't change that Lena took matters into her own hands. She had no right to decide on her own to bring in an outsider. It doesn't matter if that outsider was giving out gold."

"Yes, Mollie, we realize that," Michael added. "We're not talking about reinstating her right now. We're simply assessing the damage. You seem to think Samantha hypnotized your son, but he keeps saying she didn't."

Dwayne's mother glanced at him, but she didn't tell the board who'd told her that.

"Peter." Grey placed his elbow on one leg. "Samantha only came to the school a few times right after Elsie died. Why did you see her more than that?"

"Lena asked if I needed to talk to somebody. Lena...she's got an eye for what's really happening inside her students. I told her no, but later on, after I kept waking with nightmares and got to where I couldn't stand eating, Dwayne told me I should tell Lena I needed to talk to Samantha again. It helped." Peter looked at his Mamm. "I...I'm sorry, but when I started thinking about killing myself, I just wanted to talk to that woman again."

"Peter!" Mamm screamed. "What are you saying? That's...a...sin!"

"Let's not get into a debate on what is and isn't a sin." Grey put his hand on Peter's leg. "Nothing is a sin because one feels drawn to it. It was a temptation that he sought help to avoid. If being tempted is a sin, then where does that leave Jesus?"

Dwayne's Mamm plunked into a chair. "Ya...ya...I hadn't thought about it... That woman...she helped you?"

"A lot, Mamm. I never saw her do or say nothing that might pull someone from the faith. She only wanted to teach us some things she's learned about dealing with shocking and violent deaths, and she likes learning things I can teach her."

Leeriness crossed Mamm's face. "What did she need to know from a boy?"

"Well, she wanted to know how to measure a horse by hands and the difference between a pony's, donkey's, and horse's personality and what she should look for to know if a horse is a good one. She's been thinking about buying one for her children."

Dwayne couldn't stand Peter's disloyalty, and he refused to hear another word from any of them. Lena had cast a spell on all of them, and the only way to break it was to kill her. He slammed the door as he left, mounted his horse, and rode home. He stormed into the tool shed and found the goods he'd been hiding there.

After he placed the thick part of the baseball bat in the vise, he tightened the clamps. He grabbed the steel horseshoe and lined it up against the wooden bat. He tried it upside down, right side up, and sideways. Sideways was the ticket. It had taken a bit of effort and patience to find a heavy steel horseshoe like this one. But it would be worth all the hassle. He opened a package of screws and began anchoring the shoe to the bat.

Tomorrow would be her last day. He hoped she didn't enjoy it. And he'd just be so very sad to learn her rogue horse had stomped her to death.

❧

Lena set the pressing iron facedown on the heating plate. Her home smelled of freshly made bread. She'd opened the windows at daybreak, and even as it neared noontime, the cool May air kept the room comfortable as she baked and ironed.

Her Daed wouldn't be back from Ada's until nearly dark, and when he did get home, he would have already eaten dinner. But she wanted to take a loaf of bread to each member of the school board and apologize for overstepping her bounds. She still believed the scholars did nothing but benefit from Samantha's visits, but Lena had been stubborn and rebellious to refuse to submit to anyone else's opinions and concerns but her own. She would apologize for her lack of submission.

Other than her family, she'd seen very few people. Five days ago she'd stood in Allen's yard talking with Grey across the creek with the half-finished bridge between them. She longed to finish her half, but that awful feeling of *something* kept tugging at her. If she could get a peace about that one thing, she'd be ready to complete her half of the bridge.

She understood now what he'd meant when he'd said, *I'll build us a bridge…in every way possible.*

The structure symbolized her part in meeting him at a place where they could understand each other, but she just couldn't do that, couldn't promise to be his again until she knew what this catch in her spirit was about.

Her horse neighed loud and long. She went to the front door, but before she stepped outside, unease warred inside her. Nicky jumped up and followed her. "Not this time, ol' girl. She's spooked enough without you getting near her." Ignoring her reluctance, Lena went outside and closed the front door so Nicky wouldn't push the screen door open and follow her.

She hurried down the steps, but that odd feeling caught in her gut again. She stopped and studied the barn. Nothing looked out of the ordinary, and she commanded her imagination to quit being silly. Even as she chided herself, she stopped walking. Nicky's angry bark blasted through the air.

She went back toward her home. As she climbed the steps, a shadow fell, and boards creaked as Dwayne came around the corner of the wrap-around porch.

He tapped a baseball bat on the porch floor. "Going somewhere?" He smiled and held up the bat, showing her the attached horseshoe. "I think you've got horse problems, ma'am." He laughed. "Almost as if somebody has been taking a cattle prod to her. Of course, you make that real easy because you like her kept in the stall. Now that bull wasn't as easy to use the cattle prod on. I had to be on a fast horse that knew how to take direction. And poor Aaron thinks he didn't repair the fence good when I'm the one who undid his handiwork. But the end result was not aimed at anyone but you."

Lena couldn't catch her breath or make her body move. She just stood there trying to think of what to do. Scratching on the solid door, Nicky barked and growled, but she couldn't get out.

Dwayne flinched when Nicky lunged at an open window, knocking over a side table and kerosene lantern. "Just look at how this has turned out. That bull gored the wrong person, but this new plan means Grey can lose two women in the same way. He'll never get over the odds of that. It'll drive him nuts. Who knows, I've come to hate him so much, I just might be around to make it happen a third time."

She had to get past Dwayne and inside her home. If she couldn't get in, just getting the door open would free Nicky. That'd give her time to... to...what? Lena needed a plan.

He gestured toward the barn. "This way, Teacher Lena."

She suddenly remembered a self-defense move she'd learned while in public school. Unsure if she could do it, she felt woozy. He planned on killing her, but she didn't have to make it easy for him.

When she didn't do his bidding, he grabbed her by the arm, jerking her along as he went down the steps. She resisted his pull. "A fighter, eh? I figured on that. It'll make the marks I leave on you look more like a horse stomped you to death."

He moved to the same step she was on and towered over her like Peter had at the beginning of the school year. As he peered down at her, she arched her free hand back, jutting out the ball of it, and jammed it into his nose as hard as she could. Blood gushed, and he stumbled backward; landing on his backside on the steps, he screamed and cursed.

The dog barked and growled while lunging at the screened window. She hurried up the steps, across the porch, and clutched the doorknob. Before she could turn it, his hand caught her by the ankle and pulled her feet out from under her.

Thirty-Eight

With a clipboard in hand, Grey cataloged the shop's inventory. During his next break he'd write to Lennie. He wished he knew the words that would reach inside her heart and allow her to trust him. There were a lot of things about women he didn't understand, but Lennie's belief that men cared more about some physical feature than they did anything else baffled him.

"Grey," Ephraim said.

"Ya?"

He pointed outside. Peter stood beside his horse at the hitching post. "He's started this way half a dozen times. I asked him if I could help, and he muttered your name."

"Thanks." Grey strode outside. "Peter," he spoke softly, but Peter jolted.

"Dwayne…" Peter gasped. "He…he says I'm too stupid to know… and maybe he's right…but…"

"Peter, take a few breaths and slow down."

Peter sucked in air as if he'd been held under water. "It's my fault about Elsie. I should've come to you a long time ago. I…I'm so sorry."

"You didn't cause Elsie's death, Peter. And whatever you did do wrong, I've forgiven you."

Specks of sweat beaded across Peter's pale face. "You won't believe me, and he'll find a way to make me look like a liar."

"I…I don't understand."

"This morning I saw Dwayne with a horseshoe attached to a baseball bat. It's a weapon. I knew it the moment I saw it."

Grey's whole body jolted as if he'd been shot.

Peter wiped his eyes. "I made up an excuse and got Mamm to let me leave school early. As I came through the back field, I saw him leaving with it. Maybe he's right. Maybe I'm just too stupid to add two and two, but I got a bad feeling about this, and he hates Lena."

"You did the right thing." Knowing his own horse was way out in the pasture, Grey grabbed the reins to Peter's horse. "I'd like to get there quick-like. May I borrow your horse?"

"Sure."

"There's nothing stupid about what you've done here," Grey said as he mounted, and then he spurred the animal hard. Dwayne had a mean streak, but surely he was all talk and no action.

No matter how much he tried to convince himself of Lennie's safety, fear tightened around his throat. Thoughts of her being hurt tormented him. And when his greatest fear—losing her—danced a vision before him, he prayed for mercy.

A half mile before he came to the four-way stop, he pulled on the right rein, guiding the horse off the road and through a back pasture. Going this way would take half a mile off the trip. Images around him seemed to magnify as he flew across the field. The sky stood out as a brilliant blue. The hayfield went on for acres and acres, all filled with rich green blades of hay about two feet tall. Finally Lennie's place came into view. Nicky's angry bark echoed off the hills as Grey approached. He brought the horse to a halt, jumped off, and ran toward the house. Nicky leaped at the screen of the window, barking unlike he'd ever heard her before. The dog yapped and growled. The horse whinnied loudly. Lennie screamed. Grey ran as hard and fast toward the barn as he could.

Inside the shadows of the barn, Lennie fell back against the wooden slats of a half wall. Dwayne raised the bat. Grey bolted into the barn, coming between Dwayne and Lennie. Dwayne's bat hit Grey's ribcage, causing Dwayne to stumble backward. Searing pain shot down Grey's left side, knocking the breath out of him.

Several seconds passed before he managed to jerk air into his lungs. He glanced to Lennie. Her eyes were closed, and she hadn't budged. Alarm ran through him. Dwayne regained his footing but not before Grey took hold of a nearby bucket. He met the next blow of the bat with the bucket. The power of Dwayne's swings caused fresh pain to keep pounding through Grey's chest, and he grew weaker. "Put the bat down."

"Make me."

Holding on to the bucket, Grey deflected blow after blow, while backing Dwayne away from Lennie. The horse kicked and whinnied harder with each thudding sound. Grey saw a cattle prod in the horse's stall. And Dwayne's plan began to make sense—the bat with a horseshoe attached, the cattle prod, Dwayne fighting with Lena in the barn. "It's over, Dwayne. No one is going to believe both of us were stomped to death by her horse. Put the bat down."

Dwayne swung again and again, each time aiming for a different part of Grey. He warded off the blows with the bucket, but exhaustion and pain slowed him. Dwayne came at him again, and Grey went to his knees. Holding the bucket above his head, he withstood another hit. Something black lunged at Dwayne, hitting him square in the chest and knocking his upper body into the horse's open stall. Nicky jumped back, barking like mad. The horse kicked and stomped as Dwayne tried to get out of the stall. Grey got to his feet and reached for Dwayne to pull him out. The horse kicked again, its back hoof catching Dwayne in the temple, and he fell over. Grey grabbed Dwayne by the feet and dragged him out of the stall.

He lay unmoving on the ground.

Grey ran to the half wall where Lena lay motionless. "Lennie."

Nicky nudged her, licked her face, and whined. While going to his knees in front of Lennie, Grey patted the dog, unsure how she got out but thankful she had. "Sit." Grey pointed, not wanting the dog's excitement to jar Lennie. Nicky did, studying her owner.

Lennie rubbed her head, moaning. One arm lay lifeless, and she cradled it while slowly prying her eyes open. Fear owned him as memories of losing Elsie beat against him.

"Grey." She gasped in pain before reaching for him. "You okay?"

"Ya." He drew her fingers to his lips and kissed them. "I need to go get help. Just stay still, okay?"

"I'm not hurt bad. I promise." Tears filled her eyes. "He only managed to hit my arm, and then I hit the back of my head on that wall when he pushed me."

Grey kissed her forehead and her cheeks, breathing in the beauty of life. "I was so worried." His lips moved over hers. He cradled her face. "I need to get us some help. You've got to be seen."

"Dwayne?"

Grey turned to look at Dwayne's still body. "I think he's dead."

The sound of hoofs grew louder until Ephraim came into sight, riding bareback. He brought his horse to a halt just outside the barn. "Peter said…" He studied the scene for a moment. "Do you need help?"

"Ya. I want Lennie seen, but we need a driver to take us."

Ephraim took off for his place to make a call.

Lennie tried to stand. "I want out of here."

Grey stood and helped her up. She moaned in pain. "My ankle's hurt too. I don't think I can put any weight on it." She cradled her lifeless arm.

He gently steadied her, concerned about possible hidden injuries. After a glance at Dwayne, she buried her face against Grey's chest.

"Kumm." He wanted to carry her but feared he might make her injuries worse. Leaning on him, she slowly walked across the driveway and yard and to the steps of the front porch. The screen on one of the open windows was ripped. Nicky had jumped through it to get to them.

Lennie sat on a step. "If I'd followed my gut, I would've never stepped outside."

Grey sat beside her, and she rested her head against his shoulder. "And if you hadn't followed your instincts to have faith in Peter, he wouldn't have come and told on his brother."

Nicky put her head on Lennie's lap.

Grey ran his hands over hers, feeling the softness of her skin, so grateful she was safe. "You know I love you, don't you?"

"I want to believe that, but from the beginning I've had this catch inside me that makes me feel like you're hiding something."

She'd picked up on the lie he carried. But his life before her, the one between him and Elsie, would never be open for another woman to know about. His marriage deserved that much from him, didn't it? He drew her fingers to his lips and kissed them. "Some things are best left alone, Lennie. I'm not one of your students for you to mold. Do you trust me?"

She said nothing for several long minutes.

"Grey?"

He kissed her forehead. "Ya?"

"If you'll bring me a pot of daisies from the greenhouse while we wait for a driver, I'll show you how to land on 'she loves me.' "

He held her hand that wasn't hurt and gently squeezed it. "I'd like that."

❧

"Lena." Her Daed tapped on her bedroom door, waking her.

She moaned in pain while trying to sit up, realizing she still had Aaron's letter in her hand. The pages of the lined paper crinkled as she shifted. "Ya?"

Midmorning sun streamed through her bedroom window. Nicky lay on the bed beside her. The dog had not let her get out of sight since she'd come home from her surgery at the hospital two weeks ago. Lena had a plate in her arm, a sprained ankle, a mild concussion, and a lot of bruises— all of which were diagnosed through the proper tests and addressed without a night's stay at the hospital.

Her Daed eased the door open. "I wouldn't wake you, except Peter's here. He's downstairs, hoping you'll see him. Are you up to it?"

Two weeks of bed rest and she'd yet to have an easy day of recuperation. But she'd begun to need less pain medication and to feel a little stronger each day this week. The doctor had said the type of sprain she had meant she couldn't put much weight on her leg. He gave her a medical boot to wear, but since she couldn't use crutches because of the injury to her arm, she'd had to wait for her ankle to heal enough so she could walk using only the boot. She'd been able to get up and move around for short periods the last few days.

"Okay, I need a housecoat. Deborah and Cara washed clothes and put them away last night, so I'd look for it in the closet."

While her Daed rummaged through her closet, she tucked Aaron's letter under the covers, unwilling for anyone to catch a glance at its contents. He was doing well but knew he had a long way to go yet. He hadn't chanced returning to Dry Lake for Dwayne's funeral for fear of what it might do to him. It'd been hard for him to admit how blinded the alcohol had kept him. He'd thought Dwayne to be a better man than himself. The news that Dwayne had dismantled a part of the fence, purposefully making it easy for the bull to get into the wrong pasture, and had angered the bull with a cattle prod had only shifted Aaron's sense of guilt, not removed it. The encouraging news was that Aaron continued on, not drinking since arriving at the Better Path.

Her Daed passed her a housecoat and eased pillows behind her back. With her arm in a cast and a lot of bruises, shifting didn't come easy. After a little help from her Daed, she slid her good arm into her housecoat and hung the other side of the terry cloth cover-up around her shoulder.

"You getting hungry?"

Lena wrinkled her nose. "You doing the cooking?"

He laughed. "Ada's here."

"Again? And on a Saturday this time. That means she's missing her busiest day at Ada's House."

Her Daed's cheeks flushed. "With so many folks stopping by, she's coming whenever she can to help fix desserts and coffee."

"Well, I'm glad my suffering is working out so well for you."

"Ya, me too."

She laughed and then yelped with pain.

He placed her prayer Kapp on her head and kissed her through it. His hand rested on top of her head, and his eyes appeared to be misting.

Grey had saved her life and sustained three broken ribs from the hit he took for her. If Dwayne had hit her full force in the head, as he'd aimed to do with that one blow, she'd have died. The memories of that day were endless, rarely fading from her thoughts.

During that awful time she'd had the wisdom to stall Dwayne by getting him to talk. He'd been itching for years to brag about his genius in stealing from homes in her area, killing pets, and setting her up as his best victory yet. He saw her as no more valuable than a barn cat—to be done away with at will. She shuddered. Neither his viciousness nor his wanton desire to kill her could ever be fully explained.

He'd left a lot of bruises on her, but when he'd started swinging that bat, she dodged it, deflected it with boards, a saddle, and her now-injured arm. When he'd slung her against that wooden wall, knocking her unconscious and unable to defend herself, Grey arrived and took the blow for her.

"I'm safe, Daed."

He cleared his throat. "You keep it that way." He picked up a pitcher of water and poured her a glass before he opened a bottle of pain medicine. "Half a dozen girlfriends are also downstairs, hoping for another visit."

"Don't any of them have a Saturday job?"

He held out the glass of water and a pill. "I'm not asking that. You're the one on enough pain meds to be so candid. You do it."

She suppressed laughter. "I'd like to see Grey."

"I know, and I'm sure he'd like to see you. Discretion says to wait."

When she and Grey had returned from the hospital the day of the incident, her Daed had asked him not to stay and not to visit. While in the waiting room of the hospital during her surgery, Grey had to answer a lot of questions for the police and for the church leaders. According to her Daed, it didn't take long for the church leaders to realize Grey cared for her. When they asked Grey, he didn't deny it, and the church leaders began discussing what to do. A few hours later a preacher confided to her Daed that because Grey and Lena had been through so much together this past year, they were considering freeing him of the usual time restraints and protocol on a widower. But the preacher cautioned her Daed that Grey needed to keep his distance until a decision was reached.

Grey told Lena he was willing to stay, that the whole community could think of him what they wanted. But Lena asked him to go home. She didn't want to be the cause of trouble for Grey, so now they waited.

"Any news from the church leaders?"

"Not yet. These things take time."

She rubbed her head. With all the medications, she could barely think. "How long since Dwayne's funeral?"

"Eleven days."

"How does Peter look?"

"Rough, but better than I'd have expected."

"Send him on up."

She lay back and closed her eyes, thinking of Grey and the life they had ahead of them.

Grey was right. He wasn't a student to be molded. If he chose not to share whatever caused that catch inside her, she'd respect that. She didn't have to figure out every angle of what was wrong in someone's life and insist they become all she thought they should be. Be willing to help? Yes. Track down the source of the problem and refuse to let go until she saw the wanted improvement? No.

That was God's job, not hers.

Peter eased the door open, looking pale and shaky.

"Hi. Kumm." She motioned to one of several chairs her Daed had set up in her room for visitors.

He sat in the chair farthest from her. "Mamm and Daed said they won't be coming, but I know they're sorry. They didn't know him like I did. Christian saw it too. But we only thought he was mean. I didn't know he was...there's a word our new counselor uses...oh, ya, psychologically disturbed."

"All is forgiven, Peter. You tell them that for me, okay?"

He nodded. "I...I'm sorry I called you ugly and stupid. You're not."

"Forgiven."

Silence fell between them. She wanted to thank him, but should she? His actions had saved her, but his brother had died. "I...I'm proud of you, Peter."

He shifted. "I've been thinking...a lot, and...well...I was so busy pointing out your flaws, I couldn't see my own."

"It works like that for all of us at some point, especially teens. You aren't the first to point out my birthmark, nor will you be the last. I've considered trying to have it removed, although it doesn't sound like they can do much more than make it fade."

"No. You...you shouldn't do that. If you can make yourself perfect on the outside, where does that leave me and others like me who have marks stamped on our insides? I can't have what Dwayne's done removed by some doctor. I gotta live with it. I gotta carry that stain the rest of my life, hoping a few people can see beyond it to love me anyway."

"That's good insight, Peter. Really good. Have you and Grey talked any?"

"We had a good long visit last night. You and him got something going on?" He lowered his head. "I shouldn't ask that. But if you don't, you should. I think he likes you."

"Ya, I think so too."

Peter stood. "I need to go. Mamm and Daed get worried right quick-like these days."

"Denki for coming by."

He closed the door as he left. Last night Deborah and Cara had washed Lena's hair for her and helped her bathe. With some assistance she could manage to get dressed, visit with her friends for a little bit before sending them on their way, and maybe even bake some cookies to take to Grey. It was midmorning. Surely she could do that small list by midafternoon.

She moved ever so slowly through the next four hours, but with Ada's help, Lena went to the porch with her hair neatly done, a clean dress on, and a box of fresh chocolate chip oatmeal cookies in hand. Well, the dress was mostly on. Ada had to cut it, add material, and resew it, but the patch-work dress looked normal as long as she kept her good arm through one sleeve of her sweater and had the other side pinned in place. The top part of the boot was hidden under her dress.

She and Grey hadn't spoken of their future, but she knew he loved her. They fit. And he didn't want flawless. While drifting in and out of a drug-induced state, she had finally understood the core of who Grey was. He wanted friendship most of all—the kind only a man and woman in love could have.

Her Daed led his horse and smooth-riding carriage to her. "You sure you don't want me to drive you there?" He opened the door, and Nicky hopped in.

She passed Daed the box of cookies and slowly climbed into the buggy. "I need to see Grey. Your horse takes no effort to direct. You know that. Go have coffee with Ada. Surely she's not here just to help me and be a hostess for my guests."

Her Daed glanced through the screen door of the house. "I hope not."

"Maybe it's time you found out. I won't stay long, and I won't go again until the church leaders and community approve. But no one will frown at me going to his place to give him a proper thank-you."

Her Daed passed the box to her. "Ada and your siblings were trying to keep it a secret so you wouldn't do any of the work, but they've planned a huge dinner."

She took the reins in hand. "Sounds wonderful. I'll be home in plenty of time for that."

He closed the door to the carriage. Her Daed's horse clipped along at a nice speed. Her own horse was in the pasture. Lena planned to work with her to rebuild trust, but she didn't know if the now high-strung mare would ever be useful again.

The warmth of May soaked into her healing body. After nearly a mile she drove up Grey's long gravel driveway, parked the rig, and got out. Ivan ran outside and greeted her, saying they'd been fishing earlier. He and his Daed had cleaned the fish, and now his Daed was in the shower.

When she awkwardly climbed out of the buggy, he pointed at the cast on her arm and her medical boot, asking what had happened. She made up a story about tripping over her shadow. He laughed, and when Nicky bounded out of the buggy, ready to play, Ivan was totally and happily distracted. After they talked and played with Nicky for a bit, she passed him the box of goodies and told him to let his Daed know she was here.

She meandered to the creek and watched the pristine water flow downstream. Life, like the water drifting by, never stopped moving. She longed to embrace every moment without regard to flaws—hers or others—and to end each day knowing if it was her last, she'd loved freely.

"Lennie," Grey called as he strode toward her. His movements weren't stiff, but she imagined his ribs still caused him a good bit of discomfort. Unlike her arm, there wasn't anything that could be done for ribs except pain relievers while he healed. He came within feet of her, and his body language spoke of wanting to embrace her. "Should you be out and about like this?"

"Ya. My strength is starting to return." She looked at the stockpile of planks still sitting on the bridge. "I want to build my side."

"Now?"

She nodded.

"Lennie, with your injuries, you can't possibly be up to it."

"If I help about as much as a preschooler and you do the rest, I'm up to it. The question is whether you'll accept that as me building my half."

"You're here and doing what you can. I'll never want more."

He couldn't have given a more perfect answer, and with it he'd stolen even more of her heart. "Are you able to do that kind of work?"

"There's plenty I can't do yet, but this will be pretty easy. We'll move slowly and secure the boards with a minimum of nails for today. The job can be finished right in a week or so when we're both feeling stronger."

Grey brought a few planks at a time and laid them on the bridge next to her. She slid each one into place. With his help she hammered nails part of the way in, and he finished securing them for her. A warm breeze made the bushes along the creek rustle. The pristine water gurgled softly while glistening in the sun. His silvery voice washed over her as they worked. With most of the bridge already done, it didn't take more than thirty minutes to complete.

She stood in the middle, and he joined her. He took her by the hand

and intertwined his fingers with hers. The catch in her gut concerning him hadn't let go, but she had peace about it.

"I have some good news." Grey drew a breath. "The church leaders came to see me while I was cleaning fish. We have permission to see each other and marry next wedding season."

Without warning, tears brimmed. She put her one arm around his waist and leaned her face against his chest. "That's what I've been hoping for—freedom to choose." After the embrace she gazed up at him. "But I think we should only see each other quietly at Allen's or my Daed's until October—not out of hypocrisy or sneaky hiding, but out of respect for how hard it will be on others, like Elsie's family, if they see us together too soon. They need time, and us waiting for a year after her death to be seen out together is not asking too much."

"I think most people have figured out how we feel, Lennie."

"Ya. But people knowing and having to observe it are two very different kinds of pain. And when we go public in October, they'll be pleased we tempered our actions out of respect for the Old Ways. Besides, I think *we* need quiet visits inside Allen's or Daed's home with no stares and lots of calm, easygoing time to really get to know each other."

"Are you doing this for me—to keep folks from thinking less of me? Because if you are, I don't mind what anyone thinks. Not anymore, Lennie."

"I...I've waited so long, Grey." A tear escaped and ran down her cheek as she laid the truth of her heart open to him. "I'm sure you can't imagine how lonely it got. And now I have you. I want to enjoy being courted without feeling people's frowns or knowing I'm hurting someone."

He wiped the tear off her face before kissing her cheek. "I...need to tell you something...at least a sentence or two, just so you know." He stroked her cheek and down her neck, tracing the path of her birthmark with the back of his fingers—as if assuring her he cherished who she was.

She waited, but he said nothing. Whatever he needed to say battled with him to stay hidden. "I'll hear it as if you were inside the circle of peace."

He drew a deep breath. "My marriage was…was…" The pain in his voice said so much more than his words. "Difficult. Troubled, really. We had no bridges. No way to cross over. We'd just taken a few steps toward a second chance when she died."

What? She didn't say the word, but she wanted to. His confession didn't fit with who she'd thought him to be. He had known years of loneliness too. His words, as few as they were, changed her. The news didn't make her feel superior or more secure. Grey himself had freed her of insecurity without a word about his marriage. But what he'd confessed gave her understanding of many things about her future husband.

He rubbed the center of his chest, exhaling freely. "I so needed to say that. I needed *you* to know."

"Ya, you did." She looked up at him, desperately wanting a kiss.

He cradled her face before he placed his lips over hers. Her heart went wild as dreams of being married to him and having children warmed her. "Will you marry me before next year's wedding season is over?"

"Ya. How about February?"

"February." Grey rolled the word around as if thinking about the pros and cons. She'd chosen the end of the wedding season, giving them four months of openly courting before they wed. He slowly kissed one side of her face and then the other. "It's a good plan. In the meantime I intend to steal a kiss or two when no one is looking."

She tugged on his shirt collar, pulling him close. "Like this?" She gently pressed her lips against his.

Ada's House Series

Main Characters

Lena Kauffman—twenty-three-year-old Amish schoolteacher in
Dry Lake.

Israel Kauffman—a forty-five-year-old Amish widower. Lena's father.
He's been quietly interested in Ada Stoltzfus for a long time.

Allen Kauffman—twenty-nine-year-old brother of Lena. Close
friend of Grey's. Married to Emily, and they have four children.

Benjamin "Grey" Graber—twenty-eight-year-old Amish man
married to Elsie.

Elsie Blank Graber—twenty-seven years old. Married to Grey
Graber.

Ivan Graber—five-year-old son of Grey and Elsie Graber.

Cara Atwater Moore—twenty-eight-year-old waitress from New
York City who lost her mother as a child, was abandoned by her
father, and grew up in foster care. Cara has been stalked for
years by Mike Snell. She and her daughter, Lori, found their
way to Dry Lake in *The Hope of Refuge,* and Cara is now
engaged to Ephraim Mast.

Lori Moore—Cara's seven-year-old daughter. Lori's father, Johnny,
died before she turned two years old, leaving Cara a widow.

Ephraim Mast—thirty-two-year-old, single Amish man who works
as a cabinetmaker and helps manage his ailing father's business
and care for their large family. He and Cara became friends
during her visit to Dry Lake when she was a child.

Deborah Mast—twenty-one-year-old Amish woman who was
engaged to Mahlon Stoltzfus in *The Hope of Refuge.* She's
Ephraim's sister, but she lives with Ada in Hope Crossing.

Mahlon Stoltzfus—twenty-three-year-old Amish man who was engaged to Deborah in *The Hope of Refuge*. He ran off without explanation, leaving his widowed mother and Deborah to cope with life and bills on their own.

Jonathan Stoltzfus—twenty-six-year-old Amish man who is good friends with Lena Kauffman.

Ada Stoltzfus—forty-three-year-old widow whose only child is Mahlon. She's a friend and mentor to Deborah Mast. She took Cara under her wing in *The Hope of Refuge*.

Aaron Blank—twenty-four years old. He was raised Amish but hasn't joined the faith. His sister is Elsie. He runs his parents' dairy farm.

Michael Blank—Elsie and Aaron's father and the chairman of the school board for the local Amish school.

Dora Blank—Michael's wife and Elsie and Aaron's mother.

Anna Mary Lantz—Ephraim's ex-girlfriend and one of Deborah's good friends.

Emma and Levi Riehl—an aunt and uncle of Cara's who inadvertently contributed to her being abandoned as a child and consequently being raised in foster care.

Robbie—an Englischer who is a co-worker and driver for Ephraim's cabinetry business. He is a driver for several Old Order Amish families.

Nicky—a mixed-breed dog whose personality and size resemble the author's dog, Jersey.

Glossary

Alt Maedel—old maid

Daadi—grandfather

Daed—dad or father

denki—thank you

Englischer—a non-Amish person. Mennonite sects whose women wear the prayer Kapps are not considered Englischers and are often referred to as Plain Mennonites.

Grossdaadi—grandfather

Grossmammi—grandmother

guck—look

gut—good

Helf—help

Hund—dog

Kapp—a prayer covering or cap

kumm—come (singular)

kummet—come (plural)

Mamm—mom or mother

nee—no

Ordnung—The written and unwritten rules of the Amish. The regulations are passed down from generation to generation. Any new rules are agreed upon by the church leaders and endorsed by the members during special meetings. Most Amish know all the rules by heart.

Pennsylvania Dutch—Pennsylvania German. *Dutch* in this phrase has nothing to do with the Netherlands. The original word was *Deutsch*, which means "German." The Amish speak some High German (used in church services) and Pennsylvania German (Pennsylvania Dutch), and after a certain age, they are taught English.

Plain—refers to the Amish and certain sects of Mennonites.

Plain Mennonite—any Mennonites whose women wear the prayer Kapp and caped dresses and the men have a dress code.

rumschpringe—running around. The true purpose of the rumschpringe is threefold: give freedom for an Amish young person to find an Amish mate; to give extra freedoms during the young adult years so each person can decide whether to join the faith; to provide a bridge between childhood and adulthood.

wunderbaar—wonderful

ya—yes

zerick—back

Pennsylvania Dutch phrases used
in *The Bridge of Peace*

Bischt hungerich?—Are you hungry?

Der Gaule kann nimmi schteh.—The horse cannot stand.

draus in da Welt—out in the world

Du bischt daheem.—You're home.

Duh net schtobbe.—Do not stop.

Frehlich Zwedde Grischtdaag—Merry Second Christmas

Geh, ess.—Go, eat.

Gern gschehne.—You're welcome.

Guder Marye.—Good morning.

Gut is was ich bescht duh.—Good is what I do best.

Haldscht Schul fer die Handikap?—Do you teach at a school for the handicapped?

Heem geh?—Go home?

Ich geh in die Handikap Schul.—I'm going to the handicap school.

Ich hab.—I did.

Kummet rei.—Come in.

Kumm mol, loss uns geh.—Come on, let's go.

Kumm uff.—Come on.

Loss uns fische geh.—Let's go fishing.

Loss uns Heemet geh.—Let's go home.

Mir esse un no gehne mir.—We'll eat and then we'll go.

Net im Haus. Is sell so hatt zu verschteh?—Not in the house. Is that so hard to understand?

Was iss es?—What is it?

Wie bischt du Heit?—How are you today?

Witt du ans Allen's geh?—Do you want to go to Allen's?

Witt fische geh?—You want to go fishing?

Ya, en verhuddelder Hund.—Yes, a confused dog.

Ya, in paar Minudde.—Yes, in a minute.

---

* Glossary taken from Eugene S. Stine, *Pennsylvania German Dictionary* (Birdsboro, PA: Pennsylvania German Society, 1996), and the usage confirmed by an instructor of the Pennsylvania Dutch language.

Acknowledgments

To my family, co-workers, and friends—If life tempts me to doubt God's faithfulness, I remember you.

Our teen broke a toe in the spring of 2010, and because of that, my husband and son came in contact with a wonderful physician—John A. Alsobrook, MD, Northeast Georgia Physicians Group, Sports Medicine, Buford, Georgia. As an author writing a trauma scene, I couldn't let such a great resource go untapped. I'm very grateful to say that the doctor was willing to return a call from someone looking for help with fictional characters in trauma. Each time I needed advice, Dr. Alsobrook was truly informative, focused, and fun to work with, which means he will be called upon again ☺.

To my Old Order Amish friends, who provide insight and direction before I begin to write each story, correction on any inaccuracies in the manuscript once it's complete, and our own hiddy where we can chat, as well as good food, fun fellowship, and a cozy bed to sleep in—Thank you!

To my expert in the Pennsylvania Dutch language, who wishes to remain anonymous—Your input is invaluable. It may not feel like it to you, but authenticity gives great pleasure to readers.

To those who work so diligently on every aspect of making each book a success, my team, WaterBrook Multnomah Publishing Group—It'd take a nonfiction book to express how honored I am to know and work with each of you! From marketing to sales to production to the editorial department, you are so much more to me than time allows me to express. From the president to the newest savvy person added to the house, you're all making a difference in the lives of authors and readers.

To Shannon Marchese, my editor—I believe that if I were to write for you until I'm a hundred years old, I'd still be soaking up your knowledge and learning how to craft a better and stronger story.

To Carol Bartley, my line editor—I always look forward to the amazing polishing job you do. Your expertise, open-mindedness, gentleness, and humor strengthen so much more than the story. I trust you, and I take pleasure in working with you.

To Steve Laube, my agent—My time and creativity would be buried under the work load of business if it weren't for you. I shove things onto your plate and return to what I love doing, writing. Thank you for being so knowledgeable, trustworthy, and understanding of an author's dream—to *write*!

To Marci Burke, my good friend and critique partner—In our seven years of working together, you have yet to let me down even once.

To my sons—When I'm in isolation mode during writing, it is your taps on my office door, early-morning phone calls, and spur-of-the-moment visits to whisk me away for a meal or a game that remind me I'm loved. And to my two daughters-in-law—You are help when I need it, laughter when I don't expect it, and strength when I have none of my own.

And lastly, to my husband—Every year and decade we celebrate together, I understand more that it'll never be enough. I'm content with many things but never when it comes to having time with you.

About the Author

CINDY WOODSMALL is a *New York Times* best-selling author whose connection with the Amish community has been featured on *ABC Nightline* and on the front page of the *Wall Street Journal*. She is the author of the Sisters of the Quilt series as well as *The Bridge of Peace, The Hope of Refuge,* and *The Sound of Sleigh Bells.* Her ability to authentically capture the heart of her characters comes from her real-life connections with Amish Mennonite and Old Order Amish families. Cindy lives in Georgia with her husband, their three sons, and two amazing daughters-in-law.

To keep up with new releases, book signings, and other news, visit Cindy at www.cindywoodsmall.com.